CH00925297

BLAC
OF
HORROR

Selected by Charles Black

Mortbury Press

Published by Mortbury Press

First Edition
2007

ISBN 978-0-9556061-0-6

Mortbury Press
Shiloh
Nantglas
Llandrindod Wells
Powys
LD1 6PD

mortburypress@yahoo.com

Contents

Acknowledgements

Shaped Like a Snake first published in Ghosts and Scholars #17 1994

An earlier version of *Regina vs. Zoskia* appeared on *The Art of Grimscribe* website as *Regina vs. Sycorax*, November 2004

Lock-in first published in *Hallows Eve* 2006

Lyrics to *Jingle Bells* by James Pierpoint

Cover artwork by Paul Mudie 2007

*****

Dedicated to Herbert van Thal
1904-1983

INTRODUCTION

Welcome, ladies and gentlemen, to the Black Book of Horror.

Short stories provide a great deal of reading pleasure for little investment of time, and the form is perhaps curiously suited to the horror genre, where their brevity can sometimes sharpen a cruel point.

Yet anthologies, we are told, do not sell; but once upon a time, they did. The Pan Book of Horror ran to 30 volumes (1959-88), and sold several million copies. The 1960's and 70's in particular were a golden age for horror anthologies. As well as the Pan books, the Fontana Great Ghost Stories anthologies ran to twenty volumes, while that publisher's horror series reached seventeen volumes. There were numerous others, many edited by Michel Parry, and Peter Haining. Hugh Lamb, Richard Davis, and David Sutton notably contributed several more.

Although I do not expect the Black Book to reach as wide an audience as the anthologies of the past, it is something of a tribute to those books - right down to the blood soaked quotations on the back cover. Inside you will even find contributions from some of those involved in the aforementioned golden age.

For more information about British horror anthologies visit: http://vaultofevil.mysite.wanadoo-members.co.uk/index.html

CROWS

Frank Nicholas

Two massive stone gateposts framed the view ahead. Between rusted iron bars, all Ronson could see were unruly hedges bordering a stretch of gravel road that curled out of view, effectively blocking any sight of the house. The rain had stopped and thin sunlight struggled through slate clouds. He got out of the car. Keys jangled in his hand. Massive padlocks secured the heavy chains that snaked through and through the bars.

He turned and looked toward the town. A smattering of lights glimmered in the distance. Oldmire was further off than Ronson thought. A rusty signpost lied that the town was two miles away, when it was clearly closer to five. It was almost as though the whole town had drawn itself back from this spot, as if there were something here to be shunned.

Surely that was a pang of guilt he felt for driving on past that old man? He could have been lost. Or senile. Or criminally insane, hiding a cleaver in his coat. Or one of those wandering phantom hitchhikers?

Ronson told himself to get a grip. He, if the bundled and stooped figure he'd made out in the headlights actually was a he, wasn't even hitchhiking. The figure hadn't raised an arm or even turned its head as the car had roared past. All Ronson had seen through the windscreen was a tall, dark shape, well wrapped up for the cold, trudging along between the side of the road and the woods.

He stopped to wonder why he was even thinking so deeply about this. Was it because the thought of going to the house scared him?

No, of course not! He wasn't scared. Nervous, maybe. No, not even that.

Had it even trudged? It might have been no more than a bundle of rags caught round a stump of tree or a scarecrow of

6

some sort. And, no, he didn't think anyone would put up a scarecrow in a wood next to a road but then, what did he really know about farmers and their mysterious local rituals and their old wives with their odd tales and all that rural garbage? He was a city dweller by birth, by upbringing and by attitude and, despite the house; he would continue to be so. His few trips to the countryside as a kid hadn't exactly thrilled him and the only country folk he could say he knew - correction, could say he had known - were now dead and no doubt fertilising the land quite nicely.

Okay, he admitted, maybe he was a little bit nervous. Uneasy, even. But standing by the roadside until the last of the sunlight died wasn't going to make him any more relaxed, was it? So, without thinking too much about it, he unlocked and opened the gates and got back into the car. He wouldn't bother closing them behind himself. It wasn't like he'd be staying long. Just long enough to take another look at what had been left to him and to make sure any loose ends were tied up to his satisfaction.

He drove slowly on until he found himself looking up at the house at the end...

At the end of what? He hated it when odd questions like that popped into his head. It happened rarely but, when it did, it was a sure sign he was out of sorts. You can't be businesslike with a head full of random nonsense, he told himself, but the initial thought had already been overtaken by others.

At the end of your journey? The end of the road? The end of your world? Ronson quickly realised that as much as he didn't like the question, he really didn't like the answers. For, in his head, it was the house at the end! The House Where Nothing Lives!

It was Aunt Jess who had said it first; on that horrible week he had spent at the house, when he would cry out in the night about things moving up above his bed. She would chuckle at his fears and tell him not to be silly, that nothing lived up there in the dark above. Birds nesting and the wind in the old timbers would get the blame. Even as a child he'd hated her, standing there grinning and pink and ruddy, while he shivered palely and tried not to weep.

Corbiewood Lodge loomed high in the clearing. Jagged crags of roof and chimney and a sharply angled weather vane clawed the slate sky. Tall windows dully reflected the remaining sunlight. There was a stone patio surrounding the house, the stones furred with moss and grass sprouting between cracks. Ronson decided to get out and walk, and checking his mobile phone was safely in his pocket, he locked the car and fetched a heavy-duty torch from the boot.

All the time he kept his eyes fixed on the house, scanning the upper windows for any sign of darting movements and straining for sounds of scratching or fluttering. A single round window in a squat turret looked back at him like an unblinking eye and it was Ronson that looked away first.

There were two things that struck him as surprising about the whole place. First of all, he had yet to spot a broken window or scrawl of spray paint, nothing to proclaim some local lad as 'a poof', or some girl as 'a slag'. And the neighbourhood tramp populace didn't seem to have used it as a toilet. Old houses, in Ronson's considerable experience, attracted vandalism like a magnet, yet, despite lying empty for months, the place looked untouched. Maybe that was the difference between city kids and country kids, though he couldn't imagine the kids from the village were any less bored than the gangs of youths back home. And it was doubtful that the railings would bar the way to any self-respecting teenager looking to throw a few stones or smoke a crafty fag without their parents catching them.

Secondly, there was the lack of noise. Ronson liked the sound of traffic. The sound of movement, life, speed. And, in the absence of mechanical noise, there was another notable absence. He scanned the tree line, looking for birds, either nesting or swooping. Nothing.

"Nothing lives there..." A sigh in the wind?

Ronson smiled. Good. Mr Saville had done his job well.

Surprisingly well, even for the efficiently reliable Mr Saville. But, despite the smile, Ronson was shivering now. The cold air whipped around him and he pulled his coat tighter before approaching the front door.

A woman moaned at him out of the shadows round the doorway. Most of her face had been worn away by wind and rain, while her long dress was grey with mould and streaked white and green with countless stains.

Ronson took a step back, swearing sharply. Then he laughed. It was just a statue. It put him instantly in mind of one of the creepy angels with the clasping hands and spreading wings from the little graveyard down by the orchard. He remembered this one from before, when she still had half a face. Now the nose has crumbled leaving a ridge and the chasm between this and the chin gaped at him like a great beak.

Still not quite convinced the disintegrating woman wasn't going to suddenly shuffle toward him, he mounted the three steps to the main doors of the lodge. The shadows were deep here and he had to fish out his torch to locate the keyhole.

He put his hand to the door. It was icy and solid. Closed since the funeral, all those months back. At least, officially closed. While there were a few annoying legal technicalities to be dealt with relating to a second cousin living somewhere in the USA, Ronson had seen no point in hanging back when there were some other details that could be dealt with closer to home.

Not that this place would ever be home. Not once it was sold off, land and woods included. There were deals waiting to be considered, one of which promised to turn the property into the one thing he could see as a genuinely worthwhile use of the countryside. If the bid was right, he was genuinely looking forward to sinking a few putts on the rolling green lawns that would replace that ugly, dark, dingy forest. As long as everything had been cleaned up. Not that Mr Saville had ever left room for complaint in cleaning up any of the other awkward messes that might have delayed any previous transactions.

Stepping back from the house he pulled out his mobile phone. This was the one thing he insisted all his employees carry on pain of instant dismissal, ever since a former colleague fell through the floorboards of an abandoned warehouse and had to wait for a passing glue-sniffer to summon the police. He checked for a signal. There was one. Two bars only. Ah, the joy of country living, Ronson grumbled to himself as he took a walk round to check if the signal was any stronger round the back of the house.

Once round behind the building he located the archway and heavy wooden doors that had long ago led to enclosed stables. The door tingled under his touch, as if it was alive. The tingle became a shiver and a memory fell into place, dislodged from somewhere dark. It was a memory of his own hand, smaller and smoother, pressed against those same doors as figures flocked around, draped in black clothes that flapped and beat around them in the wind. He had been crying and the sky had been grey and things stirred in the trees.

Some distance away, that same forest skulked. And through the trees lay the family cemetery where generations of Ronsons also lay, rotting quietly. Not his parents, though. He hadn't wanted to leave them in this place for eternity after the accident and their ashes now sat in urns at either end of a fireplace that was valued at more than the flat they'd brought him up in. As for the other driver, who'd walked away from the wreckage virtually unscathed... well, he didn't know where Mr Saville had left his remains.

He searched the bare branches. The only movement was the wind. It had been different back then, when the crows had lined the branches, looking on like mourners. His first funeral. Not his last by a long chalk. Though that had been in this same spot. But he was going back decades now, not months, to the time when the grandmother he'd hardly ever met had been put into the ground. And when he'd been dragged out of school and halfway across the country to a place he didn't like or understand and where there were no kids his own age, only old people who spoke in funny, rolling voices totally unlike the clipped and nasal tones his ears were attuned to.

He'd barely met his grandmother and, despite the sympathetic looks he was getting from the grown-ups, he was really crying because his mum and dad were talking about leaving him there. He didn't understand what it was his mum had needed a break from. He knew she was sad because of the old lady in the white dress in the long box but, if they left him there, how could he try to make her happy again? Though when he'd tried to tell her his best ever joke and she hadn't laughed and dad had got angry, he knew they meant it when they said they would leave him with that tall, pink faced lady and her sturdy husband, his aunt and uncle. But he didn't know if they also really meant it when they said they'd come back for him in a week's time.

They had, of course, but a week was a long time when you were seven and such a lot happened in that week. Like the time he'd gone exploring and ended up in the cemetery and found all those black things fluttering on top of the mound of earth they'd put on top of his grandmother.

Ronson jolted back to the present, startled by the memory, and found himself leaning against the doors. From within, he could hear a steady clunk and throb of machinery. There had been a note about the stables, hadn't there? He fished it out from the folder the solicitors had provided. "Generator Room in old stable house," it read, followed by instructions on how to fire up the machinery and a diagram that looked like a cross-section of an octopus. Not that anyone would be needing that once the papers were signed and the bulldozers moved in. Still, someone, either from the solicitors' office in town or, more likely, Mr Saville, had taken the trouble of switching the power on for him. Ronson had the strong urge to phone and find out but he didn't particularly want the local legal eagle scurrying out to meet him and he never phoned Mr Saville if he didn't specifically have to. After all, good help wasn't cheap and Mr

Saville charged by the second, never mind the minute.

He wandered on, wondering what condition the wiring inside would be in. It was doubtful that any light-bulbs would actually work. But he left the power thrumming away behind him like the beat of a gigantic heart.

Eventually, having long lost count of the turns, he found himself standing by the three steps leading up to the front door. He was struck with the sensation that he had been walking in a straight line while the house had somehow revolved around him, inspecting him as he inspected it. He wondered which had observed more.

The doorway lay open in front of him. Had he unlocked it? The keys were still in his hand. He allowed his thoughts to drift slightly out of focus; a skill he found useful when making decisions he didn't particularly care to think too deeply about. This successfully allowed the various intimations of alarm that were building to be neatly shuffled away to the back of his mind. Then, pocketing the keys, he clutched his files in one hand, hefted his torch in the other and stepped into the darkness.

The air in the massive hallway was clammy and chill and he shivered as it wrapped around him like a shroud. The wind, so blustery outside, didn't even cause the slightest quiver in the hanging cobwebs, almost as if it refused to follow him over the threshold.

Once his eyes had grown accustomed to the gloom, he saw the long, wide stairway soaring up to a landing before branching off to twin staircases to both left and right. Above this landing, what little light there was filtered through the gaps in the dustsheets that covered a tall, narrow stained-glass window. He couldn't make out the figure depicted there but he was sure he recalled something with wings.

He reached for the light-switch on the wall behind him, snatching his hand back hurriedly as he flicked the tiny brass lever, half-expecting electrocution or an explosion from the decrepit wiring. Surprisingly, with only the faintest buzzing sound, dim, yellowish light streamed out of the few remaining bulbs in the cobweb-strewn chandelier.

Ronson's feet made a sharp clopping sound on the black and white tiles in the foyer. From here, five narrow steps took him down to the bare floorboards of the hall. He was acutely aware of the echo of his own footsteps. Maybe, he caught himself thinking, he was listening for a step which didn't match his own.

From the foyer, the hallway widened out around and above him. Taking care not to stand directly below the chandelier, he looked up toward the ceiling. The split stairways lead up to wooden-railed balconies before all detail was lost in the gloom.

According to the file, the room to his left used to be a parlour, leading through, he remembered, to a library, though he'd never been allowed inside it. Next to the parlour, a door in the stairwell led to the cellar. In the opposite stairwell was the doorway to the kitchens and directly to Ronson's right was the dining room.

A quick scout around revealed that the cellar was locked, while the kitchens had been stripped bare of everything bar the plumbing and he suspected the only thing that'd come out of the taps was rust. He decided not to investigate further, since a sickly, sweet, rotted smell, which reminded him of yoghurt left out on a hot day, hit him when he opened what used to be the larder door.

The doors to the other three rooms lay partially open, though he could see only darkness beyond. He shrugged off any inclination to take a look and marched up the staircase, knowing exactly where he wanted to see before he locked the door behind him and never set foot in the house again.

He'd had a dream, one night on that long week in this house, where he'd come down those stairs and gone through the parlour, looking to see if his mum had come back for him yet. The forbidden door to the library was slightly open and there had been voices from behind that door, though he hadn't been able to understand what they'd been saying. He'd thought he'd recognised the thick vowels of his aunt's voice and there had been another voice that had sounded similar but drier and croakier. And, when he'd pressed his face to the gap in the door, he'd seen his aunt talking to an old lady who he thought he'd seen before, wearing a long white dress and with mud and feathers in her hair.

That had been the same day he'd found the black feathers sticking out of the fresh grave in the little cemetery. It was so wrong, the fluttering tongues of blackness sprouting out between the green of the squares of grass and the grey of the gravestone, he'd thought it might be a joke. What do you get if you cross a crow with a lawnmower? But these feathers hadn't looked strewn randomly. They'd seemed placed.

When he'd mentioned that to Aunt Jess, she'd laughed, but in a way that made her sound more angry than happy, then told him off for using his imagination too much. So he'd crept back upstairs and decided that when he woke up, he wasn't going to tell Aunt Jess about this dream about the old lady in the library.

And here he was, still creeping up those stairs, still hoping to get to the top before someone caught him. Still holding his breath...

Ronson breathed out. Then something flapped and fluttered in the darkness beyond an open doorway and he fought his immediate urge to squeeze his eyes shut and wave his hands around his head to protect himself from sharp claws and pointed tips. Instead, he laughed when he saw the curtain edge that shifted in the breeze. The laugh was short and sharp and died when he realised that a window had been left open. After all, things could get in that way. This was not satisfactory. It was also most unlike Mr Saville.

Mr Saville wasn't his real name, of course. That was just the cover name for the man who fixed things for Ronson and smoothed out any minor inconveniences that got in the way. The subterfuge was Mr Saville's idea, since he had realised it might be an inconvenience if his employer was found to be connected to him in any way. The name was Ronson's contribution. A rare joke for him. He'd long since stopped trying to make other people happy. Whether Mr Saville found it amusing, well, who could say? Ronson had certainly never known him to crack a smile. Mr Saville rarely showed anything but attention to his employer's instructions.

Aunt Jess hadn't really been an inconvenience. It was just that after Uncle Benjamin had fallen out of that tree the old fool had been pruning at his age, well, it seemed a shame to just leave her rattling about in this big old place. And if an old lady, living on her own, was to take a tumble down the stairs, it was hardly going to lead to calls for immediate investigation of such suspicious circumstances, now was it?

Recovering his nerves after his fright on the landing, Ronson realised that he had thrown himself back against the rails. He was now aware that he teetered on the edge of a precipice, where a wooden banister no longer seemed quite sturdy or secure enough... it certainly hadn't broke poor auntie's fall... so he edged toward the doorway. He kept one arm pressed against the cool surface of the wall and his eyes fixed on the door ahead, the one that he all too clearly remembered led to the attic stairs. Silently, though, he was praying that no other unexpected doorway would open out in the wall behind his back, allowing something to reach out for him from the darkness.

There was a mixture of dismay and relief when his hand closed round the battered, brass door-handle and it turned easily in his grip. The door swung open. Dust swirled in the changing atmosphere. Grey light spilled down from somewhere above in the high stairwell.

The only way up to the attic, and whatever he might find there, was by climbing a narrow, wooden staircase. It was a spiral staircase and it was difficult to judge just how far it coiled its way above Ronson's head. The last time he had ascended it, it had seemed like hundreds of feet, but he had only been a child then.

Spiral staircases had always put a slight shiver down his spine, a tiny, but noticeable jolt of secret fear. They had done even since before his childhood visit to the attic, since he'd had an odd dream. Here was another forgotten nightmare. How many more buried night terrors would this old house bring bubbling back to the surface?

The dream about spiral staircases was simply that he was running up a very, very long flight of spiral steps inside what appeared to be a tower, with the stone walls and the curve of the stairs into darkness in either direction making it impossible to see what it was that moved upwards and unceasingly upwards either just ahead of or just behind him. This meant that he couldn't tell whatever else it was, on that staircase with him. He could just hear the scrape, scrape, scrape as it moved.

What was worse, though, was that he could never tell if he was chasing it or if it was chasing him. Would speeding his step take him further from it or more quickly into its grasp, and what would he see either looming from behind him or turning a face... or not a face at all, merely a gaping darkness... to greet him when the pursuer... or was it the pursued... inevitably fell upon its prey?

As if Ronson didn't have enough going on inside his head at that moment, he had to remember that? But there were yet more memories, these ones more tangible than nightmares. These were memories that brushed his skin and pecked at his eyes until they smarted with tears.

There was the memory of the false bravery of childhood. Of Aunt Jess's smiling reassurance that there was nothing in the attic. Of the need to find out for himself, just to be sure. And of arming himself with a pointed stick, which seemed to be the only type of plaything he could find in abundance away from the city, before tiptoeing up the steps.

It had seemed a long way to his seven-year-old self, but he'd finally stood nervously at the door to the attic. He stood there for a long time, staring at the handle, waiting for it to twitch and turn and for the door to fly open and the darkness to descend.

Finally, more fearful of Aunt Jess or Uncle Ben finding him sneaking about, he'd prodded the door open with the end of the stick. As it had opened into the gloom beyond, he'd squeezed his eyes tightly shut, and froze. It was only when long moments had passed, in which nothing had reached out of the attic and dragged him in, that he'd dared to open his eyes and step inside.

He hadn't been able to believe it. There really was nothing to be scared of. The attic was just a long room with some boxes scattered round the edges and a roof that sloped down on either side high over his head. He'd poked about in the boxes for a bit, finding nothing more interesting than some old clothes and books without pictures that were full of words he'd not been able to read, before deciding to see what the view was like from up there. The door at the end had to lead to the turret with the porthole window. From this height, though, it would have been more like a lookout post or the crow's nest on a pirate ship!

The door flapped open and a circular shaft of light fell in from the window. It was open and cool air poured in. Then there was a clap like thunder from the sudden beating of dozens of pairs of wings and he was being buffeted by a flurry of air as dark shapes lifted up and crashed into his face and arms and chest and his ears were full of noises that his yell of terror didn't cover.

He'd flailed around with the stick, slicing through air and hitting the rafters, the walls and the floor with sharp cracks that had merely sent the swooping forms swirling in even more frenzied circles, like a harsh, black whirlwind that thrashed around him, till the stick sunk into something soft and wet.

The pigeon had struggled feebly and the boy dropped the stick, horrified by what he'd done. The other birds had gone, escaping out into the afternoon sky. And, even though the pigeon was finally still, he couldn't take his eyes off its crookedly twisted neck and the deep red stain on the grey chest feathers.

When he'd gone downstairs again, he'd left the pigeon propped up on the end of the stick, a warning in the window to keep the other birds out. He couldn't see it from outside and he'd hoped no one else but the birds would. But when he'd come in from pretending to play, his uncle had been holding the stick in one hand and a scraggy mass of feather and bones in the other and muttering something to his pink-faced wife. And while he hadn't known what the word "carrion" meant, he'd been able to guess what "picked clean" entailed and realised that, no matter what he tried, the scrabbling and scratching would be there again that night.

It would have been no use explaining to his aunt or uncle about his fears and, although neither had said anything to him over dinner, Aunt Jess had looked in on him while he'd read in bed. She'd brought him a book, one with pictures. At first he'd been grateful for the gift, until he saw that it was full of pictures of birds. And she'd told him how there had been birds of all sorts in those trees out there since long before the house was built or any of the houses that had stood there before it. And that even the name of the woods had a word meaning a type of raven in it. And she said how her family, who knew about nature from long times past, had sworn to protect the creatures of the air for this was their territory and humans were only guests there. And then she'd gone and, in the quiet darkness, the noises above him had sounded like beaks trying to scratch their way through the thin plaster that was the only barrier between the attic and his bedroom.

Ronson thought of creatures of the air as he pictured his aunt toppling through space to land at the foot of the stairs. It cheered him slightly. And if Mr Saville had completed the second half of his assignment, there would be nothing but air, cobwebs and maybe a touch of damp waiting for him in the attic. After all, red tape and conservation orders only applied to the living and if it somehow seemed that his careless and possibly senile old relatives had foolishly stored hazardous material in their attic and it had wiped out some flying vermin, well, boo-hoo!

But there were times and places for gloating. Behind closed doors after he'd offloaded some overpriced, redeveloped hovel or after he'd seen acres of green and pleasant land filled up with identical homes that were compact in size but not in price. He decided to put his mind to more immediately practical things. The planks that formed the stairs were old, buckled and mouldering. He wasn't a shivering, scrawny slip of a kid now. Time and some very expensive private gyms had seen to that. So, would the stairs still support his weight?

Probably, he thought, yes.

Maybe.

The ancient wood protested loudly under his feet as he slowly ascended the stairs. He couldn't locate a light-switch and wasn't so sure his relatives had even had the attic wired up. So, the beam from his torch performed a jagged dance ahead of him, as he tried to hold onto the damn thing and also press his hands to the walls to help distribute his weight. The circle of light slid up the beaten panels of the old door at the top of the steps. He had to force himself not to make a run for the door and the slivers of grey light that surrounded it.

There were only a dozen steps to go but suddenly that seemed far too far. The steps screeched but still he ran, afraid to slow down in case the additional seconds of pressure would cause the wood to crumble beneath him.

He heard a loud snap and hurled himself through the doorway. The brittle wood of the frame shattered as he hit it but at least the floor below him was solid. He took a gasping breath or two then shone his torch back to the staircase. Just over half a dozen steps back, the timber had snapped. Ronson made a note to remember that on the way back down.

The room he found himself in was long and narrow and criss-crossed with shafts of grey light. Silvery patches of sky could be seen through dozens of holes in the sloping roof above him. He now had to crouch to move forward. The space had seemed so much bigger when he was so much smaller.

And there was the door up ahead that led to the tower. He moved toward it, slowly, steadily. Then, "Damn!" The torch beam suddenly dipped, the yellow light turning brown and murky before flickering back on. Ronson switched it off, not fancying the stairs with no torchlight at all. Besides, there was just enough light to get him to the door and there was the round window beyond that.

The beams beneath his feet seemed spongy and something cracked, like a bundle of dried up twigs. He looked down and he was glad that the light wasn't strong enough to let him clearly see the corpses under his feet. What he saw was enough: tiny skulls, fragile and brittle, ribcages and stunted legs protruding from decayed, fleshless bodies.

Stomach lurching, he staggered back toward the wall, his voice rising in an angry chant that didn't quite cover the snap and clatter of bones. He raised his phone, focusing his anger, punching in the number. This wasn't good enough, he told himself. This should have been dealt with weeks ago, as soon as it was safe to go back in! This wasn't professional. Professionals cleaned up. They didn't leave a mess like this behind. They also answered their damn phones when their employer's called. How long was it since Saville had confirmed everything was in hand, with only the tidying up to be done? A fortnight and no contact since. But that was normal. This mess was not!

He was about to terminate the call when he heard the ringing. Muted, but close by. Behind him, in fact, just through the wall.

Ronson grabbed the handle but the door wouldn't budge. The ringing continued and he rattled the door violently, calling out Saville's name. Then he dropped to his haunches, crouching carefully, not wanting to let his suit come into contact with what was on the floor.

At first, what he spied through the keyhole made little sense. Was that a shape? A colour? Then he saw that what he was spying on was spying on him.

He jumped back, startled. "Hello?" He almost laughed at the ridiculous politeness of the enquiry.

There was no reply, not even a whisper of breath.

Despite everything his nerves were screaming at him, he looked again.

The eye still stared. A startling blue, even through the film that was forming on the surface. It didn't blink, like the eye of a porcelain doll. He'd only ever seen eyes this blue once in his life.

"Saville?" He yelled the name and pounded on the door until he heard something shift inside. And, when he looked back, his fix-it man had fallen back from the door and, for the very first time in their association, the hired man was smiling at his employer. At least, he appeared to be smiling, though that might have had something to do with the fact that his cheeks had been eaten by the same thing that had picked his carcass clean. What remained of his hand was curled round the handle of the flick-knife that protruded from what remained of his throat, and his throat, like his mouth, appeared to be smiling!

Ronson scrabbled backwards from the door, whimpering, and only screamed when his hand brushed against something that tumbled loudly out of the corner. He dimly recognised it as a bag of industrial strength poison, the kind pest controllers used, which now spilled what remained of its contents over the floor. It had all been in hand! That's what Mr Saville had said. He'd just needed to wait for the fumes to disperse before coming back in and finishing it off. But had something been waiting for him? Was that why he was lying there with a knife in him?

Ronson crawled, the powdery contents of the bag turning his suit grey. But he was far too concerned about that other thing that rolled out of the darkness and tumbled toward him like a scarecrow uprooted by a hurricane before seeming to break apart into dark fragments caught up in their own storms, to worry about stained silk. Then he was out of the door,

21

slamming it behind him, hoping it would stay wedged shut in the broken frame, and racing down the stairs, his torch flaring into life just in time to reveal the broken step as a strip of darkness under his foot.

For a split second, he froze.

Then, instinctively, he stepped back, heart hammering. Only his foot came down with more force than he had expected and he stamped down hard on the stair. It gave way with a crack! He could feel only empty air beneath his foot for an instant. But only for that instant and no more. Then, arms flailing for something to grip, his entire body tilted and spun, his right foot crashing down behind him. Wood splintered and his balance went completely.

Beams, rotted with age, tumbled around him as he fell. Then, with a wrenching jerk, his descent came to a sudden halt. The torch jumped from his hand, rolling away only to snag between two posts, shining a feeble spotlight on the door he had just fled through. His mobile phone slid from between his fingers and, as it shattered somewhere below him, the distant ringing from the attic tower was silenced.

The beam that pierced his torso and suspended him like a rag-doll over a black, oily puddle of darkness, was slick with his internal fluids. Its jagged, spiked edges reminded him, almost dreamily, of the spires and turrets of a house...

Which house?

Was it important? That phone had cost him a fortune. And his suit was ruined. The stains would never come out and it'd need more than invisible mending. And, as for things that needed mending, who would fix the fix-it man, now all his troubles had come home to roost?

Ronson laughed so hard he passed out.

Had a grey face, the cheeks no longer pink from the open air, leered down at him and laughed, it's crowing cackle spilling out of a dark maw in amongst the hair that was matted with black plumes?

Would someone plant black feathers on his grave?

22

Delirious. He had to be. He had to be businesslike. Assess the situation. File a damage report. He had to focus. How badly injured was he?

There was little pain. No doubt about it, then, his spine had been severed.

His blood smelled warm and sweet.

He was only distantly aware of the pounding in his ears. When he did, finally hear it, he dismissed it as his blood pumping its way round toward the hole that went all the way from his back to his chest.

But it wasn't. It was coming from behind the door. Scratching and pounding! The slivers of light broke apart and reformed. Shapes were moving behind the thin wood. The panels began to bulge. Chinks of light glimmered through cracks in the surface as something pushed to break through from the other side. The scratching became a determined chipping and sharp splinters of wood rained down on him. Ronson tried to lift an arm to protect his eyes but his limbs remained limp and useless.

He was already screaming, even when the thing beyond the door came into view as more wood splintered away and he realised that he was mistaken. It wasn't a thing that scrabbled so desperately to be free. No. It was things, dozens upon dozens of scratching, snapping, clawing, misshapen, twisted things. And Ronson instantly realised that no-one had used the knife on Saville, that he had turned it on himself while he'd still had the chance, and he wished that he too had a knife rather than face these things as they poured out toward him, pushing and biting until the first wave of them tumbled through the torn door

They tumbled because most of them could no longer fly. These birds had been dead for a long time. A collection of bones and matted grey feathers, they moved in a tide toward him. Beaks clacked like scissors. Fleshless wings flapped in his face.

The worst was a mother bird that lurched toward him. Or,

23

rather, it was what she carried with her that was the worst of it. Between the stringy, gristly strips of withered organs, a whiteish, bulbous mass, fully formed but unlaid, shifted. Then the semi-soft skin of the egg bulged and quivered. A web-work of tiny cracks radiated out and the white surface ruptured, spilling a teeming mass of black-legged spiders, which chittered and scurried up the corrupted innards of the mother bird, shredding and rending dead flesh and pouring out around Ronson.

The mother bird spasmed and her bony beak sliced down into the soft skin beneath his eye. His numb paralysis seemed to stop just below his neck, as a white-hot needle of pain seared his nerves. Yet still he managed to clamp down on the scream as those eight-legged monstrosities tumbled past his lips.

The fresh blood on his face attracted some of the birds that had been drinking from his torn chest. Skin was stripped away, hanging in bloodied beaks like fat, pink worms. It was gulped down, only to fall through hollow ribcages, a useless feast for these cannibal crows.

At long last, both his eyeballs were gone but, in the instant before darkness finally, mercifully descended, he clearly saw his torn clothes and skeleton hanging on a piece of wood, and realised what he had become… the most useless scarecrow in the world.

REGINA vs. ZOSKIA

Mark Samuels

A blast of cold, damp air outside Chancery Lane Underground Station was sucked down into the depths of the ticket hall and the surrounding passageways. Dunn met its full force as he was carried upwards towards the surface by the escalators. He found the wind refreshing after the sweaty confines of the train and the platforms. However, once he'd emerged onto High Holborn and into the grey morning, all it did was to chill him and increase his dissatisfaction. He glanced at his watch. It was just after 10am.

He was already thirty minutes late for the office, despite trying to make up time by catching the tube from Bank instead of walking. At least his boss, Mr Horace Jackson, was rarely in before 10:15am on a Tuesday morning. He was carrying on a relationship with his legal secretary, Miss Jenkins, and usually stayed over at her place on Monday nights, dragging himself into the Gray's Inn chambers in her wake so as not to arouse suspicion. The fact that Dunn obviously knew about the affair anyway seemed not to worry Jackson as much as the need to not acknowledge that such was the case.

He doubted that Jackson would arrive for another ten minutes at least.

The archway next to The Cittie of Yorke pub was dripping wet and two barristers in peri-wigs and black gowns sheltered in the short passageway beneath, smoking cigarettes. Both glared at Dunn with inhuman eyes as he passed by, snarling as if they were a couple of Doberman guard-dogs.

He crossed the square, which he could not help associating in his mind with a vast prison courtyard, passed through a long narrow passageway, until he finally stood beneath the soot-caked tenement that housed 7B Coney Court Chambers. Jackson's offices occupied two small rooms on the top floor and Dunn's heart sank as he gazed up and saw that the lights above were already lit to ward off the morning's twilight gloom. The old lawyer had arrived before him.

Dunn began to climb the circular flight of stairs that led to the attic chambers. The wooden steps were hollowed over hundreds of years by the tread of visitors though none wearier than the man who now made the ascent. Doubtless, Dunn thought, Jackson would be sitting behind his desk facing the panelled entrance door, drumming his podgy fingers on the desktop and staring at the clock. A little vein on his right temple, close to one of his bushy eyebrows, would be pulsing with resentment. Emily Jenkins would be sitting in the adjoining office, clad as usual in a tight pin-striped skirt suit, applying make-up, somewhat tired after satisfying Jackson's desires the night before.

Dunn passed the landings and the entrances to the other chambers, F, E, D, C, and then reached the top where A and B faced one another. He paused to catch his breath and put his ear to the door. He heard the muffled sounds of Jackson and Jenkins flirting with one another.

Dunn took a step back, lost his footing, and his shoes clattered against the stairs behind him. Almost at once the door flew open and the corpulent figure of the white-haired Jackson appeared. He glared at Dunn ferociously from behind bi-focal eyeglasses. The vein on his temple seemed fit to burst.

"Well," he thundered, "Mr Dunn! Good of you to grace us with your presence, at last!"

"Sorry," Dunn mumbled, "the trains, Mr Jackson, delays on the Central Line..."

Jackson stood back and crooked his finger at Dunn signalling him to enter.

"I'm not interested in your excuses Mr Dunn. As I've told you before; if you left earlier for work you'd be here in plenty of time."

Dunn's desk was situated in the corner of Jackson's office, squeezed into a little nook beneath a sagging shelf weighed down with dozens of dusty legal tomes and briefs bound with red ribbons. It looked as if it might collapse at any moment in an avalanche of pages infested with bookworms and silverfish and crush anyone stupid enough to sit under there.

As Dunn settled himself into his ramshackle chair, Jackson shifted from foot to foot like an ape that was ill-at-ease standing upright for long periods.

"Don't get too comfortable," he said, "while you were idling your way to the office I received a telephone call from our client Dr. Zoskia. We've got to visit the premises and pick up a new series of documents relating to the 'Regina vs. Zoskia' case. I suppose that we'll have to drive there and should leave in about ten minutes or so. They want us by 11:30am"

Wiping his mouth with the back of his hand, so as to disguise a nervous smirk, Dunn nodded his head in agreement. 'Regina vs. Zoskia' was an interminable case that he had only ever heard Mr Jackson mention obliquely, and of which he had scant knowledge. Certainly it had been dragging on for many years and, in an unguarded moment, Miss Jenkins had once hinted to him that it was this case alone which enabled Jackson to continue with his legal practice. Gigantic fees were involved. It had been thus since the time of Jackson's own father, also a solicitor, who had originally taken on the defendant's case on a plea of justification. Dunn thought of it as strangely akin to 'Jarndyce vs. Jarndyce'.

"I'll need you to navigate," Jackson said, as the effort of standing finally overwhelmed him and he slumped into the leather-upholstered chair, "I too easily get lost in all these stupid modern one-way systems."

Miss Jenkins giggled. It seemed to be a private joke.

*

"I know," Jackson said, changing up from third to fourth gear with a convulsive motion, "that you're probably full of curiosity about the 'Regina vs. Zoskia' case. Well, there's no secret about the thing. It's just a bit confusing that's all and it's

27

been going on for a very very long time."

Jackson's battered old motor-car, a Jaguar XJS model that had seen much better days, sped along the dual carriageway. Its interior was dank with the smell of stale cigars. Dunn looked up from the street-map nestled on his knees.

"I expect," Jackson grumbled, "that the case will finish me off. It did my father. Not that the family hasn't made a pretty penny from it, mind. We certainly have; it's just that… well, it can be easily misunderstood. But it's important. More important than anything else in our files."

There was a weird tone in the old man's voice. It was as if he was opening up to Dunn, cautiously of course, but without any trace of the scorn that had so often characterised his speech.

"Umm," said Jackson, "it'll be clearer when we arrive there. I won't be around forever you know, Dunn. Not getting any younger. Might be better if you did this trip in future."

Dunn's sense of confusion deepened. He looked at Jackson with an expression of complete bafflement.

"I'm really sorry Mr Jackson, but what you're saying makes no sense to me."

"Not surprised, when I was first told about it I can remember being as confused as you must be."

The car was passing through a particularly desolate part of the city. All the shops were boarded-up. Flanking the sides of the road were great expanses of run-down housing estates. Their tenants seemed to have departed some years ago. It looked as if the entire region had nothing to expect from the future except a merciful wave of demolitions.

Jackson's fingers worked along the panel of the car radio and he adjusted its FM wavelength. His middle digit was adorned by a garish onyx signet ring with his initials inlaid in gold. Dull static issued from the speakers. For some reason Jackson appeared to enjoy listening to this crazy, meaningless noise and he kept it on in the background during the whole of the trip.

"It's just around this bend," Jackson said, the first words

he'd spoken for several minutes, "up there on the hill. It'll come into view any moment now."

The series of dreary housing estates on either side of the road had begun to thin out, and what few buildings that had been erected (either unfinished or abandoned) were overrun with weeds. The whole area reminded Dunn of those seemingly endless bombsites in the Docklands before the mass redevelopment during the 1980s. Then the hill came into view. It was covered with a profusion of bare trees; their long thin branches swaying in the wind, appearing to rake the leaden sky like claws. At the very summit, above the top of the trees, one could see a domed and weather-beaten clock tower of Byzantine design.

"Impressive, isn't it?" Jackson said, "You know, back in the 1960s, they put the inmates to all sorts of tasks."

"What do you mean, inmates?" Said Dunn.

"Well, it started off as an insane asylum and now... let's just say something else altogether. The Director of the place, Dr. Zoskia, believed in collective therapy, in a self-sufficient community formulating its own diagnoses and ethos."

"How did our firm become involved with them?"

"When the inmates decided they no longer wished to be classified as insane. They've been challenging the legal basis on which the definition rests for the last forty-odd years. Dr. Zoskia contends that the hospital is for the sane and that it is the outside world that is occupied by the mentally disturbed. Proving this contention in law became the 'Regina vs. Zoskia' case."

"Surely it's obvious whether or not these people are crazy? If they can't function in society..."

"It's not just that. The thing is that they've trained themselves not to sleep. They're suspicious of those who do. Some of the inmates in that place have been awake, non-stop, for several years. They've been using sleep deprivation to break down the barriers between so-called sanity and madness."

The car exited the dual carriageway at the next junction. The turnoff itself was not sign-posted and the pock-marked road the vehicle ascended had vegetation growing out of its cracks and hollows. The banks on either side were not properly maintained and wild foliage blurred the boundaries between the road and its surroundings. The climb was steep and tortuous, and Jackson had to drive at a crawl in first gear, brake often and occasionally reverse to avoid the wheels and axles becoming entangled in roots and vines.

The road terminated at the entrance to the Zoskia Establishment. A high lop-sided wall crowned with barbed wire enclosed it. Most of the crumbling brickwork was home to a rapacious species of ivy. The entrance gates were rusted and hung at an absurd angle due to uneven subsidence, and were sealed by a huge padlock and chain wound between its central bars. Beyond was a gravel driveway that curved out of sight.

"We're expected. Don't worry, they're all harmless" Jackson mumbled, "We just need to give the right signal to get into the place."

He sounded the car's horn three times in quick succession and then two times in longer bursts. There was silence for a couple of minutes after which Dunn heard footsteps coming along the path, crunching across the gravel in an uneven, slow rhythm. An aged woman dressed in a patient's gown appeared behind the gates, and peered at them with bulging blue eyes that seemed too large for their sockets. Her face was skeletal and fissured by a confusion of deep-set lines. A few strands of stray dark-grey hair hung down across an emaciated cheek; the rest of it was tied back in a ponytail. She was horribly thin, and looked more like a scarecrow than a woman. Her feet were bare and filthy. Her arms and legs were little more than skin covering bones.

Jackson waved at the grisly apparition.

"That's Dr Zoskia," he said, "she hasn't changed a bit."

Dunn said nothing by way of response. He sat there staring

in dumb astonishment.

Zoskia took out a key from a pouch at the front of her dirty smock and unlocked the chain binding the gates closed. She dragged open one of the huge portals so that Jackson's car could pass through. As the car rolled slowly forward across the gravel drive, Dr. Zoskia opened the back door and clambered inside the vehicle, carrying with her the cloying scent of cheap perfume and an under-odour of stale sweat. She mumbled something to Jackson that sounded as if she had said; "you can fuck me later as well if you like". Dunn turned to look at Dr. Zoskia and found that her face was a mask of innocent vacancy.

Once they were inside the walls Dunn had his first glimpse of the hidden citadel in its entirety. Between the overgrown foliage that covered the grounds Dunn saw several low buildings in a ruinous state of dilapidation. They seemed to be former chalets, shops and other out-buildings. There were even deserted tennis-courts.

In the centre of these weird holiday camp ruins was an abandoned Olympic-size swimming pool filled with stagnant weed-choked water. Discarded objects had been dumped there; a few mattresses, a wheelchair, what looked like an old operating table, and a couple of filing cabinets. On the far side, a man sat on the edge of the deep-end of the pool, clad in a doctor's white coat. He was kicking his feet back and forth in the swamp, licking his lips and laughing inanely at the splashes he made. He had long black hair and a grizzled beard that grew down to the top of his chest. The man was like some mad Russian mystic from the Tsarist era.

Elsewhere there were the remains of huge pyres, blackened mounds of vats, drums and jars. All manner of junk was littered in the spaces between the tall, bare trees; broken chairs and benches, discarded and battered respiratory apparatus, head restraints and other surgical appliances.

The main building lay straight in front of them. Dunn now saw the whole structure that supported the Byzantine clock tower that had been visible back on the dual carriageway. It was an immense four-storey building at the centre of over fifty acres of land. Parts of the sloping, tiled roof had caved in and many of the arched windows were either completely broken or riddled with cracks. The white paintwork was peeling away from the outside walls, driven from the brickwork underneath by weathering and an untreated infestation of mould.

The car pulled up beside the steps to the front entrance - a rotting faux-Greek portico whose pillars were strangled by half-dead vines. As the three of them got out of the vehicle Zoskia said, "Let me show you inside."

With Zoskia leading the way, they passed into what had once been a reception area. However no-one manned the admissions desk and the tiled floor was littered with empty tins of food, torn and soiled clothing, used syringes and broken chairs.

Jackson and Zoskia began to discuss the new documents that the latter had collated as evidence for the interminable court case. Zoskia gestured towards objects on the other side of the hall. A pile of six cardboard boxes sat at the foot of the stairs leading to the upper floors. The advertising logos on the sides showed them to have once contained cans of baked beans. They had since been scrawled over with a black marker pen. The childish handwriting read: 'INPORTENT LEEGUL PAYPAS FUR REJINA/ZOSKIA'.

Dunn wandered around the chamber as the other two spoke and was drawn to a huge poster, yellowing with age. Its edges curled away from the wall. It had been displayed up there for decades no doubt. He could scarcely believe that what he had seen was not an absurd joke:

THE ZOSKIA REFUGE FOR THE TRULY SANE
THE CURSE OF SLEEP DAMNS THE OUTSIDE WORLD

"If you wish to take a look around Dunn, go ahead," Jackson called from the other side of the hall, "we've got one or two details to iron out."

"Try not to get lost though," Dr. Zoskia added.

Dunn nodded back at them as he picked his way around the debris. Although he feared for his own safety, he also felt a sense of irresistible curiosity to see more of this bizarre community. He passed through a double-door with portholes, and then entered a long, deserted corridor. This took him deep into the heart of the institution. On both sides of the passageway were cell doors hanging off their hinges, and beyond, in shadow, the inmates' rooms. The doors looked to have been torn open from outside. Dunn peered into the interiors and could make out graffiti scrawled on the walls, all manner of useless junk and one or two human forms crouching in the corners. These figures chattered away, holding paranoid conversations with themselves in eerie, discordant accents. The stench from these cells was almost overpowering; a mixture of sweat, shit and urine. Dunn had to cover his mouth and nose with a handkerchief to prevent himself from gagging.

After passing through a series of unlocked doors further along the corridor, he reached some kind of shipping warehouse deep inside the building.

The interior was a mass of activity. Oblong wooden crates lay scattered and piled up on the bare floorboards and inmates in hospital gowns fussed over the objects. They were too intent upon their work to pay any attention to Dunn as he mingled with them. He was overcome with a mixture of nausea and horror at the scene and felt as if he had stumbled onto the set of an expressionist horror film.

There were dozens of emaciated people working in the chamber. All of them were quite obviously mentally disturbed. Their eyes were either dead or manic and surrounded by deep black rings. Yet despite this they laboured as a well-drilled unit. A corner of this vast chamber was filled with banks of manual typewriters. The inmates that worked away on them by candlelight were wholly absorbed in their tasks. In fact, as he drew closer, Dunn saw very clearly that the crumpled papers they produced were passed to the examiners. After glancing at their contents, they raised the crates' lids and inserted the bundles of documents.

Dunn had forgotten about Horace Jackson. Zoskia was, however, now close at hand and looking over a pile of papers covered with a mass of gibberish. The typewriters used here were out of date, rusty with many missing some of their letter keys. Dunn saw examples of the texts being produced: they were schizophrenic ravings typed upon stacks of old HMSO affidavit forms.

"Listen," Zoskia said, "Jackson told me to tell you he'd arranged for you to take over from him. He was persuaded to retire, to stay and seek refuge from the world."

"To seek refuge from the world? You mean *here*?" Dunn replied. He had to lean a hand against the table to steady himself.

"Yes," Zoskia babbled, sucking at a toothless gap in her gums, "He agreed that he might as well stay. Anyway, we felt he had lost interest in our case. Lack of enthusiasm over time. No good to us outside anymore"

"Look," Dunn said, "I want no part of this, no matter what Mr Jackson's decided. I'm going back."

"You will live in that world of darkness for a myriad of years and no-one will know of your existence." She said.

Without responding, he turned away from Dr. Zoskia and caught a glimpse of four inmates carrying a heavy crate into the warehouse. Something stuck out of the gap between one of its sides and an ill-fitting, bent lid. Before he had time to think about what he'd seen, an inmate pushed the obtrusion back inside the box. It appeared to have been a lifeless flabby hand.

"The legal papers are in the boot of Jackson's car. You'll do your job, you'll carry on with our case, and anyway you have no choice. Everyone has to make sacrifices don't they?"

*

Dunn returned to the offices alone using Jackson's car. He had one of the porters of the Inn assist him in carrying the boxes of legal documents up to the top-floor offices of Coney Court Chambers.

Miss Jenkins expressed no surprise at the sudden transfer of power from Jackson to Dunn. Over the next few days, as he took over the running of his former employers' legal practice, she even began to flirt with him. There was no difficulty in the matter of Dunn now assuming full control over business affairs. Amongst the papers he had brought back from the Zoskia Institution was a codicil signed by Jackson naming him as sole beneficiary.

Despite his horrible experiences, Dunn realised that it was in his own interests to at least maintain the pretence of continuing to pursue the 'Regina vs. Zoskia' case. As well as taking over Jackson's less-than-onerous workload, he was also to benefit from additional income provided by the terms of the codicil, provided he remained. However, the immediate consequence of this was that he had to examine the papers he'd brought back with him from the pseudo-asylum, correlate their contents and determine how useful they were in relation to previous statements already bearing on the case. So, working at home on the papers until well into the morning, Dunn sat up every night for the next two weeks in his little flat hidden away in a maze of railway arches, renovated warehouses and alleyways close to Fenchurch Street Station in the City. The gibberish he was forced to read coincided with the onset of a prolonged case of insomnia. At least it spared him from nightmares about the Zoskia Institution.

Dunn's flat, which he had been bequeathed by his uncle Charlie whom he had met only a few times as a child, was situated within the attic of a mouldy building. Perhaps this had been his late uncle's idea of a joke, for the place was scarcely fit for human habitation. Dunn doubted whether his relation had ever used it during his banking career, though an aunt dropped hints that a prostitute with whom Charlie had become infatuated during his last years had lived there. She'd been

35

forced to vacate the place after his death. Weird, unwelcome legacies seemed to have become a defining feature of Dunn's life. He had no choice when it came to his career and home.

The ceiling of the flat was low and the passageways cramped. From the dusty back window Dunn had a view over the small, hidden churchyard of St. Olaf's. A high brick wall topped with iron spikes hemmed in the burial ground. On a triangular lintel above the gateway there was a bas-relief depicting three horribly grinning skulls. These three were, to Dunn's mind, a most effective reminder of mortality. The churchyard was overrun with weeds and half a dozen stunted trees. Close to the edges of the wall lurked shapeless grave-mounds, eroded by centuries of weathering. The tombstones were lop-sided; the names of those whom they commemorated obliterated by circles of lichen. The buildings that surrounded the churchyard were all like that one in which Dunn had been forced to dwell, half-derelict and threatened with demolition and urban redevelopment. What businesses that had operated from the premises had crept away to healthier environs over the course of the last few decades. Yet for some unaccountable reason, the tenements still stood, overlooked monuments to decay and neglect, in defiance of all the glass and steel skyscrapers in whose shadows they hid.

During one of those long nights, as he laboured into the small hours of the morning poring over certain of the statements, Dunn happened to glance out of the smoky window that overlooked the churchyard. That night was lit by a full moon. Down amongst the ancient tombstones and the weeds he saw a group of figures digging up a patch of the mouldering soil with spades. Resting against one of the stunted trees was a ladder that they had doubtless hauled in after them once they were inside. Somehow the men had also managed to get a crate over the wall despite the spikes. It seemed that their purpose was not to disinter one of the graves, but rather to bury the oblong wooden box.

Dunn watched their activities with a horrified fascination. He

36

thought of calling the police and was on the verge of getting up to do so when one of the figures happened to glance upward, giving Dunn a clear view of his face in the silvery moonlight. His skin was dead white, the features framed by long black hair and a grizzled beard that grew down to the top of his chest. It was the man he'd seen by the swimming pool in the Zoskia Institution, the man with the appearance of a mad Russian mystic. He was laughing without making a sound, like an actor in a silent movie. He gestured to one of his companions and between them they levered open the lid of the oblong crate. Dunn knew that, for whatever bizarre reason, this mummers' play was being performed for his benefit.

Inside the crate was a mass of papers. Dunn could see a ruinous face, protruding like the tip of an iceberg from the turbulent sea of crumpled pages.

Dunn could not tear his gaze away. He didn't doubt that it was a warning from his clients. Then a bank of thick cloud passed over the moon, plunging the churchyard into total darkness.

Later, exhaustion must have overtaken him for he awoke just after dawn slumped at his desk, and surrounded by papers from the 'Regina vs. Zoskia' case. As if in a trance he descended the narrow staircase to the streets, turned the corner and passed into the churchyard via the gateway from whose lintel leered down the three carved skulls. At the spot where the men had been digging, there was now a small mound of freshly turned soil. Dunn was under no illusion that what he witnessed last night was a dream, or even some hallucination brought on by overwork and lack of sleep. Although there was not a single scrap of paper littering the churchyard, he spied a glinting object nestling in a clump of weeds that confirmed his worst fears. It was a signet ring with a large onyx stone into which were engraved the gilded initials 'H.J.'

*

Regina vs. Zoskia

A few days later Henry Dunn stood upon the mosaic pavement of the immense central hall of the Royal Courts of Justice in the Strand. Heavy rain lashed at the high windows and cast a funereal gloom over the interior. He was relieved to be inside and out of the downpour, for the great clock tower and arcaded front were so drenched that the whole structure seemed to have lately risen from watery depths. The members of the legal profession who passed Dunn by cast baffled looks at the dishevelled, soaked little man who stood regarding a painting of the Anti-Slavery Convention of June 1840 with a distracted air.

Down the maze-like corridors of that imposing Gothic pile, with more than a thousand rooms and containing over three and a half miles of passageways and stairs, there is an out-of-the-way little chamber with green tiles on its walls. It is unknown to all but a handful of those who use the law courts. Dunn had only learned of its existence since examining the gigantic brief for the 'Regina vs. Zoskia' case. This chamber was part of an almost forgotten division of the law courts, one scarcely used but still forming a tiny, rusty cog in the vast machine of the English legal system. It was to this room that Dunn made his way, clutching his heavy leather bag stuffed with typewritten papers. His boots left sodden footprints in his wake.

Dunn had to consult the hastily scrawled map previously prepared by Jackson when he had been obliged to make the same navigation of the Law Courts' innermost recesses in search of the green chamber. Most of the offices Dunn passed were long-abandoned, and there were even a number of ghostly Victorian courtrooms given over to decay; relics from another epoch, their docks, benches and galleries occupied solely by shadows. He walked alone, not having seen another person on similar business for the last twenty minutes. The lighting was atrocious. Many of the lamps were broken and those that worked seemed to emit only a dim, often intermittent, glow. The arched ceilings and gothic niches, the

38

narrow flights of worn steps, the echoing and serpentine corridors lined with cracked tiles; they seemed to be endless. Certain passageways even led nowhere, save to darkness. If Dunn had not been in possession of the map he believed it likely he would never have been able to retrace his path out of the labyrinth.

The dereliction around him reminded Dunn uncannily of the Zoskia 'Asylum'. He realised that here, in the bowels of the Law Courts, the flip side of the interminable case was revealed; an official legislature as deranged as his clients' and their inner sanctum. Plaintiff and Defendant were distorted mirror-images of one another, unyielding, forever locked in a grotesque dance, each attempting to overcome their nemesis whilst in their own death-throes.

Finally, Dunn reached his destination. He stood in front of a panelled door on which a notice hung. It was written on a foolscap sheet of aged paper, and held in place by a single nail. Scribbled on the sheet were the words:

'Regina vs. Zoskia 1964, 7 Q.B. 323. Master of the Rolls, Lord Justice Hirsig, presiding.'

Dunn knocked on the door twice and heard a muffled voice from within. He supposed it indicated that he was to enter.

It was so gloomy inside the green-tiled room that his vision took a few moments to adjust. Then he saw the legal briefs everywhere, some piled in towers tottering under their own weight, others massed in scattered heaps. Yet more loose papers littered the floor, ankle-deep, and Dunn could not avoid trampling through them as he advanced into the cramped, vaulted chamber. On impulse, he bent down to pick up a random handful of the pages, scrutinising them as best he could in the appalling light. One passage read:

'—such application of the hidden laws of the universe being incomprehensible to men even though their strict enforcement is imperative—'

This is a rubbish-dump, Dunn thought, for all the paperwork connected with the 'Regina vs. Zoskia' case. He stifled a hysterical laugh that bubbled up in his throat.

A faint rustle in the sea of papers to his left made him start. Someone appeared to have been buried underneath a heap of rotting affidavits, summonses and writs. Dunn saw a shoe and part of a leg sticking out from the bottom of the pile and began clearing away the papers hiding the rest of the body. He uncovered an old man, his face squashed with age, his skull almost turned to jelly. The ancient was toothless and his uncannily bulging eyes were closed. He was dressed in a Judge's legal garb, dusty black robes and a peri-wig. However, a vestige of life still remained in his carcass for he murmured something and Dunn bent down to catch the words. Drool oozed from the revenant's puckered lips as he spoke in a voice like dried leaves:

"Henry Dunn acting for both the Plaintiff and the Defendant, what have you to say?"

The Judge opened his eyes to reveal that the sockets had been hollowed out and then stuffed with crumpled paper balls covered in writing. Perhaps the whole of his cranium had been filled with brittle documents.

Dunn removed a huge brief in a buff folder bound with red ribbon from his bag. He began to present his case; both for and against. He scarcely noticed that he was no longer sane, at least in any recognisable sense of the word.

THE OLDER MAN

Gary Fry

Jack Preen had been standing outside his flat for twenty minutes that Friday morning before the truck arrived. RAPID RELIABLE - PAINTING AND SCAFFOLDING read the sign on the door of the cab; well maybe, yet today they would be late for the new job. Still, Pat Stone was an amiable enough boss, and there were certainly worse ways to make a living. Better too, but more recently, Jack had tried not to think too much about that. As the vehicle chugged off, he suppressed a playful resentment of the third man up front: a sociology undergraduate at the local university, Louis Fluck was almost half Jack's age. The metal piping that rattled in tow served only to remind Jack of essential cosmetic renovations...

Dear, dear. Thank fuck it was near the weekend. Even though they were working tomorrow, there was the gig to look forward to this evening. He resigned himself to his least preferred, if more regular, source of playboy funds.

"So Jack, what time you on stage tonight?" His fifty-year-old frame struggling with the transmission, Pat steered into a tree-lined grove. "Me and the missus were thinking about coming down, see."

"What's the name of your band again?" Louis wanted to know.

"We're called Fatal Inversion. I'll be there at the mike about nine."

"I was thinking about bringing a few friends myself."

"You all going to give my vocals a critical analysis, eh, Louis?"

"It's his bird they'll all be, ahem, studying," Pat cut in, pulling up at the kerb of a cul-de-sac outside a leafy overgrown garden. "Don't know how you've managed to keep a young sort like that."

"If she's tasty, it must be his rock star sensibilities - you

41

know, the image. Women tend to find status desirable in their partners, whereas for blokes it the way she looks that's more important."

"Hey, why don't you guys just talk about me as if I weren't here!" Yet despite his secret discomfort, Jack was smiling. He ran a wrinkling hand through his cropped dyed hair, tweaked an earring, and then glanced out the window. "This the house? Who lives here?"

The driver briefed them on the task ahead - something about an old lady who had died or was dying, and her daughter and son-in-law moving in. The couple wanted the stuccoed exterior painting white. After the scaffolding had been erected, Jack would take the top floor, Louis the second, and Pat the ground on account of his periodic arthritis.

As the guys climbed out of the van, Jack thought he'd seen a movement at an upstairs window - pale and rapid - but when he looked more closely, there was nothing.

The property was a neat detached with a square of lawn to the front and a snaking tangle of undergrowth at the rear. As Jack and Louis began to assemble the steel, Pat went inside to announce their presence. After a while an attractive woman, thirty-something and dressed with panache, was seen in the lounge window. She smiled when she caught the singer's eye and he reciprocated, a gesture that didn't go unnoticed by the student.

"So much for this stunning girl you're seeing!" The lad gazed back at the pane, but the homeowner had disappeared. "You're out of your league there, mate. This place must be three-hundred-K. I'm told she's a solicitor. Wonder what her husband does."

"I thought females of a superior status liked a bit of rough. That puts a shadow on your theory, don't it?"

"Not necessarily. Some argue that attraction is an evolutionary imperative. By seeking out a hard chap, she's ensured good stock - that is, strong kids. Alternatively, this might all be a social construction, because others believe that as gender roles shift, the successful woman becomes less concerned about the ability of her man to provide. In short, suddenly it's the blokes who have to *look* the part."

"Louis?"

"Yes, Jack?"

"You're incredibly dull and a bastard. Did you know that?"

"It's been hinted at previously, yes."

"Then let me raise such protest to a yell!"

The conversation dissolved into laughter, and when Pat returned from his glorious consultation, his eyes were knowing too. "Fucking hell, lads," he muttered in an undertone, gripping one arm at its bent elbow, "if I were twenty years younger..."

The hilarity raged anew, though soon there was the solitude of individual divisions of labour.

Jack was instructed to go into the basement to prise the lids off the paint and give the tubs a stir. The lowest room of the building was a grotty little quarter. Spiders scurried along the concrete underfoot; the corners were dark and dirty. There was stuff leftover presumably from the previous occupant - the solicitor's mother, had that been? Here was an old photograph displaying a couple not unlike his own late parents, if perhaps a class above, since these two were groomed and standing beside an expensive car. She was pretty and slender, and he was stoutly important. Yes, the sociological rule was holding there: the older bald fellow hadn't pulled such a sweet wife on account of his appearance!

Had matters changed really? Using a stick to thicken the glossy liquid, Jack found himself staring into a broken mirror. He hadn't let himself go, yet how much of this was a reaction to the contemporary world? He wondered if Stella, his girlfriend of nearly two years, stayed with him on account of his position in the rock band or his efforts cosmetically. He'd managed to keep the weight off, despite his fondness for the bottle. He wasn't very tall, but he was broad; good dress sense too. So what if he was forty next time? He didn't seem to be.

His reasoning was growing increasingly desperate; the wood in the paint went round more vigorously.

His almost extinct pop ambition could not be rescued by self-deception. And his power over the opposite sex, the one element that singled him out from obscurity, was hanging by a proverbial thread...

Just then he heard footsteps somewhere inside the building.

Jack Preen stepped outside with three tubs and welcomed the opportunity to lose himself in graft.

By lunchtime the scaffolding was in place, and after venturing into the nearby village for fish and chips, the team made a start with its brushes. Jack climbed a sequence of ladders to the upper platform, waving through a window at the man of the house in his first floor office. Earlier the husband had made them hot drinks, explaining that he was a writer whose first book, an exposé of supposed ghostly sightings, had been delayed by his publisher. His wife had taken a week away from her chambers in order to tackle the interior, though she hadn't been seen again that morning. Jack wondered how this rather plain unsuccessful character, in his comfortable cords and woolly sweater, had managed to hold the attention of such a beauty. It wasn't fair; Jack had more than him. Maybe the modern woman desired something of which he was unaware...

The top floor was cramped, its gables shallow triangles. There were three windows, one of them thin and frosted, the second giving on to a cluttered storeroom, and another around the back that Jack had yet to reach. The paint went on in clotted pleats, which were smeared about with the considerable wedge of bristles. He was enjoying himself, even when he reached the tricky bit at the frames.

As he concentrated on attaining a neat edge, he heard a noise from within. Through a distorting pane he saw movement at a lavatory, a pinkish narrow figure reduced to an emaciated mass. Was this the gorgeous woman who'd given him the eye earlier? It was nearing 5pm - time to finish up. Jack gathered his tub and flew to the rear. Before retreating, the shape inside had made a sound like the smacking of wet firm lips.

The largest window of the third flight revealed a poky bedroom bearing a single mattress on a threadbare base. Sheets lay a-tangle upon a mucky slipcover; they appeared to be enfolding debris, like a tissue over the carcass of a consumed chicken. Who slept here? Probably nobody. These were arguably the remains of the former owner, the old lady who'd either died or was dying, possibly in a hospital or a rest home. Jack looked left at a gaping entrance, leading on to a hallway. There was a shadow shifting along this uncarpeted tract - it grew longer, deeper. It was headed for this area of the house.

Perhaps he should glance away, descend the metal framework. The early autumn evening had dropped its murky portent; Jack saw his ripening reflection in the glass.

The visitant shuffled to the jamb, and then hobbled across the threshold. It was indeed a woman, though not the one he'd anticipated. She was naked, her distended breasts flapping above a sagging belly. Her pubic hair was alopecic, dividing unsteady legs. Stunted toes clawed at the boards, just as fingers worked feebly. Jack examined her face: it was a rotting parody. The cheekbones had nigh on imploded, her forehead supporting a thatch of wire. Nevertheless, as she staggered closer to the pane, he realised that the compressed rheumy eyes were somehow familiar. Although greatly advanced in years, this was the lady from the photograph in the cellar: the solicitor's mother.

Maybe she hadn't seen him - was she blind or senile? Jack turned away as the messy sheets were manipulated. He hurried down to the ground where his colleagues were packed and ready to depart. The couple had come to the front door to see them off; they stood a significant distance apart. As the van was started, Jack was glad to be gone. He didn't say a word on the way back; he needed a drink.

In his flat, he stripped and washed at the kitchen sink. During the last few months, stretch marks had appeared on his hips and buttocks; his teeth had gone a hue more yellow than

45

enamel. His pectorals had developed orange-flesh, and his knees were dangling several folds of skin. The bags under his eyes were getting fuller, while hair was fed in an infuriating loop from his nose, and rather less so, his grey faltering scalp. He was in short falling apart.

Jack Preen put on his most forgiving leather outfit and struck off up the lane for his local pub. Ten minutes later he had supped his first pint.

Stella arrived at 8pm, just before he was due to start warming up with his band. This was a competent outfit; drummers and guitarists had come and gone. Jack had taken song writing seriously when he'd hit thirty - a sure indication of the clock ticking away - though he didn't have the talent for either words or tunes, so he'd decided to concentrate on performance. He was an able vocalist, popular among younger age groups; his repertoire included pop and rock. Woman were particularly captivated by what he reckoned must be his raw lyricism, a kind of lay-Rod Stewart (and lay him they had in his prime!) who was running to seed. In truth, he was very ordinary, a nice guy who traded on image.

But how long would this modest status last? Oh, he had a string or two to his bow yet.

He opened with 'Candle in the Wind', a melancholy rendering that had the audience swaying in unison. Pat and his wife had showed, as had Louis and a bunch of his mates. That pleased Jack almost as much as seeing his girlfriend gawping at him, undeniable lust in her big brown eyes. She was by no means the only female wearing such an expression. As he warbled on with 'Ghost Town', he noticed that many of the prettiest had somewhat nondescript partners, while none of the good-looking guys was with a plain companion. He glanced again at the sociology student. Could the clever lad be right about attraction between the sexes?

At the end of Fatal Inversion's stint, he stepped off to applause, hoots, and whistles. He joined a select few at the bar and ordered drinks all round from his fifty pounds fee. Stella was all over him, clearly suggesting that they might move on soon, to his place since she shared a rented property with her hairdresser pals. Jack was aroused by the prospect, though couldn't this wait a while? He was relishing the after-show buzz. It *wasn't* that he was eager to postpone the removal of his clothing until he'd drunk enough not to care. Near last orders, he found himself engaged in rather fragmented conversation with the colleagues of his real job.

"That house we're at," Jack was shouting above the din of the jukebox, "that woman!"

"Cor, yeah, if I weren't married..." Pat answered with less volume, since Mrs Stone was loitering behind them, chatting to some of Louis's very drunk tagalongs.

"Whatever it is you're thinking, don't!" the singer added, breaking into laughter. "I'm not ref-, referring to her."

His boss and the student exchanged a puzzled stare.

"Ah but of course you didn't see her, did you, the pair of you? On the top floor. B-bare as the d-day she was b-born. Hideous sight!"

"What was?"

"The old lady. Whoops, shush, here comes more of them!"

Pat's wife and Stella had encroached on the trio. Jack just had the opportunity to hear Louis reply in an alcoholic slur, "There was only one in the prop-, prop-, property. The mother d-died a fffffortnight ago..." And then he was jerked to one side, just as his boss had been. Both attached men, and the enviably youthful undergraduate, decided to call it a night.

Back at his flat, Jack switched out the lights before preparing for bed. In such a state, there wasn't a great deal of effort involved; rather, his girlfriend tugged off his pants, and he lifted her dress as they collapsed together on the clean duvet. Moonlight tumbled in through the drawn curtains, and immediately Jack was conscious of Stella's smooth pert body. She wouldn't always be this way, of course. Curiously the thought dismayed him, made his penis droop a little. Was there something on his mind, something he'd been told recently?

Suddenly all speculation about old ladies was occluded by the mouth at his groin. Stella was gripping his flabby thighs; she didn't seem concerned that these had seen their best days. Didn't women care? He recalled his own parents: his always-tidy mum, his grubby little dad. Perhaps relationships *were* changing, though not very noticeably.

As he came ungracefully, he considered the solicitor at the house. Was she content with a superior position to her husband's? They hadn't seemed happy in one another's company. Perhaps it all came down to the class system, Jack thought. A man from his own lowly background was less able to break the old traditions than a woman with her status. He'd ask Louis about it tomorrow. Perhaps the lad would have a simple answer for a change.

It took him half-an-hour to get into shape before leaving for work. His girlfriend tied up her hair and scraped on a light coat of makeup in five minutes. In the street he kissed her flawless complexion, and as she wiggled away, the truck appeared; he climbed onboard like an old man, his ageing frame in protest after his exertions the previous evening.

There was no talk for several miles, but when the driver steered the rickety vehicle onto the grove, Jack was jolted into an enquiry.

"Hey, Louis, what the fuck were you on about last night?"

"Which bit?" Pat interrupted. "We all talked a lot of bollocks, didn't we? My missus hasn't spoken to me this morning. She must have overheard us referring to the, ahem, delectable lady of this house."

"Well, that's who I mean - not her, the other one. The, er, horrible crone." He twisted to the student, inexplicably nervous. "What did you say as we left?"

Again, their boss cut in. "Yeah, I remember. You'd got some weird idea that the old dear was still living here. Well, as the chap said, she died two weeks ago. That's why sexy and her hubbie are moving in."

"Wh-who told you?"

48

"I got talking to the guy late afternoon - the writer. He's a ghost debunker apparently. There're age-old rumours that this place is haunted. What better method of ensuring sales than living in a spooky dwelling?"

"I- I—"

"What's up, Jack?" asked Pat with a teasing smile, as he slumped out for fresh air. "Mortality tapping you on the shoulder? You should think how *I* feel!"

"Years in me yet," the undergraduate gibed, joining his elder outside.

Jack, left alone in the middle of the cab, had started to shake, and not only as a result of alcohol.

He was able to stabilise himself by stirring the paint for the day. The cellar thrust forth seasonal shadow; he heard a voice above, a female protesting. Now he noticed the staircase in one corner, leading on to a connecting door. Setting aside the stick, he trotted up the flight, creeping through the entrance. He found himself in the hallway of the rundown building. The front entrance had just been slammed, and through a window in a lounge, Jack could see the husband stumping angrily for a car: a dated hatchback beside a sparkling Mercedes. The kitchen lay off to the left; Pat and Louis were chatting beyond the greasy pane. On a chair ahead sat the glamorous woman, her dark hair falling on casual clothing, and a cloth in her palms. She was in a flood of pitiful tears.

"Hey, hey, what's wrong?" His lingering disquiet allayed, he stooped to the homeowner, grinning as she raised her head.

"Personal problems," she explained, a mite stiffly, though her features had brightened, too. She added with more gentleness, "What are you doing in here anyway?"

"Is this a cross-examination?" Despite the pain in his skull, the charm hadn't failed him. "Okay, I confess. Guilty as charged: first degree compassion."

Now she chuckled. She dried her face with one sleeve, exhaled sharply. "Thanks for that. You're nice."

"Nice? Me? Through the day yes, but at night…"

49

"You should speak to Michael - he'd soon rationalise your delusions."

"He's your—"

"Yes. Oh, I'm sorry. I shouldn't be setting any of this on you. It's just that my mother died recently and I'm having a difficult time. The release of *his* book has been delayed again. He's feeling useless, I'm overwrought." There was only a brief hesitation before she added, "Jesus, I could do with a good shag!"

"Huh? Wha—"

"Do I shock you? What can I say? I love the way you dress."

"Oh I, er—"

"You're doing the top floor, aren't you?"

"Erm, ye—"

"There's a bedroom up there - it used to be my dad's office. He was a solicitor too, yet mum didn't have a problem with that. She was a housewife for most of her life, but she's been - *was* a widow this past decade. Anyway, you don't need to hear this. How about it?"

"Eh?"

"Climb in the window; we can do it on the bed. My father used that to figure out his cases. It's an inspirational item of furniture!"

"It's filthy," Jack replied feebly.

The woman stood, drawing him to his feet. "I know I'm confused and vulnerable. That doesn't make me a fool. I saw the look you gave me yesterday; I read it well. It's what I do every day in court. You want me and I want you. So...*come on.*"

It was very flattering: even at his worst he was able to pull the best of them, regardless of social rank! He glared at her, noticing wrinkles around her mouth: she couldn't be much younger than him; he was tempted. Nevertheless the thought of his appearance beneath the trendy denim had him backing off, headed for the cellar and muttering, "I'm sorry, I can't. I'm, er, not available."

That was an excuse. He lifted the tubs, before rushing for his waiting colleagues who said, "Thought you'd died in there," and, "Or gone stir crazy, ho, ho!" before Jack ascended the scaffolding with his brush, the better to get the task done, leave, put this whole midlife crisis behind him.

It hadn't been that he'd feared the sight of a naked older female. What was pressing at his memory was merely an illusion caused by too much drinking. He tried to recall Stella's body, the faultless flesh that rendered his own comparatively repulsive. He couldn't reveal that to the lady of this house. Jack painted maniacally, closing in on the broadest sheet of glass. He heard speech lower down.

"...so what you're saying, Louis, is that us more ancient folk - couples, perhaps I mean - have firmer understandings: we know what's what, and how to relate to one another?"

"Yeah, that's it. This is not necessarily a good thing - certain entrenched inequalities, et cetera - but at least it seems to function in a fluid manner. Man does right by woman - am I talking about finance, particular home comforts? - and she does right by him. I'll leave the last bit to your very capable imagination, Pat!"

A lewd growl followed, yet Jack had stopped listening. He was almost at the frame. It occurred to him that his mental activity was an attempt to hold aside a most troubling perception. It was all nonsense; he only need glance inside the bedroom. He did so, his heart hammering audibly in the chill midmorning.

There was nothing on the bed save for the grubby, stuffed sheet. This had been redistributed, presumably by the solicitor as she'd cleaned the interior. Was she apt to return? Surely he'd made his decision clear. Jack continued to run bristles along the line of the lintel. His arms betrayed will, reducing his standard to slipshod.

There was somebody coming along the unseen hall passage.

Maybe she'd heard him trembling on the metal. Would she be dressed as he'd seen her on the ground floor, or nude as she'd been earlier - no, no, that hadn't been her, had it? Rather someone who'd resembled her, far in advance of that age; older than Jack, double his years; decrepit, disgusting, dirty—

The newcomer crawled around the jamb, sticklike limbs taking in the air. He watched, hypnotised and stationary, as the bare cadaver made its sluggish way towards the mattress. It was she who he'd been spying upon the day before, and similarly she didn't acknowledge him. In such a condition, she was surely eager for rest. She gripped the wrinkly covers, misshapen like disease, and he thought: there has to be some mistake. Another guest was lodging with them, a favoured aunt or possibly Michael's mother. It was only a little insensitive of the solicitor to offer her dad's ex-office. The dotard was climbing in now.

In fact, *on*.

Suddenly Jack's qualms had resurfaced. A chap must have something in order to guarantee the ladies, and that factor-X was changing as tradition was eroded. Once he'd relied on his status, and this still held true in some sense, but what of the future? Jack scrutinised the fading looks of his reflection, yet he was unable to gaze away from the travesty inside the chamber.

The sheets had been pulled back, and now the stripped woman, her putrefied breasts dangling like organic pendulums, straddled what remained on the mattress.

There wasn't a great deal left of him. He'd gone thoroughly black with the ravages of a passing generation. His torso was haggard, a hunk of dissolving meat that sprouted arms and legs like wasted potato buds. When the head came up in receipt of pleasure, Jack saw a toothy smile barely repressed by flesh. Perhaps the senior solicitor wasn't actually seeing him, but as his comparatively appealing wife continued her dry-moist gobbling at a stunted disaster of genitals, his eyeballs bulged in the bone, the pupils that ought to be dead slowly dilating, indicating ecstasy, a knowing stare.

If there'd been anything attached that resembled lids, Jack

fancied that the man, his old-fashioned boundaries firmly in place, might have winked his way.

POWER

Steve Goodwin

I

The first time I saw Marek he was pissing into an unmarked grave. Tottering unsteadily on the edge, the soft soil crumbling beneath his booted feet as he rocked drunkenly backwards and forwards. It wasn't an empty grave but sometime over the course of the last sixty or seventy years the loosely compacted and rotted earth had begun to subside, leaving a shallow trough about six inches deep which sent the acrid stream of beer-coloured piss splashing back up onto his heavy boots and turned-up jeans.

From my vantage point behind the tree, I stood dead still, a cold sick fear spreading through my stomach and chest in case I should make even the slightest noise. It was quite dark now and I was unlikely to be seen there in the shadows, but one injudicious movement of the foot, one small snap of a twig, could still alert the shaven-headed figure to my presence. I could sense his anger, his hatred, even through the numbing effect of the alcohol and I didn't want him to get the wrong idea. I hadn't gone to the old Jewish cemetery in the forest to peep at skinheads with their cocks out but I couldn't very well expect him to believe that.

And the real reason for my regular nocturnal visits there was even less likely to convince. I liked it there. It was a tragic place. Obscene almost in the extent of its neglect, unchecked decay and deliberate desecration and vandalism. But somehow I found comfort there. Amongst the weeds, the broken headstones and the collapsed graves half-filled with beer and vodka bottles. It confirmed some belief I held. About the world. About People.

After what seemed like an unnaturally long time, the pale steaming arc of the skinhead's urine finally spluttered and dipped. Marek shook himself, cursed, spat loudly into the shadowy hole in front of him and began to lurch off into the trees, fumbling awkwardly with the buttons of his fly as he went. I stayed where I was, still not daring to move as I listened to him making his way deeper into the forest. Into the surrounding night.

I'd first come across the old cemetery by accident. A walk with Magda in the forest near her family home. A beautiful snow-drifted day, bright and keen. We walked holding hands while she told me at some length how to tell edible mushrooms from poisonous ones and how once, when she was about eight years old, her and a friend had found a packet of Russian cigarettes and come into the forest and smoked the whole pack. My head full of childhood and old wives' tales I'd decided to wander off on my own for a bit, half hoping I'd come across one of the wild boar that someone had told me still lived wild in the area.

I hadn't recognised it as a cemetery at first. Just an uneven patch of ground with some broken stones scattered here and there across it. It was only when my foot slipped into some kind of shallow leaf-covered depression and I nearly stumbled and fell that I began to pay more attention to the details of my surroundings.

"A cemetery," said Magda who'd come up behind me. "A Jewish cemetery - but they haven't used it since the war."

"But how could people let it get into a state like this?" I was genuinely shocked.

"There are no Jewish people here anymore," answered Magda simply.

"Someone else then. Whoever does live around here now." I checked myself before continuing, not wanting to be seen as making any explicit, or even implied, criticism of her family who lived nearest to the forest. "They don't have to be Jewish. It's a cemetery for God's sake, you could at least keep it… decent."

"No one really comes here anymore. Only drinkers. And

55

children."

I was staring down at my right foot which I now realised I'd inadvertently planted in an untended and decaying grave. Amongst the rubble and the brittle, frosted leaves, I could just make out the damp, curling edge of a discarded red and white cigarette packet.

I couldn't bring myself to look up at Magda.

I first came back to visit the old cemetery on my own a month or two later. *Zaduszki*, the day to pray for the souls of the dead. I'd been to the main cemetery in S------- with Magda that morning. She'd wanted to visit the grave of her friend who'd been killed in a car crash when they were sixteen. She'd bought some flowers and a large, red candle at the cemetery gates and we'd found the plot with a minimum of searching, standing, heads bowed, by the immaculate black flower-wreathed marble bearing the small sepia-toned photograph of her friend. A school photograph, taken shortly before the accident. No trace of a smile. Had he known? Magda prayed quietly under her breath. To herself.

After what felt like a decent amount of time had passed, I told her that I was feeling unwell and would have to leave. No, she wasn't to worry, I was sure I'd be alright. Yes, I would call her. I stopped by the gates on the way out to buy another candle and started to walk hurriedly, anxious not to be observed, in the direction of the nearby village where Magda's family lived.

I spent several hours in the old Jewish cemetery in the forest that evening. Lighting the candle and watching it burn slowly away. I didn't pray but I did do a lot of thinking. It was easier to think there for some reason. Something about the place made everything clearer somehow. About ten o'clock I made my way back to the unlit road, slipped quietly past Magda's house and started the long walk back to town. It was very dark now and after I'd nearly been killed by two careering drunk drivers, I decided it might be better to look around for somewhere to spend the night.

Power

The bus shelter smelt of ammonia and stale smoke but it was dry and went some way towards keeping the wind out. The wooden slats of the peeling, knife-marked bench dug into my ribs and meant that sleep was a long time coming. But there was just enough light to make out the graffiti and crudely-drawn genitalia on the wall in front of me and, after I'd read and re-read the various inscriptions: FUCK, SKINS, SZATAN 666, I finally slipped into numbness.

II

On the roadside my apartment overlooked a small green & yellow painted corrugated metal kiosk and the local Maxi supermarket. From about mid-day onwards a small crowd of jobbing drinkers would gather around the entrance to the supermarket to squabble and smoke. Two or three would squat in the dust and pass round a bottle, ritually wiping the neck on their sleeves between swigs. The rest preferred to stand, occasionally engaging in spitting and pushing games to break the monotony.

From the kitchen at the back the view was altogether more imposing. By the river on the other side of the park stood the town's Teutonic castle.

Allenstein Castle was built in the 14th Century as a stronghold for an order of monastic knights. It had withstood countless sieges and a couple of major wars. Had been the scene of several important scientific discoveries and housed - until it was finally plundered of most of its treasures in the first few decades of the last Century - some of the finest works of art in Central Europe.

On my first evening in the flat, I'd been disturbed from my cold impromptu meal by the noisy passage, just outside the back window and then overhead rustling and flapping across the roof, of between fifty and a hundred bats coming from the castle tower. My life certainly didn't want for Gothic flourishes.

I'd never have gone to Viking Pub if I hadn't have run out of cigarettes. The kiosk always closed early and even the supermarket shut around nine o'clock. Viking Pub lay at the bottom of the hill as you walked down into town. I'd walked past it many times but never thought about going in. Even if you couldn't see inside from the street, it was clear from the swastikas and other insignia sprayed and daubed on the blank dirty-white wall outside that the regular clientele consisted largely of local skinheads and soccer thugs. But that night I was just desperate enough.

All eyes didn't turn. The music didn't stop. The conversation never lulled. But still I knew that my entrance had been noted by everyone there. Eyes fixed straight ahead, I approached the bar with a purposeful stride and what I imagined was an air of measured confidence, which hopefully stopped just the right side of arrogance not to get bottled or glassed.

"*Piwo*," I demanded. The first word of Polish I'd learnt. Why not have a drink now that I'd come this far. "...*i paczka Marlboro.*"

The barman raised himself off his stool just high enough to reach up and take down a packet of cigarettes which he placed on the bar, then he took down a glass, wiped it, and steadied it under the single pump.

"A large beer?" he asked in English, beaming broadly at me.

"Er... Yes. Thank you."

"You are English?" This question came not from the bar, but from the end of one of the long low tables around which some dozen or so shaved and jacketed skins huddled conspiratorially. At the head of the table a face, I recognised. They say that if you don't want to be intimidated by someone, you should imagine them sitting on the toilet with their pants round their ankles. I remembered how the last time I'd seen this bloke he'd had his knob in his hand. It didn't really help.

"Manchester?"

All eyes on me. Expectant. I had to admit it. Yes.

A nod. "Do you have any gadgets?"

"Gadgets?" Boss skinhead's English wasn't too bad, but now he'd lost me.

"Hooligan gadgets."

I reached across the bar and took a sip of beer. Sweating casual disinterest. "I don't know what you mean."

By way of an answer, the skinhead reached into his jacket pocket producing a vicious looking object, which glinted in the dim interior light as he slipped it almost lovingly over his fingers and down to the knuckles of his right hand.

"No... I don't have any gadgets."

"So. You are not a real hooligan."

"No." Another determined swig. "I don't like sport." I fumbled with the Marlboro packet trying to find a way into the plastic... found it at last... and, counting silently from one to ten and back again, drew out a cigarette - holding it between dry, bitten lips. To my relief it lit first time.

All the time his steady gaze never left me.

"Join us."

Marek was a natural leader, you could tell that right away. He had authority. He was possessed of power. I was introduced to some of the others. Radek had blond hair and blue eyes and the face of a young boy. Pawel was missing one and a half fingers due to an accident with a power-saw at work he said, proudly. Kuba had just come out of prison. Something to do with a cache of unexploded bombs left over from the Second World War. We smoked and drank, and talked about hooligan gadgets until two or three in the morning when I left, promising to come back and see them again.

The next day I'd arranged to meet Magda at the castle. She had a friend who worked as a part-time tourist guide in the season who'd agreed to take us on a private tour at a reduced rate. Apparently the friend knew someone who worked there who would let us see parts of the castle that the public never normally got to see. I'd often thought about visiting the castle but had somehow never got round to it so this seemed like a good opportunity.

There were six of us making up the party - the guide, Magda and myself, a middle-aged Canadian couple and a thin, tired looking man who it turned out was one of the caretakers.

I wasn't in the best of moods. Something had happened that morning as I made my way across the park. Something which unnerved me for no particular reason that I could identify. Just before the wooden bridge which crossed the river at its narrowest point, a youngish man sat cross-legged on a bench testing veins in his arm with a needle. He looked up at me as I passed and smiled. Not so much friendly as... knowing. He had something strange about him. Something... not right. His upper body was naked. His bare chest smooth and hairless. He wore only an extremely baggy pair of stained, nylon track-suit bottoms. His hair was a dirty golden colour and fell about his neck and shoulders in long, unkempt curls. He eyed me expectantly for a moment and then his gaze fell back to his left arm, fixed intently on his needle and the single drop of blood which began to swell at the point where it now entered his skin. His feet, I noticed, were also bare and had the toes curled over lending an almost animal aspect to an appearance which already seemed somehow less than human. A mythical figure. A young fawn with a syringe. I moved on quickly.

The climb up to the top of the castle tower was a long one. The floor was inches deep in feathers and bird shit and the smell was rank and pungent but the view was impressive.

Apart from one or two nice paintings, most of the rooms in the main part of the castle offered up little in the way of cultural treasures. We were shown a medieval toilet and then led down into the cellars.

On first impression, the cellars didn't look that promising either but it soon became apparent that under the castle lay what seemed like miles of passageways linking together a series of large subterranean rooms each, no doubt, with some long forgotten purpose. One such high-vaulted room had a number of other much smaller rooms leading off it. Most were padlocked or nailed shut, just one door stood slightly ajar.

"What's in here?" asked John, one of the Canadians, pulling open the door.

Our guide shone her torch through the narrow opening, casting a dim, yellow light down the walls and across the floor. On the stone flags in the middle of the room lay an empty vodka bottle, a half-burnt candle and a large piece of cardboard on which had been carefully inscribed various symbols and words I couldn't decipher. They weren't Polish.

And there was something else. Stains that may have been rust marks. Or may not.

"I thought these cellars were always kept locked," said John.

By way of an answer, the caretaker closed the door.

"We go now."

III

If you want to get a quick overall impression of the kind of place you're living in, you only really need to read the first three or four pages of the local paper. The *Gazeta* that day revealed that violent street crime was on the increase - the latest victim being a young woman who'd sustained serious neck injuries when her shoulder bag and gold necklace had been ripped off in a street attack. The attack had happened just after mid-day in the town's busy main square. There had been several hundred witnesses and one man had even attempted to chase the attacker, without success. The lone attacker was described as being young and very slim with fair, shoulder-length hair and dressed in casual or sports clothing. The woman was still recovering from her injuries in the local hospital and was also being treated for shock. Elsewhere a forty-year-old club owner had been shot and killed in his own club when a group of masked men, armed with pistols (and in one case, a Kalashnikov assault rifle) had burst in and shot him in the back and head at close range. The man with the Kalashnikov had then turned his weapon on the bar, causing extensive damage and wounding two bar staff. An ambulance was called, but the bar owner had died of his wounds before reaching hospital. Russian mafia were suspected. The front page was given over to the disappearance of a child of nine who'd last been seen playing outside her family home four days ago. In international news, another man had died in South East Asia after exhibiting symptoms of a new strain of some kind of super-virus, bringing the death toll to thirteen, and war continued to rage in the Middle East and elsewhere.

Viking Pub was all but empty in the afternoons, never really filling up until after dark when the local industrial plants and factories closed. I was sitting in the corner furthest from the bar reading the paper when Marek came in.

He nodded a sharp, curt greeting, bought himself a drink and came over.

"We say; 'No news is good news'," I offered, folding up the newspaper and dropping it on the table.

Marek placed his beer next to it and sat down pulling the ashtray towards him. He fixed me with his eyes as he always did, reached into his jacket pocket for his cigarettes, took one himself and offered the packet to me.

"You are weak man," he told me with a trace of a smile. "But I like you."

I'd only just put a cigarette out but I took another one anyway.

"These... things," he indicated the newspaper. "These killings, attacks... wars, diseases. They are good things. How you say...? Like gifts from God... but you cannot understand." He flipped open his Zippo lighter with the embossed Death's head and offered me a light. I'd just been holding the cigarette in my hand, rolling it between my fingers and tapping it distractedly on the tabletop. Almost as if obeying an order, I put it in my mouth and accepted the light.

"A strong man is afraid of nothing," he continued. I noticed his hands for the first time, they were both heavily marked and stained with cuts and tattoos; the symbol of a cross in a circle, a word in Polish; SILA - strength or power. The Sila in Arabic mythology, it also occurred to me, was something like a Ghul or a Djinn. Strong hands.

"You are afraid of everything... so you will die. This is the law. The strong survive. The weak die always. Not just you, the whole world. The whole world must die."

I wanted to look away but I wasn't able to.

"So how do I become strong?"

Marek smiled. "Fuck everything."

I'd agreed to meet Marek again the following weekend. He'd promised we'd do something special. There was something in his manner that was almost evangelical. As if he wanted me to be saved.

I walked through the town turning everything he'd said over and over in my head, but the crowds of tourists made it impossible to think. I resolved to go out to the old cemetery at the earliest opportunity to try and clear my head.

It kept coming back to me that almost the first words Marek had said to me the other night in Viking Pub were; "Join us." Had he meant anything by it? Had I been chosen for some reason? Some hidden purpose.

I stopped walking suddenly leaving the crowds to push and jostle around me. Coming towards me from the other side of the square was the boy with the needle from the park. He was still smiling, still barefoot and still shirtless. No-one else seemed to notice him, it was summer now and as the days and nights had become warmer and closer, most of the visitors had cast off their anoraks and heavy jumpers in favour of T-shirts and shorts. He seemed to be coming straight to me but, at the last moment, he altered his course very slightly, just brushing my arm as he passed. Even through the sleeve of my shirt, his skin felt cold and damp. Not with sweat but with something... thicker, stickier. I looked down at my arm expecting to see a stain of some sort but there was none.

There was a smell too, sweet yet sickly and unpleasant. In my nostrils. In my mouth and on my tongue so that I had to spit on the cobbles to try and get it out.

I turned around quickly to see him disappearing into the crowds and noticed something else for the first time. Across his back, he had... not a tattoo exactly - no ink had been used, large letters had simply been scratched into his back with a needle or some other sharp implement. A knife? Four words had been carefully spelt out: GDZIE SĄ MOI LUDZIE? - 'Where are my people?'

IV

I followed the trail of bones through the trees, the whole time telling myself that they were probably animal bones but knowing full well that they weren't. Knowing already where the trail would lead me.

In the paling dusk, the old cemetery looked much as it had the last time I'd been there. Closer inspection however revealed that several of the graves had been recently disturbed and the name of a local football team sprayed over one of the few headstones which still remained upright and unbroken. A small grave near the centre had been roughly excavated and now appeared to be completely empty. Two others nearby showed further signs of digging and other interference. There were also traces of blood and faeces and a couple of discarded black plastic refuse bags.

I don't know that I'd ever felt such a complete sense of sadness and loss. Of total defeat. I lay on the ground, buried my face in the loose soil, and cried until my guts hurt and breathing was reduced to a series of short, painful jerks. I must have lain there for an hour or more, my senses slowly returning; the feeling of insects crawling over my arms and legs, twigs scratching the side of my face, the cold of the earth.

I made my way back to town by the longest route possible, taking my time and avoiding the main road. Avoiding civilisation. I didn't want to see anyone, speak to anyone, or even admit the possibility that there might be anyone else alive in the world apart from myself. The last person I wanted to see was Marek. But he found me.

The city streets and squares were largely deserted but, after I'd ignored his shouts and quickened my step, he grabbed me, pushing me down a small alleyway between some dark, silent shops and a block of dilapidated apartments.

My eyes still burned and stung and for the first time I found myself able to avoid his gaze.

"Look at me!"

"No!"

"So... you are brave man now, uh?" He punched me hard in the stomach, propping me up against a wall with his other hand, not allowing me to fall. His face pushed up against the side of my head, his mouth next to my ear. "It hurts?"

I nodded, the side of my face scraping against the brickwork.

His teeth closed over the lobe of my right ear. Just nibbling at first, then slowly he began to bite.

I gritted my teeth, holding back for as long as I could. I counted in my head. It was more than a minute before I started screaming.

He stopped immediately.

"It hurts because you are not dead. That is good, no?"

I nodded.

"I like you," he added, licking the blood off the side of my face. "Listen to me...

"Pain means you are alive, OK? You... you spend too much time with the dead. Like all the others. You forget you are alive. You... you..."

"Might as well be dead?" I suggested helpfully.

"Yes!" he punched me on the shoulder encouragingly.

"You've been spending a bit of time with the dead yourself though, haven't you?" I challenged him. I knew he wasn't going to kill me and felt somehow stronger now.

He grinned, showing my blood on his teeth. "The dead cannot hurt you and you cannot hurt the dead... but you are scared of them. Why?"

65

I thought for a moment. Any question which Marek put to you, no matter how obvious the answer might have seemed, had to be thought about carefully before answering. Demanded your full consideration.

"I'm not scared of the dead... I'm scared of death, of dying."

"No!" He grabbed my collar and shouted into my face. "No! No! No!"

"Okay! Okay... maybe I am scared of the dead... because they remind me of death. '*Memento mori* - remember thou shalt die'."

"*Nunc est bibendum, nunc pede libero pulsanda tellus,*" said Marek smiling - or rather, the words came from his mouth but not in his voice. "Face... your... fear," he told me - his old self again - punctuating each syllable by slamming me bodily into the wall. "Show them you are not afraid...

"The castle... tonight... midnight."

V

"*Aaargh!* Live now... dead soon!" a friend once wrote to me following the break up of a particularly harrowing relationship. Sound advice.

The strange thing was that I was beginning to think of Marek as a friend. I knew he was dangerous. Violent. Possibly insane. Probably a desecrater of graves and God only knew what else. But somehow, I felt that he had my best interests at heart.

So I went to the castle.

I was waiting by the main gate in the rain just before midnight when a whispered voice called for my attention.

"*Hej!*" A hand beckoning me to the far corner of the castle wall.

"The door is open for us at the back." In the dark, I couldn't see the speaker's face, but the voice wasn't Marek's. Maybe one of the others, Radek and Kuba both knew some English. I followed the figure through the darkness and rain around to the back of the castle where Marek and the rest were waiting, each clutching a plastic shopping bag.

Marek acknowledged me with a smile that looked almost relieved. "This is for you," he said reaching into his bag, rummaging around and taking something out, holding it out for me to take.

I hesitated.

"Take it!" he hissed.

I did as I was told, feeling my fingers close around something cold and metallic. A can of lager.

"It's raining," he pointed out.

"We say; 'Pissing down'"

"'Pissing down'," he repeated and gave a little chuckle to himself. He translated to the others in case anyone hadn't got it and they all laughed together.

"Drink," said Marek passing beer to everybody, then holding up his own can in the gesture of one making a toast. "Drink."

We drank. Standing in the rain at midnight. Only the moon and stars hanging between us and heaven. Nothing to keep us from hell. The evening was just beginning.

"The others are already inside, waiting for us," Marek informed me as we readied ourselves to go into the castle.

As we passed through the small gate and crossed the courtyard, making our way towards the heavy, wooden door which led down to the cellars, I wondered who the *others* might be. Radek, Kuba and Pawel were all here with us. Who else had Marek invited? Or maybe it wasn't his party.

On my last visit, I'd been told that the cellar door was always kept locked and bolted to keep out unwanted visitors. It had been left open tonight. We began our slow descent.

Kuba and Pawel both held torches but made no attempt to light them as we made our way down the worn stone steps. They'd obviously been there before and Marek held onto my shoulder, guiding me as I felt my way blindly in the close, warm dark. The atmosphere was stuffy, lifeless, and not just from the summer heat. It seemed to me that the air was slowly being extinguished, consumed by something that waited

67

silently for us somewhere deep in the cellars. Marek pushed me forward.

Only when we emerged into a space large with echoes, did Kuba and Pawel turn on their torches. I recognised the room as the largest of the cellars, the one served by several smaller rooms. In the centre of the floor, the shirtless youth from the park sat cross-legged. Thick streams of blood ran down his arms, pooling on the flagstones beneath him. He looked much the same as the previous times I'd seen him except that, between then and now, he'd grown a sparse, wispy beard which just covered the end of his chin. He smiled in welcome but didn't speak. Arranged all around him were various objects; a case of vodka, a portable CD player, candles, a can of petrol, a selection of knives with a few assorted medical instruments mixed in, and several black refuse sacks. It was clearly going to be quite some party.

In one of the smaller rooms something was moving, pacing impatiently.

"Put some music on," said Marek softly and Kuba complied enthusiastically.

It was some White Power skinhead band hurling racist abuse in German over a backing of buzz-saw guitars and pummelling drums. I remembered the words of Marek - or whoever it had been - from earlier that evening, *Nunc est bibendum, nunc pede libero pulsanda tellus*. I didn't feel much like dancing but I certainly needed a drink. In the twenty minutes or so it'd taken us to make our way down to the deepest part of the cellars, I'd conceived of a plan which might just be my salvation. Get very drunk, very quickly.

"Stay here," commanded Marek at last releasing my shoulder. He walked towards the smaller room, pausing and bowing his head before entering. The music ended abruptly and in the sudden silence, I could hear low murmuring and the shuffling of feet inside.

Pawel opened a bottle of vodka, took a swig, and passed it to me, while Radek busied himself lighting candles. Kuba kicked the CD player and the music started again.

Marek emerged from the other room carrying a large piece of cardboard similar to the one I'd seen last time. He laid it carefully on the floor in front of the bearded, golden-haired youth and came over to me, pushing me gently into a corner.

"This is honour," he stressed, poking me with a tattooed finger. "You understand?"

I nodded and drank some more vodka.

As the candles began to illuminate more of the room, I could see that the walls had been hung with white sheets, each one bearing some sort of painted symbol or insignia - the same cross in the circle that Marek had on his hand and which could be seen sprayed over many of the town's walls, another cross - each arm ending in an arrowhead, the ubiquitous swastika. Others I had difficulty making out.

Marek returned to the centre of the room and knelt down before the golden-haired youth who had still not spoken or risen from his seated position on the floor. The blood still flowed from his arms, collecting now around the large piece of cardboard and the worn knees of Marek's Levis.

From the inside pocket of his jacket, Marek now produced a marker pen, dabbing it carefully, reverently, in the blood from the youth's outstretched arms. Hesitating, hand shaking, as he held the marker above the cardboard. Something about the awkward, unnatural way he held the pen in his tightly clenched fist made me realise - Marek was illiterate. The youth touched his cheek gently and Marek began to write.

As Marek completed his task, the music was turned off and Pawel took my hand and lead me to the middle of the room, where we removed our wet jackets and shirts and sat forming a half-circle around the young man's bare, misshapen feet. He regarded us for a moment across the cardboard altar, still smiling contentedly, then gestured to Kuba with his left hand.

Kuba rose from the circle, returning with one of the black plastic bags. He retook his position and opened the bag. Marek bowed his head and gestured to me to do likewise.

I could hear Kuba take something from the bag and pass it to the blue-eyed, innocent looking Radek who was sitting on his left. Radek opened the bag, took something from it and passed it to Marek in turn. I daren't raise my head or even risk a quick glance to my right to get a better look at what was happening. Marek passed me the bag.

The smell from the sack was dank and musty and I suppose I already knew what was in it. I closed my eyes and placed my hand inside. My fingers closed around something hard, but oddly weightless and slightly brittle to the touch. Quite smooth but porous in places, with some sharp edges and cavities on one side.

"No fear," whispered Marek, each word separate and distinct.

I removed the object and opened my eyes. It was what I'd thought it was. The skull of a small child.

Marek gave a satisfied nod while Pawel reached over, took the sack from me and began to root around inside. When he was satisfied with his own choice, he placed the bag and its contents on the blood-stained flagstones, reached round to pick up something which lay on the floor to his left, then turned and tapped me on the arm.

I started, flinching at the touch.

"Drink?" he grinned, offering me the open bottle of vodka.

I drank.

The ceremony lasted about an hour and was conducted mostly in silence. We were obliged, each in turn, to perform a series of acts to demonstrate our personal strength, our complete lack of fear and, above all, our unconditional obedience to the young man who sat silently before us.

All things at the young man's bidding.

Then with a blessing, he left us lying in our own blood.

As he turned to leave, I saw that the words which had been carved into his back had changed, replaced now by three letters: VIS.

In the silence that followed the departure of the bearded youth, Marek lay stretched out on the floor apparently deep in thought. Brightening suddenly, he got to his feet.

"*Chłopaki...* let's have some fun!"

Kuba and Pawel ran like excited children over to the smaller room and flung the door wide open. There was no movement inside the room. It was quiet and empty as far as I could see. They disappeared inside, quickly found what they were looking for and dragged it eagerly and unceremoniously into the light.

Laid out on the cardboard altar, the sickly glow of the candles played dully on its pale, yellow skin.

Someone turned the music back on and they all began to take off their boots and jeans.

Marek slapped me on the back and handed me a bottle.

"You first," he said.

CORDS

Roger B Pile

"Why don't we go in?" Jenny said. We'd been walking down Treswithen Street, which is really just a narrow lane running parallel to the main street, connected by labyrinthine alleys and quiet roads. It had led between shops and run-down tenements, and had emerged close by the cathedral, when we'd seen the notice on the cathedral door.

Contemporary Warfare, we read, *Its Glories and Terrors.*

The cathedral had been closed years ago; fallen victim to subsidence, its congregation had dwindled, the arched windows with their stained glass had been boarded over, and for two decades it had been left to crumble in its own way. But now its doors were open, and the notice was pinned to a board at the foot of the steps.

Jenny gave me a questioning look. "Why not? It could be interesting."

I shrugged. Why not, indeed? It was always Jenny who initiated things. I hated making decisions. Some people wondered what we saw in each other, I know, we were so dissimilar, but they missed the point; it was precisely this dissimilarity which defined our relationship. Jenny had a love of the extravagant and unusual; she needed less to share this with anyone than to exhibit her own fascination, like a child showing off a new dress. And I was a willing observer. I like to think of myself as being solid and supportive, but in fact it was always Jenny who led the way, while I merely followed in her train - and sometimes picked up the pieces. Now I followed her up the cathedral steps and into the small antechamber.

There was no-one waiting inside the double doors; only a bare folding table with a collection plate on it, empty. I decided the exhibitor was foolishly trusting, but put down some coins anyway. Jenny was already eagerly pushing open the inner door. I followed her through.

Cords

We stepped through the doors into a jungle.

I'm not sure what we'd expected. Perhaps some newspaper photos, paintings; empty shell cases, a uniform or two. But we saw none of those things; we had pushed our way through the heavily studded door from the antechamber into a blackened jungle of huge dripping leaves.

The leaves glistened under an equatorial moon. I looked up and I could swear that I saw stars. Reason told me straight away that they could only be clever illuminations. All the same I was unnerved when I looked behind me for the door and couldn't find it. But then my hand found sweaty wood, flat, planed, behind a curtain of lianas.

"You know, Alexander Korda once built a jungle in a studio. It was so humid one of the actors kept getting asthma attacks."

I'd heard that story, but of course I knew she was right. We were looking at a clever set piece, props, stage trickery. The hanging lianas seemed real, but they hung from clever imitation trees. The thick bunches of leaves were convincing, but I'd seen equally convincing ones in the foyers of public buildings, where the interior designers had tried to soften the hard, uncompromising lines of modern architecture. But they hadn't used as much artificial foliage as surrounded us here.

We moved forward into the 'trees'.

Jenny stumbled in the dark on a snaking root, and it crossed my mind that the creators of this exhibit needed to worry a little more about Health and Safety in this age of litigation. A flicker of wings caught my eye, high up in the hanging vegetation, as some bird or bat that had found its way into the building flew through the leaves. I wondered if this was intended to be Burma or Cambodia. But the sign had stated 'contemporary warfare,' so surely a Middle East setting would have been more appropriate?

Red light flared as a crown of mud, smoke and flame erupted against the blackness. I heard the dull thud of the explosion a few seconds later. The trees shook and rustled as the wind from the blast stirred the leaves. There was the sound of the thrashing of huge blades rotating like some mechanical flying reptile of the Palaeozoic age, hovering low over us, but invisible of course.

We nearly turned and went back right then. It was pretty damned convincing.

I reminded myself that this was an exhibit. There was a sunlit street only yards away. And in any case, Jenny's hand was gripping my own, pulling me forward through the jungle, the exhibit.

Her voice came back to me. "Whoever did this is good. I can't tell if these trees have been planted here, if they've dug up the floor, or if they're fake."

"Remember Alexander Korda," I said.

I had to suppress laughter. From the excitement in her voice I knew straight away that she was in her element; the place appealed to her passion for showmanship. Jenny wasn't a culture snob; she just loved spectacle. The loudest music, the grimmest drawings of Klinger, paintings by Bacon, bloody and beautiful comics. She got turned on by those awful Italian movies.

A turn in the track brought us to a stockade. The gates hung ajar. As we pushed them wide and walked in, pale green moonlight filtered down through the surrounding trees.

Far to the right of us a woman was crucified to a tree, her front drenched black in the moonlight, the white rags that were all that remained of her clothes, stiff with dried blood. She had been savagely mutilated: even when we walked closer it was impossible to tell the rags of her breasts from her clothing.

"Gross." Jenny's voice was a whisper.

The woman moved. A shudder ran through her frame as she tried to raise her head. The movement was slightly unnatural, a series of barely perceptible jerks. It had to be some sort of ingenious mechanism. Jenny didn't say anything, but I could hear her breathing, slow and shallow. She turned and said: "What's over there?"

It was a pit. A swarm of flies hung over it, glittering in the beams of artificial moonlight. Something told me that I didn't want to look into it. These effects were becoming a little too convincing, and I didn't quite have Jenny's taste for the Grand Guignol. She caught my expression and said: "It's only a show. Like a waxworks."

A sudden eruption of gunfire sent leaves and twigs spraying from the dense bushes on the other side of the clearing, and a ragged line of small explosions ripped up the ground a yard away, sending us running for a hut, tumbling through the open doorway. "It's just a show," I said, when I was able to breathe again. "Like a waxworks."

But as I looked out, back at the ground we had crossed, I could see the scattered leaves and the thin branches and twigs with ends showing white where they had been smashed through.

"Waxworks don't fire at people. Damn it, I think someone out there's got a real problem."

Silently, I agreed; but our own problem was more immediate. Given time, it wasn't difficult to figure out how any of these ingenious, if grisly, tricks were performed; but I was beginning to have serious doubts about the sanity of anyone who would stage them.

"Welcome to the Experience." The voice came from behind us. We turned, but there was no-one there. "This is a non-profit making exhibition, staged for your enjoyment and edification. It will bring you the reality of conflict in a subjective way."

Looking up I could see that there was a speaker fixed up inside the hut. The voice was a man's; a cultured voice, it sounded as if he did voice-overs for car commercials or easy-listening classical music compilations for people who don't really care for music.

"No pains have been spared in this presentation," the voice continued. "The gunfire you have just witnessed was real gunfire. You are advised to take all possible precautions whilst attempting to return to safety."

"He's shitting us," Jenny said.

"Please consider this advice very seriously," the voice said.

We looked at each other. Then we looked out at the compound with the ragged scar of torn earth and the woman bound to the tree. "What's he mean, 'Attempting to return'?" I knew we were both thinking the same thoughts, wondering whether to call this madman's bluff and just walk out. Real gunfire didn't necessarily mean a thing if it wasn't aimed at you. But the big question was: Just how crazy was the genius who had created this?

Crazy enough to plant a jungle in a church.

Crazy enough to train a machine gun within a yard of us.

I was turning over phrases from the little speech: 'The reality of conflict.' 'In a subjective way.' 'Attempting to return.'

I didn't like the sound of any of them.

"We can force our way out through the back of this hut," Jenny said. "It's just hardboard and thatching." She was levering a panel loose. "Don't push it out. Someone might see it lifting. Ease it back into the hut."

Eventually we freed the panel. We saw a yard of hard earth, then the stockade itself, about six feet high, topped with roughly cut spikes. It would be difficult to surmount, but not impossible. I could hear the helicopter again. Back through the door I could see the compound and the trees rising over it. Above that, at what looked like a distance of about a mile but had to be a clever illusion, I could see a searchlight blinking on, sweeping the tops of the trees, blacking out.

When it blinked on again it was closer.

I said: "I'll go first. I'll get on the stockade, then I can swing you up."

Sweat was beading her face; I could feel it trickling down my own. She was licking her lips with quick snaky movements of her tongue. Her eyes looked almost feverish, unnaturally bright. She nodded her head. I took my jacket off; moved out through the opened back of the hut, slowly in case someone was watching, ready to duck back in. Everything was still, apart from the sound of the helicopter, which was growing closer. I ducked through, hared it for the stockade, threw my jacket up over the spikes and jumped; grabbing the tapering tops of the piles, I levered myself up. The sharpened ends scraped at me through the jacket as I got on top and between them.

Looking down I saw her standing below, arms extended. Catching her by one wrist, I lifted her until she could gain leverage and climb up beside me. We turned to drop down the other side, and at the same time the sound of the helicopter grew to a rumble, and the hut and the stockade shook as heavy shells began to eat into them. The searchlight caught us for an instant as splinters flew all around. Then we were down into the deep foliage on the other side, feet sinking into the loam, ignoring branches and sharp leaves that tore at our clothes and skin. We hid behind a huge tree bole while the brilliant light flickered through the leaves, hunting. Then the helicopter was moving away, circling, and widening its search pattern. I knew that it had to be illusion, a thing of lights, cables, synchronised gunfire; but it was a perfect and deadly illusion, and I had not the slightest doubt that we had barely escaped alive.

Jenny was down on her haunches, working up one leg of her jeans. Blood was trickling down her shin, and I could hear her quick breathing as she pulled splinters from her leg. When I got out of this place, someone would suffer for this!

We found a small hollow by the roots of a tree near a stream. The water splashed over a little fall into a pool. I was fascinated to see tiny fish moving about in the depths of the pool. We had lost any sense of time; my watch had been broken climbing the stockade, and Jenny never wore one. I said, "If we keep heading in one direction, we must reach one of the walls. We could follow it around and find our way out."

If they hadn't hidden the door by now. Or blocked it up.

"Why is this happening to us?" It was the first time Jenny had said anything in what seemed like a long time. She was looking towards me, and the feverish, excited look had left her eyes. Her hands picked at her jeans where the blood stuck them to her legs. With a determined effort she got to her feet. "Anyway, we can't stay here." Her usually musical voice was ragged and hoarse.

Almost in the same movement, she turned and waved her arm, gesturing at me to stay down. There was something moving out there; I heard slow cautious steps, the sound of feet, heavy-booted, crushing twigs and leaves. I moved carefully up beside her and strained to see what she was looking at.

Soldiers.

There was a line of them, moving along some barely defined path. They looked hardly human, shadowed hump-backed shapes under huge rucksacks, massive men in ragged uniforms, twigs and leaves bristling from their helmets and webbing. They moved a little unnaturally, almost mechanically, heads turning to peer into the undergrowth, gripping their automatic weapons tensely. One of them stepped into a stray patch of moonlight, and I saw his broad leathery slab of a face, eyes narrowed and glinting in the shadow cast by his helmet. His tunic was in ribbons and great cords ran under the skin, down his arms and across his chest. The cords twitched abruptly and he was gone, out of the moonlight, back into the shadows. Then I saw trees growing up between us and the soldiers. The jungle was moving.

It was a sudden and merciless ambush.

The densely camouflaged soldiers who had been waiting, so still and silent that we had mistaken them for part of the forest, fired on the patrol, ripping away the darkness with jagged bursts of gunfire that sawed through leaves and branches and filled the air with flying wreckage. One of the men on the path kicked backward and fell out of sight, while others were falling to the ground or to their knees. Someone lobbed a grenade and the black and green forest turned deep red as flame and human flesh rained outwards.

Returned gunfire raked through the trees around us, and on the patrol, turning leaves to confetti. I felt something tug at my shoulder as I moved back behind a tree trunk. I looked down and saw that part of my shoulder was gone. There was a whirl of movement at the corner of my eye, and I saw Jenny start to run. She splashed through the stream. I started after her; she was already up the bank and fighting her way through the bushes. There was a narrow path just the other side and I pounded after her, the sound of her dragging breaths coming back to me. She was about six feet from me when she stepped on the mine.

The explosion hurled me back but I glimpsed her arms and head raised, black in the gout of fire that lifted her cart wheeling high over my head.

When I recovered consciousness I saw the tall shapes of the soldiers towering over me.

*

I turned my head, trying to find the source of the endless high keening sound cutting through my ears and my brain. Jenny was lying on the ground by the still-smouldering crater. She could not stop screaming, except now and again to draw a breath, when the noises she made became sobbing. Her hair had burned away in the heat of the blast. I noticed one of her shoes on the other side of the path. Then I saw that her foot was still in it. Her legs were gone, her thighs ended abruptly in ragged bloody stumps a few inches below her waist. Two paramedics were doing something, but she kept on screaming.

My vision kept blurring, and it was difficult to see, but I could make out some men in city suits standing at a short distance. One of them was lighting a cigarette. He puffed smoke. "There's no major damage to the internal organs, we can still use her," he said.

"The other one?"

I blacked out then.

My memory's a bit hazy. I don't remember them fitting the cords. There have been blank times, like sleep, but I don't remember dreaming. I think they know my thoughts, can steal them somehow. Then when we wake, we go to another place.

Sometimes there are streets, but usually it's jungle. I don't think about what I have to do. There are no decisions to make. The cords do that. They help me move.

The doors are opening now. The cords twitch and tug under my skin and I check my weapon and step out with the others. We push through leaves and see a ruined city half sunk in water. The patrol's begun. I hope I don't see Jenny this time. She can't talk now, but she makes noises. She just lies there in a hole in the ground and makes noises. I know she can't help it, but I don't like the noises she makes when she sees me.

THE SOUND OF MUZAK

Sean Parker

There was no light. There was no dark. Nothing was visible. A sense of suppressed energy and invisible movement surrounded everything. It was neither hot nor cold. Either nothing was solid or everything was.

There were no stars.

What lived there may not truly be alive. It might have been at one time, before it entered this state and this place. Alternately, it may merely be waiting for the next phase in its development to begin. For however slowly, however incomprehensibly, the nature of things is to change. Even here that was the case.

This place may be vast, it may be microscopically small. It may exist in space as we mere mortals know it, or outside it. Its occupant may be sentient, driven by some purpose, or it might be nothing more than another example of existence for its own sake. Maybe there is more than one of them. Maybe they have emotions, maybe not.

It is possible that they are aware of our little planet. On occasion things pass between there and here, harmful things. It is likely that it is not intentional. It could just be caused by weak areas between the two planes of being. The traffic is always one way.

They could be attempting to understand us, or attempting to communicate in some way. They could be blissfully unaware of us, or just indifferent. It is entirely possible that we are completely irrelevant to them, that the chaos which is generally caused when something from there reaches the earth, is not worthy of note. Or goes unobserved.

From the viewpoint of humans however, it is always fairly traumatic.

On this particular occasion, it started here:

The Sound of Muzak

Ian was noodling aimlessly around in the key of D minor when he thought he heard the noise again. Cursing quietly to himself, he stopped playing. There was silence, interrupted only by the chirping of birds and the occasional rumble of a car in the near distance.

He decided to take a break, and wandered into the kitchen to grab a coffee from the machine. He took the steaming cup and a packet of the cigarettes that he was, as always, seriously considering giving up and ventured out into the garden. It was more than a little neglected.

Ian had moved into the rented cottage a couple of months earlier. Freshly painted a dazzling white, it sat snugly amongst idyllic surroundings, chocolate box perfect. He had found some problems with it, certainly, mainly with the plumbing. And the draughts. And he was not used to having such unreliable television reception. And there was no twenty four hour garage. And... But these minor gripes came from being accustomed to life in the decaying city where he had spent the last few years. He liked it here, and fully expected to be able to get on with his work, such as it was, with the minimum of disturbance. The garden could definitely do with a bit of a spruce-up though, but that wasn't likely to happen.

The unexplained noise irritated him. He'd first heard it the previous day whilst he was working on the newest piece of soulless muzak crap that he was financially bound to create. He worked on his own music in his spare time, when he wasn't too dispirited to do so, or when he wasn't doing cash-in-hand manual work or signing on. But the time for his own projects seemed to be diminishing with the passing of years, as was his confidence in them. He dreaded the day may come when he ceased to strive, when he could no longer be bothered, when the battle had been lost.

Ian detested listening to muzak whenever he heard it in shops, and always felt vaguely guilty about his part in creating it. He cringed when he occasionally managed to recognise a sickeningly bland example of his work amongst the other bland pieces of nothing. This was music completely drained of emotion and excitement and everything else that made it enjoyable. Unfortunately, artistic integrity was something he could ill afford, and this trash helped paid the bills. Well, some of them. Sometimes.

His musical equipment was set up in a room just off the kitchen. To all intents and purposes it constituted a cheap and cheerful home studio, certainly more than adequate for what he was unleashing on the world. Yesterday he had programmed a simple, loping drum pattern into the sequencer and had started to record some basic keyboard parts over the top of it when, literally out of the blue and in complete silence, something had struck the garden just a couple of feet from the window. Some kind of lightning or other strange electrical phenomena, maybe. St Elmo's fire, perhaps. He had leapt up in surprise, knocking his chair to the floor. He rushed over to look, then hesitated for a second, wondering if it was safe, or if there were going to be further displays. After a short pause in which nothing happened, he'd approached the window. All seemed quiet. Then what sounded like a baby crying but was probably a cat had caused him to jump, but he continued to stare at the lawn.

He had only seen the lightning or whatever it had been out of the corner of one eye, and he had an impression of both purple and turquoise, brilliantly bright, flashing downwards. Whatever it had been, it had left a large black patch in the lawn.

Ian had gone outside to inspect it at closer quarters.

The patch was pretty much circular, and contained no plant life at all. The grass surrounding the dark shape was completely unharmed, not even the blades closest were so much as singed or withered. He'd touched the dark, burnt looking soil, ready to withdraw his hand quickly, but the area gave off no heat at all. If anything it was possibly colder than he would expect the ground to be on such a warm day as this.

Above him, the sky had remained a clear blue, not a cloud in sight, no sign of any coming storm, nothing. A little puzzled, but at a loss as to what he should do, if anything, he'd returned to his music.

The fragment had found itself in a different place. The journey had lasted for almost eternity, or almost no time at all. Squeezed through insurmountable distances less than the width of an atom, both faster than light (something it had never experienced) and slower than the flow of rock on a planet frozen to absolute zero.

With whatever form of awareness it possessed, the fragment took stock of its new surroundings. Everything was different. It would be unable to cope with this strange landscape without making some very major adjustments.

Tiny flickers of consciousness surrounded it on all sides. These were much too small to bother with. Then, it became aware of something that contained a little more of what he needed.

In its own way, it moved.

In rapid succession, several unfortunate creatures dwelling in the garden met completely unexpected deaths.

First to go was a beetle, crawling through the grass near where the fragment had come to rest. Its limited consciousness was suddenly overwhelmed by something else far too complex and large for this little scrap of life to hold. The beetle ceased functioning without fuss.

Finding itself in the open again, the fragment threw itself into the nearest hiding place it could.

A sparrow, happily pecking the ground for grubs suddenly fell sideways as its tiny heart well nigh burst with fear. Then another sparrow fell out of the air, followed swiftly by a blackbird that toppled backwards off the hedge.

A rabbit was next, its brain large enough to feel that something was terribly wrong before its life ended. A neighbours cat, sunbathing on the shed rood, did slightly better. She had time to yowl once, and claw frantically at the things that had suddenly surrounded her before she too succumbed.

Here, Ian had a stroke of luck that he never aware of. It did him no good in the long run, and it would have been far better for thousands upon thousands of people if the fragment had simply latched onto him at that point. But it did not.

Casting about for a place to inhabit, it found the computer.

Five minutes later, Ian, blissfully unaware of events transpiring just metres away from him, had started to re-record the keyboard part that he had been working on before the interruption. Then he'd heard the groaning noise.

Maybe groan was the wrong word. It somehow felt like a groan, but it was in all probability a faulty lead or a computer glitch or *just one of those things*. Annoyed, he had brushed a stray strand of his speedily receding hair out of his face and fought the urge to kick something. He did not want to spend time playing nursemaid to a bunch of temperamental gadgets. He merely wanted to get his work done quickly so he could meet his deadlines (looming as they were) and go and get royally pissed every evening without having that guilty nagging feeling of things left undone.

As soon as he had heard the stray sound, he'd stopped the program he was recording through and played back the last few seconds he had committed to virtual tape. There was only his dreary keyboard part to be heard, nothing more. On the monitor, the graphic representation of the sound-wave had showed no spikes or troughs, nothing unusual to indicate where the noise should by rights have appeared.

Irate at having ruined, for no good reason at all, what was up to then a perfectly good take, he had wiped the useless part and started to record it again. He had played the part through perfectly on the next attempt, and it had been cleanly recorded, with no little audio surprises.

Then, after a short while perfecting a suitably cliche'd guitar line, Ian had called it a day and ate a hearty microwaved meal before strolling to the village pub, and, several hours later, staggering back.

This morning, Ian had woken feeling more than a little queasy, with an orchestral percussion section rehearsing in his skull. He'd wasted a couple of hours drinking coffee and nibbling gingerly at toast until he felt up to placing nose on grindstone. It was then that the noise had returned. It had improved his mood not one iota.

Sighing rather more theatrically than was strictly necessary, he tipped the dregs of his coffee onto the scorched patch of lawn, dropped the still glowing cigarette end into the tiny steaming puddle, and wandered back into the cottage (almost stepping on the mortal remains of a small bird) where, with little enthusiasm, he tried to continue with his recording.

The noise did not re-appear.

That day.

Since moving to the cottage, Ian's days had quickly settled themselves into a predictable routine. A late start, some work, frozen dinner and then an evening at the pub, where he was still a novelty, a new face, and would, he guessed, be one for as long as he stayed here.

Unfortunately, the recording was beginning to play on his mind more than necessary. The noise was beginning to make itself heard almost every time he tried to record anything. He'd messed around with all the various leads, wires and connections, but to no avail. He didn't want to call out anyone to check the computer over, as he couldn't see how that could be causing the problem.

Although he could hear the noise, it never showed up on any of the recordings, so, after ruining a couple more takes by ceasing to play when he heard it, he merely tried to ignore it instead. Thank *Whatever* that the bulk of the job was done, and he was working on the last piece he had to produce.

The Sound of Muzak

The noises didn't vary much. Sometimes he thought he could distinguish a stray syllable of an almost recognisable word, mumbled or whispered in the background. This was, he thought, merely his imagination trying to impose order on something completely random and meaningless. Occasionally, when the noise sounded like it was trying to speak, he could almost credit it with some emotional resonance, but this could surely not be the case.

Wherever it was now, the fragment was, if such emotions were available to it, feeling more secure, and happier. The biological machines had not been able to house him, but this comforting logical setting (a completely alien logic, but it could sense the patterns and the rules of the place) did not appear, as yet, to have even noticed its guest.

It floated through numbers. It was not quite physical, not quite pure information. It wandered in the hard drive, the memory became its playground. On the whole it kept silent, and attempted not to disturb its surroundings.

Sometimes this was not possible. It could sense that it was accidentally sending signals to the space outside. The concept of sound was new to it, but it could sense part of itself being torn away and reduced to vibrations that were broadcast through the system designed for converting information into noise. Each tiny part of itself fought to survive, in files, in programs, in folders and, incidentally, in the music being recorded. It hid.

With each lessening of itself, the main fragment itself grew weaker. It tried to draw energy from sources outside itself, but with only limited success. It gave up when a large part of itself broke away was lost to a fate unknown.

Although the weather had been fairly pleasant for the last day or two, Ian began to feel the cold. The studio appeared to be especially susceptible to draughts, although this struck him as odd, for there was no wind. Little mysteries like that were only to be expected though, he supposed. The place was, after all, a couple of hundred years old.

At the moment, he was taking a break and watching the afternoon news program on the portable set in the front room when he heard something that had become unwelcomely familiar to him. Certain that he'd shut all the equipment down, he leapt from the sofa and ran to the studio. He found that everything was indeed switched off. Then he heard the noise again. It seemed to be coming from everywhere.

Feeling more rattled than he would care to admit, Ian made for the front door. Maybe it was coming from outside. But before his hand reached the latch the noise ceased. All there was to hear was the sound of bad news being read aloud by someone at a desk in a studio somewhere in London.

Bewildered, Ian tried to ignore a slight flickering which seemed to be affecting his vision and helped himself to a small whiskey before returning to work. And then another, just to be on the safe side.

It was a Sunday afternoon, and he wanted to get the completed discs posted and out of the way by the following morning. Ian set about completing the mixing on the final song with, if not enthusiasm, at least with some determination. Clicking open the various programs needed, he first played the drum track in isolation. A low humming noise covered the whole four minutes of percussion.

Ian felt an odd sensation tickling at the back of his mind, an unease he didn't want to acknowledge.

"Shit," he muttered, his conscious mind not concerned with anything except the possibility of a sleepless night trying to re-record all this crap on a machine that clearly had some unresolved issues. Hoping for the best but fearing the worst, he re-started the track, now with the bass-line added. The humming, slightly different, pitched a little higher, with a hint of a crackle, covered it all. Blended together, the two noises seemed to be trying to sound like something else entirely.

The Sound of Muzak

As the song, accompanied by the unwanted sounds played on he added a keyboard track, another keyboard track, and the nauseatingly polite guitars. The tune became whole, each part adding to the whole, but at the same time adding strength and form to the increasingly suggestive noises, which had coalesced into something that wanted to be a voice. Possibly.

Voice or not, it bubbled and muttered, like a pure audio representation of misery and loneliness, strangeness and madness, all accompanied by a pleasant, if entirely nondescript, little ditty.

Frustrated and annoyed, Ian sat staring at the moniter as the song gurgled to its end. There was something seriously not right about all of this. He tried to think it through rationally, but deep down the feeling that he wanted to be anywhere else but where he was grew stronger.

With a vicious click of the mouse, Ian started the tune playing again, and heard nothing but the muzak itself. Fuck it, he thought and grabbed a spindle of blank CDs from a nearby shelf, and then quickly burnt a couple of copies of all the finished tracks in the machine. When the last CD popped out a few minutes later, still slightly warm, he took them into the front room and put one in the stereo. He zapped forward to the problem song and listened. Christ, he was getting tired of that tune, strange noises or no strange noises.

There was nothing out of the ordinary to be heard.

Quickly, Ian labelled the discs with black marker, found a couple of cases for them, typed a brief letter, printed it, and shoved the whole lot in a padded envelope, which he sealed and addressed. Job completed.

If only the sense of something being terribly wrong would go away.

He growled comically at the studio in general as he went about shutting everything down. Before he got to the computer, the moniter screen went blue, then, a few seconds later, black, and nothing Ian could do would get it to work again.

Some of the fragments betrayed themselves and were caught out in the open. They were lucky, though, as they were able to hide themselves deeper. Some found themselves transported into a nearby form of life, and were surprised when it didn't immediately keel over dead.

In the machine, many of them were gathered in one place, isolated by file walls at first, but then reunited, and able to join together again. Then they were reproduced, and this new version of themselves was removed, containing, to all intents and purposes, exact clones of the originals.

Those left behind went on a rampage. The larger part of the original fragment flared up, and, sensing parts of itself nearby, attempted to reach them. In a frenzy of activity, they all followed the urge to become whole again.

This was too much for the computer. It died, and whatever had dwelled inside it faded to nothing.

Mid-morning the following day, Ian took a leisurely stroll the mile or so into the nearby town and sent off the discs by registered post. Feeling at a bit of a loose end, he popped into the first pub he came to that he liked the look of for a lunchtime pint or three.

He ordered his drink at the bar, and idly looked around, taking in the somewhat smoky atmosphere of the place until his drink was placed in front of him.

"That'll be..." started the barman, and then his voice changed abruptly. His lips moved as if finishing the sentence, but what came out sounded slowed-down and menacing and completely incomprehensible. His entire face seemed to shift subtly, each feature arranging itself to play its part in displaying expressions that seemed alien on it. His body appeared to have become somehow bloated and unpleasant.

Ian stared.

"Two pound twenty, please," said the barman, both his voice and appearance returning to normal. Then, after Ian made no immediate move to do anything except to continue standing there, he added "Are you alright, mate?"

"Fine, fine," said Ian in a voice that sounded anything but. He managed to give the barman the correct change, being careful to make absolutely no physical contact with him when doing so.

Vague concerns about his mental health ran through his head. Ian picked up his drink, found himself an unoccupied table and made himself at least physically comfortable. He drained half of his pint in one mouthful, lit a cigarette and sat back, trying not to look as shaky as he felt. He surveyed the room, looking for any other hint of unnatural changes occurring. He could see none.

Relaxed slightly by the drink, Ian patted his pockets until he located his mobile, intending to see if he could get someone to come out to make his computer feel better. He found the number of a technician in his virtual phone book, pressed the green button and held the phone to his ear, then let out a squawk of surprise.

The phone was producing similar noises to those the barman had seemingly voiced. Behind it, he could just about make out a voice asking how they could help him. "I don't think you can," he said distractedly, and cut the connection. As he did so, the phone's digital display lit up and dozens of words chased each other across it. They all appeared totally alien to him, their unfamiliarity apparent even as they sped across the screen.

Then the phone seemed to soften in his hand. It became elongated and started to stretch down towards the table.

Ian dropped it quickly. It landed on the table with a clunk, and sat there, just an ordinary mobile phone on a pub table. He eyed it warily. He had had enough. Now he was seriously worried. Pausing only to drain his glass, he stood up with no idea what to do or where to go, but instinct, the simple ancient fight or flight mechanism, told him he had to get out of this place. He left his phone where it had fallen and lurched in the general direction of the door.

The door itself was wedged open, letting in a glimpse of shopping-crowd bustle and sunlight. The door-frame was wavering, as if from an extremely localised heat-haze. The dark brown varnished wood was becoming redder as the line of the grain writhed. Distracted by this, he walked straight into the back of a stool which was occupied by a young lady with a shifting, distorted face, who looked up at him and spoke with a voice that seemed to come from everywhere, for now everyone was talking like that. As her companions at the table, all muttering in the same manner, glared at him through eyes filled with something awful, he felt the first stirring of blind panic.

He forced his legs to move, and managed to make it out into daylight, ducking to avoid the top of the door-frame which had now sagged down a foot or more in the middle. The outside world was too bright. The few clouds in the overly vivid blue sky were swirling into suggestive patterns that broke apart before becoming anything definite. Something tapped on his shoulder.

Ian yelped, but at least he still sounded like himself. Unwillingly he turned around. There stood the barman, seemingly taller than he had been, holding something out towards him. A struggling black and green object that hissed but was still just about recognisable as Ian's mobile. The barman creature spoke, if what he uttered could be called speaking, his face exhibiting shadowy hues of green and red as he did so. The furrows on his brow became deeper, pressing a ridge of skin down towards his eyes, transforming them into half-closed slits. His nose grew wider and his mouth turned downwards as his cheeks sagged. His teeth were rotten and misshapen and his neck seemed to be becoming shorter and thicker, almost disappearing.

Ian turned and ran.

The street was still recognisable for what it was, but it flickered, and turned liquid at the edges. He tried not to look at any of the people, but he could feel them staring at him. The normal everyday sound of hundreds of aimless conversations was reduced to a choir of lunatic shrieks and groans, all slowed down to the point of incomprehensibility.

Ian tried to shout for help. He didn't know what the hell was going on, whether it was in his mind or actually happening, but he knew that he was well past the point of dealing with it all alone.

His cries were identical to the rest of the cacophony, deep and full of misery and pain, with a whining hint of fear woven in.

The sheer horror of it all, or possibly something else, took over. Ian ran faster, knocking what had only a short time ago been people out of his way if they strayed into his path. He bounced off shop windows which tried to drag him in, he ran through the traffic when he reached a busy road, and continued running when, against the odds, he reached the other side uninjured. On he went, straight out of the lives of all those who had ever known him.

One thing was certain; he never made it home.

What had taken up residence in Ian's brain meant him no actual harm, not through actual malice. The otherness of it was just too great. It distorted his thinking, it altered his perspective of what he heard and saw. It generally fucked-up his usual patterns of thinking.

It also developed a taste for serotonin, which helped matters not one bit.

Ian, in fact any life on this planet, was just the wrong vehicle. Whatever was driving him, too small and insignificant to cast about for further hosts, remained stuck in him when he finally crashed.

The Great British postal system performed its duty wonderfully, and the CDs of what had turned out to be Ian's final musical achievements were delivered to their destination by Wednesday morning, along with whatever else was lurking within the encoded digital information. The good people at Marshmallow Muzak Inc. never did realise that anything had happened to Ian. They weren't likely to chase up the fact that someone couldn't be bothered to cash a cheque, that is if indeed one was even sent. All records of a financial nature were lost when the company folded a few months later.

Marshmallow Muzak Inc. was a small concern. That morning, Old Jeff was busy. At the moment he was listening to the new consignment of musical pap. He was also making a show of moving some paperwork about, solely for the benefit of the other two people who wandered in and out of the office. He also answered the phone on the one occasion it bothered to ring.

Old Jeff hadn't in fact passed his mid-forties, but looked much older due to years of drink. A headache was creeping across from one temple to the other, and his nerves were jangling as they sometimes did when he was in the throes of a really dreadful hangover. However, he put it all down to his enforced abstinence from his favourite pastime, brought about by severe stomach pain.

Mid-afternoon, Jeff pleaded ill health and left early (not an uncommon occurrence) but not before okaying Ian's CD to go to the pressing plant. Just a couple of hundred copies would be made and distributed as muzak was hardly an admired sub-genre of the musical world. So many shops just had radio these days, but enough didn't. Enough to make the business worthwhile.

The following morning, poor old Jeff made it to the office, situated above a shop that was apparently willing and able to stretch your pounds for you. A little late, but not bad by his standards. He seemed a little disorientated, but his fellow workers put it down to a relapse and guessed that he hadn't quite recovered from a heavy night. This was not the case.

As the morning wore on, his behaviour grew increasingly odd at an alarming rate. At around half-past ten, by which point he had started to scream at the walls, his co-workers called a doctor. When the doctor said that he wouldn't be able to get there until some time in the afternoon, they called an ambulance instead. By the time the ambulance arrived, Jeff had wandered off, unsteadily and loudly, leaving behind broken furniture and a slightly bruised and very pissed-off young secretary. He whereabouts were only discovered later that afternoon when he was arrested for public order offences.

After some struggle Jeff was taken to the nearby police station. Here, nobody could get a word of sense out of him and medical assistance was called once again. The doctor took the medical equivalent of one quick look at him and left to inform the psychiatric services. Jeff was then transferred to a ward in a nearby hospital where he was heavily sedated. This helped with the immediate problem, but made no overall difference to his condition.

Thus started what would have been the long process of putting Jeff back together again. That was if the shit hadn't hit the fan in the manner that it was shortly about to. But for now, it is time to leave him almost (but not quite) sleeping in the psychiatric ward, desperately trying to keep some hold on reality, and failing, keeping silent because he never wanted to hear that sound emanating from his lips again.

Days passed, the world continued undisturbed on its orbit and all the usual wars and murders and different varieties of bloodshed and natural disasters continued as normal. A CD pressing plant in the north of England lost two of its staff to completely unexpected breakdowns of some kind. Regardless, a batch of CDs was sent to the office of Marshmallow Muzak Inc. and orders were filled and money was moved about by cheque or electronic means, and the discs were distributed, and all was well. Up and down the country various supermarkets and chain-stores received their copies, and their unlisted extras. Eventually the disc received its world premiere.

Here's the scene, in what could be any town or city centre. A large shop, maybe not as huge as those out-of-town aircraft hanger affairs, but large enough. It sells food, drink, electrical goods, clothes, bits and bobs you may need for your garden and much more besides. The place is teeming with shoppers, the willing and the unwilling. They consider purchases, compare prices, they consult lists, their children run and scream and ask for things they don't need and their parents cannot afford. Harassed staff man the check-outs. Security guards stroll the aisles. There is probably the occasional shop-lifter going about his business as inconspicuously as possible. As a background to all the hustle and bustle can be heard the unobtrusive muzak, calming and nondescript. No-one notices it, except perhaps as a minor irritant.

Nothing out of the ordinary takes place. The dance of the Saturday shoppers continues without missing a beat. Tills continue to ring, money and goods continue to change hands. Whatever hides between and below the notes takes a short while to make itself known.

The muzak is on a loop, so the entire selection starts to play through again and again. Hundreds more hear it, without really hearing it. Before closing time it has been played five or six times.

This is just one shop, in one town.

Whatever had found its way into Ian's muzak would, if it had functioned that way, be well within its rights to feel pleased. A selection of hosts presented itself, and it sent a little of itself into each and every one. Rejuvenated whenever the song was played again, the process could continue almost indefinitely. With no communication from its splinter-selves (selves is probably the wrong word), it could not realise what the fates of itselves and its hosts would be. Regardless of its nature, or purpose, its effects were starting to be felt.

The beast was loose, on wings of song.

"What's up with your face?"

"Jesus, you're a charmer. What the hell do you mean?"

Pause.

"Sorry, I didn't mean it like that."

"Well, how did you mean it?"

"I don't know, what I mean is I'm not sure. Its hard to describe. You just looked a bit strange there for a second. It was probably just the light."

"Are you pissed already?"

"No! Jesus Christ, I've only had three."

For a while there is only the background waffle of a television and the occasional sound of a meal being prepared in the kitchen. This is interrupted by a muffled crash, and the clatter of broken glass.

"What the fucking hell was that?" comes a shouted inquiry from the kitchen.

"Something crawling behind the telly. I nearly got it, but..." Pause. Then, "Oh shit," in a much quieter voice.

The sound of someone approaching from the kitchen.

"You idiot! We're still paying for that!"

Silence.

"Hey, are you okay?"

More silence. Then a scream of complete terror followed by the sound of someone staggering to the front door which is opened and then slammed shut. Then footsteps and more screams, fading quickly into the distance.

Indoors, the sound of a woman sobbing. This doesn't last long. She now has more immediate concerns. It appears to her that the meal she was preparing is trying to crawl out of oven, pans and grill towards her. The patterned wallpaper looks on and chuckles.

Tim and Jeremy were screaming in the back seat of the car. Really howling, making an absolute bloody racket.

"Will you stop that this minute, you two?" Mum shouted from the front. Dad cursed and tried to concentrate on the road ahead, which was becoming increasingly difficult. He must be

97

over-tired, his eyes were playing tricks.

The children did not stop. They did not even understand the words. They were both in hell. Both had watched their Mum and Dad (and each other) turn gradually into monsters with scary voices. They were both strapped in and the car was shrinking in on them and growing stranger and stranger and there was no escape.

Tim was five years old, and big brother Jeremy was seven.

Daddy turned to Mummy and screamed something awful out of his new mouth. Tim stopped howling and began to weep uncontrollably.

"Can't you keep them quiet for Christ's sake?" is what Dad had said.

"Of course I can, I'm just letting them carry on simply to annoy you and make you even more fed up than you already are," retorted Mum. The children heard this exchange as a hideous growling from the depths of their worst nightmares.

Jeremy could take no more. He struggled with what had been the seat-belt and managed to undo it. Guessing that the black finger poking up next to the door window was still the lock, he forced himself to reach for it and popped it up. Then he opened the door and jumped out.

The car was travelling at around seventy miles an hour on the M6 at the time.

Mum screamed. On instinct, Dad hit the brakes immediately. He felt something thrown forward by the sudden deceleration, banging heavily into the back of his seat. Behind him, Tim's sobbing ceased abruptly.

Then the car travelling behind slammed straight into the back of them.

Rob was travelling by tube when he started to feel more than a little out of sorts. He had indulged in a few miscellaneous chemical entertainments in the last few days, celebrating the fact that he had lost one job and had another one fall into his lap unlooked for in less than a fortnight. He attributed this rather odd feeling to his more than usually excessive weekend. Or maybe he was just getting old.

His ears were playing up. Every snippet of conversation that he could make out above the noise of the train itself seemed to be taking place at a much slower speed than normal. Rob shook his head slightly, as if trying to clear something out of it.

At the far end of the crowded carriage, someone started to make a whole variety of strange sounds. Great, a nutter, thought Rob. Just what he didn't need.

Suddenly, the mass of swaying people started to shift and Rob was able to see what was going on. A young man was flinging himself about wildly, all the time giving vent vocally to whatever ailed him. Passengers tried to push away from him, but there wasn't the room to do so. The noise of the crowd grew angry in tone, and a little frightened. It all sounded wrong to Rob.

He watched with some apprehension, ready to do what he could to avoid getting involved, hoping the scrum that was developing didn't come any closer to where he was hedged in. On top of all this, something was wrong with the light. It was too bright, somehow more white than usual. Rob wiped his eyes. He felt pretty bad. Everything around him was grating on his nerves, the nutter, the noise, the lights, the feeling of too many people in not enough space. The faces of the folk nearest him were making him edgy. God, he felt bad. The need to get away was almost irresistible.

With a suddeness that would have surprised him if he had been able to think logically, he lost control and in seconds there were two disturbances taking place.

Rob fought the horrors that had replaced the people around him with every ounce of his strength, but they fought back and they were stronger. By the time the train halted there were many battered and bloody and bruised and frightened and angry passengers. There were also two corpses.

Back at the shop which had the dubious honour of hosting the first public airing of the rather dangerous tune, another fine selling day had dawned. A couple of staff had not turned up or phoned in sick, but no more than there would be if a nasty bug was doing the rounds. Some that did turn up felt a little under the weather, but were generally okay. Business as usual, in other words.

On the second floor (mainly clothes and bedding) Kelly was trying to spot the little brat that had been hiding in amongst different racks of clothing for the last half hour or so. She sensed movement behind her and turned quickly, but she was too slow again. Sighing, she wandered over to the nearest cashier point to talk to Helen, who wasn't looking quite herself, whoever she thought she was this week.

Kelly waited while Helen finished taking money off a couple of valued consumers, aimlessly pretending to adjust a nearby display until all transactions were completed to the satisfaction of both parties.

"Have you seen anyone messing about with the displays? Someone is, but I can't find them," Kelly said.

"Can't say I have, but God, have we had some weird looking people in this morning. There was this one bloke who..."

They were interrupted by a commotion from the direction of the checkout that Josh was operating that day, halfway across the shop floor. A group of not-so-happy shoppers were running away, screaming and knocking over racks of clothes as they did so. They were being pursued by Josh himself, all five foot nothing and one hundred and ten pounds of him, glasses askew, wild eyed and silent.

Helen gasped and quickly pressed the button under the till that would call for security, but, unknown to her, the guard on this floor had locked himself in a toilet cubicle half an hour ago and was quietly weeping to himself. In the meantime, a burly middle aged fellow with a bristly head accompanied by a teenage version of himself launched themselves at the unlikely figure of the manic Josh, knocking him to the ground. Josh struggled silently as more people helped to subdue him.

Occasionally someone would curse and move back as one of Josh's limbs flailed outward and connected. The burly fellow's groin was on the receiving end of a stray kick. He doubled over briefly and then set about punching Josh in the face until he stopped moving.

It all happened with the terrible speed typical of random acts of violence. Since security seemed unwilling to make an appearance, Kelly readied herself to go over, if only to see how Josh was, but before she had taken more than a step or two, she heard Helen muttering "Oh god help me, oh god help me," and in the second that it took for Kelly to turn back, Helen had started to bang her head repeatedly against the cash register. Little drops of red sprayed in an arc, vividly coloured in the fluorescent light. Running on instinct, Kelly reached to restrain her. Helen looked up, eyes blank, face awash with blood. Snarling, she bit a chunk out of Kelly's arm. Kelly fell backwards with surprise and pain and watched from the floor as Helen brought her head forward to the till again with all her strength and, on impact, collapsed bonelessly.

Kelly staggered to her feet and reached for the intercom mouthpiece at the side of the gore-covered till. She grabbed it by the wire, which slipped in her hand and then tried to coil around her injured arm. She flung it down and it landed on Helen's prone form, which was shifting and trying to reveal some new form. The tiny puddles of blood on the floor were gathering together and pushing themselves forward in her direction. She could feel hundreds of eyes looking at her, and could hear some dreadful noise that had no place here or anywhere.

She screamed once in somebody else's voice and ran for the elevators, desperately trying to ignore the scenes that surrounded her. She stabbed at the buttons which tried to evade her until the doors finally opened, like a robotic mouth into which she dived. She hammered at more buttons until the doors closed again and then, panting, she threw herself into a corner and crouched, making herself as small as possible,

101

attempting to blank out everything she could see or hear, trying to even avoid thinking and the thoughts that couldn't possibly be hers.

What may have been seconds or possibly hours passed and the doors slid open, displaying a scene of absolute chaos. Alarms had started to sound, several different varieties of siren were drawing closer outside, pockets of mayhem were scattered throughout the place. Terrified people ran from real or imaginary horrors, and incident after incident escalated and spread until the whole place was playing host to a completely insane riot. Somewhere, somebody had started a fire, and as the black smoke started to billow upwards the sprinkler system clicked into action, soaking the insane and the merely terrified alike.

Eventually, the elevator doors closed once again, leaving Kelly in isolation with only her thoughts for company.

This situation was not in the least bit unusual. It was repeated up and down the country at various times. Jokes exploring the sanity or otherwise of shop workers sprung into being from wherever jokes come from. It wasn't just the staff, of course. Everybody that heard the muzak was affected to a greater or lesser degree, usually greater. Even animals were at risk, although since they rarely came into the shops this was not much of a problem, but there was at least one case involving a guide dog which ripped out its owners throat.

The media did not know what to make of it all, although they had a damn good time reporting the bloodier incidents, presenting ill thought-out theories, and printing angry editorials. In the following weeks, the emergency services did not know what had hit them. The number of people directly affected by what seemed to be a spontaneous eruptions of lunacy around various towns and cities was, percentage of population-wise, pretty small, but the effects started to snowball with extreme rapidity. Unfortunately, new occurrences were still being reported all the time.

The Sound of Muzak

In the surrounding area of each of the shops where someone had been unlucky in their choice of easy listening, hundreds upon hundreds of incidents of varying severity took place, some ending with death or injury, many ending with some poor soul wandering the streets terrified out of their mind or huddled in a corner at home trying to convince themselves that it would all go away soon. For instance, old Jeff still lay in the psychiactric ward as far removed from the world as he could make himself, as chaos reigned around him. The medical staff were swamped, and at least two of their nurses seemed to have developed similar mental problems.

It was the hospitals (first at A & E and the psychiatric units, then the general wards themselves) that first found themselves unable to cope. There the cracks became apparent quickest, along with the shopping centres themselves a little later when health officials eventually figured out that many of the primary victims (as opposed to the people injured by these victims) had recently visited these places. The unfortunate people themselves were not able to divulge this information themselves, as it was impossible to engage them in any kind of conversation, coherent or otherwise.

Theories, all wrong, were presented, demolished and replaced with new theories. Food poisoning (possibly ergot based), a new kind of viral infection, a hallucinogenic terrorist attack, wrath of God or gods were all suggested causes. Absenteeism from the workplace reached an all-time high, due to those affected obviously being indisposed to work, and their immediate families, friends or loved ones attempting to cope with them with or without the help of the quickly collapsing medical services.

The country as a whole was afflicted by sporadic electrical blackouts, interrupted water supply (the main problem being in Birmingham where two dead bodies had been found in the cleansing plant), a record number of air disasters, more major road accidents than could possibly be imagined, a murder rate that was truly astronomical, a potentially apocalyptic incident

103

at the Sizewell B nuclear power station in Suffolk, a major riot at a football game at the Millenium Stadium that left twenty three dead and hundreds injured, massive disruption to all businesses of all kinds, outbreaks of arson and a huge number of accidentally started fires, countless unprovoked attack of varying seriousness, accidents involving tall buildings and the ground immediately below, a bizarre situation on an army testing range involving a runaway tank, a terrible incident where a young mother ran amok in a maternity ward, several rail crashes, a ferry disaster, an appalling episode involving a surgeon butchering his patient and several nurses. The list could go on and on. Each small incident caused ripples, each larger one produced waves.

The World Health Organisation were at a complete loss, too. Their teams, taking many elaborate precautions whilst carrying out their investigations, eventually made the connection to shopping centres, but as to the actual specific cause, they were in the dark. Questions were asked in Parliament, and, as an unfortunate demonstration of the problem at hand, the Speaker of the House suddenly went beserk. The incident was not reported in *Hansard*.

Most of the population tried to carry on as usual, although they were scared, bewildered, inconvenienced and occasionally injured or killed. Many that could left the country ahead of the strict quarantine laws that were introduced on the assumption that the problem was contagious.

The majority of the dead amongst those affected were, at least in the first couple of weeks, killed by their own actions or of those around them. They provided numerous specimens for post-mortem study, but whichever way they were sliced, brain and body yielded up nothing out of the ordinary. Several large towns and cities gained a wandering population of increasingly bedraggled victims. As the days and the weeks passed, the sudden outbursts of violence grew less, as if they were slowly accepting their new world and way of life. The violence still occurred, but they were as a whole becoming worn down. As the days and the weeks passed they almost became feral in their actions, shy but vicious. Many survived, but many succumbed to hunger and exhaustion.

Drastic measures would be needed to deal with those that lived, although rumours of an implicit shoot-to-kill policy were vehemently denied by the powers that be.

The muzak discs, with their digitally encoded intruder, still existed. Only the closing of so many large stores, and the general disruption to the entire country stopped them being played. Slowly, its effects would begin to fade away, as it had on all the other occasions when leakage had occurred. But there could, and would be, other isolated incidents over the next couple of years.

Kelly coughed harshly, spitting a lump of phlegm onto the pavement outside the doorway of a long abandoned shop where she was crouched. Almost at once, the small globule started to slither away. She ignored it.

Her clothes were little more than rags, covered in soot and all the other muck and filth that had accumulated on her since the demons had arrived. A burn on her face which had gone untreated had become spectacularly infected and several deep cuts on her arms showed no signs of healing. She was much more than tired, she was absolutely exhausted. She had passed the point of hunger some time ago and was well on her way to becoming severely malnourished. Adrenalin and sheer panic had worn her down into a defective shell of a person. She no longer remotely cared that the world was a place of evil and terror, she no longer even looked at the awful things that were faces of those around her, now that the masks had been lifted. Maybe, she thought in the disjointed, slow and detached manner which was all she was capable of now, the world had always been like this. Maybe it hadn't changed all that much, maybe it hadn't been that sudden. But she was fairly sure she could remember a time when it had all been very different. She could recall talking and laughing and crying and all the things that make up a life, but she couldn't remember why she did those things, and certainly couldn't manage them now. All those things were gone. She lived in a sinister shifting world where nothing stayed still long enough to comprehend. Too many strange sights, too many strange sounds, too many fight or flight situations had all played their parts in wiping out the majority of her reasoning power. All that remained was the occasional memory that floated to the surface, the occasional half-formed thought. Even her dreams were distorted.

Living as an animal in the city, attempting to feed and shelter amidst the nightmare had proved impossible. The biological machine had broken down.

Coughing again, Kelly curled herself into a ball and shivered, Soon a wave of complete exhaustion overcame her and she slept.

She never woke up.

SHAPED LIKE A SNAKE

D. F. Lewis

I needed Time to be a moveable feast, so that I could mould it
to my purpose, bend it to each and every whim. Time endured
more than its intrinsic length but, otherwise, was shorter than
mere moments laid end to end in widdershins motion. What is
the present moment other than a series of timeless moments?
The past, contrariwise, was replete with nothing but alternating
longueurs. The future - what of that? It would replicate the
past, no doubt, but with newer and, hence, tawdrier, more
uncharacterful pauses between its own present moments. For
me, the flexibility of Time was all important. Still is. I live at
the corner of sight or am the very mote in the eye as it stares
beyond the edge of a sunlit land-locked meadow during an
endless childhood summer holiday that has yet to begin. I was,
am, will be one of Pan's creatures who outlives Pan, outlives
even the memory of Pan having ever existed in or out of make-
believe...

*

Dr. Tom Magri folded up the piece of paper with a sigh of
frustration, having read it several times, without grasping any
degree of sense from its oblique paradoxes. He could only
work properly at night. Peering from his hotel bedroom
window, he tried to imagine the endless sunlit meadow,
knowing full well that what was presented to him in the guise
of impenetrable darkness was really the bunkers, hump-backs
and dune-shaped greens of the golf course sweeping down to
the fenced-off cliff top (over which balls were often wildly
pitched by guests, much to the detriment of their scorecards).
He could hear the swish of the sea, even ensconced here
behind the window at the desk. He must appear a strange sight,
he thought, to anybody wandering the links - seeing Dr. Magri

bent under the anglepoise, spectacles at the end of his nose - but why so strange? The onlooker must be an even stranger creature of the night - to be thus out of doors peeping in.

The hotel was not at all what he had expected, after having travelled a great distance here from his home in Oxford for a holiday - but, as he knew full well, the trip was more than for simple capricious pleasure. Several independent sources had apprised him of items of historical and antiquarian interest in the area: particularly St. Luke's Church which sat back from the village houses, of which the hotel was the largest, previously the manor lord's abode. All the other guests seemed related to each other, so much so he felt himself to be an intruder at a family gathering. The heavy breakfasts were also a sight to behold. Never was there such a mound of bacon, kidneys, mushrooms, tomatoes and fried egg on someone's plate, he thought, the first morning, after a long night with his paperwork.

He was irritated by guests continuously approaching him with long-winded accounts of their ills, believing him to be a medical doctor. However many times he informed them that he was a Doctor of Philosophy, they maintained their onslaught of aches and pains - to such an extent that his own body began to feel phantom versions of the very symptoms they described. But even Doctor of Philosophy was a misnomer, his area of discipline being closer to history than the meaning of the Universe or the Existence of God. One elderly gentleman exposed a bee in his bonnet - that the past, unlike the present, possessed magical qualities, all ignored by historians and even primary sources.

Still, such irritations were thankfully missing after the others had retired for the night. Yet, there was one person with whom Dr. Magri found himself conversing. Her name was Myrtle, the woman who looked after many of the domestic chores. She had lived in the village for the whole of her life. Albeit with a tongue that ran away with itself, she possessed an inherent wisdom which her manner of speech belied - and a wide, if simple-minded, knowledge of many of the area's facets in which Dr. Magri was interested. She it was who had given him the piece of paper which he had just perused in such a non-plussing manner. He tried to go over in his mind the dialogue with Myrtle...

Yet, he was tired. He had managed very little sleep, if any, since arriving two days before. At home, he was able to catch up on his sleep during the day - his housekeeper being fully aware of his habits. At the hotel, however, guests were expected to vacate their rooms - so that hoover hoses could be wielded and bedding changed. Even if he had made special arrangements, the daily bustle of the place would no doubt have kept him awake. Time enough for sleep later. Life was too short for long-cuts, he thought, as his mind temporarily muddled his normal equilibrium.

What had Myrtle said?

"You're interested in old things, Dr. Magri? My brother has this old book, which goes into many old things. Older than I think it's in anyone's right to go. But, there you are. My back's been giving me gyp. I know you're not a proper doctor. So I won't bother you with that. Lugging all those hoovers about don't do it any good. And all that bedding stuff that looks as if it's wings off things God threw out of Heaven as my brother says. If you don't mind my silly ways. Yes, I know, I was telling you about his book. It has all sorts of peculiar pictures - drawings, more like, about old wives tales in these parts. But why they had to be wives to tell them, I'm sure I don't know. Parts of St Luke's that've fallen down and used for stones somewhere else. For things to live under. What's that, Dr. Magri? With pleasure, I'm sure. I'll bring it tomorrow. If I remember. My memory's not so good as it was, but how should I know, when I can't remember! I sometimes have to laugh as what goes on in my mind. If you were one of those other doctors - a psycho-ologist is it? - well, I'd tell you a few things that would make me a proper case. My brother says I have a nose short of a head. Still, that's his way of talk. You wouldn't believe it. But whilst I think of it. There's a piece of paper kept in the reception desk. Been there ages. Certainly *looks* old. With brown stains. Full of fine words that are too much for the likes of me. Part of a longer thing, I think. Might be interesting to someone of your leaning. Makes me feel queer to read it. About Pan. Have you heard of Pan? Yes? I know about Pan because my old granddad had a notion about something he called Pan. A pagan God, he said, that was taller than real God. If you ask me, a pan's what you cook breakfast in."

At that point, she had left to fetch the piece of paper in question. It turned out to be precisely as she had described it. While he scanned its printed out handwriting, Myrtle resumed her ramblings.

"Found it easy as pie. Don't know why it's kept there. I somehow remember there being two pieces of paper like that. The other one did a disappearing trick about two year since, when we had a gent staying here who hadn't booked. He only stayed three nights. Yes, it's all coming back to me now. He wandered the golf course without playing golf. Didn't seem right, him getting in the way of the proper players. Someone told me he wandered there at night, too, and when warned about the dangers of the cliff in the dark, shrugged it off. Whether he left that piece of paper you're now holding and pinched the other two from the drawer, I don't know. But I have a vague idea that what the paper *once* said was that one of Pan's servants or whatever lived outside before it was a golf course and now they're its eighteen breathe holes - like drains, as well. Comes out on special nights, squeezing up shaped like a snake."

Dr. Magri had made little sense of her speech, if speech it were, bearing in mind its air of not having been rehearsed. Nor the words on the paper. But she had continued after only a short break to deal with the egg deliveryman.

"So, he must've left that piece of paper in place of the other two. Some hereabouts reckoned he was related to the owner of this hotel (who we never see, I have to say) - and didn't want anything to rub off on the place. People are so easy to believe things. Didn't want any talk of ghosts or whatever. Wouldn't have done. Left that piece of paper so people wouldn't notice anything was missing. But he didn't bank on me noticing that there were two before and then only one."

It was strange how her words held more meaning now that he was remembering them in his room at the dead of night. The topsy-turvy atmosphere that night bears, in contradistinction to day, adds a telling perspective. Tomorrow would be his third day at the hotel - a most peculiar fact to dawn on him. He could have sworn this was his third night. He was urged to wander outside even before he realised that he felt the urge. There was something he must do to circle the square. A deed undone. An explanation yet unexplained. Something that he had noticed but not noticed during the two breakfast sittings he had witnessed, if not fully shared: the thin slivers of shaped meat, with mauve filaments, that supplemented the rashers of bacon and which he wished he had the good sense to have eschewed.

On his way out, Dr. Magri slipped the paper into the reception desk drawer, without pausing to see if another similar sheet was already there. He hoped the fresh night air would ease the aches and pains in his limbs.

ONLY IN YOUR DREAMS

David A. Sutton

It was not before the title music to some bittersweet sit-com finished that Margaret noticed her daughter, kneeling halfway down the stairs. She was staring forlornly through the ribs of the banister. Sophie's eyes, caught in the darkened stairwell by the dancing images off the TV screen, appeared to flicker madly from side to side.

"What is it, Tuppence?" Margaret asked, rising from the sofa. Her husband, deeply immersed in the files he'd brought home from the meeting in St Kitts, grumped quietly at the interruption.

"Will the child never learn that bedtime is *bedtime*?" he whispered, but loud enough for the six year old to hear.

"Donald, *please*." His work, on developing strategies to overturn the IWC's moratorium now that Iceland had recommenced whaling, was undoubtedly complex, but he shouldn't take it out on his children. At least *he* could swan off to foreign climes to attend conferences whenever it suited him.

She reached the staircase, which overlooked the spacious living room of their recently acquired country house. Before she could say anything more, Sophie quickly ran to the bottom step.

"Can I stay up tonight, mummy?" she asked; her words a strident plea. Margaret could see her lips quivering.

"No you can't," Donald said, not looking up from his papers. "If William is willing to obey the house rules, and he's four years older, then I can't see any reason to allow you to break them."

Donald was so insensitive these days, Margaret winced, but she did not respond. He just didn't seem his old self any more. "C'mon, Soph," she bent to her daughter, holding her close, "I'll tuck you right back in bed, read you something?" Then she added, "There's nothing on TV for you at this time of night anyway."

"But mummy, I don't want to watch TV."

"Well—?"

"Mummy, it's the jelly man."

"Good grief," her father shouted. "Who's been filling her head with nonsense?" He finally stood up from the dining table at which he'd been working and switched the chattering television to standby.

"Has your brother been saying things?" Margaret asked her softly, wishing her husband had finished decorating the room that was to become his home-office. Then he would be out of the way and not upsetting Sophie.

"William doesn't know about the jelly man. He's too old." She began to cry.

"Too old...?" Margaret asked.

"Bed, young lady. *Now.*" Donald was suddenly hovering close, making his daughter squirm, as if she was caught on a fish hook, unable to respond to her mother.

"C'mon, Tuppence, let's go up and you can tell me all about it and I'll show you that there is no monster." Margaret took her daughter's hand and led her tearfully back up the stairs into the dark cavern of the landing.

She wanted Sophie out of her father's way; he wasn't helping at all. He'd been neglectful of both their children for some time. She knew he was under a lot of pressure with his job. After all, he was bringing more of it home with him, along with his moods. He never said that the job was getting him down, but if not that, then something he was unwilling to divulge was affecting him. He had become less tolerant of the children. Less interested in her, too, Margaret thought dismally. She told herself she *must* talk to him; get him to open up.

In Sophie's bedroom Margaret saw that the quilt lay strewn on floor. Two favourite teddy bears, which normally kept her company at bedtime looked as if they had been thrown angrily to the far corners of the room.

113

"Well, Sophie, let's tidy this up first!" Margaret tried to make her voice light-hearted, expecting Sophie to respond now that Donald was out of earshot. She began to spread out the quilt. "Were you having a bad dream, love?" she asked.

"No." Her snivelling began to subside and her mother hugged Sophie close, lifted her and slid her under the covers.

Sometimes kids couldn't distinguish between dreams and real life, Margaret reminded herself. "I can tell you that the jelly man only... only lives in our dreams. He's not real—"

"He is, mummy, he is! And he's coming to see us!"

Margaret stared at Sophie, shocked by her outburst, thinking hard what to say that would defuse her daughter's terror. Wondering, too, how on earth Sophie had invented or heard of such a thing. It wouldn't have been William's doing, would it? It must have been one of her friends, telling her creepy stories.

"Who told you about the... the jelly man, love? Was it someone at school?"

"Nooo," Sophie insisted, shivering, her eyes wide as if seeing hobgoblins hovering above her.

Her mother wasn't convinced. She asked, "Do you want me to leave the big light on tonight?" The night-light hardly made any impression on the dark.

"Mmm-m. Please." Margaret could see that Sophie was fighting her drift to sleep. "The jelly... the jelly man!" she called, momentarily wide awake again.

"Shush, honey, there's no one here."

Sophie's eyes were wide with fear. "But he's coming tonight, mummy." Margaret could see drowsiness was fighting with her desire to stay awake, to nurse her fright.

"Only in your dreams, love. And he can't hurt there, can he? And," she added, to try to tame her daughter's fear, "if you think about something nice, something really good, then even the bad dreams will become good dreams. F'rinstance—" she paused to think.

"He's seen William, but he was too old to believe in him. Like Daddy."

"Oh, honey, Williams's all right. He's fast asleep, like you should be. Now, let's think about Ted and Ned here—" She realised that Sophie's teddy bears were still lying in separate corners of the room. She picked them up and placed one each side of Sophie's head. "Ted and Ned will bring you beautiful dreams. Because they love you just like me and dad."

"Daddy doesn't love us anymore."

"Shush, shush." Too right she wanted to say. Instead she said, "Daddy *does* love you, it's just that he's so busy at the moment. Just you wait until the school holidays... How about Ted and Ned telling you all about when we go to Spain?"

"Can they come too?"

"Of course, honeypot."

Sophie was slipping back to sleep. She must be dog-tired. She herself still felt wide-awake, because her daughter's antics this evening had upset her.

"Ned and Ted went to Spain when they were both two years' old," she began a story that she knew she wouldn't need to finish.

"He's coming, mummy..."

"Now, there, relax. Ted's going to tell you about the aircraft flying through the clouds and the seaside and the beaches. Ned, well he'll be talking about the shops and the funfair and how daddy's been waiting twelve months, working so hard so that we can all go on holiday—" Sophie was fast asleep.

Margaret rose gratefully from the bed. When she turned to face the door, William was standing, sleepy-eyed just inside the bedroom.

"Well, young man, what are you doing up?" his mother whispered, beginning to shoo him out.

"Heard shit-head crying."

"*William!*"

She quickly turned him by his shoulders and wheeled him out, quietly pulling the bedroom door to behind her. When she had returned William to his own room, she angrily flung him onto his bed.

115

"How *dare* you use such language in front of your sister? Is that what they teach you at school?" She realised she was beginning to trot out the same old clichés as her own parents had. Of *course* you learned bad language from your peers, nothing new there. She told herself to calm down.

"No," William replied sheepishly, hanging his head in shame at last.

"That *has* to be a lie." She felt herself becoming annoyed enough to want to slap him, and wishing she'd never thought it even as she brought the feeling under control. "You certainly didn't pick up words like that from me or your dad - or Sophie."

"I'm sorry, mum." Suddenly he was looking at her fiercely, his blue eyes sharp, and the exact opposite of apologetic.

Margaret decided to end the conversation, though not before one more question. "All right. But let's hear no more swearing. Will, you must have heard what Sophie was saying? Did you mention this jelly monster thing to her?"

He was quite vehement about it. "No! There's no such thing."

"Well somebody told her that Santa Claus didn't exist last Christmas!"

"So, if I told her that Father Christmas doesn't exist, why would I tell her that the jelly monster does?" he offered logically.

He seemed so adult sometimes, she thought. Senior school next term, so still plenty of growing up to do. Deciding the discussion really should be at an end, she said, "It's getting late, Will, try and get back to sleep, eh?"

"You're not still angry with me, mom?"

Margaret realised that she was still on edge. "No, not any more, scout's honour!" She smiled, saluted, and ran her fingers through his hair as he lay down. He shrugged her hand away, not out of spite, but because he wanted to appear grown up.

"I'll make sure Sophie doesn't get frightened if she says anything to me," he said with brotherly bravado.

116

Margaret was about to say 'good boy', but instead said, "There's my little man! Thanks."

"Night-night, mom."

She began to breathe more easily as she went back downstairs. "Any chance of a bit of quiet, now," Donald snapped when Margaret returned to the living room.

"It wasn't *my* fault, Don," she tried to placate him by keeping her voice measured. Then, holding her breath she said, "D'you think you're taking on too much responsibility?" She wanted to say more, to alert him to his irritability, his changed personality.

"We have to eat, don't we? Pay the mortgage..."

A folder smacked against the table. Margaret felt as if he'd slapped her face. She sighed, picking up the remote. She was about to select a channel. "Would you rather I didn't?"

"It won't interrupt me," he spat out. No, she thought, but the kids do.

Margaret jabbed at one of the buttons at random, now wanting to do something to really justify angering him. She needed to tell him that their marriage was suffering, the children too. When she'd exhausted about eighty channels, the screen turned to hissing snow, and she snorted and banged her fist on the remote. The screen imploded into standby again and she left it, throwing the commander onto an empty chair.

At about two-thirty Donald came to bed. He looked exhausted and was sweaty. As if he'd been out for a ten-mile hike in the middle of the night while she'd lain awake, waiting. He was soon snoring, however, leaving Margaret lying in the dark, listening to her breathing steadily rising in frustration.

She toyed with the idea of masturbating, but then she heard Sophie talking in her sleep from her room next to theirs and she felt compelled to look in on her daughter.

When she put her head around the door she could feel the brush of cold on her face. The window was wide open, a breeze lifting the net curtain as if it were a fat ghost drifting into the room. The lower half of the sash had been pushed

117

right up. Sophie must have done it herself. Maybe in her sleep? That seemed unlikely; the wood was rather tight in the frame. Margaret gently eased it right down, finally pulling the top half of the sash open a few inches to allow in fresh air; but not a gale.

She decided to check on William as well, although she was loath to admit she was beginning to feel apprehensive. With relief she saw that he was asleep, his window closed.

She was no longer tired, so she decided to make herself a drink. The smell of instant coffee and the quiet roaring of the kettle soothed her thoughts somewhat. But she still felt vulnerable now that Donald had become so unreliable. The country house was isolated. Anyone could have been watching the property for an easy way in. She was unnecessarily sensitised because they had been forced to move house, because of the, as yet un-apprehended, animal rights people. Woolly-headed criminal terrorists, Donald called them. They had learned what Donald was doing for a living and found out their address. Their former home had been daubed with graffiti, along with some obnoxious, decomposing substance. Perhaps Sophie was remembering those incidents and had translated them into her imaginary monster?

Walking with cup in hand, she began methodically to check downstairs doors and windows. Damn it! She shouted to herself. Donald had left the back door unlocked. She'd always left him to deal with the security unless he was away on business. But since moving, he'd his mind on work, work, work! He was neglecting everything else. Family life. Being amenable. Realising that she had desires even. Unless he was having an affair, which might account for a lot. He used to be so meticulous, before this damned work for the Icelandic government intervened. She wished that the 'North Atlantic Whaling Research Group' had never promoted him and the work hadn't caused them to need to buy the new house to escape persecution.

But her mind quickly returned to the night fears. The jelly

man… As daft as it seemed, she wondered if maybe Sophie *had* seen something at her window. An intruder? Or had the animal rights mob caught up with them? They really *were* isolated. Burglars would find easy pickings. Shouldn't they have had an alarm system fitted sooner? If not a thief, perhaps an axe murderer was lurking outside. She shuddered.

She decided to lock Sophie's window before she returned to bed. Doing so might have seemed over cautious; there was no drainpipe outside her window, no way up except by ladder and they didn't own one. But for her own peace of mind, she would latch the window.

Returning to the breakfast bar, she could feel cool air on her skin, the tug of the fabric of her knickers. Her hand touched her crotch briefly, pushing up against the satin. Between her legs was becoming hot and wet. She allowed her fingers to play. The coffee cup fell out of her other hand, spilling its remaining contents onto the kitchen work surface. She wandered back into the living room and lay down on the sofa.

She thought about Donald's sweating body upstairs, wondering where his sex-drive had gone. It had to be job worries that were the cause of his lack of responsiveness.

Margaret thought she could hear Sophie getting up again. But then it might have been William going for a pee. Or Donald, stirring in his sleep. Abruptly there was a loud double thump from upstairs. Serve him right if he comes down and catches me masturbating, Margaret thought triumphantly. Might even turn him on. But what if it was William? And *he* came downstairs? She realised that she might be the more embarrassed. But there were no further sounds from the upper storey.

She turned her heard to one side and gasped as she slipped off her panties and spread her legs. On the coffee table beside her Donald had placed his folders, casually left open. As her fingers went deeper she idly read the typescript that Donald was editing. About CITES and the Icelandic government permitting the taking of fin whale for commercial purposes.

119

Hunting disgusted her, but she had no say in her husband's job, and his efforts to reel in countries that would support an end to the moratorium.

Later, she tiptoed to the upstairs landing. William's door was firmly closed. The master bedroom door open. Hadn't she closed it earlier?

Margaret's nervousness returned as she stepped along the corridor. Pausing outside her daughter's room, the door seemed to stare at her, willing her to pass by, unwilling to let her in.

Nonsense! Her mind screamed.

Then the door was caving inwards with the press of her body, as if a weight on the other side had suddenly moved. She scrambled, thrusting herself along the wooden floor, its squeaky polish burning her knees. The room was in darkness, yet hadn't she had left the light on? Something was wrong. "Get up!" She said quietly, not quite understanding what she was going to do next.

"Mummy," she could hear Sophie saying. Partial relief began to flood through her. Then it was frozen solid in her veins. "See, it really is the jelly man."

Margaret frowned, dragged herself to her feet. *Something* was in the bed with Sophie. She couldn't see what it was properly. The darkness clung to her daughter. She *had* left the main light on before, she told herself as she threw herself across the room and flicked the switch. Sophie was throwing back the covers and bringing up her knees.

"It's all right, mummy," Sophie stated calmly. Too flat, her voice was emotionless. Then she began to slide on something wet on her sheet. "William's had a visit."

But she was all right. *She was all right!*

In a panic, running to William's room, she turned the cool porcelain of the knob, feeling the mechanism creak. The hall light sent a weak shaft across the room and over the bed. William must have been wriggling in his sleep, because his duvet was all bunched up. Then she was moving into the room, fussing at the quilt, except that it wasn't the bedspread at all. It was moist. William was waking up now, sleepily opening his questioning eyes.

Margaret whimpered. Her daughter's night terrors echoed in one half of her mind while the other tried to deny what her hands were touching. She was pulling on something slippery and wet, trying to tuck Will back comfortably under his duvet. He didn't need to see what it was. But he was safe. *He was safe!* Wasn't he safe?

Abruptly she realised that she had left Sophie alone. She turned, falling onto her hands and knees, unable to stand up. Scuttling back along the corridor, slipping on something smearing the hall floor, she was unable to reach the doorknob of Sophie's room. Her fists thumped the wood, one hand after another, a drumbeat that measured out her growing terror.

"Sophie!" she hissed, her voice unable to shout, because her throat was as thin as a straw. "Come. Out. Here. At. *Once!*"

The door opened hesitantly. "Mummy, mummy. The jelly man. He doesn't like daddy, *not one bit.*" Sophie was reluctant to move into the hallway, as if there might be something there she did not want to see again. "He asked me where daddy was and I told him. We's innocent, but the jelly man says daddy is not nice. He's gone to see him now."

Standing up at last, Margaret stumbled towards hers and Donald's room. Donald's naked body was spread-eagled on its stomach. She found herself tugging at something that uncoiled from between his legs. It was still very warm and she realised that the slimy loops really should have been coiled up *inside* her husband's belly. He didn't wake up. There was the smell of brine in the air, like rotting seaweed. The room contained another inhabitant, but she didn't wait to see what it was.

Margaret screamed only after she saw the colour of the handprint she left on the wall outside the bedroom as she flung herself through the doorway.

Slipping on the hall carpet, she fell heavily, batting her head against the antique pine of a bookcase, her wet hands leaving a smear down her thigh as if she'd begun her period. She felt giddy and distant from reality. Her lungs flapped asthmatically inside her chest. She hoped that Sophie was correct, but if not perhaps there was still time for her to escape from the house with both her children.

THE WOLF AT JESSIE'S DOOR

Paul Finch

The first time Adam saw the animal, he was slumped drunk in the armchair in his lounge. It was about five in the morning, he thought, and he'd been dozing for several hours. The chill in the room and a cramped neck had finally conspired to wake him properly, and he found himself gazing bleary-eyed across the can-strewn floor, finally focussing on the window, which, being uncurtained, was now filled with a dingy February light.

The animal was peering in at him.

It had reared up on its hind legs, and was resting its front paws on the windowsill.

His first thought was that it was some kind of stray sheepdog, though what a sheepdog would have been doing loose on the Trapp Hill estate at this hour, he couldn't imagine. Besides, this thing was bigger than any sheepdog he'd ever seen, and there was nothing even vaguely cute about it. It was covered with shaggy silver-grey fur, streaked with what looked like dirt or oil, and, balanced on two legs as it was now, it stood at least five and a half feet tall at the shoulder. Its head was large, flat and anvil-shaped, and its ears pricked up like a wolf's (something else which, now that he considered it, rendered it distinctly unsheepdog-like). A long pink tongue hung from its slightly parted jaws, draped sideways over sword-like teeth. But more menacing still, its eyes, which were fixed unswervingly on Adam, were like holes in dirty snow: dark, depthless blots that were completely unreadable.

For a moment Adam thought he was dreaming. He knew he was in that semi-delirious state between wakefulness and sleep, when all manner of bizarre hallucinations are apt to strike, and for this reason he didn't at first react. The animal continued to stare in at him, its hot breath misting the glass. When he finally stirred in his armchair, it let out a long, low growl that he heard clearly. That was when Adam realised that he was actually wide-awake.

He jumped to his feet… at least, as much as he was able to, being cramped, stiff and abominably hungover.

The window was now empty.

Though what looked conspicuously like a fog of breath was still visible on it, albeit fading rapidly.

A second passed, then Adam lurched his way across the room, kicking through the detritus of last night's solo booze-fest. Stumbling out into the tenement's downstairs corridor, he was immediately bitten by the cold. He was only wearing Y-fronts, after all, but for the moment even that didn't stop him. He went up the passage, opened the front door and scanned the deserted housing estate. A minute passed, then he stepped out and walked warily up the paved path towards his window. A dusting of snow had fallen the evening before, but temperatures had plunged during the night, transforming it into a brittle carapace of ice. It stung appallingly as he trod it barefoot.

When he reached the window, he scanned the estate again. Nothing moved. In the icy chill and grey dawn light, it was a dismal and deserted scene. Finally satisfied that he was alone, he glanced back at the window and noticed that in the central area of its lower frame, two portions of frozen snow were missing - as though they'd been wiped away. Adam instantly understood that these were the points where the animal's paws had rested.

*

"Hello, Greater Manchester Police at Mullacroft," the voice on the line said. It was clipped, very efficient. "Area Office, Sergeant Lloyd speaking."

"Sergeant Lloyd," Adam said. "This is Adam Verricker. You may have heard of me, I used to be in the job."

There was a very brief silence before the officer replied: "Sorry, no I haven't. What can I do for you?"

"Can I speak to WPC Gornall?"

"WPC Gornall's not on duty at the moment. What's it concerning, please?"

"I think I may have some information for her."

"Anything *I* can help you with?"

"Not if you don't mind, sarge. I used to work with her, you see. I know her quite well. I really think this is something she personally will be interested in."

"She's on this afternoon. I'll leave a memo for her. Can I have your full address?"

Afterwards, Adam did what he could to tidy up his ground-floor flat. It wasn't too difficult. The newspapers went in the rack, the beer-tins and pizza scraps went in the bin. He vacuumed the carpet and threw all his dirty pots into the sink, and then, as an afterthought, went around the lounge with a duster, though this drew his attention to the higher corners, where there were cobwebs he couldn't reach, and to the stained and generally unsightly wallpaper, which, again, there was little he could do to put right. Shortly before two o'clock, he took an envelope from a draw in the kitchen. It contained two items: a faded, dog-eared Polaroid, and a newspaper clipping. The Polaroid showed a much younger, much sturdier version of himself, clad in knee-length shorts and a vest, holding up a pint of beer and shouting. Beside him in the picture, a youthful Jessie Gornall, wearing an unbuttoned blouse over a dark swimsuit, was having an equally fun time of it. She had an open bottle of champagne in one hand, and a glass in the other, which she was in the process of filling. Other people were crowded around them, all bellowing, laughing and pushing each other, but Adam and Jessie were without doubt the central figures.

Adam smiled. That picture had been taken at a beach party at Bruche, North West England's police training centre, many years ago. It was all the more amusing, he considered, as Bruche - a bleak complex of concrete blocks and military-style parade grounds - was at least ten miles from the sea, and the

125

several months he and Jessie had spent there had run through a bitter winter that had seen everything from frost and fog to heavy snow and driving rain. The so-called 'beach party' had been held indoors, in the bar. But that hadn't stopped them having one hell of a good time.

The second item in the envelope, the newspaper clipping, was more recent in origin; only two or three weeks old. It featured one grainy photograph, a close-up of Jessie, smiling prettily from under her uniform hat, the entrance to a police station close behind her. Above it, the strap read: 'Heroine policewoman transfers in'. The accompanying story went on to say how WPC Jessie Gornall, a serving officer of twenty-one years' experience, who'd made national headlines in 1988 by tackling and arresting a robber armed with a knife, and in 1991 by jumping into the River Irwell to rescue a small child, was joining the Area staff of East Manchester's Mullacroft sub-division.

Adam had been overjoyed on seeing the newspaper story, for two main reasons: firstly, Mullacroft was the local nick to Trapp Hill; secondly, Jessie was using her maiden-name again. Only a couple of years after passing her probation, she'd married some twattish chief inspector from Traffic, called Carver, but by the looks of it, that relationship was over. For all this, of course, Adam knew that he couldn't rush things. They hadn't spoken in he didn't know how long. In truth, he found it hard to believe that she was actually coming to visit his home. With that thought in mind, he went round the lounge one more time, then dashed into his bedroom, rummaged through the spilled heaps of clothes and at last found a pair of jeans and a sweatshirt that were reasonably clean and uncrumpled. At around two-fifteen, she arrived.

Adam went out front, while she parked her unmarked car by the kerb.

Though part of the uniform branch, WPC Gornall was an Area officer rather than a beat officer, and this meant that her main task was to present the public with a friendly and attractive face. Her daily duties, while they might on the surface seem easy - attending residents' committees, speaking to schoolchildren, advising little old ladies on nuisance neighbours, and the like - required skills of communication that not every police officer was born with. They also required patience, understanding and, if possible, a natural pleasantness of personality that even the most suspicious punters could eventually come to trust. As such, it was always important that Jessie looked good. But in his wildest imaginings, Adam hadn't expected her to look *this* good. A uniform that had never been devised to accentuate the female form fitted her trim and shapely figure like a glove. The fact that she was wearing a skirt rather than trousers, and higher heels than would usually be permissible, helped of course. But even so, the lithe and pretty Jessie Gornall that Adam had known in her early twenties had now bloomed, at forty, into a truly beautiful woman. Her soft blonde hair was tucked neatly under her prim hat, but he imagined it would unravel to glorious length if she unpinned it. Everything about her appearance, though still efficient and stern, was feminine. She wasn't wearing any body-armour, for example, and in the fashion of the old-style WPCs, carried a black handbag rather than a hefty belt laden with manly accoutrements like handcuffs, truncheon, gas canister, and such.

Adam stood at the front door as she came up the path. When she reached him, she halted. For a moment she didn't speak, and he thought she hadn't recognised him. But then she said: "Jesus, you look terrible."

Adam understood this. He'd lost a lot of weight since she'd last seen him. His hair was unkempt and grey, he hadn't shaved recently and his face was lined and blotchy through his years of alcohol abuse. He smiled all the same, and nodded as though to make light of it. Then he invited her inside. Once in the lounge, she looked around with distaste - he'd thought he'd tidied up, but immediately he began to spot patinas of dust that he'd missed, crumbs along the edge of the carpet, beer cans

127

lying only partly concealed. When he offered her a brew, she declined, which was a good thing in retrospect, because it might have meant that she'd accompany him into the kitchen, and he hadn't had time to even start dealing with *that* shambles.

"So what's this information you've got for me?" she asked, sitting down and taking her pocket-book from her handbag.

Adam sat opposite, took a deep, melodramatic breath, and then let forth about the animal, giving her as much detail as he could, ensuring to underline the horror of that moment when it had risen up to gaze into his flat. A couple of times as he spoke, Jessie glanced out of the window, though he knew that wasn't because she was looking out for the beast, herself; it was because she was looking out for her car. Leaving any decent vehicle - and in this case it was a brand new Saab - unattended in a place like Trapp Hill wasn't a good idea. When he'd finally finished, however, he was surprised at how generally uninterested she seemed.

"So why are you reporting all this to me?" she asked.

"Why do you think?" Adam said. "If there's a dangerous dog loose on the estate, doesn't that fall into Area's remit?"

"Well, first of all, you don't know it's a dangerous dog, do you. I mean all it did was look at you. Secondly, you don't know that it's loose on the estate. Suppose someone was taking it for a walk?"

"At five in the morning?"

She put her pocket-book away, having written nothing in it. "I don't have all the answers, Adam. But as long as this dog hasn't attacked or menaced someone, there's not really a lot I can do." She stood up.

He stood too. "You're not just going to ignore it, Jess, surely? I mean this thing was monstrous. It was like a wolf."

She eyed him dubiously. "You sure you weren't just having a dream?"

"I'm absolutely sure. Look, it left its paw-marks on the window-frame."

"Let me see."

He led her outside, but during the course of that day there'd been a thaw, and any trace of marks on the window-frame had vanished.

"Look, I'm not lying!" Adam insisted. "This thing frightened the life out of me."

"All the more reason to consider it a nightmare," she said. "If you see it again, and it clearly is a stray, call the RSPCA. They're much better equipped to deal with this sort of thing than we are."

"And in the meantime, what if it rips someone's throat out?"

She gave him a frank stare. "Why on earth would it rip someone's throat out?"

Adam couldn't really answer that. Not in any way that would make sense.

"Still writing horror, are you?" she asked him, which was a pleasant surprise. So she'd kept tabs on him after he'd left the police, after all.

He shrugged. "I'm writing anything that'll sell."

She glanced up at the two-storey Council block where he lived. Its façade was basic cement, decorated under each front window with alternate blue or yellow boarding. He knew immediately what she was thinking: *You can't be writing much that sells, living in a place like this.*

"So was it worth it?" she wondered. "Leaving the job, I mean? To become an author."

"That wasn't the reason I left."

"No," she agreed. "How's the neck anyway."

"It still hurts when I get cold."

"That's the way it goes, I suppose." She clearly didn't want to talk further. "Got to go now, Adam. Been nice seeing you again."

He hurried after her, as she walked down the path. "You think I'm making it all up, don't you?" She stopped, glanced round at him. "I mean about the dog?"

Jessie's expression wasn't warm; in fact, it hadn't been since

129

she'd arrived, which puzzled him a little. When he'd read in the paper about this policewoman who wasn't just brave and handsome and clever, but who was pleasant as well, and kind and sympathetic, he'd expected her to give him a little more time, especially considering the relationship they'd once shared. If anything, though, she regarded him suspiciously.

"I don't for one minute think you're making it up," she said at last. "At least not consciously. But... well, to start with, your living room smells like a brewery."

That caught him by surprise. "I can have a few drinks in my own home, can't I?"

"Sure. But do you leave it at a few drinks?"

"Oh. You mean am I an alky? Or maybe am I on drugs? Was I tripping at the time?"

"Well were you?"

"For God's sake, no. Bloody hell, Jess, I've not fallen that low."

She glanced around at the encircling buildings. Trapp Hill was basically a cul-de-sac, a semi-circle of Council tenements ranged around a run-down playground. Most of the exteriors were covered in graffiti; a couple had boarded windows. "You'd be one of the few round here who hasn't," she finally replied. "Anyway, I've got to go."

"I'm glad you're working up here, by the way," he called after her.

She was now unlocking her car. "Sorry, what?"

"It's very cool."

"Okay, good." She climbed in. "See you round, Adam."

By her tone, that final comment had sounded like a figure of speech rather than a genuine belief that she *would* see him again, but it didn't matter too much, he thought. It was a start, and that was as much as he'd hoped for. A couple of moments later, however, he was reminded, as he had been so often in life, that any vaguely pleasant thing tends to have a price-tag attached. In the communal corridor, someone was waiting for him.

130

It was the guy from upstairs, a balding, thick-set individual, who always wore tight T-shirts that showed off his massive, tattoo-covered muscles. Adam knew him simply as O'Gara, but thought his first name was something chavish and trashy like 'Dane'.

"What do the fucking coppers want?" O'Gara asked. He was leaning against the door-jamb in the open entrance to Adam's flat, his arms folded.

"Do you want to move out the way?" Adam said.

"I'll move out the way when I'm good and ready. I said what do the coppers want?"

"What's it got to do with you?"

O'Gara chuckled to himself, then straightened up and stuck a fat, be-ringed finger in Adam's chest. "Look pal, you don't want to get on the wrong fucking side of me. I don't fucking like you, as it is."

"I didn't think you even knew me," Adam said.

"I know you well enough. Fuck around with me, and I will fuck you up. You got it?"

Adam wasn't so ring-rusty that he couldn't recognise a genuine threat when he faced one. At close glance, O'Gara's tats had prison written all over them. He also had a good three stone advantage, and his face was pig-mean.

"Well?" O'Gara prompted. "What the fuck did that fucking sow want?"

For a moment Adam was tempted to respond: *You've got an amazing vocabulary, do you know that. With such a broad range of terminology, you should write scripts for Joe Pesci.* But, as he'd already told himself, he knew when real danger was staring him in the face. "She came here because I made a complaint," he said.

O'Gara scowled. "Not about me?"

Again it was tempting to smart-mouth, to say*: Jesus, you've not done something illegal, have you - not someone like you?* Or: *Wow, so the people visiting you all hours of the night are not calling in for a cuppa after evensong?* Instead, he said:

131

"No, it was a complaint about them. I got locked up the other day for shoplifting, but it was mistaken identity. Didn't stop them giving me a shit time down the nick, and then releasing me without charge. Afterwards, when I complained, they said make it formal. So I have."

"You didn't mention me?" O'Gara asked him again.

"Why would I mention you?"

"Good attitude. Keep it that way." The hoodlum gave Adam another surly once-over, then turned and ambled down the passage to the stone stairs at the end.

Adam went back indoors and stood in his lounge. He hadn't been a policeman for seventeen years, so that natural street-toughness that came with the job had worn off him some time ago. Which made it all the more curious that he didn't feel unnerved by what had just happened. There was no sweat on his brow, his heart wasn't thudding. Why, he wondered, had an ogre like Dane O'Gara not scared him more? The answer was elusive at this moment. Not that Adam was giving it a great deal of thought. Before anything else, he had a romance to re-ignite.

*

Later that evening, Adam received another visitor, but this was one he hadn't been expecting, so when the buzzer rang he was half way through a rancid chip supper.

The lady at the door was very large - an impression enhanced by the enormous Parka she was wearing - plump-cheeked and smiling broadly. She immediately offered him a plastic ID card, which said that she was Sheila Southerby and that she worked as part of a civilian support unit for the Greater Manchester Police.

"You're the gentleman who reported the dangerous dog, yes?" she said, her friendly smile never faltering.

"That's right."

"May I come in?"

She already had one foot on the step, so he let her in the rest of the way. The state of the lounge had degenerated somewhat since Jessie's visit, and Adam didn't feel particularly inclined to tidy up again. But for the sake of appearances, he snatched the wrapper of brown, shrivelled chips, scrunched it and tossed it at the already overflowing bin, which, in the way of these things, promptly rejected it back onto the carpet. The television was still on, but he didn't bother to turn the volume down. Not that this would have made a great deal of difference. It was an old portable, and none of its controls worked very well; he didn't even have an aerial for it (nor a licence, if he was honest).

He indicated the woman should sit, which she did. "So what's the score?" he asked. "You had other complaints about it?"

"No, no. I'm just here to ask what you, yourself, thought you saw."

"I didn't *think* I saw anything," he replied. "I *know* I saw it. It was at that window over there."

"And it was a large dog?"

"Yeah. Look…" Adam couldn't help but feel aggrieved; his tea had been interrupted and he still didn't know who this person was. "I gave all this to WPC Gornall earlier on. Though I suppose if she'd actually bothered to write anything down it would have helped."

The woman was unperturbed by this. "Is it okay if I take my coat off?" she asked.

Adam nodded, but was now starting to feel vaguely suspicious. This lady was being way too polite, which suggested that something was afoot. He dropped into his armchair, took the beer tin from the top of the television and had a long, hard swig from it.

"I'm assuming you haven't seen this dog on the estate before?" she said.

"No, thank God."

"Do you not like dogs?"

133

"Look, this wasn't just a dog, it was..."

"Yes?" Suddenly she was staring at him keenly, genuinely interested to hear more.

"The main thing is it's gone," he continued. "I haven't seen it all day." For some reason, he didn't want to talk about the dog any more. It was already fading from his memory, as though it really *had* been just a dream.

"How'd you feel in yourself about what happened?" his visitor wondered.

"I don't know what you mean?"

"Were you badly shaken? I should think you must have been to have called the police."

"I still don't know what you mean."

"Well... people who live in places like Trapp Hill are often hesitant to contact the police. Either because they don't like them through prior experience, or because they're concerned about what their neighbours might think."

Adam remembered the conversation with O'Gara. Now that he considered it, perhaps he *had* let emotion get the better of his common sense. Not that the emotion in question had been fear of the dog; that incident had sparked a momentary fright, but nothing more.

"So you were obviously fairly disturbed?" the woman went on, nodding as though to encourage him.

"It put the wind up me, that's all."

"Hmm." She pondered this, and then, to Adam's astonishment, reached into her handbag and produced a clipboard. She flipped through a couple of typed documents that were attached to it. "According to WPC Gornall's notes, you said the animal was 'monstrous, like a wolf.'"

Adam was cheered. Jessie had paid more attention to him than he'd thought. But even so, to selectively quote him like that was deceptive. "Turns of phrase," he explained.

"Yes. Well that doesn't surprise me." Mrs. Southerby smiled again. "You're a writer, aren't you. Must be a very interesting job?"

134

"Sometimes. Most of the time it's bloody frustrating."

"Oh, I see. Well, would you like to talk about *that*?"

"No I wouldn't."

"Would it be easier if I put the kettle on?" she suggested. "It might relax us more."

"What do you mean 'relax us'... hey!" He stiffened in his chair. "You're not some kind of social worker, are you?"

"Not as such."

"Not as such!"

"I'm actually a volunteer. As I said earlier, I'm with the Civilian Support Team. We make follow-up visits to victims of crime."

"But I'm not a victim of crime."

"No, I appreciate that." She smiled again, and leaned forward as though to reassure him. "But WPC Gornall thought it might be useful, in your case, if one of us came to see you. We're really just here to lend moral support. You know, provide a friendly shoulder to cry on."

Adam was trembling as he rose to his feet. "Get the hell out of here."

"Don't take that attitude, please."

"I want you to leave," he said, just about managing to contain his temper.

"Alright, no problem," she said, still smiling but hastening to put her Parka on. "And there's no insult taken. Believe me, you're not the first person who's shown me the door. Just as long as you know we're around. Can I leave you my card?"

"Fine, leave it, whatever."

She handed him a paper version of the plastic one she'd flashed earlier. "It's only the last few years that we've really been doing this," she said. "I mean, there are hurt and vulnerable people all over this city who never get to talk to anyone."

He marched stiffly to the door, opened it and let her out into the communal passage. "It's very public-spirited of you," he replied, "but for your information, I'm neither hurt nor

135

vulnerable. And I'm sorely pissed off that Jessie thinks I am."

"I doubt she considers it in those terms."

"I don't care what terms she considers it in. Just go. I don't need anyone to talk to."

The woman started down the passage, but then halted again, and Adam was suddenly conscious that he'd heard what had sounded like a door creaking open upstairs. "It's a strange thing, though, what you reported," she added, her voice no doubt carrying clear up the stairwell. "I mean, any normal person would've been alarmed at something like that. It's no wonder you got in touch with the police."

"I reported a dangerous dog!" he shouted. "It was nothing at all, a complete waste of time." A second passed, and seeing the peculiar, rather shocked look on his visitor's face, he managed to lower his voice. "And now it's over and done with. Yes? Don't you agree?" And with quick motions of his hands, he shooed her down to the front door.

A moment later, Mrs. Southerby was waddling down the path to her car, which in the darkness Adam couldn't identify, though it was a long vehicle, pale in colour and with dark markings on its flanks. It wasn't a police vehicle, but it looked unnervingly like one. Overhead of course, the curtains would no doubt be twitching.

The lady turned once more to speak, but Adam cut her dead.

"It's over and done with!" he said so forcefully that she nodded, smiled again - rather half-heartedly this time - and clambered into her vehicle. As she drove around the cul-de-sac and headed off the estate, he added to himself: "It's definitely over and done with."

But later that night, it became apparent that this wasn't the case at all.

*

Adam's bedroom was the size of a closet. With his bed taking up at least half of it, and the space near his wardrobe occupied by his desk and computer, the spillage of papers from which completely obliterated the remaining section of floor, it was claustrophobic in the extreme. As it had no radiator, it was also damp and cold, though he always slept soundly in there; he'd long ago acclimatised to such harsh conditions (his night in the armchair had been a mistake - the result of drinking even more than usual).

It was about four o'clock in the morning, however, when he heard the snarling.

It woke him instantly. He threw the quilt off and stood up.

The snarling continued. It was so loud that, for a spine-chilling second, he thought it was coming from his lounge. Instinctively, he stuck his hand into his cluttered wardrobe, rummaged around and found his old baseball bat. With this raised to his shoulder, he ventured out into the passage and then into the lounge itself.

Glacial winter moonlight filled the disordered room. But there was nothing untoward in there; nothing he could see. Adam stayed where he was for several seconds, scanning each corner. He could still hear the snarling, and now that he listened to it carefully, it was the weirdest, most blood-curdling thing he'd ever heard: it was powerful, gutsy, gruesome, as though emitted by a deep throat and a huge pair of lungs. Yet it was also faltering, as though choked or constricted. For an incredible moment, he thought about a movie he'd watched only the other night: Oliver Reed in *The Curse Of The Werewolf*. After his first horrific transformation, the hairy hero of the title had made a sound just like this. Slowly, stealthily, the carpet ice-cold beneath his feet, Adam padded across the room to the window and gazed out.

And that was when he saw it.

The dog.

This time it was standing amid the skeletal wrecks of the playground. It looked even larger than it had before; it was maybe seven feet from its nose to the tip of its tail. It stood rigid on all fours, yet was quivering violently as if having some

137

kind of convulsion. Dark streaks ran haphazardly down its body to its hind-quarters, which, compared to before, were now completely black. And then, when it suddenly ceased its quivering and its snarling, and it turned abruptly to face him, Adam saw that there were other changes. A prominent, pointed nodule had sprouted above each of its eyes.

Horns?

Dear God, the thing had horns?

And then it came. Weaving its way out of the playground with pantherish speed, it bounded across the road, heading straight for Adam's flat.

He backed from his window, shouting. He raised the bat, but knew it was futile. As the thing came swiftly closer, the eyes that had previously been dark blots now gleamed a feral crimson. Froth and spume flew from its gnashing jaws.

"Someone help!" Adam shouted. *"Help me, please!"* But it was already here.

It leapt straight for the window. It would barrel clean through. The glass would explode into a million fragments.

Yet none of that happened.

Adam found himself sitting up in bed again, morning light pouring down from the high letter-box window. He was breathing hard, and soaked with freezing sweat. But only a few seconds passed before he was able to chuckle to himself, to laugh at his own foolishness. Unfortunately, another few seconds passed and then those chuckles faded.

Adam stared down astonished... at the baseball bat in his hand.

*

The Chadwick Arms was essentially a police pub. It was close to Mullacroft Central, the sub-divisional HQ, and as such, though it fronted onto a market square and would normally be filled with hucksters, hawkers, and, on weekend nights, drunken revellers, it was a no-go zone for serious troublemakers. Externally it was tall and narrow, and made from dingy red brick. Inside it was very traditional, all brass, polished wood and framed, sepia-toned photographs of townscapes past. What it lacked in breadth it made up for in depth: running backwards from its front door, it consisted of five different but equally spacious and ornate rooms, each one with its own bar. It was in the rearmost of these where Adam found Jessie.

He spotted her in a seating bay with two other men. Like most of the rest of the clientele, the two men were in civilian clothes, but were clearly coppers. The first was middle-aged and heavy built, with a saggy, jowly face but also a telltale crew-cut. The second was younger but plumper, with red hair shaved to the bristles and a trim red moustache. Adam thought he recognised this second man, but he wasn't sure. A moment passed, then he walked over there.

"Fancy meeting you here," he said to the woman.

She eyeballed him warily. "Hello Adam."

"Mind if I grab a seat?" he asked.

He'd have been more likely to secure a warm welcome if he'd offered to get a round of drinks in - the threesome's glasses only contained dregs - but life on the dole didn't favour generosity. He thus placed his own, full pint glass on the table, and sat down. The two men regarded him curiously but didn't seem overtly hostile. Adam now realised that he *did* recognise the younger one. Though much heavier than he had been as a youth, he was Billy Prentiss; he'd joined the force as a young constable around the same time Adam and Jessie had. "Don't remember me, I bet?" Adam asked him.

Prentiss shrugged. "Should I?"

"Adam Verricker." Adam offered his hand. "Four Relief at Central?"

The red-haired copper shook hands with him, but seemed none the wiser. "Sorry, no."

"Adam injured his neck in a car accident a few years back," Jessie explained. "He had to leave."

139

Still, Prentiss shook his head.

Jessie continued: "Adam, you already know Bill." She turned to the older man. "This is Frank Tamworth, DI at Shetland Street. Bill's the DS there now."

"Good to meet you," Adam said.

The DI nodded, but was already looking bored with the new-arrival.

"So what can we do for you?" Jessie asked.

Adam shrugged. "Nothing. Just bumped into you."

"Come to The Chadwick Arms a lot, do you?"

"Now and then," he lied.

"It's a bit of a hike from Trapp Hill," she pointed out.

The words 'Trapp Hill' provoked an immediate reaction from the two detectives, who glanced at each other furtively. Adam knew what they were thinking: *Trapp Hill? Exactly who the fuck is this guy?*

"I don't socialise around there, Jess," Adam said, laughing. "It's a bit rough."

She nodded. "Well, it's good to see you again, Adam, but we were having a conversation, and it's kind of private."

"Oh… right." Used as he was to police bluntness, this rather took him by surprise, though her apologetic smile was quite endearing in its own way. "No probs." He stood up and pushed his chair back. "I'll leave you to it."

He walked away, and the moment he did, heard a snigger of partly suppressed laughter behind him. When he glanced backwards, he saw the two detectives chuckling. Jessie was grinning and becoming animated as she told them something that he couldn't quite hear. She was shaking her head very pointedly.

It didn't put him off.

"You don't get rid of me that easily," he said later, when she emerged from the Ladies, putting her coat on, and suddenly found him blocking her path.

"For God's sake!" she snapped. Appearing out of nowhere, like that, he'd made her jump.

"For God's sake?" He feigned astonishment. "Am I that disagreeable a surprise?" He glanced down at himself. His leather jacket and stonewashed jeans weren't quite as smart as Jessie's pearl blouse and black skirt-suit, but his shirt was clean and he'd combed his hair, and by his normal standards, that was going to town.

"Adam, what do you want?" she asked.

"More straight talking, eh. Okay, well... what I want is to know why you've suddenly decided I'm a charity case?"

"Oh, that." She seemed to understand, and now finished putting her coat on. "I heard you'd sent the Civilian Support volunteer off with a flea in her ear."

"Of course I did. I've got some pride left, you know."

"Just out of interest, how did you find me here?"

"It wasn't hard. You're back at Mullacroft Central, aren't you? This is where we always used to come after shift."

She shook her head. "I'm not sure I'm comfortable with this."

"With what?"

"Adam!" Her voice hardened. "You're not one of us any more. You haven't been for a long time. You're a punter, and that means you don't go around pestering us when we're off duty."

He shook his head. "Am I not a special case?"

"Why on earth would you be? Look, thousands of people have left the job and gone back to civilian life." She added as an afterthought: "Most of them left under considerably less of a cloud than you did."

"Whoa, hang on... I had an accident!"

She rolled her eyes. "Yeah, we all know about that."

"I was injured out. I broke a bone in my neck."

"You broke a bone in your neck because you crashed your car while you were driving drunk. The brass gave you the opportunity to resign gracefully."

She was glaring at him, and suddenly Adam himself felt angry. "Just out of interest, whose fault is it I was driving drunk?"

"Oh, I've had enough of this," she said, heading for the pub's back door. "That was seventeen years ago. We've all got on with our lives since. It's time *you* did as well."

She marched outside into the car park. Adam followed her as far as the door and stood gazing after her. And then saw the dog.

He froze.

A split-second later it had vanished again.

But he wasn't fooled.

The car park was extensive and filled with vehicles, but he could have sworn he'd just seen the animal slip past a gap between a Peugeot and an Audi. It was even larger now than it had been before: immensely long in the body, deep in the chest and moving at a lazy trot, its head hung low, its hyena-like ruff visibly bristling. It had now turned black all over, and without any doubt, he'd again spotted its two horns projecting up and curving outwards from just above its bony eyebrows.

"Jesus," he breathed. "Jesus, no." Then he shouted: "Hey Jess!"

He dashed forwards across the tarmac.

Jessie was in the process of opening the driver's door to her Saab when he threw his body over hers like a human shield, slamming her against the vehicle's flank.

She squeaked in momentary fright, then wrestled her way around and pushed him back: "What the hell do you think you're doing?"

Adam craned his neck to scope out every corner of the car park. Sweat suddenly glistened on his brow. "I saw... I mean I thought... shit. Shit, it can't be!"

And he was right; of course it couldn't be. Trapp Hill was nearly three miles away from here. Then he realised that Jessie was staring up at him, bewildered and not a little frightened. He snapped back to reality, lurching away from her. "I... I'm sorry. I think I made a mistake."

"Yes, I think you did."

142

The woman was pale, and looked more than a little shaken, which was hardly surprising. For a moment then she could have been about to be raped, murdered, anything.

He tried to explain: "When I heard you'd transferred in, I wanted to... I just thought it'd be nice to see you again." The words tailed off and he could have kicked himself. He hadn't intended for it to sound so weak.

"I see," she said. "So does this mean the mysterious dog was a total fabrication?"

"No, no... not a fabrication. But, well, I've always had a vivid imagination, as you know."

There was another moment of silence, and then she shook her head: "What happened to you, Adam? Look at the state of you. I mean, you're a shadow of the man I knew. Where's the *rest* of you?"

"The rest of me?"

"You were a go-getter once, a real killer. Top exam grades every week, best in the class at self-defence, first-aid, PT." She shook her head. "You had the whole of a lucrative career ahead of you - you could have been a superintendent by now. But you just couldn't stop partying, could you."

"That's the way the job was in those days," he protested. "You know what it was like? Pre-PACE, no such thing as political correctness. We could do what we wanted."

"Yes, but you were worse than many," she said. "I mean, you took terrible risks during your day-to-day work. Cutting corners, breaking rules. And every night it was wine, women and song, didn't matter what time you were on in the morning."

He smiled wolfishly. "There was only one woman for me."

"Oh for Christ's sake, don't give me that. We had sex. *Once.* At Bruche, after that beach party."

He smiled all the more. "I see you've not forgotten."

And for half a moment she smiled too. "Hardly. It was our passing-out parade the next morning. I had to sneak out of your block at six o'clock, so I get could get back and sort my

143

uniform out without anyone noticing."

"And then we got posted to the same nick, afterwards. Great days."

"Yes, but they ended, didn't they." Her smiled faded again. "For most of us. Though not for you, it seems. I mean for God's sake, how can you live on Trapp Hill?"

He shrugged. "I can't afford anything else."

"Then get a real job, stop playing around."

"I'm hardly playing."

"You are actually. Playing is exactly what you're doing."

"You've seen how I have to live. I take what I can get."

"Yes, but the up-side of that is it's stress-free. Responsibility never darkens your day, Adam. Anyway..." She waved a hand. "I've said enough. Just do yourself a favour, and me: grow up." She unlocked the car door, made to open it.

"Did it ever enter your head, Jess," he wondered, "that I might have crashed deliberately that night?"

At which she looked sharply around. "Excuse me? No it never did!" Her anger was short-lived, however. "Look, you're not going to keep doing this, are you? I mean now I'm back at Mullacroft, you're not going to keep turning up... like some grim spectre of the past?"

"Not if you don't want me to."

"Don't want you to? I told you a dozen times back then, Adam - we weren't right for each other."

"You mean I wasn't a chief inspector like Paul Carver? I didn't have the five-bed detached in the suburbs and all the influence necessary to get you any posting you wanted?"

She stared at him as though she couldn't believe he'd just said that. Then she shook her head again and opened the car door. "I'm going home now. I don't expect to see you again."

"Jess, I'm sorry."

She ignored him, climbed into the driver's seat.

"Look, you're right," he added. "We went through all this at the time, and it's inexcusable to bring it up again. It was just the surprise of seeing you, you know. How good you looked...

144

after all these years."

She was now behind the wheel, but she didn't start the engine.

"I guess I just got carried away," he said.

There was still no sympathy in the woman's face, but suddenly she looked tired with the confrontation. "You've no transport, I suppose," she said. "Can I give you a ride somewhere?"

At this time of night, with several drinks fermenting inside him, and a long slog home, especially up Trapp Hill itself, he was strongly tempted. But then he thought about Jessie's car stopping outside his house again, and yet more curtains twitching. "No thanks. I can use the fresh air."

As he walked out of the car park a few moments later, she drove up alongside him and rolled her window down. "Adam, don't come bothering me again, okay. It's no good for either of us."

"Maybe you think I've something else to do with my life."

"I'm sorry?"

"I said I swear it on my mother's life."

*

Adam had always regarded Jessie with more than pure lust, but she'd offered him a ride, and that night, boy, did she give him one.

They were back at Bruche again, the way they had been before, only this time it wasn't sexy beach-wear that he stripped from her supple body after he got her back to his room; this time it was full policewoman garb, or should that read *fantasy* policewoman garb? He pushed the tight black skirt up her firm thighs, exposing black stocking-tops and suspender straps, and nestling between these, a full cunt of lush golden hair. His mouth meanwhile was all over her breasts, the nipples prominent as finger-tips in her white blouse. He sucked them through the sopping linen, bit them, chewed them, and

145

then with his sharp, canine teeth, plucked loose one button after another, finally tearing the garment open. Beneath it, glory of glories, a flat white tummy and two enormous breasts sheathed in a barely-there brassiere of black satin. By now his fingers were playing sweet music between her thighs. He plunged his thumb in and out of her - vagina then rectum, vagina then rectum - a timely rhythm to coincide with her gasps. His other hand was on her breasts again, clawing the flimsy bra down. His mouth followed it, feasting on the succulent flesh underneath.

Jessie cried out hoarsely, threw her head from side to side. The efficient policewoman's hat came off and her blonde hair spilled in a shimmering frenzy on the pillow. He licked his way up onto her throat, then forced his open mouth upon hers. Their tongues entwined, and she gripped the back of his head with both hands. Urgently, he worked his trunks down, his member springing free like a steel ramrod, which, without preamble, he nudged first against her womanhood and then against her anus. She was now choking on his tongue, her hands tangling in his hair as though ready to wrench it from his scalp. With a single, brutal thrust, meanwhile, he was inside her. He didn't care which aperture he'd penetrated, but began to piston feverishly, bucking against her so hard that the head-board started slamming on the wall, the feet of the bed clacking on the tiled floor.

Behind them, he was vaguely aware of the door to the room swinging silently open. This had happened all those years ago too: one of the other lads in his group - he wasn't sure which one - had sneaked a couple of crafty peeks. Adam hadn't bothered at the time, and he doubted Jessie would have done either, even if she'd known. But this time, of course, it wasn't one of the other lads. This time it was Paul Carver, a tall, lean figure, immaculate in his pristine chief inspector's uniform, yet somehow ludicrous at the same time. The iron-rimmed spectacles on his beak-like nose always made the piercing blue eyes beneath them too large for his face; and underneath his

146

pompous, white Traffic officer's hat there was his balding pate with that ridiculous combed-over sidelock.

"Why would you want him instead of me?" Adam growled into the girl's ear.

Her nylon-clad legs had now locked around his waist, the black, high-heeled shoes hooked together in the small of his back. She said nothing, just rolled a slippery tongue up the side of his face, then groaned deeply as she received his first jet of sperm. Behind them, meanwhile, the door swung closed again and the heavy footfalls of the tall, ungainly Carver receded down the passage. No doubt he was off to make a report. Fraternising between girls and boys was strictly prohibited at Bruche in those days.

But he never got that far.

As Adam ejaculated a second time into Jessie's womb, he heard the Traffic commander get taken down, probably near the front door to the building: his brief shriek was swiftly lost in a whirlwind of snarls and a berserk rending of fabric and flesh.

Abruptly, Adam woke.

He had a pounding hangover, and when his eyes unglued themselves, the grey miasma of another dull winter morning hung over him. Grunting with disappointment, he turned beneath his quilt, half hoping to find Jessie snuggled alongside him. But on this occasion, the dream remained just that - a dream. His rod had now wilted in the front of his underpants, which were caked with numerous sticky discharges, and these, like the sweat still drenching his torso, had chilled discomfortingly in the low temperatures of the flat.

Adam sighed and rolled onto his back again. He tried to recall what he could of the night's entertainment, but instead found himself gazing at the ceiling, once formulaically white and bland, but now cracked and water-marked in a series of greenish, flower-like blotches. In one corner of it, a rather large section was missing, revealing ugly lathe-work beneath. Absurdly, Adam found himself concentrating on this particular flaw. He didn't remember it happening; he didn't remember a time when it could have happened without his noticing. That thought alone would have made him angry, had he not been so drained from his nocturnal exertions. In truth, he should be angry about a great many things, he realised. The way his life had gone in general: so many of his former contemporaries now respected, valued, empowered, and he, who'd been worth fifty of them, marooned in this drear outland of the lost and forgotten; that social worker woman implying that he couldn't cope, yet knowing nothing at all about his high-energy past; Jessie ditching him the way she had, and now calmly telling him to stop bothering her, calling him names - a mess, a child, a God-damned 'spectre of the past' for Christ's sake!

He certainly should be angry. Well and truly angry.

But for some reason, he wasn't.

Not really. He was bitter, irritated, annoyed... but not angry.

He looked for it in himself for several minutes, but he was getting hungry now so he finally gave up and trekked off to the kitchen to see if there was any bread that didn't have mould on it.

*

As the new Area constable for the district, Jessie was to hold her weekly surgeries on Thursday mornings in an office just off the atrium in Mullacroft Town Hall.

The atrium was a tall, airy chamber located beneath a stained glass ceiling that bore various illustrations symbolic of the city's prosperous industrial past: hammers, anvils, mill chimneys and the like. Suspended over the arched double-doors connecting it with the main Council Chamber, there was a large coat of arms in painted brass - a medieval picture of a peasant holding a pitchfork standing back-to-back with a knight holding a serrated sword, and beneath that the township's official motto, *United We Stand, Divided We Fall.* At the same time, numerous portraits of deceased aldermen, all elderly, grandfatherly figures in dark suits and high collars, gazed down implacably from the lofty, teak-panelled walls. In this stern and sobering atmosphere, the public - whoever they were there to see - would sit quietly on the seats provided and humbly await their turn.

Adam was about tenth that morning, but at last his moment arrived.

He licked his hand and flattened his hair, then jumped up and went into the office. Jessie, now uniformed again though with her blonde locks down to affect a friendly, informal look, was seated behind a desk and several piles of forms and leaflets. She was busy writing something in her pocket-book, but when she saw Adam the pen almost dropped from her hand.

He plonked himself down in the chair facing her. "The dog's real."

"You know, Adam, this is getting beyond a joke."

"I said the dog's real. It came again last night."

"In which case, I told you to contact the RSPCA, or even the Council. If there's a problem with stray dogs on your estate..."

"This dog isn't stray."

"Adam, I've been patient with you up to now..."

"You're my community constable," he interrupted. "I can report a crime to you if I think one's been committed, can't I?"

"A crime?"

"I think it might be an attack-dog."

"An attack-dog?"

"You know, a trained killer."

"I know what an attack-dog is. Why the devil would there be one on Trapp Hill?"

He laughed. "You know some of the people who live on that estate?"

"I'm getting a better idea by the minute."

"It only seems to be around at night," he added. "That's when you need to stake the place out."

"Adam, there are people waiting out there with serious problems."

149

"Oh, and I don't count as one of them?"

Jessie laid her pen down. She sat back. "Am I being punished? Is that it? That thing you said two nights ago, about deliberately crashing your car. Does that have…"

He smiled, waved it aside. "Don't worry about that, just a throwaway comment. I didn't deliberately crash the car. I mean, it was a shock when you broke the news to me. A real shock, a complete stunner. I thought I was going to faint - I think I almost did." He paused. "But that's because I was crazy about you. And you know I was. I had been ever since that time we got it together at Bruche. But no, I didn't crash deliberately. I was just drunk. Drunk out of my mind, remember?"

It would have been difficult for either of them *not* to remember. At the time, their relief had finished an early shift and they were looking forward to a long weekend off. They'd all gone to the pub together, The Chadwick Arms in fact.

"I'd just asked if you'd go out with me properly," he reminded her.

"And I'd replied to you," she said sternly, "for the umpteenth time, 'No Adam. I don't want to go out with you'. To soften the blow, I then added that I was seeing someone else. Someone I'd just met that week. But, despite that, you proceeded to get aggressively pie-eyed and later on, against everyone's advice, insisted on driving home."

"We all did it in those days," he said defensively.

"We all did everything in those days, Adam. But not to the excess that you did."

"Look, the dog…"

"Forget the dog," she told him. "Adam, I'm not coming to Trapp Hill and spending a night in your flat, staring out of the window."

"Is that because the place is a shit-hole?"

"No, it's because I'm just not doing it."

"What if I proved to you there's a fucking dog?"

"And what if I arrest you right now for being drunk and

disorderly? You *have* been drinking, haven't you?"

"Two or three tins, what's the problem?"

"The problem is it's not even eleven o'clock in the morning yet."

He made an awkward gesture. "I had to pluck up the courage to see you again."

"Well take a good long look," she said, "because this'll be your last chance. I'm leaving."

For a second he thought he'd misheard. "What?"

"I'm joining CID, moving to Shetland Street."

It was as though a cold hand had suddenly tightened around Adam's heart. His throat constricted, his mouth went dry. Shetland Street was the other side of the city - twelve miles away at least.

"W-what about all that guff in the paper?" he finally stuttered. "About you never taking your sergeant's exam, never looking for any kind of promotion, because all you ever wanted to be was a community bobby?"

"I'll still be a community bobby?" she replied. "Those guys you saw the other night: DI Tamworth, DS Prentiss. They want me to join their Offences-In-The-Family unit. It'll involve a lot of the kind of work I do right now."

Adam was almost lost for words. "Are you doing this because of me?"

"No Adam. Like everything else in my life, this decision has nothing to do with you."

"So, when... when do you leave?"

"The transfer comes through in two weeks time."

"So that's it then?"

She nodded. "It is indeed. However, you were correct the other night. You said that because we'd got on so well together when we were young, you should be a special case. And after some consideration I decided you were right, you should be. So here, this is for you." She took a form from the nearest pile and handed it to him. "Take this away and fill it in - everything you know about this dog."

151

Adam glanced down. It was a 'Notification of Community Nuisance'.

"When you've done that," Jessie added, "post it to Mullacroft Police Station's Area office, and I will personally see that it gets in-trayed for the attention of my successor, who will be in place in about one week's time."

Adam studied the form for several moments, then got abruptly to his feet. "You think this whole thing is just going to disappear, don't you?"

She gazed boldly up at him, all pleasantries dispensed with.

But he was unfazed. "You want to know the problem with the police service now, compared to when I was in it, Jess? It's actually not a service at all. It's a sea of red tape, it's officialdom gone mad. And you - *you've* become part of it. You're not Jess Gornall any more. You're an official, an automaton who juggles paper all day and gives stock responses."

"Why don't you go home and sleep it off, Adam. You can fill the form in tomorrow."

He wanted to tear the form to pieces, but instead he folded it neatly into quarters and dropped it back on her desk. "Were you addressing me, officer?" he enquired. "Well you can't have been. Because I don't know who you are."

Back in the atrium, he had to halt in mid-stride just to get his breath. He scanned the room, but barely saw any of it, aside from a door in a corner, signposted 'Conveniences'. Unable to form any other plan of action, he lumbered off towards it, so heated that he didn't even notice the two men detach themselves from the rest of the waiting public and follow him.

The door connected with a long corridor, at the end of which two arched brick entrances faced each other from opposite sides. Adam went through the one marked 'Gents' and stood staring at himself for several moments in the mirror over the first wash-basin. His complexion wasn't as sallow as usual. In fact, for the first time in quite a while, he looked pink, almost healthy. His eyes were bright, and the usual unshaved stubble had actually become a beard and moustache, which, now that he considered it, rather suited him. He straightened his shirt collar, brushed a few spots of dandruff from his shoulders.

And then went cold.

In the arched doorway behind, again reflected in the mirror, he saw Dane O'Gara.

The hoodlum was wearing a denim jacket over a hooded sweatshirt, and from the inside pocket of this, even now, as Adam watched, was drawing a length of steel pipe. There was another man with him, dressed in a green canvas overcoat: this guy was taller than O'Gara but broad as an ox, with short, silver-grey hair and an extravagantly large ring in one ear. His pallid face was disfigured by an old and hideous razor scar, which ran across his mouth diagonally, bisecting both his lips.

There was Hell in that face.

Adam swung around, but they were already onto him. Before he could resist, O'Gara had one hand on his throat and had slammed him back against the wash-basins.

"Mr. Verricker, how fucking good to meet you again!" the criminal said. "Allow me to introduce my associate, Mr. Cleaver. That's not his real name, of course. But it's all *you* need to know about him."

Adam raised both hands in prompt surrender. He couldn't fight his way out of a paper bag these days, but even if he'd been in shape, these two were clearly bruisers of the first order. Not that he intended to simply subject himself to whatever they had planned for him. "Listen," he said urgently. "Listen! This is not smart! I strongly advise you..."

"You advise us!" O'Gara spat, pushing Adam backwards all the harder. He raised the pipe. "You've got a nerve. You fucking lied to me. I trusted you and you fucking lied."

Adam shook his head. "Lied? I've hardly ever spoken to you."

For a moment O'Gara looked baffled; it was plainly a new concept to him that he could accost someone in a corridor of their own home and threaten them, and it not be the most

153

significant event of their week. Behind him meanwhile, Cleaver had taken a position in the doorway, to watch the corridor outside.

"We've been keeping tabs on you, Mr. Verricker," O'Gara said, though 'ranted' might have been a better description. Chillingly, his apelike face had blanched white, while the top of his bald cranium was glowing red, like a volcano set to explode. "And you've been busy, haven't you. You've had two different lots of pigs up to your flat recently. A couple of nights after that, you're in a pub where they all hang out. And now you're bloody *here!* What exactly are you talking to them about, eh?"

"It's nothing to do with you," Adam said. "You don't need to worry."

"I'm not worried. You're the one who should be worried. You're about ten seconds away from a battering so severe that you won't believe it's happening."

"I'll get the law," Adam warned him, but O'Gara shook his head.

"As I suspect you've already done that, it doesn't bother me much. But before I smash your fucking bonce in, I want all the gritty details. I want to know exactly what you've told them, so fucking shoot!"

And then something occurred to Adam, something so obvious that it amazed him he hadn't thought about it before. "Are you with the dog?" he suddenly asked them.

There was a brief silence. O'Gara looked puzzled. "What the fuck are you talking about?"

"The dog," Adam said. "Is it you with the dog? Is he part of your operation? Is that where he comes from?"

O'Gara's puzzlement had turned briefly to bewilderment. But just as quickly, it now turned back to anger. "I've had enough of this shit. I'm here to kick the crap out of you anyway, so I might as well get started."

And that was when they actually *heard* the dog.

A growl so savage that it stopped even O'Gara in his tracks

154

sounded from the farthest end of the lavatories. It was so unexpected and so shocking in its low-key ferocity that Cleaver abandoned his sentry-post and came curiously into the room. O'Gara stepped back from the row of wash-basins and gazed down the narrow passage between the cubicles and the urinals. The growl had only lasted a couple of seconds, but it had definitely come from somewhere down there. Nothing was visible, yet even as they stared, they heard another growl. This one lingered longer, and if anything, it was even more blood-curdling than the first. What was more, it grew both in volume and intensity, until soon it seemed to be coming from all around them; the polystyrene tiles on the ceiling began to shake, the mirrors on the wall to rattle.

As one, O'Gara and Cleaver started retreating. A third growl followed, this one of such timbre that it was difficult to listen to it without clapping one's hand to one's ears: the toilet cubicles vibrated in response, plaster dust trickled from above. And then a mirror cracked, with a noise like a gunshot.

That was too much for them.

Without a second glance, the two hoodlums turned and fled into the corridor.

Adam gazed after them, breathless, his heart still hammering. Almost immediately on their departure, the growling ceased, simply stopped - as though a switch had been thrown. But even then it was several moments before he could straighten up and go, himself, to look down the aisle between the lavatories and the urinals. Still there was nothing visible down there. He advanced, determined to investigate. But each cubicle was empty, and at their far end, they halted at a bare wall with a frosted window in it. The topmost panel of the window was slightly open, but when Adam climbed up and peeked out, he saw that it was a good ten feet down to the Town Hall car park, which, though it contained a few vehicles and had the odd pedestrian strolling across it, was bare of any animal life.

*

There were two conclusions to be drawn from that day's experience.

First of all, the dog was real: O'Gara and his pal had clearly heard it. That at least proved that Adam wasn't going nuts. Secondly, the dog was on Adam's side. Perhaps it could even be deemed *his* dog. That one was more of a stretch, admittedly, but hadn't it gone for Carver in Adam's dream? And now, hadn't it menaced his real-life foes, only vanishing when the danger had abated?

Adam visited one or two town-centre pubs afterwards to celebrate. For the first time in a long time, he felt he had some power in his corner. In fact, he felt so much better than normal that he extended his lunchtime session until well into the afternoon. Ordinarily, he would leave some money over for his gas and electrics, and so that he could do a meagre weekend shop. But on this one-off occasion he threw all caution to the wind, as a result of which it was dark when he finally set off home. The streets where heaving with rush-hour traffic, but a thick February fog had descended, each pair of headlights appearing through it like luminous fish-eyes as they shunted slowly along. For his part, Adam didn't even feel the cold; the alcohol had insulated him nicely. It had also relaxed him, as had the fog if he was honest. There was something strangely soothing about winter fog, he thought. It was icy and dirty and it seemed to get into your lungs, but it muffled the harder edges of reality. Passers-by were little more than hooded spectres. The monolithic structures of the tower-blocks were lost in gloom as he wove his way between them. This didn't make the walk up Trapp Hill itself any the less exhausting of course, and despite the weather, the usual crowd of rodent-like urchins were hanging around the twisted frame of the bus shelter at the entrance to the estate, smoking cigs, slugging tins of lager, kicking shards of glass.

"Got any spare cash, mate?" one of them asked as Adam sloped by.

"Fuck off you little shit," was his only response.

"Oy, you gangly twat!"

Adam didn't even glance back. He'd never been frightened of these kids, but they were a permanent fixture in the neighbourhood and it wasn't sensible, as a resident, to fall out with them. On this occasion, though, he couldn't have cared less. He even felt pleased with himself. But when he approached home, his upbeat mood soured rapidly. The first thing he noticed was that the light was on in his lounge - and he never left his lights on. He hurriedly let himself in through the front door, and instantly saw the door to his flat standing ajar, its lock visibly bent.

With a curse, he lunged inside... to find his home wrecked.

Everything in there had been vandalised: books and papers were scattered, the furniture was slashed, the television lay bashed in, whirls of spray-paint covered each wall. When he glanced into the kitchen, he saw that the little crockery he owned had all been smashed. The fridge had been overturned, the oven door ripped off, and a foul stench was soon traced to human excrement, which had been smeared all along the work-tops and then poked with a stick down into the inside of his toaster. Most hurtful of all, though, was what awaited him in his bedroom.

Adam hadn't written anything of consequence in many years. When he'd first started out writing, he'd managed to sell a single script to a police soap-opera. He'd made a few thousand quid out of that, but in the end his inexperience had told; he'd found the constant rewrites laborious, and though the episode had finally been polished enough to go to air, the programme makers had decided there'd been too much difficulty along the way. As a result they'd never commissioned him again, and ever since that amazing start to his new career, his list of successes consisted of a few short story sales to magazines that the vast majority of the public would never see let alone read. Despite its shortcomings, however, this scant body of work *belonged* to Adam more than anything else he possessed. It was intimately his, the product of seventeen years of *his* toil and tears, and perhaps the most personal and therefore most precious thing he owned.

More fool him, then, for neglecting to make back-ups.

He stood in the doorway to the closet-sized room, a cold feeling in the pit of his stomach as he stared at the battered casing of his PC, its wire and circuit-board intestines having been dragged out in handfuls through its now-shattered screen. Underneath the desk, the hard-drive was in a similar condition. It had been broken open and completely gutted. All that remained of its memory were myriad silver fragments strewn on the crumb-impacted carpet.

Under normal circumstances, the wannabe author would probably have fallen into a heap and wept. He might even have had a breakdown and woken up in a mental ward somewhere, mercifully obvious to his past. But things had changed for him during the course of this day. He stood stock-still for several minutes, his gaze roving back and forth over the disembowelled computer-ware, slowly letting the painful knowledge of what this signified seep through him. Then, he went stiffly to his wardrobe.

His baseball bat was an old-fashioned Toledo Slugger. He'd bought it over a decade ago from a second-hand sports shop, when first having to face the necessity of living on Trapp Hill.

A moment later he'd opened the front door to the building and left it on the latch, then he advanced upstairs to the first storey. O'Gara's door was the only one up there. Like Adam's, it was painted a shitty blue colour, which somehow proclaimed that it was attached to substandard Council property. It stood on a narrow concrete shelf, with only a wrought-iron railing fencing it off from the actual stairwell. There was still room, however, for Adam to step to one side after he'd knocked.

A second passed, and then he heard movement. A bolt was drawn back and O'Gara stood there, gazing truculently out.

The hoodlum didn't even see the Slugger until it detonated in the middle of his face.

It was a good shot: very accurate, with plenty of muscle behind it. But Adam's main mistake was in not using *crushing* force. As a young PC, he'd wielded his staff many times, quite effectively, as he'd confronted the city's yobs. But there is a certain skill required to successfully hitting someone with a baton. From a police perspective, you have to use sufficient force to stun or disable, but by the same token, you must take care not to inflict life-threatening damage. On this occasion, Adam wasn't concerned about the latter, but for some reason, he couldn't manage the former. It was a good strike, but it wasn't as forceful as it could, or should, have been.

Inevitably then, O'Gara leapt back to his feet, blood spouting from his ruptured nose, his eyes like chips of hot coal; and Adam wondered for the thousandth time why, even on days like today - when he was on such a high - he'd become a pussy-cat in his middle age.

Not that it mattered terribly. He hadn't planned to *personally* be the agent of vengeance.

O'Gara now took him by the hair and dragged him inside. Adam immediately smelled chemicals. He saw walls that were bare plaster, floors that were naked planks covered with stains and other filth. Before he could see any more, however, Cleaver ghosted into view, still dressed as he had been earlier in his green canvas overcoat, but now wearing a pair of thick leather gloves. Before Adam could say anything, the guy's big fist had smashed into his cheek. O'Gara, meanwhile, who was screaming like a thing demented, had managed to wrestle the bat from Adam's grasp, and was swinging it hard at his legs. Each blow was agonising, but Adam tried not to register it. Another hay-maker then swept in from Cleaver, catching his nose side-on, breaking it cleanly.

He'd once have welcomed a set-to like this, Adam thought, as he collapsed to the floor. It had all been part of a job, the cowboy aspects of which he'd enjoyed perhaps more than he should have done. Of course time passes, people change, and he wouldn't have stayed a wild youth forever, even if he hadn't

159

been fired. He accepted that.

They were now kicking his head, stamping on the back of his skull. "Get him into the bathroom," he heard O'Gara say. "Fucking snout bastard! Get him in the fucking bath!"

They hauled him through into another room, then humped him up and dropped him into a metal tub. His broken nose slammed on the bottom, which sent pain like white needles through his head. Rough hands then grabbed him from behind, dragging him over. Adam found himself gazing up through bloodied eyes, to see O'Gara discard the bat, lean down and start raining in blows with his bare fists. At the same time, Cleaver lifted his leg over the rim of the bath so that he could recommence the stamping.

It was impossible not to flinch from each explosive impact, but Adam tried his best to speak, and though blood bubbled from his mouth with each slurred word, it was with great glee that he told them: "Any thecond now."

They didn't even pause, but it didn't matter. Fur was already bristling, a hot breath was throbbing in the night. Large paws were skittering at speed up concrete steps.

O'Gara was swiftly exhausted by his efforts. Sweat was soon dripping from his face as liberally as the blood (both his and Adam's), so he drew back for a second, before reaching down for the bat again.

Adam gave a toothless jack-o-lantern grin. He could smell the animal's drool, could hear its panting, its fur-flushed belly-growl. "Any thethon now..."

O'Gara glanced sideways at Cleaver, who'd dropped to a crouch and had produced a claw-hammer. They nodded at each other. "Kill him!" O'Gara said.

And the dog struck.

Adam could only lie there and listen to its fevered snarls, to the slashing and ripping of its jaws, to the rending of flesh and gristle, to the hideous, hapless shrieks as it mauled and mutilated with all the gusto of a true jungle predator.

Only after several torturous minutes did it finally end.

160

For both of them.

Afterwards, their bodies lay undisturbed a long time into the night; two mangled, contorted forms, their mouths locked open, their eyes glazed over, their gore congealed like jam in the deadening winter chill.

Adam was in O'Gara's bath, his skull pounded to pulp; Jessie lay on her garage steps, her throat in tangled ribbons.

SIZE MATTERS

John Llewellyn Probert

"For the last time, Mr. Walker, there is no way on God's green earth that your penis enlargement surgery can be subsidised by Britain's National Health Service."

Mr. William Harding, for such was the specialist's name, removed his spectacles and rubbed his aching eyes. He had forty-three patients to get through this morning, and five minutes in which to see each of them. Harry Walker, middle-aged, bad tempered, and his first patient of the day, had already taken up forty-five minutes of his time.

Harry scowled at him from the other side of the desk. With his prominent black eyebrows and mop of unruly greasy black hair, he struck Harding as an unpleasant sort of fellow. When Harry spoke, it was with the nasal drawl of someone with a permanent sinus problem.

"I still don't see why—"

"As I have already explained," said Harding, wishing he had taken another tranquiliser before starting the clinic, "this sort of surgery can be fraught with complications."

Harry banged a fist on the desk.

"But my penis is only—"

"Six inches long," the consultant nodded. "Exactly the same as the vast majority of men. A few are a little larger, a few a little smaller, but most are precisely the same size as yours. Operating on you would be neither sensible nor ethical. Good day."

*

That evening Harry Walker sat in his little flat above the pet shop in the high street and planned his next move. He was not the sort of individual who could be dissuaded easily once he had his heart on something. He had waited eight months to be

162

seen by a consultant after a confrontational visit to his general practitioner to organise a referral. During this time his desire to have a penis at least seven and a half inches long had grown into an overwhelming obsession.

After leaving the hospital that morning, he had popped into a nearby newsagents. Leafing through several publications he had no intention of buying, trying his best to commit to memory all the undraped female forms depicted within, his gaze had chanced upon the 'Women's Interest' shelf. Sandwiched between a sheaf of copies of *Women's Realm* and something about styling your dog's hair was a perfect-bound periodical entitled *Modern Chat*. It was not the pretty nineteen year old on the cover that grabbed Harry's attention (although she was very attractive and, Harry thought, obviously wasn't just there solely to garner the interest of female customers) but rather the magazine's headline, which announced its lead article in vibrant bold red lettering. *'The A-Z of Plastic Surgery!'* it cried, *'What You and Your Fella Need To Know!'*

Harry definitely needed to know, and immediately set about the problem of getting the magazine out of the shop and past people who might recognise him without losing face. Eventually he sandwiched it between a copy of *Huge 'n' Hairy* and a magazine about tractors. On the way home, the vicar asked him if he was intending to buy a farm with the money, his recently deceased mother had left him.

Back in the safety of his flat, and having donated *Huge 'n' Hairy* to the grateful pet shop owner who had a penchant for that sort of thing, Harry sat down to study the relevant pages.

Between *O* for *'Obvious Stretch Marks'* (Harry thought that was cheating a bit) and *Q* for *'Quite Saggy Breasts'* (Harry thought this was cheating a lot, but looked at the pictures anyway), he was relieved to find *'P is for Penis Enlargement'*. He skipped the paragraphs about vacuum pumps and the warnings about using weights, and went straight to the section on surgery. There were several types of operation described, and Harry thought that the one where fat was taken from another part of the body and injected under the skin of the penis sounded best. He pinched at the mass of blubber around his waist with some pride. He had always thought it would come in handy - there was easily enough for an extra couple of inches. Or even a couple of feet.

The article usefully listed the addresses and telephone numbers of practitioners offering such a service. If Harry had looked at it more closely, or more critically, then he might have noticed that no mention was made of the success rates or complications of the operations which were described. He might also have spotted that the article itself just happened to be sponsored by the same individuals whose names he was now perusing. But he didn't, which to some extent is why we have a story to tell.

*

Harry eventually picked Mr. Gerald Lockhampton, who seemed to have a nice, safe, professional-sounding surname, and arranged an appointment. Mr. Lockhampton's private rooms were in a part of the city Harry had never been to before. As soon as he knocked, the door was opened by a smart-looking young lady in a navy blue double-breasted jacket and matching skirt. Harry was shown into a snug oak-panelled antechamber where he sat in a leather armchair to wait. He barely had time to make a mess of the copies of *Horse & Hound* and *The Lady* that had been arranged in neat fans on the mahogany coffee table before he was being called through.

Mr. Lockhampton was an immaculately dressed gentleman in his late forties whose three-piece pin stripe suit had obviously been made to measure, such was his portly build. The light gleamed off his bald head as he gestured to Harry to lie on a plush divan upholstered in red velvet that Harry thought might be put to better use by a psychiatrist. It was, but only on mornings when Dr Cruickshank could manage to steal it and push it into his own consulting room further down the corridor before Mr. Lockhampton arrived. The plastic surgeon sat with his hands clasped over his considerable waist as Harry told him his story.

Harry Walker was one of those individuals who felt that he had been treated unfairly in life. Following the death of his mother, and the subsequent discovery of the considerable quantity of money she had managed to save up over the years, he had decided that it was time for him to start enjoying himself. Never having had much success with the opposite sex, Harry had decided to tackle that problem first. Unfortunately, rather than direct his efforts towards such worthwhile areas as improving his personal hygiene and etiquette, and perhaps then registering with a couple of suitable on-line dating companies, Harry had decided that what would really make him a hit with the ladies was the size of his penis.

He had decided on his ideal length after much deliberation and the examination of numerous moving and still pictures obtained from Eddie's Erotic Emporium, down by the bus station. It seemed to Harry that seven and a half inches was a reasonable and fairly obtrusive size that should show itself nicely through the skin-tight trousers he intended to wear after the bruising had settled down.

After a cursory examination Mr. Lockhampton said that he would be more than happy to undertake Harry's surgery, Harry wouldn't have to wait, and Mr Lockhampton preferred cash if that was at all possible. Harry went home to collect the funds while the necessary arrangements were made.

*

A little prick with a needle (yes, the anaesthetist really did use that joke) and the next thing Harry knew he was waking up in a soft bed in a room he didn't recognise with Mr Lockhampton beaming down at him.

"All went well," said the specialist. "You should be able to go home tomorrow. We'll just take the bandages off and have a look at-ah."

"What?" asked Harry. Despite the fact that he was still quite groggy, he could tell that the surgeon didn't look too happy.

"Oh nothing, nothing," said Mr. Lockhampton, taking care to keep his hands away from Harry's groin. "I'm sure things will settle down in a few days' time."

Harry looked downwards.

"Is it supposed to look that black?" he slurred before collapsing back into dreamless sleep.

*

Harry was discharged the next day as promised with a large bottle of painkillers, an enormous bandage over his nether regions and some antibiotics 'just to be on the safe side'.

The first twenty-four hours went well. Harry rested and took the tablets as instructed. It was on his second night back at home that he woke, just after midnight, with the feeling that his genitals were on fire. He switched on the bedside lamp and, despite the instructions he had received to the contrary, began to unwrap the bandages.

The area they had taken the fat from had healed very well - in fact he hardly noticed the little scar just below his bellybutton. It was when he started to unwrap the area around his crotch that he realised something might be amiss. The smell of rotting cabbage that arose when he removed the sticky cotton wool pad from the operation site did little to reassure him. Steeling himself, he forced his gaze downwards.

His penis looked like the huge maroon salami sausage that he had seen on Nigella Lawson's cookery programme last week, right down to the runny brown gravy she had poured over the end. He dipped a finger into the crease of his right groin where the fluid was starting to pool. The pungent odour that arose set off a spasm of violent nauseated coughing.

Sliding off his bed and trying not to drip on the floor, Harry picked up the telephone and dialled the number for Mr. Lockhampton's private clinic. The answering machine explained that Mr. Lockhampton was out of the country for the next two weeks. If he would care to leave a message after the beep, they would try and fit him in after that.

Seriously worried that a festering pool of brown evil-smelling liquid might be all that was left of him by then, Harry dialled the emergency services.

*

"What on earth have you been up to?"

The doctor who saw Harry was a young chap named Matt Sims. He did his best not to look too horrified as he examined Harry on a trolley out in the emergency department corridor. Harry winced as he was prodded with a gloved finger.

"I'm not much of an expert with this sort of thing," Dr Sims admitted, "but it looks as if you've got gangrene down there. I'll ring the specialist on call who'll have to decide whether or not you need emergency surgery."

Mr. Harding was not impressed, neither with being yanked out of bed at three in the morning nor with the particular patient responsible.

"I warned you," he said, as he got Harry to sign a consent form. "The consequences of this sort of surgery can sometimes be dire."

Harry nodded sheepishly as he handed back the piece of paper and crossed his fingers. And everything else.

*

If he had been one to appreciate irony, Harry may have found some small amusement in the fact that after everything had healed up he was left with a penis seven and a half centimetres long. Although it had been explained to him that it was remarkable they had been able to save any of it, he still felt

167

hard done by. His plan to sue the specialist concerned also ended in disaster. Mr Lockhampton proved untraceable after he failed to return from his two-week holiday in the Bahamas and it was discovered that there was no such person registered with the United Kingdom's General Medical Council.

There our story might have ended, but for the fact that when Harry was on his way back from the pub one evening, much the worse for several pints of strong beer, he took several wrong turns and found himself wandering down the old abandoned railway line.

Harry stumbled over hidden sleepers and tried not to get too entangled in the briars and groundsel that grew thickly over the wasteland. To give him due credit, he persisted in trying to find his way home for half an hour, trusting to that innate sense of overconfidence in one's sense of direction that an abundance of alcohol can sometimes instil. Finally realising he was completely lost; his attention was drawn to a tumbledown brick shack at the end of a siding. He was sure he could see a fire burning through the many gaps in the crumbling brickwork. Rubbing his hands as the alcohol started to wear off and he began to realise how cold it was, Harry trudged over to see if he could find someone who could point him in the right direction.

He tentatively pushed aside the grey woollen blanket draped over the entrance. Despite being sure he had seen a fire earlier, he found he couldn't make anything out in the gloom of the hut.

"Is there anyone there?" he asked.

A voice like a needle being scraped across a record croaked a reply.

"If ye're from the council ye can fuck off! Ye should know better by now!"

"I'm not from the council," he said in slurred, meek tones. "I need help."

He could vaguely see something moving inside the hut and he found himself having to crouch before he could take a step forward. As his eyes adjusted to the gloom, he saw a very old woman hunched in a far corner.

"What d'you want?" she asked.

Harry explained that he was lost, and then, perhaps because he had not had the opportunity to talk to anyone since the whole business had started, he told her everything. Unfortunately, because there was still a fair bit of alcohol in his system, he showed her as well. He was none too pleased with the cackles that followed his disrobing.

"They've done for ye a treat, haven't they? And tell me, *little* man, how long would ye like to be?"

Harry told her and yet more cackling ensued.

"Can you help me or not?" he asked, still meaning about being shown the way home.

He saw the figure nod and hold out a withered claw. A small bottle hung suspended between its thumb and index finger.

"Take it," she urged. "When you are home tonight, and only when you are absolutely sure that you want what you have told me, you must drink it all down. All, mind you, if you wish to benefit fully from its effect."

"What do you want for it?"

"I will ask that of you in my own good time."

Harry left clutching the bottle. Having been failed by modern medicine, Harry saw no reason why he shouldn't place his trust in more traditional therapeutic methods. He cannot really be blamed - after all, he had little experience of dealing with the supernatural.

*

The bottle was in the shape of a rose hip and contained a volume of fluid similar to a measure of spirits. Harry held the murky green glass up to the light and hesitated briefly before unscrewing the tiny brass cap.

The liquid tasted surprisingly of oranges.

When Harry was woken once more from the depths of his

slumber by a tingling in his groin his first response was to panic. He threw back his nylon sheets and yanked down the bottoms of his blue and white striped pyjamas.

The scarred stub of penis sat there looking up at him.

He felt a mixture of emotions. First relief at there being no further harm done, and then anger as he realised that the old woman's medicine had not had any effect. He was reaching to switch the light off again when he felt sure he saw something moving out of the corner of his eye. He returned his attention to his groin, and this time there could be no mistake

His penis was moving.

Or rather, it was stretching. As he watched, it appeared to be struggling against the scar tissue which encased it, but with a little more effort, it increased its length from three inches to three and a half inches.

Four and a half inches.

Six and a half inches.

Now Harry would actually have been perfectly happy with this length. A wonderful length. A length that almost made him feel as if he was welcoming back a long lost friend. Six and a half inches was absolutely fine.

Of course, he had asked for it to be a little bit longer.

There was another twinge in his groin. Ah, he thought, here we go. The icing on the cake.

His penis increased in length by another inch while Harry looked on in wonder. He was about to get up and pour himself a drink to celebrate when another, more violent sensation caused him to keep still. He tried to stay calm, telling himself that it was just everything settling down.

When he looked back at his penis, it was ten inches long.

What was going on? Had he taken too much of the liquid? The old woman had told him to drink it all, hadn't she?

Mind you, it wasn't as if he didn't appreciate a bit extra. He made little satisfied noises as he looked at it, hanging down to just above his knee.

And then it was just below his knee.

170

Now he felt the first few pangs of worry.

An encroaching tightness turned to discomfort as another couple of inches were added. His scar tissue, far more rigid and inflexible than normal skin, was doing a Herculean task of holding out, but surely that couldn't go on for much longer?

It didn't.

Perhaps if his skin had been unsullied by the ravages of gangrene and two surgical procedures, there would not have been a problem. Sadly, this was not the case, and so poor Harry watched in horror as, with a sickening tearing sound, the scar tissue anchoring his member to the skin of his groin tore away to allow the head of his penis to continue its journey towards the foot of the bed. Covering the muscle tissue which had become exposed, he used his other hand to dial a now-familiar number.

*

"What the hell have you been up to this time?" asked Dr Sims, hardly able to believe what he was looking at. An ambitious sort of chap, he immediately overcame his shock and began mentally composing a case report that he felt sure would help him towards achieving a position in the academic institution of his choice.

"I don't know - it just won't stop growing," complained Harry, who now looked anything but happy about the organ currently dangling between his ankles.

At a loss as to what to do, Sims called Mr. Harding, who denied knowledge of any such phenomenon and came in to see it for himself. The exposed muscle was rapidly being covered with new, healthy skin, but in view of the fact that Harry's penis was still increasing in length, he was admitted to a side room for observation with strict instructions that only male nurses were to look after him.

The gossip spread like wildfire.

Specialists from all over the country came to visit. Pictures of him (or rather, the part of him that was of interest) were published in the *British Medical Journal*. Harry would probably have been most perturbed to learn that he could have earned a considerable amount of money if he had allowed the pictures to be published in rather more downmarket (and top shelf) publications instead.

Two days later, when things seemed to have calmed down a little, Mr. Harding came to see him again.

"More pictures, doc?" asked Harry, who through all of this was rather enjoying himself. Mr. Harding shook his head and sat on the edge of the bed.

"We've decided that we need to keep you in for a little longer, just to make sure it doesn't grow any more."

"Fine with me, doc."

Harding smiled.

"Excellent. We will, of course, have to move you from here. This is our emergency admission ward and I think you'll agree you don't quite fit that description anymore. I've made arrangements for you to be transferred to a more comfortable ward where things should be a bit quieter."

Secretly Harry was quite pleased. The constant attention of the press could be rather wearing.

"When do I move?" he asked.

"Right now," was the reply. "If you'll follow me I'll arrange for your things to be brought over later."

Harry got off the bed, pulled on a dressing gown, and followed the consultant out and down a long corridor where they turned right and left so many times Harry lost count before coming to an elevator. Harding pressed the top button on the display and Harry felt his stomach surge as they ascended.

When the doors opened again, Harry's mouth dropped open in amazement.

If he did not know better, he would have said that his new ward was a private luxury studio apartment. He had no idea hospitals had anything like this.

"Do you like it?" asked Harding.

Harry walked over to the large window on the left that gave him a view of the city.

"Like it?" He said. "I could stay here forever."

"Well it's funny you should mention that, but that's kind of the idea," said Harding as two rather burly looking gentlemen emerged from the kitchen.

"What do you mean?" he asked. "Surely this can't be for my own good?"

"Oh it isn't," said Harding, stepping back into the lift. "It's for everyone else's"

Harry frowned.

"What do you mean?"

"We can't have people like yourself parading around in public. The media have already done their best to exploit your situation. Can you imagine what would be next? Docudramas and reality TV? Interviews with you and about how happy you are with your new image? We can't have that."

"Why not?"

"Don't you know how many miserable people there are in this country who think their problems can be solved by having cosmetic surgery? Do you realise that every time there's a programme about it the number of requests for treatment goes up? This nation is obsessed with physical perfection, and with abnormal excess that is paraded as normal by the media because they know the public's fascination with what they want done to their bodies is never ending?"

Harry still didn't understand what Harding was getting at.

"Is that so bad?" he asked.

"Yes," said Harding. "Yes it is. Or at least I and some of my colleagues think so. That's why we've set up this little apartment. You don't realise it but you'll be doing mankind a far greater service by staying here that you ever could by being a free man."

The elevator doors closed. Harry turned back to look at his new luxurious accommodation.

"I suppose you two are here to make sure I don't leave?" he said to the two orderlies standing either side of the kitchen door.

"Yes sir. And, of course, to fetch whatever you would like from the outside world."

Harry still couldn't decide whether what had happened to him was such a bad thing. Certainly this was a hell of a lot better than where he had been living before. And the concept of being waited on hand and foot appealed as well.

"Is that a new one? Where is he? Will someone tell me what he looks like?"

The voice came from the kitchen. A woman emerged, her face half obscured by the most enormous, balloon-like pair of lips Harry had ever seen.

"Hi," she said. "I'm Daphne. I'm a patient here, too. Some of us thought we'd come and welcome you."

Harry sat on a nearby sofa and tried to make himself comfortable between two huge cushions.

"How many are there of you?" he asked.

"Oh only a few. We've all got rooms just like yours. You'll meet us all in time. Just make yourself comfortable."

Before he could stop himself, Harry asked,

"So I suppose there must be someone here with unfeasibly huge breast implants?"

There was a titter from behind him.

"You're sitting on me," said a voice.

SPARE RIB: A ROMANCE

John Kenneth Dunham

It was the spider crawling across his eye that finally woke him.
He twisted wildly on the sofa, gibbering and trying to lash out
with his dead right arm. It took him a few moments to realise
why the arm wasn't responding. The night before slowly came
back to him in bits and pieces. In shards. He'd been drinking.
Heavily, for him. Mixing it too. A tumbler of Irish cream with
ice. Another because the first one had gone down so easily. A
bottle of sangria after that, then some beer with blackcurrant
cordial added. Anything he could find that would get him
drunk but didn't actually taste of alcohol. He sat and rubbed his
arm until some of the feeling came back. His head felt spongy
and tight at the same time and he wanted to puke.
    He puked.
    He didn't feel any better. At least not at first. Then he
plucked up the courage to look down and saw that he'd
managed to puke on the spider. It's long, hairy legs thrashed
impotently at the yellow mess, unable to free itself. It's black
body buried under small lumps of partially digested chow
mein. Vengeance is mine. Next time he'd have the sweet and
sour pork balls though.
    He pulled himself to his feet and, stepping carefully over the
resurrected body of last night's dinner, made his way
unsteadily towards the bathroom. He knew, even before he'd
reached them, that he'd never be able to negotiate the stairs in
his present condition so he changed course and headed for the
kitchen and the back door.
    It was still dark outside and biting cold. A warm, almost
sensual, feeling of relief flooded his body as he began to empty
his tingling bladder. Then suddenly he was hopping backwards
as it dawned on him that he was pissing all over his socks. His
frantic leaping didn't help a great deal but merely meant that he
ended up pissing down his trouser leg as well. Oh, you bastard.

175

They were his work trousers too.

He swore to himself that this would be the last time then, almost immediately, remembered the last time he'd sworn the same thing. The last 'last time' he'd woken up on somebody else's floor in a pool of his own sick and had shat himself during the night into the bargain. He shuddered as the scene came back to him. Luckily, everyone else had still been asleep and he'd managed to creep down the corridor to the bathroom and into the shower without being seen.

Or at least he hoped he had. To make things worse, his friend's parents had been visiting at the time and he had this horrible part-memory of the door opening quietly, while he'd still been lying on the bedroom floor half asleep and covered in his own filth, and his friend's mother's face appearing in the doorway bearing an expression which turned rapidly from motherly concern to utter disgust. He told himself that it'd just been some sort of anxiety dream but the fact remained that Mr and Mrs Bartlett had made their excuses and left hurriedly the next day.

At least this 'last time' he'd only pissed on his socks and thrown up in the living room (thank God for laminate flooring). He was showing definite signs of progress.

His own parents had been dead for about three years now. His father had died first followed, about nine months later, by his mother. He didn't miss them as much as he'd always thought he would. And nothing like as much as he missed Alison. No comparison. You could choose your friends and lovers, at least to some extent, but with family you just had to make the best of it.

He went back into the kitchen and decided that he couldn't face clearing up now. Better to leave it until morning when he was likely to be less of an idiot.

He didn't often drink. Mostly he could block everything out with a simple combination of take-aways and late night Reality TV. He liked Reality TV because it wasn't real to him. It represented a means of escape, nothing like his own real life at all. Aspirational is what it was. People who were desperate to be someone. To be the constant centre of attention. To be loved. People with dreams. He had precious few opportunities to dream and no time for aspirations. No time for anything much after the two-hour journey home after work every evening. This was his life, an endless round of vegetable spring rolls and weekly evictions (maybe a bit of porn when his bollocks got the better of him) and he'd learnt to content himself with that.

The weekends were the worst. Most of the time he could convince himself that Ali was just away during the week, working or maybe on some course or other like she always had been. But at the weekends he ran out of excuses as to why she wasn't there with him. In truth - in reality - she had the perfect excuse of course. She was dead. Taken away. God had voted her out of the house and left him alone. She hadn't even had time to collect her belongings so they were all just left upstairs. Hanging in the wardrobe, thrown over the bed, the chair, the floor, or lying unwashed in the washing basket. He'd never been able to bring himself to sort them out. That was one reason why he always slept downstairs now. That and the TV. Oh, Ali.

He rubbed his eyes.

Ali.

Ali.

Ali.

That Sunday she came back to him.

He was poking about down the back of the sofa looking for the remote control, hands sticky with spare ribs, when she appeared in the room.

"Look at the state of you," she said.

He'd wiped his hands on his shirt before he realised what he was doing then sat sheepishly as she chastised him with her dead, black eyes.

"Well, aren't you going to say anything?"

What do you say to your wife when she comes back from the

177

dead after eighteen months?

"You're late."

"And you've put on weight," she said. "How do I look?"

Another difficult one. Honesty, he knew from long and bitter experience, was not always necessarily the best policy.

"Be honest."

Ali's hair hung lank and matted around her sallow face. Her burial gown did nothing to hide her almost skeletal thinness. The yellowing nails on her calloused hands and feet appeared to have carried on growing while she seemed to have lost most of her teeth.

"You look... fine."

"Do you want me back?"

For the third time that evening, he didn't really know what to say.

"Prawn cracker?"

*

They slept together that night, or at least shared a bed, and he did his best not to shudder every time she touched him. She begged him to take her in his arms and, as he held her, she felt much lighter than he remembered, strangely unsubstantial, and her elbows and knees dug into him uncomfortably. She always did have bony knees.

The next morning he got up early and made her breakfast in bed before he left for work.

"And they say romance is dead". She laughed her little, hollow ringing laugh. "Can't you phone in sick or something?"

He fingered the knot of his tie and looked absently around the bedroom as she struggled to balance the fully-laden breakfast tray on her all but non-existent lap.

"No... I've never been able to do the voice," he offered feebly.

"What *voice*?"

"You know, the 'oooh, I'm really not very well at all' voice that people always put on when they're phoning in sick. Even if they're pretending they've broken something."

"You could say you have to go to a funeral," she suggested with the ghost of a smile.

"I've already been to the funeral of everyone I know," he said without really thinking. "Even the ones who aren't dead yet. My Auntie Noreen died twice last year, once during the summer and then again just before Christmas. If it happens again, they might start getting suspicious."

"I promise I'll never leave you again," Alison said.

"I have to go now... I'll miss my train." He started to make his way out of the bedroom.

"Bring me some flowers!" she called after him. "I used to like it when you brought me flowers!"

FAMILY FISHING

Gary McMahon

When I was twelve years old, my parents went through a rocky patch in their relationship. There were fights, silences, total communication breakdown. So they decided it best that I stay with my grandad one weekend late in the summer, to give them the space to sort things out between them; to mend the cracks that had suddenly opened up in the formerly smooth wall of their marriage.

I had no firm evidence, but somehow felt that I might be the cause of much of this strife. I was self-aware enough to realise that my behaviour was at the very least erratic - and possibly even bordering on the antisocial. I was afraid of becoming what used to be called a "problem child" but these days is merely an average teenager.

Dad dropped me off at grandad's place late that Friday afternoon, his long face stern and pale and twitching under the skin as if a swarm of butterflies was flapping around inside his balding head.

"Be good, Dan," he said to me before driving away in the big old red Renault. He kissed me lightly on the cheek before climbing quickly into the car, and didn't once look back as the dusty distance swallowed him.

Grandad stood in the doorway of his big old crumbling detached house; he and dad hadn't even spoken. Just nodded silently to each other, as if passing and receiving some mysterious unspoken message.

"Come on, boy. Let's get you settled," he said in his deep, grating voice that sounded like he washed out his mouth with a cheese grater. Then he stood to one side and pushed open the door with a gnarled oak hand.

I glanced back along the unmade road that led to the distant motorway, and eventually to home, and then reluctantly went inside.

My grandparents had lived in that isolated house all their married lives, and even after grandma died of cancer when I was still in nappies, grandad refused to sell it. Even though the place was far too big for him, with too many empty rooms, he wanted to remain there until he died. Until that day came, he haunted the house like a ghost, pacing through the rooms and hallways and reliving old memories.

The house was located five miles outside of a small North Yorkshire village called Fell, and the closest neighbour was about a mile away. The surrounding countryside was beautiful, but bleak. Grandad had always cherished that desolate aspect: it was in his nature.

I followed the slightly stooping but still substantial figure of the old fellow along the gloomy hall and into the cluttered living room. The walls were hung with dark oil paintings - spooky landscapes and dour, staring portraits - and little piles of ancient paperback books lined the blistered skirting. Grandad didn't own a TV; there was a radio in the kitchen, but that was his only concession to modern communications. The old man preferred to read.

"I've made up a bed for you in the small room," he said, glaring at me as if I was an unwelcome guest. "Other than that, you have the run of the house until suppertime." Then he left the room, and short a while later I heard the muted gabbling of the radio and the clattering of pots and plates.

The small room. The term was actually something of a contradiction: every room in the place was huge, the one I'd been allocated was simply the least spacious.

I tiptoed back out into the hall, those unfriendly portraits watching my back intently as I tried hard not to make a sound to disturb them.

The stairs loomed above me, shadows dancing across the thin treads like small questing creatures. Directly above, on the wide landing, stood the upstairs bathroom; a place so damp and mildewed that even grandad no longer used it. The main bathroom was downstairs, adjoining the kitchen, where he was

181

singing quietly to himself and preparing some hand-me-down family recipe too rich for the limited tastes of a developing pubescent boy.

A thin, bulb-headed hat stand that stood by the door was a bulky figure bowing towards me as I began to climb the stairs, and those capering shadows scattered beneath the soles of my feet. Darkness hung heavy, like a vapour, and I attempted to shrug off the cloying atmosphere of gloom.

The stairs creaked loudly under my thin feet, and when I grabbed the ancient timber handrail, it wobbled dangerously. I couldn't imagine grandad coming down here in the night and the darkness to take a pee; it was unbelievable that he hadn't fallen to his death on this decrepit staircase.

I turned right at the top, heading towards the small room. My plan was to inspect my bedchamber, and then nose about in the other rooms on that floor. Like my father, grandad was a hoarder, and there were always treasures to be found tucked away in the corners of this house: armless shop window mannequins, battalions of lead soldiers, rusty bicycle frames, arcane gardening tools and instruments for mending clothes and shoes... the place hadn't been cleaned out for decades, and even then I knew that some of those heirlooms might be worth a small fortune if sold as antiques.

The small room lay at the far end of the landing, to the right of the small stained glass window that never seemed to let in any light from the front aspect of the building. I approached softly, aware of the sound of old boards, and opened the door. Grandad had done a good job; the room was actually quite light due to a large table lamp that was positioned next to the bed, and it looked like he'd changed the tatty old bedding for a modern quilt.

Closing the door behind me, I unpacked my rucksack and laid out my clothes for the morning. I'd been told to bring along a pair of old jeans, a warm sweater, and some Wellington boots, as we were going fishing early Saturday afternoon. I'd never known that grandad was a fisherman, but it didn't surprise me. He seemed to have tried his hand at most things during his long and eventful life.

The same books that dominated the rest of the house were also present in the room: stacked on wall-mounted shelves, piled against the pitted walls, and stuffed into the top of the wardrobe. I was something of a voracious reader myself, but the titles of the books that I inspected put me off ever attempting to read any. There were volumes of esoteric medical, anthropological and natural history encyclopaedias; heavy books of quotations; masses and masses of poetry. My horizons stretched as far as the odd Stephen King or James Herbert novel, and even most of what I read within those giddy pages was too adult for me to fully understand.

I left the small room and poked my head around the door of the other first floor bedrooms. The most interesting thing that I could find was what I recognised to be a battered ouija board, most of the letters that were printed upon its creased cardboard surface faded to indistinct and wholly indecipherable markings.

"Supper's ready!"

Grandad's voice boomed up the dark stairwell, and filled the empty spaces of the house. Twitching in shock, I left the room that I was in and ran down the stairs, the smell of something hot and spicy assailing my nostrils.

The stew we shared was too plentiful, and its ingredients far too stodgy for that late an hour, so I went to bed with a heavy stomach and a sense of being too full to sleep. But I did sleep, and it was dreamless for the most part, but accompanied by the fear that my parents wouldn't be able to settle their differences, and I'd be consigned to stay here forever; or at least until I was grown up and able to leave of my own free will.

I have a faint memory of grandad entering my room in the darkness, and placing a cool hand on my brow. I think that I may have been tossing and turning in my sleep, fighting imaginary demons, and the words that he spoke came to me through a miasma of conflicting emotions.

183

"Get some rest, boy. We're going fishing the morrow."

And then he was gone, and the shadows were closing in.

Morning arrived with the smell of frying bacon. In those days, a fried breakfast was still considered part of a healthy diet, and my family had always prided themselves on cooking the best. Huge strips of crispy bacon, delicately prepared scrambled eggs, pork sausages fatter than a baby's arm, and golden bread that had been fried in the juices.

I dressed in my warm clothes and went downstairs to eat; grandad was already serving up, and had on a thick roll-neck jumper that made him look a little like a ship's captain.

"Eat up, boy. You'll need the energy today."

I sat at the table in the kitchen, and wondered how I'd get through such a huge portion of food. Then, magically, my plate was clear and I thought that I could perhaps squeeze in another of those sausages before my plate was taken away.

At home, I'd be pressured by my mother to clean my teeth, wash my face and neck, brush my hair, but grandad lived his life by different rules. In grandad's house I was an individual - a man or thereabouts - and could be trusted to do my own thing without being constantly prompted.

"You about ready?" he asked, clearing the table.

"Yes. Just about."

"Good," he said, his eyes coming to rest upon me. I saw a light in them that might have been love, and then it died as quickly and mysteriously as it had flared into being. A sad smile hung on the old man's lips, and then he turned away. "Today we make a man of you," he said. And I didn't have a clue what he meant.

Later, motoring along uneven country roads in his open-backed truck, grandad broke the silence and told me something that I didn't really expect.

"Back when your dad was your age, I took him fishing too. Same place, same kind of overcast weather."

"Really?" I asked, welcoming any stories of my dad as a boy.

"Aye, it's sort of a family tradition. Like living in that old

184

house. Y'see, in our family the women always die first, and we men folk stay in that big old house to welcome in the new ones that get born. Tradition, boy: it's important. When your mam dies, your dad'll move in there, long after I've gone. I expect you'll do the same, when it's your time."

This was the most I'd heard him say since I'd arrived the day before; the most I'd *ever* heard him say. He had a nice voice - a storyteller's voice. I liked it when he spoke, even if sometimes the subject matter seemed to go over my head.

We drove for what seemed like hours, grandad piping up with little homilies and pointing out anything of interest we might pass along the way - the pond in which he'd almost drowned as a boy, the clump of trees where he'd smoked his first cigarette, the barn where he'd once been intimate with a local lass named Molly Malloy. It was a good time; a comfortable journey, and my lumbering and featureless fears from the night before were largely forgotten.

I hadn't spent much time with grandad over the years, but he seemed to be warming to me with each passing minute. Treating me almost as an equal. He even offered me a tug off one of his cigars, which made me cough until my eyes ached. He enjoyed that, the old rascal. Probably thought he was teaching me some great lesson of the world.

By late afternoon I was beginning to wonder where this was all leading, and then grandad finally stopped the truck.

We were at the end of a narrow dirt track that finished in thick foliage. Grandad sat at the wheel and stared into the dense greenery, an unreadable expression crossing his face.

"Where are we?" I asked, afraid of the sudden soundless atmosphere, and the way that the clouds and the trees blocked out the light.

"Almost there," he answered, still staring through the windscreen.

I sat next to him in silence, not knowing what else to say.

"Come-by, lad. The fishing spot is just up there, through those trees. It's a bit of a hike, but you seem fit enough to

185

handle it." And he climbed out of the truck, heading for the back where he'd packed his stuff.

I followed him like a puppy, filled with uncertainty and trepidation.

Grandad had hauled a big empty potato sack from the back of the truck, and was picking up what looked like a short boat hook as he slung the sack over his broad shoulder.

"Where are the fishing rods, Grandad?" I asked. "The nets? The bait?"

He looked at me and laughed, but there was a sort of heavy weariness in the laughter that made me want to run and hide.

"We have all we need right here, boy. This is our kind of fishing, and we don't require any bait."

When he tramped off towards the huddling trees I assumed that I was meant to follow; I had to take two steps for his every one, but managed to keep up because of the weight of the gear he was carrying.

We walked for an hour, following vague forest trails and new ones that grandad cleared with his boat hook. The sun was beginning to set by the time we stopped, and the air was turning sooty, as if somewhere nearby there was a fire. Country darkness comes quickly, and early; and when it arrives, it is total. I knew that night wasn't too far off, even though these were the long summer days. Sometimes the darkness comes of its own accord, disobeying the laws of the season.

It was like that then. The night was descending like a blade across the sky, and already stars were blinking into existence in the clear and distant heavens.

Soon we came to a tall, rubber-insulated gate set in a high, humming electrified fence. Grandad reached into his pocket, took out a slightly rusted key and opened the gate, letting us inside some kind of compound.

"Fishing spot's through here," he said, gripping my forearm and guiding me across the steel cattle grid that was set in the ground just inside the gate.

We carried on for several more minutes, ducking under some

low bushes whose branches trailed across my face like spider's legs, and then grandad suddenly dropped to his knees, pulling me down with him. He placed his big hand over my mouth, and shook his head. I crouched there in the gathering darkness, unable to move.

"Follow me," he whispered. "And *be quiet!*" Then he took his hand away, and tapped me on the shoulder.

I stayed low to the ground and followed him through the smelly undergrowth, sweat pouring into my eyes and my jeans getting filthy from the loamy earth. I felt like a soldier lost deep behind enemy lines: a man on a mission, with only his wits to aid him.

Then grandad stopped, and reached behind him to grab my arm; he dragged me up alongside him, and pointed into the clearing that had appeared ahead. Initially I didn't realise what I was looking at, but then the details became clear and I was scared all over again.

There seemed to be some kind of shantytown set up in the clearing, with tiny, hastily assembled lean-to structures and jerry-built dwellings made from corrugated iron sheets. I saw a few caravans dotted here and there, with their doors hanging off the hinges, and no glass in the window frames. They were jacked up with their axles resting on bricks and rocks, the wheels long since removed.

People were sitting at small fires, or wandering around the clearing. Their faces were filthy, and they were dressed in rags. Malnourished bare-chested children ran in and out of the paltry dwellings; bellies distended by starvation, hair falling out in tufts.

A tall woman with prominent ribs and a deformed left arm was breast-feeding a baby outside one of the ruined caravans. I stared at her saggy breasts, feeling my burgeoning sexuality rear its ugly head. I was disgusted to find that I had an erection. Then, when I looked at the woman's face all thoughts of pre-teen lust were forgotten. She was haggard, drawn, barely even there at all. Her eyes were as dead as those of a

187

fish on a slab, and her down-turned mouth revealed stumpy teeth that were black as tar.

None of these shells of people spoke to each other; they seemed too tired, too defeated. It was as if they'd simply given up, and were waiting here to die.

"Let's go fishing," said grandad, and I suddenly remembered where I was, and who I was with.

He leaped to his feet and charged into the clearing, silent as an assassin, quick as a speeding bullet. He headed straight for a group of young girls who were gathered around one of those pitiful fires warming something in a dented baked bean can on the rocks that surrounded the flame.

There was a pause before any of the bedraggled folk realised that anything was amiss, and then the breastfeeding woman noticed him and began to groan.

All hell broke loose: the tattered people scattered like antelope before an attacking cheetah, fleeing and leaving their belongings, running and wailing incoherently; darting into the cover afforded by the trees. Grandad scampered in a straight line towards the girls, intent on his task - whatever that may be.

He grabbed a small one, and tucked her under his arm. Then he turned, and bellowed at me: "Come on, boy! *Come on!*"

I ran to his side, feeling a strange kind of power as people fled before me.

"What about this one?" yelled grandad, manhandling the girl onto the ground. She was young - probably about ten years old, perhaps even younger. I stared at her wide frightened eyes, then up at my grandfather. I didn't know what to say.

"Too small," he muttered. "Have to throw her back."

Then he was away, running back into the fray. I saw him grab a lanky woman with dirty black hair and pale blue eyes; he tagged her with the boathook, swinging it so that the point sank into the bare meat of her shoulder. He tugged her towards him. She was screaming hoarsely, strangely, tears gouging clean lines through the layered dirt on her face. And grandad was laughing, his eyes blazing with a distinctly unhealthy light.

He wrapped her up in the potato sack, trussing the whole package with rope that he pulled out in a neat coil from inside. The woman squirmed quite a bit, but after a few hefty whacks from the boat hook, she went still. I could see the sack rising and falling rapidly as she breathed; it's a sight that has stayed with me, haunting my dreams and staining my waking hours.

Back at the truck, grandad threw her in the back, securing her there with a chain that was attached to a small motorised winch meant for dragging heavy objects. Her breathing was deeper now, and I thought that she might have passed out.

It was only then that I noticed the hooves. Where the woman's legs poked out of the frayed end of the sack, a pair of cloven hooves could be seen in place of human feet. And then it clicked, just like that. They had all had hooves instead of feet: the ones that had fled before grandad, the little one that he'd cast aside in favour of this older female...

As we drove back to the house full night began to bloom; thick black petals of darkness erupting and spreading across the irrevocably altered landscape. I could hear the woman's hooves skittering in the back of the truck, sense her fear, taste her hatred.

"Our family used to own all this countryside, boy. Long ago, in another time. Your great-great granddaddy was a very rich and famous man. Well respected - so much that a great writer even wrote a book about him, making a story out of his work. He was a scientist, you see; studied genetics. But that was before the government came in and made us sell them everything we had."

I felt him turn his head to look at me as he spoke, but I couldn't face him. Not yet.

"But we still have special *privileges*. License to go where we like, to fish where we want. To continue the family traditions."

He fell silent then, realising that it was too early for me to respond.

When we reached the house he sent me on in ahead of him, and I heard him grunting as he struggled to unload his catch

189

from the truck. I went into the cold living room, and listened as he dragged her up the stairs. She made tiny yelping noises as he coerced her up each step, and grandad muttered a constant stream of obscenities to her, or perhaps to himself.

After about half an hour he came back down to find me.

I was sitting in an armchair; my arms wrapped around my middle, and shivering. Grandad stood above me, casting me in his shadow.

"Okay, boy," he said. "It's time"

He reached down and took me by the hand, pulled me to my feet, and led me upstairs to the small room. There was a key in the lock, and he turned it and pushed me inside.

"I'm locking you in here with her. By the time I come back for you, you'll be a man. Don't disappoint me, boy. This is your rite of passage, your route to manhood. We've all gone through it, every male of the clan. Now it's your turn."

As the door closed slowly in my face, he gave me an exhausted smile.

I turned hesitantly, almost too afraid to face what waited for me inside the room, and couldn't even find an echo of surprise within me when I saw the hoofed woman sitting naked on the bed. Her wrists were clamped together, and another thick metal chain bound her legs to the iron frame. Her hands were clasped tightly in her lap, as if in prayer, and her eyes were downcast, staring at the floor.

At last, I allowed myself to admit what I was expected to do. It was horrible, vile; tantamount to rape. I was supposed to enter adulthood by coupling with this poor dumb beast, and thus carry on the proud traditions of my forefathers, the bastards who'd owned this land long before my father was even born. Had he done this? If grandad was to be believed, they all had. Every man who had been born into the bloodline.

I tried to speak to the woman, to reassure her, but the words wouldn't come. I was mute with horror. Instead, I crossed the room towards her. As I got closer, I could see that she was silently weeping; and when I put out a hand to wipe away the tears she flinched as if expecting a blow.

"You're safe with me," I said, silently cursing my grandad, and every male who had been here before him. Damning the family name of Moreau.

"*Shushshshsh…* it's okay," I whispered, caressing her sweaty forehead and pushing damp hair out of her eyes.

She looked up at me at last, those cool pale eyes heating up with a glimmer of something that could have been hope. Chest hitching, throat constricting, she opened her mouth and tried to communicate. The cauterised nub that had once been her tongue flapped mutely in her slack jaw; it had been cut out long ago, perhaps on the day of her birth, rendering her speechless.

That was why none of them had spoken back at the compound. Why they'd just sat in silence, waiting for whoever or whatever came for them.

Shocked and numb and ashamed of who I was, I took her in my arms, felt her trembling warmth against my flesh. I could hold it inside no longer, so I let the rage out in a flood of remorse. I wept and wept until, a long time later, I finally fell asleep in her dirty arms.

Grandad stormed into the room early the next morning, dragging the woman from my bed and carrying her back downstairs. I was unable to read his expression when he looked at me, but was convinced that I had glimpsed pride in his eyes.

As I changed my scruffy clothes, I heard the truck pull away outside. A short time later, while I was making coffee in the kitchen, grandad returned alone. He hadn't been gone long enough for a return journey to the compound. My heart sank and I refused to contemplate what he might have done with the woman. When he entered the kitchen he was breathing heavily and his face was flushed a deep shade of red. He looked like he'd been exerting himself, carrying out some intensely physical task.

I felt like stabbing him with one of his carving knives, or

191

smashing him over the head with the kettle. Instead, I poured him a coffee and we sat together without speaking until my dad arrived later that morning to take me home.

That weekend was never mentioned again; not by my grandad on the rare occasions that I saw him afterwards, nor by my dad. And certainly not by myself. The subject, it seemed, was taboo, *verboten*. So much remained unsaid.

Grandad died five years later, succumbing to a quick and reasonably painless heart attack whilst reading a book on genetics. I wasn't sorry; I felt little, if any, grief.

My mother went not long after, continuing the legacy of the women in our family dying first. Dad was distraught, and moved into the big old house near Fell. He became a hermit, a recluse; didn't even turn up for my graduation from university, or my wedding.

He did, however, surface when my son Teddy was born. The old man made the long drive south when the boy was six months old, bearing gifts and smiles and congratulations. Sarah, my wife, was pleased that the family was together, but I just wanted the grizzled old bastard out of my life for good. I certainly didn't want him anywhere near my son, and after two days of silent pressure he got the message and returned to his house of memories.

Now Teddy is approaching his twelfth year, and my father has started writing to me. Long, rambling letters about tradition and manhood, and anecdotes about when I was a little boy. He even mentioned grandad in the last missive; and suggested that I let Teddy go and stay with him for a weekend. That he could take the boy fishing, like grandad did with me.

He even guaranteed that my boy would return to me a man.

Even after all these years, I'm afraid to tell him the truth of what went on in the small room that distant summer night when I was twelve years old. It was always assumed that I had done what was expected of me. Become a man. But the truth of it is that I will remain forever a small boy, crying hot tears into

Family Fishing

the grimy, sweat-stinking breasts of something only partly human - a beast I'd thought existed only in cheap fictions, and whose shabby progenitors had been created long ago in my families own tawdry House of Pain.

Last week I went back there for the first time since that weekend. I told Sarah that I was going to visit my dad. That we were trying to work things out. Instead, I took his key and went looking for the compound. The fishing spot. It took some doing, but eventually I found it. A clearing within a dense band of trees and heavy foliage, lean-to shacks and flyblown shelters clustered in little groups. Raggedy, semi-naked figures sitting by waning fires, dragging their chipped hooves on the dusty ground, scratching their mangy hides against the rough-barked trees, or just staring mutely at a purely conceptual space located somewhere beyond the great electrified fence.

Soon the time will come when my son will be summoned to go fishing with his grandad. Part of me knows exactly what I'll say when that call comes; another, deeper, much younger part of me isn't so sure. Perhaps that's the time when I will truly become a man after all.

SUBTLE INVASION

David Conyers

The invasion began on the same day that my eight-year-old daughter was stung by a wasp. Nikki came running across the back lawn, from the native scrub where Australian bush encroached on our quarter-hectare property. With teary red eyes, she showed me a red wrist, clutched by her opposite hand.

"What happened, Nikki?" I asked, as she fell into my arms terrified and hurt. "Let me have a look."

I took her reluctant hand in mine, observed the lump of redness swelling on her skin. In the folds of her dress, a half crumpled wasp fell loose, which I quickly put out if its misery. Nikki was crying but she was still breathing, so an allergic reaction - thankfully - was not forthcoming. It would sting a little, but that was all.

"Let's take you inside, and fix you up, okay?"

My wife appeared in that moment, pulling into the driveway in our four-wheel drive, returned from her yoga session. Kathy was more terrified than I was when she saw that Nikki was hurt, and superseded me as the parent who would fuss over our little girl. Our home medical guide told to clean the wound and then apply a block of ice wrapped in a damp towel, so we did that. Afterwards I gave Nikki a strip of her favourite chocolate, and within minutes she was smiling again. Nothing bad had happened at all.

"That was lucky," Kathy expressed her relief.

"It was just a wasp sting."

She made a face, mothers were supposed to fuss. "You better check for a nest, see how close it is to the house."

"Good idea."

I wandered casually towards the back of our property, a modern family home on the far outskirts of Melbourne along the Yarra River. We'd chosen this place for its seclusion and its natural beauty, but we'd forgotten about the snakes, spiders and other poisonous animals who shared the property, wasps included. We warned Nikki often enough, but children rarely listened to reason.

I found the nest quickly. It was a hole in the dry earth where buzzing warriors in their exoskeleton armour excited the air, fearlessly warning me away. Then my heart skipped a beat. Behind it was something far worse.

I had no idea what that something was, but even though my thoughts that followed seemed ludicrous to me, they also felt right; that this was an alien intruder, hiding out in our very back yard. It was something from another world.

Stepping backwards in fear, I realised that the wasps were not angry at me, but at the grey shape of organic flows, of hooked and barbed intrusions like the thorns on a dead rose. The thing's texture disquieted more than any other aspect of its ugly nature, reminding me of old meat left to rot in the sun. Oddly, it didn't have a smell, and it was as still and silent as stone.

I returned to the house in a daze, informed Kathy of the wasp nest, and made myself a cup of tea.

"You going to make me one too?" she asked, stacking the dishwasher. Nikki was watching her favourite pop stars on the television, her injury already forgotten. Inside our house, everything was normal, and I wanted it to stay that way.

"Sure," I grabbed a second mug, aware of the ethereal nature of my voice. I hoped no one else noticed, but that was not to be.

"What's up Carl?" Kathy asked half angry, half concerned.

"Oh nothing... I'll organise a pest exterminator tomorrow, sort out those wasps once and for all."

She accepted my answer, even though she knew I was hiding something. I didn't want to tell her about the unnatural infection in the bush. I was hoping that I imagined it, and when the morning came, it would be gone. As if it had never been.

*

The pest exterminator was a man named Bruce, who turned up three hours later than he said he would. He pulled into the driveway while Kathy was out with friends and Nikki was at school, in a van covered with uninspired self-advertising. I was working at home today. One of the joys of architecture is that with a good computer, you can achieve more at home than you do in the office. He asked me where the nest was. I told him, at the rise at the back of our property, in the bush.

"You gonna show me then?"

I nodded, wiping my brow because I didn't want to. I hadn't been back there since yesterday. I never wanted to see that awful shape again, and if this exterminator could remove it as he killed the wasps, then all the better for me.

"Well, show the way."

We walked up the rise, slowly. I was trembling, not that my companion noticed. Bruce was explaining that I probably inherited a nest of European Wasps. "*Vespula germanica*," he struggled with the Latin. "Did you know that the little bastards arrived in New Zealand during World War Two, in transported war material, and since then they've spread to Tasmania, Melbourne and Sydney. They'll be all over Australia before long, upsetting everybody."

"Really?"

"Fascinating little buggers though. In Europe, the cold weather kills off most of their nest during the winter frost, but not here. Here in the heat they just thrive. With no natural enemies, they just keep spreading and spreading. That is, until I come along. What the fuck is that?"

At first, I wasn't looking, but because of his shock, I did. It took courage to steel my mind and stare upon it again. The intrusion had not been a fantasy, and I had not expected it to have grown. Twice as large as yesterday, today I was reminded of an angry cactus crossed with a thorn bush, but constructed of rusty metal washed over with fatty grime. It was ugly, and it wanted me to know so.

"Bloody hell!"

"I don't know what it is." I felt sick. I didn't know what else to say.

"You've got more than a fucking wasp problem mate."

Tense, Bruce worked quickly, first spraying the angry airborne wasps, next poisoning the nest, and finally smothering the tunnel entrances with a thick white powder, which as he explained, the wasps could not dig through. "They won't even know what happened to them, and within days they'll all be dead."

I paid him quickly with cash, not arguing over the price. Then he burnt off down the drive just as fast, without even a quick goodbye. The sweat he left on my drive could have filled a swimming pool.

Wandering again in a daze back to my yard, I looked towards the thicket of trees. It was still there, that thing, growing uninvited inside our home.

*

"I don't think we should let Nikki play in the backyard for the time being," I said, clearing the dinner plates while pouring us another glass of Shiraz. I'd drunk three glasses to Kathy's one, just to calm my nerves. Outside, the singing of cicadas and the beat of bat wings filled the evening air, reminding me that there were still external comforts in life.

"I thought the wasps were dead Carl?"

"They are."

She twitched an eyebrow and I just stood there, staring at her, just staring through her. I realised then that I could no longer hide the truth from my wife, to what was growing just outside our home.

"What's the problem, Carl?"

I gulped when I said, "Kathy, I think it's easier if I just show you."

Being daylight-saving time and the midst of summer, it was

still light at eight-thirty in the evening, but I took a flashlight anyway. Sunset was not far off.

Amongst the shadows cast by the tall stringy gum trees, I pointed to the chaotic shape, larger still. No longer did its barbs and decayed coils grow from a single source, for the intrusion now sprouted from numerous openings in the earth. It had even begun to claim our trees, shearing through their branches, and had likely consumed the wasp nest long before that.

Kathy covered her mouth, suppressing her shock, "Oh my god Carl. When did you first see this thing?"

"Yesterday, but it was much smaller then."

"Haven't you been watching the news?"

I said that I hadn't, so she grabbed my hand and forced me to sit in front of the television. This was the first and last time in our relationship that she had to make me switch it on.

I was immediately stunned, then transfixed. The same intrusion dominating our backyard was on every channel, covered by frantic news reports streaming in from around the world. Ukraine had them, Israel, Syria, Nigeria, Norway, Japan, Indonesia, Canada, Brazil, the United Kingdom, France... the list never stopped.

"They just started to appear," Kathy squeezed my hand, "three days ago."

We watched for hours. Fox News reported from Oregon. In a small town, the Centre for Disease Control and Prevention had one of the growths surrounded like it was *America's Most Wanted*. By men and women in biohazard suits, and further a field, by Marines armed with assault rifles and bigger weapons. They were spraying it with poison, igniting it with flame-throwers, blasting it with explosives, burning it with lasers, and nothing seemed to be making a dent. "A spokesperson from the CDCP," said the voice-over, "in an official statement this morning, said that the source of the alien plant life is still undetermined, as it has been impossible to acquire samples for analysis."

Kathy switched channels. A BBC report showed an aerial view of the Amazon rainforest, where an alien growth the size of a house was blocking a tributary of great tropical river. Fresh water dolphins impaled and rotting on its offal-like texture seemed as stunned as we were, despite their unnatural deaths.

"Where are they coming from?" I asked.

"No one knows."

No one on the television did either, a common consensus on all channels. Interviewed experts from NASA and the SETI program claimed it as an invader from another world, but no one wanted to accept that explanation just yet. People were disappearing too, all over the world and in their thousands.

"This is scary, Carl, real scary." She clutched a couch cushion so tight to her chest, her knuckles shone white.

"I'll make us a cup of tea."

"Is that all you can say?" she screamed.

I shushed her, reminding her not to wake Nikki. Our little girl had recovered from the wasp sting, but the encounter had left her frightened of our backyard. Now I could only think of this as a good thing, and I hoped that Nikki didn't have to learn about the strange menace before the governments of the world dealt with the problem.

"I'm sorry," I rubbed the back of Kathy's neck, "I'm scared too."

She grabbed my hand softly, to say that she understood. "There is a free call number they keep flashing on the screen, to report intrusions to our government as they occur. Do you think we should call it?"

Again I stared at and through the television, realising that I was still numb from shock. In my heart I didn't want to do anything. I just wanted it all to go away of its own accord, even though my mind understood the folly of my convictions. "Nikki's asleep, and if government agents turn up tonight they're not going to let us stay?"

"You mean they'll kick us out, from our own home?"

"Yes, and maybe even quarantine us. Wouldn't you rather do that after a good night's sleep, than now?"

Kathy agreed, but I don't think she liked the idea of a night spent next to that thing. We slept on opposite sides of our bed, not cuddling as we usually do. I mumbled that I loved her, but I don't think she heard me. We were so scared we couldn't even comfort each other.

*

I woke to a horrendous crashing, splintering wood tearing through the night's stillness. A tree had just fallen in the back yard.

In shock, I leapt out of bed, pulled on a pair of pants and T-shirt, and was stunned to find that I was locked in. During the night, the alien growth had occupied one half of the bedroom, creeping up on us unheard and unseen.

In the next room, Nikki was screaming. As for my wife, I almost lost my mind when only her naked legs and abdomen survived on the outside of this invasive monstrosity. Half of the bed had disappeared with her too.

When I hoped to pull her free, she came away cleanly. Only there was nothing to the rest of her. Blood gushed from open veins, a spinal cord revealed the bones of vertebrae, and Shiraz mixed with last night's half-digested dinner spilt from her neatly sliced stomach. The growth hadn't eaten her; it had *replaced* the space that she had once occupied.

I screamed, sobbed, screamed again and pulled at my hair.

Nikki was screaming too. Only her calls brought me back to my senses. So I forced open the window, the only exit, and raced to her room. I was relieved to see that she was unharmed - physically - but she was crying worse than from the wasp sting, pounding at the window desperate to escape. The alien was in there too, boxing her in, like it had with me.

"Daddy, Daddy, Daddy!"

"Open the latch." I pointed desperately, hoping that she

would pay attention. I was unwilling to break the window to gain entrance. There was nowhere for her to shield against broken glass.

Eventually she complied, unlatched her freedom, and I grabbed her face to kiss it hard. Immediately I ran with her in my arms, first to get my wallet, keys and mobile phone, and then down the street, to pound upon our neighbour's door with a desperation that I had never experienced until this night.

Nikki kept asking me where Kathy was.

"Mummy had to go away for a few days," was all I could say. Not yet ready to tell her the awful truth, I don't think she was ready to hear it either.

*

"Emergency services are pushed to the limit, Mr. Sutherland," the government official spoke to us at the back of the ambulance, where we'd just been checked over by paramedics. He was desperate to send the vehicle on its way, to the next accident scene.

By the time help arrived, the seemingly motionless monster consumed the rest of my house and most of my property with it, but only when we were *not* looking at it. Of Kathy, I knew now that there would be nothing left of her remains.

The government official looked dull and exhausted. It was as if tonight was nothing new for him, that this was the umpteenth alien intrusion he'd investigated this evening. "You got somewhere to stay?" He waved the ambulance away.

"Our neighbours said they'd put us up, Mr.?"

"Jacobson, Ryan Jacobson," he gave me a card which said he worked for the Federal Government, but not which department. "That's not going to be possible I'm afraid. At the rate this thing is growing, your neighbours won't have their houses either by tomorrow night."

"You've measured how fast these things grow?"

He nodded. The flashing lights of remaining police cars and

fire trucks lit up his face with violent flickers in the pre-morning dawn. They too were moving on. There was nothing they could do but warn people away.

"I'll move into a hotel."

"Good luck," he said it like he didn't believe it.

Then Ryan Jacobson left us.

I was thankful that the government specialist team had saved our four-wheel drive. So when they had no further questions and nothing more to tell, I took what was mine and drove into the sunrise. No one seemed concerned that we were going.

"What's happening Daddy?" Nikki sitting in the passenger seat was sucking her thumb, and clutching her teddy-bear Norbert with the other hand. These were two habits she had not undertaken since she was five.

"We're going to stay with your grandmother."

"Is Mummy there?"

"She'd like to be. We'll see if she can come too when we get there."

"I miss Mummy."

"So do I honey, so do I."

At nine o'clock, I telephoned the office and told them that I wouldn't be coming in. I gave no explanation and they didn't seem to care. Kathy was dead. I'd lost her forever and that was reason enough, but I wasn't ready to admit it, not to anyone. If I did, I'd never stop crying, and I didn't want Nikki to see me like that.

At an automatic teller machine I withdrew all our savings, bought us some clothes, and a hamburger and a coke each. We sat down in the corner shop to eat it. Nikki seemed to like this moment's rest, and she told me that Norbert did too. Above her, the alien menace plastered itself across the screen of the suspended shop television. For a few seconds what remained of our house featured in a brief report - local news for local tragic colour.

"It's scary," responded the shop owner while we ate our lunch. I agreed with her.

After the hamburgers I bought Nikki and I ice-creams. She ate hers but it didn't bring a smile to her face, like it would on a normal day. She kept talking to Norbert, assuring the bear that everything would work out fine.

"Does anyone know what it is yet?" I asked the shop owner.

The woman behind the counter just shrugged. "Alien invasion is what people are saying around here, but governments and religious organisations across the world are denying it. But they would, wouldn't they?"

My smile for her sentiments was weak, "What do you think it is?"

"I tend to agree with them, the people around here I mean."

"Then where are the little green men?"

She caught my eye and held it, understanding what I meant. "That's a good question, isn't it?" Quickly she returned to wiping down the food preparation bench, our conversation suddenly at an end.

*

Every hotel, motel and guesthouse in Melbourne was without vacancies. Every other form of accommodation inside and out of the city was similarly booked up. We weren't the only family made homeless by this catastrophe, and now I was beginning to see signs of the invasion in the streets. Grey thorns were growing out of cars, replacing trees, blocking the roads, and pressing against power lines. Traffic was near standstill, and soon I became desperate.

"Are we going to Grandma's? Is Mummy there?"

I smiled weakly at my daughter, took her hand in mine. I didn't have the heart to tell Nikki that I'd phoned Kathy's mother a dozen times this morning with no success. Or that I'd discovered via the Internet on my mobile phone, that the town of Ballarat where she lived, was overrun with the spiky tendril-like mess of knotted growth. There were no known survivors.

"Grandma and Mummy are going to meet us in the country,

up north. But first, let's go shopping."

I shouldn't have been surprised that inflation and panicked buying had inflicted the city. Two thousand dollars barely bought us enough food for a week, a full tank of petrol, and two sleeping bags. Strangely, I didn't care. With anarchy on the rise, money would soon be useless.

Nikki and I decided on the backstreets to get us out of the city, eventually finding a path through the chaos, and drove north-east into the high country. Even on the main roads there were delays, huge queues at petrol stations, and too many car accidents to stop at them all to offer assistance.

I finally sobbed when I saw the mountain, not of rock and trees, but of tangled rotten grey, strangling the horizon like an angry instrument of torture. It was growing too fast.

"Don't cry Daddy. Norbert says everything will be okay, and that Mummy still loves you."

I hugged Nikki close, thankful that she was still with me. I didn't ask if she was okay, because I knew she was not, just like me. At least we had each other.

Desperate now, I siphoned three abandoned cars of their petrol, filled my tank and a jerry can for later. Then we took to the dirt roads, cutting gate chains and driving down barbed-wire fences as we went. Seen occasionally from a distance, the highways were choked and the drivers scared. Fragments of news still filtering into my mobile phone suggested riots, and that people were now shooting each other.

Two days ago, Kathy, Nikki and I were enjoying a quiet weekend at home, a loving family. Now the world had gone mad and Kathy was no more, because we were under invasion by an alien species we could not understand, and could not see. Nothing felt real.

We drove along an unmarked road, until we reached a valley surrounded only by eucalyptus forests and rolling natural hills, and stopped there for the evening. Here everything seemed normal. There were birds in the trees and ants on the earth, oblivious to the intrusions far from us in this paradise.

"I'll make a fire, and we'll camp here tonight?"

"Camping? We've never camped before, Daddy. I don't want to."

I smiled for her benefit. "We'll sleep in the four-wheel drive. We'll be safe there."

"Are there any wasps here Daddy?"

I laughed with her, remembering what it was like to feel joy, teary and smiling at the same time. What a relief it was, that Nikki was more concerned with insect monsters than the sickly grey intruders. At least I could understand and protect her from wasps, and promised that I would. "We'll melt marshmallows, and tell stories around the camp fire like they do in the movies. What do you say to that?"

"Where's Mummy?"

"She's coming. She just had a few things to do first."

"Like yoga?"

"Yeah... like yoga..."

Later that night I checked my phone again, but there was no signal and no Internet. When the battery finally died, it would be for the last time. Its telling companion, the night sky was the brightest I'd ever seen it, because I knew there were no lights on earth anymore to dampen their luminosity. This evening, the beauty of the Milky Way spoke only of horror.

*

Tranquillity was not meant to last. In the morning light, the grey thorn tangles had found us even here, as gigantic bulbs a hundred meters or more into the blue sky. They were joined together with their fibrous tentacle strands, as sick and decayed as the rest of it. I could see that the invader grew only when they were unnoticed, at an accelerated rate, and I did not wish to ponder upon this implication.

Only luck had saved us, for the area where I parked our vehicle was untouched. Trees around us now fell and sheared, where the thorny monster replaced their existence with its own

205

unnatural matter.

Nikki and I packed quickly, ate packaged food for breakfast and prepared to set off. Where we were to go I had no idea, but I still hoped there was a corner of this world that would always be untouched, and we could make a home there.

In the eerie silence - absent of animals - I heard the motorcycle engines long before I spied the biker gang. A dozen angry men, four with trashy girlfriends hanging onto their decorated leather jackets, encircled Nikki and I, and threatened us with shotguns. I hid my special girl behind me, told her to be silent. It was all that I could do.

"We're going to take your food and your vehicle," spat their leader. He didn't even threaten me, knowing that he could just do with us what he wanted.

"Okay," I nodded, holding Nikki close. As far as I was concerned they could take anything, except my daughter. Several of the fat ugly men examined the contents of my vehicle while I watched, nodded approvingly, and then indicated that their four trashy girls should drive the vehicle out of here, following the dust trails of their oversized motorcycles.

"You want cash," I offered them my wallet. I wanted these thieves out of sight as fast as I could, and I didn't want them to have any reason to come back looking for me.

The scraggly bearded leader laughed at me, "Nothing to spend it on mate, nothing at all."

"You mean...?"

"Yeah, the world's dead. We'd bring you with us, but when it got tough, you know you'd be the first to go." He winked with a bloodshot eye, and indicated his holstered revolver.

They left Nikki and me in the mélange of bush and alien thorns, with only the clothes that we wore and each other for comfort and security.

When the motorcycles buzzed us, Nikki screamed words I did not properly hear, pulled her self from my grip and ran towards the disappearing four-wheel drive. I screamed at her, told her to come back to me, but I was already too late. One of the gang members didn't see her, or didn't care, and flung her body five meters through the air when he hit her hard.

She stopped flying when she hit a log.

I heard bones break.

When I reached my daughter, the thieves were long gone. They were vanished in the tangles, and Nikki was dead.

I only understood then what my daughter had called for, what she had been desperate to hold onto; Norbert the bear.

*

I sobbed, I cried, I screamed, I wailed. Mostly I walked - one long step after the other.

The bush became alive with panicked animals. Kangaroos hopped madly from any sound; myself included. Cattle wandering in a daze, complained that they had not been milked, and that this world was as strange to them as it was to me. Beyond the native bush, alien tangles with their revolting decayed texture soared as high as skyscrapers, and I had to walk through their newly formed tunnels to escape. Soon the living were gone, replaced by corpses of cats, kangaroos, wombats and cattle that littered every edge, sliced in twos, threes and fours where the invaders had snatched them. The only smell in the air was that of blood.

Eventually I reached a small country town, and quenched my thirst with cans of soft drink, stolen from a deli where the power no longer kept them cold. Biscuits and melted chocolate became my diet. Corpses of men, women and children became my scenery. In time, I came to understand that many had taken their own life, judging by the sleeping tables, poisons, knives and guns that had fallen with them.

My four-wheel drive was there too, in a petrol station alive with flames. Four female corpses black and dead and eye sockets wide with fear, spoke of their passing.

Norbert kept them company, staring up at me from the

207

asphalt. I picked him up with the revolver next to him, the weapon that the bikers' leader had left behind, discarded where he had forgotten it in his pain. It still had two bullets. Two bullets would be enough. And Norbert agreed.

In the sky, in the sunset, all I could see were the alien tangles, higher than any mountain. It had finally encircled me.

*

I found a bed and breakfast cottage, and it was intact. No one was home. No one was coming back. The property was on the edge of another bush heartland, so it was just like home.

Solar power gave me light, and gas bottles gave me a stove. I made myself a fine dinner, a roast with potatoes and greens. I opened a '78 Shiraz which I'd found in the well-stocked cellar, and treated myself to a meal fit for kings. Norbert joined me. He told me he wasn't hungry, but that he would stay with me until the end. I told him to stop being morose, so to liven our spirits I sought music.

The previous owners had jazz records, not CDs, so I started up the turntable and we listened to the soulful tunes, a replacement to the absent cicadas and bats.

After dinner, I smoked a cigar on the veranda, with Norbert for company, and coughed as I enjoyed the unusual texture. It was dark outside, except for the tiny circle of stars. I knew why this was so, the alien world was closing in on us fast, claiming the sky. Until it did, we would have our moment of peace.

While I poured the last of the Shiraz, the best wine I will ever taste in my life, I thought back to the wasp that had stung Nikki. That had been my last normal event, before this horrible process of annihilation had interrupted my life. Those wasps had no idea what we humans would do to them, not realising that they had encroached too closely upon *our* territory. We poisoned them, destroyed their home and brought death to their entire colony. Was it sad that they didn't even know it was we humans who had killed them, or that they could never possibly understand why we did so?

In turn, what had we humans done to offend these grey thorny aliens in their subtle invasion, with their ugly growths determined to replace *everything* that had once been our world? How had we strayed too closely to their territory? Was it the testing of too many nuclear weapons? Did we peer too closely into the many secrets of the cosmos and the quantum universe? Had we split too many atoms in our particle accelerators, and thus somehow caused them pain in those unseen dimension from where they must surely observe us now? In their eyes, something about us *had* changed, something that no longer classified us as a harmless species, but as a bothersome pest intruding upon *their* home.

What had we done?

Norbert didn't know, and I didn't either. We would never know the answer. Worse, we would never know the love of Nikki or Kathy ever again.

Later, when I finished the Shiraz and smoked the last of the cigar, I looked out upon the tiny circle of night sky one last time.

When I'm done, I will go and find that revolver. Like I said earlier, two bullets will be enough.

A PIE WITH THICK GRAVY

D. F. Lewis

A pie with gravy didn't make much sense to George - unless, of course, the gravy had spilt from the pie inside. Did meat generate its own gravy or was gravy forced upon it by use of dissolving Bisto or Oxo in boiling water? Meat came dry - its natural state, with the juices burned off in cooking. So the gravy was false dressing. A sauce in all but name. Like Chicken Tonight or Rogan Josh. The pie in gravy seemed to imply that the pastry itself exuded curds of brown sweat, rather than from the meat inside the pie. The crispy pastry coating of the meat was indeed swamped with gravy - as George crossed his fork with his knife and dug in. The gravy slowly began to vanish into the pie's wound that George had gashed. It was as if the pie itself was swallowing the gravy - or taking back into itself something that it felt belonged there.

George made another, this time more careful, incision to see the pie further gobble down the thick gravy. The pie had a live creature inside - despite the cooking. This was George's next thought and he was frightened.

The crispy pastry coating was starting to crack all over like an earthquake as whatever was inside continued to thirst for what it considered to be its own belongings: the lifeblood that was loosely called gravy. George could see porous membranes and gristly marrowbone mouths eager for each gooey gulp, twitching with each satisfying quenchment of an eternal famine that the pie's innards had suffered. Evidently, the cooking had not killed it, but woken it. The snout was the first definite proof as it poked through the decorative fork-holes in the pie's crusty roof. Sniffling around for further doses of the thick gravy. George's gorge rose. He was about to be sick.

He was sick. And the snout fed further upon the stream of diced carrots that had emerged from George's mouth upon the quaking pie. George was being milked to the bottom of his stomach - and beyond to where deep bowels of even thicker gravy lurked.

LOCK-IN

David A. Riley

"Nobody expects anything really dramatic to happen at Christmas."

"There was Caesescu. He got toppled at Christmas. That was pretty dramatic."

"And they shot him. Which was even more dramatic."

"Along with his wife!"

"Then we had the Tsunami on Boxing Day."

"I know that, I know. But - and it's a big *but* - it's still true that no one expects anything to happen at Christmas. When it does, it takes us by surprise."

"But you could say that about any day of the year. You could say no one expects anything really dramatic to happen on the twenty-fifth of July. Now there's a boring date for you."

"And if you said this to the vicar he'd soon tell you that the most dramatic event in the history of mankind happened at Christmas."

"Oh, put a sock in it! You'll have us singing carols next. For God's sake…"

"Anyway, Bob, what exactly are you getting at? Why does it matter whether, rightly or wrongly - depending on your point of view - you think no one expects anything really dramatic to happen at Christmas? Apart for the usual domestic break-ups and rows and everything else you might expect when most of the population over indulges in alcohol."

"Never mind all that. Whose round is it next? I'm drinking without." Arthur Renshaw banged his empty beer glass on the table between them, emphasising his point. The four old men, the Grudgers they called themselves (after the district of town they were all born in, Grudge End), burst out laughing, while Bob Beesley fished in his wallet for a ten pound note.

"Barman," he called out. "Another four of your best, please!"

They were a distinctive group, even in the Potter's Wheel, one of the few unrefurbished, unmodernised pubs in the district. Its dark wallpaper first saw the light of day - such as ever penetrated this far - over thirty years ago, much about the same time the paint dried on its woodwork. There was a luxurious atmosphere of dilapidation about the place, with its damp beer mats that often stuck tenaciously to the scarred wooden tables and the old fashioned, barrel-shaped glasses.

Bob Beesley heaved himself up off his stool and waddled to the bar, where he picked up their next round of drinks and passed them, one by one, to eager hands held stretched from the nearby alcove that was literally their own reserve spot in the pub. "And a bag of pork scratchings," Bob added. "I'm feelin' a bit peckish."

By the time he'd sat down again, panting from the effort, the others had taken at least two or three gulps of their beers and were busily arguing once more. Bob pushed his thick, horn-rimmed spectacles back up the broad bridge of his nose and glanced at the darkening sky outside the nearest window as he nimbly unfastened his pork scratchings. It looked as if there was a storm brewing, which probably meant he'd have to hurry home later to avoid getting soaked; he'd left his raincoat hung behind his front door, along with his brolly. Typical the weather should change like this, he thought. Just his luck.

"Anyway," Tom Atkins said to him; his sallow cheeks had gained a faint, almost healthy flush from the two pints he'd drunk, "what's all this about Christmas? It's weeks away yet. It's bad enough all the shops start putting up their blasted decorations as soon as we've just seen the back of bonfire night, without you going on about it."

"You old humbug," Arthur scolded him. "You get more miserable by the year."

"So would you if you'd thirteen grandchilder to buy presents for - and none of 'em cheap."

"As if you didn't really love it," Bob told him. "I've seen you, hiking off to Eddison's Toy Shop on Market Street.

213

You're like a child yourself when you get in there. And I'll bet you make sure you help some of those grandchilder of yours to play with their toys!"

The others laughed, including Tom, who had to admit that he did, sometimes, have to help them out. "But only when they're not sure how to play with them properly," he added. "Some of these modern toys are very complicated to use, you know."

Paddy Morgan, his brick-red cheeks like very old slabs of beef, shook his head sadly. "You never grew up, Tom. I've always said it."

"Some of us grow up too fast," Tom told him. "I envy my grandchilder. They've some wonderful toys these days. Far better than we'd to make do with when we were kiddies."

There was a rumbled chorus of agreements to this. Then Tom said: "I'd better get in another round. I see Arthur's about to be drinking without again."

"Drinks too fast. Always has. Like a bottomless drain," Bob grumbled good-naturedly. He glanced at the clock, hidden above the bar amidst a line of almost empty optics. Nine thirty and he felt tired already. Getting old, he thought. Getting far too old. Not like the old days when the four of them would paint the town red. A long, long time ago now, he added to himself, sadly.

Apart from the four of them there were only a few regulars in the pub tonight. Midweek, though, it was always quiet. Which suited the Grudgers. None of them cared for the weekends, when the Potter's Wheel was crammed with youngsters, and Sam Sowerby, the landlord, switched on the normally silent juke box.

"What's going on out there?"

On his way to the bar, Tom glanced at the speaker, a terse old farmer who drove down to the pub at night in his battered Land Rover for a pint or two by himself before going home to bed.

"What is it, Jim?" Tom asked as he leant against the bar and nodded to the landlord for another four pints..

"Outside. Looks like some sort of commotion." Jim Bartlet slammed down his beer and sidled over to the frosted glass door. Frowning, he placed a hand on the door knob to pull it open.

As he watched him, Tom felt a faint premonition that something was wrong, something worse than just a commotion outside. And for an instant he had an urge to tell Jim to ignore it, to let go of the door and go back to the bar. But it was an urge he ignored. Not only would Jim think he was being absurd, but he would take no notice of him. In fact, he'd be even more likely to go ahead with whatever he was going to do if he said anything to him. And quite rightly so. If someone told Tom something as ridiculous as that he'd ignore them as well. Tom shuddered, though, as the irascible old farmer pulled the door open and stepped outside. There was a brief hint of fog and a noise like someone snapping twigs. Less than a minute later the door burst open and Jim Bartlet fell back into the pub, blood streaming from his face. He made a half turn, as if to steady himself against the bar, then slithered to the ground. Tom reached for him, but his reflexes were slow these days and he missed. Sam Sowerby, though, for all his own weight, was round the public side of the bar within seconds and knelt beside the farmer, cradling his head. Jim's face was unrecognisable. A red, raw ruin of sinews and veins and stripped, naked meat. It was as if the skin had been sliced from his face, cut away from deep into the flesh and muscles and down into the bone. On instinct Tom went to the heavy, wooden outer door, hurriedly closed it with a solid thud, then snapped the locks shut, top and bottom, though it seemed a feeble enough defence against whatever had attacked Jim Bartlet.

The rest of the Grudgers had scrambled to their feet, even Bill, though he trailed behind the others as they gathered about the body on the floor.

"I'll phone for the police," Arthur said. He hurried to the phone behind the bar. A moment later he looked at the others,

215

a crestfallen expression on his long, thin, lugubrious face. "It's dead," he told them.

Bob frowned at him. "What d'you mean *dead*?"

"It's dead," Arthur repeated. "The phone's dead."

Sam laid the farmer's mutilated head back on the floor. "Let me try," he told him. He hurried behind the bar and stabbed energetically at the buttons on the phone, as if force alone could make it work. In the end he slammed it back on its cradle. He looked over at the locked outer door. The others, watching him, looked over too.

"I ain't going out there. Not till there's at least a vanful of police outside. Preferably a SWAT team," Bob muttered.

"I don't think there's much chance of a SWAT team in Edgebottom," Tom told him. "Not for hours anyway. They'd have to send to Manchester for one - and that's more than fifteen mile frae here."

Paddy nodded at the dead body of Jim Bartlet. "What the 'ell did that to him? We can't just stand here while there's someone out there who killed poor Jim like that. It's horrible. Horrible. We've got to contact the police. Somehow."

"Barring smoke signals - which no one would see at this time of night anyway - what would you suggest, Paddy?" Sam asked, shaken; he looked down at his bloodstained hands, then went to the sink behind the bar to wash them clean. "What would you suggest?" he muttered to himself as he vigorously tried to wipe them dry on a wet bar towel.

"There's a lunatic out there," Bob said. "A lunatic with a butcher's cleaver. What else could have done that to Jim Bartlet's face?"

They all, reluctantly, looked down at the farmer's head, laid in a spreading pool of blood. The only other customer left in the pub beside the Grudgers was Harold Sillitoe, a retired schoolmaster with literary pretensions. But he seemed speechless, sat on his barstool with his eyes closed against the horror only three yards from him, his single malt whisky untouched on the bar in front of him.

216

"What did he hear that made him go outside?" Paddy wondered out loud.

"Whatever it was I couldn't hear it." Tom shook his head. "But I did feel something was wrong. I almost said that to him. That he'd be better off ignoring whatever he'd heard and stay here. I don't even know why I felt that. Though I wish I'd said something now."

"And do you think Jim would've listened?" Bob asked. "He'ld've told you to stop being soft. And gone out."

"At least I would've tried. I feel guilty somehow."

"Bollocks! Only the bastard as did that to him is guilty of anything. How were you to know someone would chop off his friggin' face?" Bob reached for his pint off the table behind them and took a long swallow.

"We've still got to do something," Paddy insisted. "We can't just stay here while whoever attacked him is still out there, roaming about."

The landlord shook his head. "And what would you suggest? I've tried the phone. And that's dead. What else is there?"

"You've got a mobile, haven't you?" Paddy asked.

Sam swore, then hurried to the stairs. He came back again only a minute later, mobile in one hand. "No signal. No bloody signal."

A tense silence settled on the men. Then Bob asked if Sam had the remote for the TV. There was an old, eighteen-inch set in the games room, usually used by some of the locals to watch horse racing on Saturday afternoons, though none of the Grudgers had ever watched it.

Sam disappeared behind the bar, then came out with the remote and went into the games room, with its pool table and darts board. They heard him cursing to himself. The old men exchanged worried looks, then Sam strode slowly back into the lounge, his broad face even paler than usual.

"You aren't going to believe this," he said to them.

"But you can't get any channels," Bob answered. "The TV's dead as well."

217

"No reception on any of its channels." Sam flung the remote onto the bar. "It's as if we're cut off from everything."

"But how?" Bob asked.

"And why?" Tom put in with a shudder. "Why?"

Bob wandered slowly to the window and peered outside, the others watching him intently. He moved his head cautiously from side to side, but the darkness looked impenetrable. He couldn't even see any street lights down the road. Not far away should have been the illuminated clock tower on St Paul's Junior School. He couldn't see that either. Nor the traffic lights at the end of the block. Nor any traffic. No traffic at all. As if the world outside had ceased to exist.

Shuddering, Bob backed away from the window. He looked at the others, unsure what to say.

"This is freakin' surreal," Sillitoe suddenly said, reaching for his whisky. "Freakin', freakin' surreal."

"Calm down, Harold," the landlord told him. "No need to panic."

The others eyed him in disbelief.

"If this isn't cause enough to panic, what is?" Bob asked.

The rest added their agreement.

"I'm just about ready to panic myself," Tom said. "And that's without even knowing what 'freaking surreal' even means."

Perhaps in an effort to show some kind of moral control, Sam slowly walked towards the front door.

"Are you sure what you're doing?" Tom asked.

"We can't just stay here, can we?" Sam said, uncertainly.

"But if you go out, the same might happen to you as happened to Jim Bartlet. I wouldn't risk it."

"Nor me," added Bob.

Sam looked round at them, seeing the concern in their faces. The fear.

"We can't just wait around for something to happen," Sam told them, insistently.

With less resolution than he allowed himself to show, Sam

took a firm hold of the upper lock of the front door, then clicked it open. Bending his knees, he reached for the lower lock and clicked that open too. Licking his lips, Sam paused for a moment to rebuild his determination, before reaching for the door handle, his palm damp with sweat as he tried to grip it as firmly as he could.

The door opened with ease. Outside all was black, the solid, impenetrable black of absolute nothingness. No street lights, no traffic, no hint of the stars or the moon or the pavement or the rest of the town or anything of the outside world at all. Just an endless, eternal black, like everlasting night, that went on and on till his eyes ached from the strain of staring into it.

Even so, Sam stood at the pub doorway for a long, long moment. He wanted to reach out into the darkness, but something warned him not to do it, that not only would it be wrong but dangerous. Perhaps Jim Bartlet had felt the same urge and leant out to peer into the darkness too, and in doing so lost his face. Sam shuddered, unable to cope with the bizarre ideas that rushed in at him about what he was looking at, then he stepped back into the warmth and light and shabby cosiness of the pub; he slammed the front door shut behind him and returned to the lounge.

"What did you see?" Bob asked, a tremor in his voice.

"Come on," Tom added. "Say something. You're worrying me."

Sam stepped behind the bar and poured himself a stiff whisky from the optics. He drank it in one gulp, then poured himself another. He drank this too in one gulp.

"Sam!" Bob rapped on the bar to catch his attention. "What the hell did you see?"

"See?" Sam shut his eyes for a moment, his plump face blank. "I wish there had been something to see. But I couldn't see nothing more than you could see through the window. There's nothing. Nothing out there. Nothing at all."

"Stop talking nonsense," Paddy snapped at him. "What d'you mean, nothing? D'you mean you couldn't see anything because we've had a power cut?"

"A power cut that's affected everywhere apart from the Potter's Wheel?" Sam laughed humourlessly. "You're a genius, Paddy. How come I couldn't think of that!"

"Then what?" Bob asked. Feeling queasy with fear, he sat down on one of the old bar stools and leant against the bar. He felt in need of his pint of beer again.

"There's no 'what' about it. Not so far as I can see - so far as I can reckon," Sam said, almost to himself. "I looked out of the door and there was nothing there. Just a deep black void that went on and on forever."

"Steady, Sam," Tom told him.

"Steady? You should take a look out there yourself," Sam said. "But be careful, 'cause I reckon it's a blackness you shouldn't even try to touch. Not unless you want to end up like Jim."

"I thought some madman did that to him. Hacked him with a knife or an axe," Paddy said, as they looked down at the farmer's body by the bar.

Sam shook his head. "I don't think so. There's nothing human, mad or otherwise, out there, Paddy. Whatever did that to him wasn't human. More likely it was just the blackness that did it. How, I don't know."

The six men sat round the bar for some minutes in silence as each of them tried to digest what had happened.

Suddenly, his face white with fear, Harold Sillitoe knocked over his whisky and rushed for the door. "I don't care what rubbish any of you say, I'm not staying here," he shouted at them. "I'm not staying here to be trapped."

Sam tried to grab his arm, but the schoolteacher was too fast. The next moment he reached the door, snapped its locks and flung it open. Arthur Renshaw was the nearest to him; he tried to pull him back, but Sillitoe was too determined to get out of the pub, and slipped past his fingers. The moment he reached beyond the doorway into the darkness, though, he screamed. At that instant Arthur managed to grasp hold of the collar of his coat, then grunted with the effort as he tugged him back. Together they fell into the lounge, tumbling across the floor, as Sillitoe writhed in abject agony, the stumps of his arms jetting blood over the two of them. Tom moved in and pulled Arthur free, then stood back as the schoolteacher's body spasmed, then stilled, and the blood ceased pumping from the severed ends of his arms.

A look of horror on his face, Arthur said: "What the hell did that to him?"

"I told you," Sam answered. "The darkness. He touched it. He put his arms into it. And, somehow, in some way, it destroyed them."

"Like acid?"

"Or worse."

"Much worse," Bob added sombrely. "I saw what acid can do when I worked at Watson's Chemical Works in Thrushington and that's nothing like as bad as this, believe me. Nor anything like so fast." He shuddered, and sat down again on his stool. Then reached for his beer.

Meanwhile Sam knelt beside Sillitoe. "He's dead," he told them, though they knew this by now. The schoolteacher's body had jerked only once and become so still there was no room for doubt in any of them that he had died - that and the stemming of the outpouring of blood from what was left of his arms.

Sam nodded to Arthur, and the two of them dragged Sillitoe's body away to one wall. They then dragged Jim Bartlet's next to it, away from the bar.

"Place is beginning to look like a friggin' morgue," Tom muttered.

"Aye, and it's us who are creatin' it," Bob added.

Sam went behind the bar, filled five glasses of whisky, then passed them out to the four Grudgers, before sitting down himself and taking a deep gulp of his drink. "I hope that's the last attempt any of us make to get out through that door."

With an exchange of glances the four men nodded their

221

heads as they raised the whiskies to their lips.

"What are we going to do?" Bob asked. "We can't just sit here, pleasant though it is, forever."

"Well, I'm just glad my wife decided to leave me last month," Sam said. "Otherwise the nagging bitch'd be going at us relentlessly by now."

"What d'you reckon it is?" Paddy asked.

Sam shrugged. "I've no more idea than any of you. I doubt our schoolteacher friend, for all his learning and degrees and suchlike, had any more himself. Which is, perhaps, why he panicked."

As the hours passed the five men slowly relapsed into silence. It was only when it passed eleven o'clock, when he would normally lock the front door and call last orders, that Sam remembered his lodger. Ever since his wife left him, he had supplemented his dwindling income in the pub by letting out one of the spare bedrooms upstairs. An odd old bugger, his current lodger called himself Albert Durer, though Sam was sure this wasn't his real name somehow. Still, the money was welcome each week - and he paid it on time every Friday.

"Have any of you seen Albert?" Sam asked, though none of the men remembered catching sight of the lodger all evening.

"Perhaps he couldn't get in 'cause of that stuff," Paddy suggested, with a vague gesture at the door.

"I'll go take a look in his room," Sam said.

It was less than a minute later that he shouted down to the rest of them to "come up here! For Christ's sake, take a look at this!"

As the four men gathered about the open doorway upstairs, panting for breath, Sam stood at the far end of the room in front of the curtained window. Between them the threadbare carpet had been rolled back to uncover the floorboards. On these there was a large, painted circle in white and a five-pointed star. All around the edges were peculiar symbols and the burnt-out stubs of candles, their melted wax lying in off-white ridges on the floorboards. In the centre of the star was

222

what horrified them all the most: it was a nailed-down body of a rat, its ribs and stomach sliced open.

"The dirty bastard," Bob muttered, wiping sweat from his forehead. "The dirty, *dirty* bastard!"

"Filthy pervert, more like," Tom put in. "Who'd do a thing like that?"

"Albert Durer, that's who," Sam said. "And here's me, cookin' his breakfast for him every morning, and the bastard does that in my own home."

"What is it?" Paddy asked. "Satanism?"

"I don't know," Sam said. "It's something horrible, I know that. Whether it's Satanism or not, I haven't a clue. Ask me something a know something about and I'll answer you. This… this is just friggin' disgustin', whatever you call it."

"There's some kind of old book over there on the dresser," Tom said, pointing.

They followed his finger, and Sam stepped over to the dresser, gingerly keeping his feet outside the painted circle. He touched the open book, its pages crackling beneath his fingers like very old parchment. He stared at it hard for several moments, his brows puckering with concentration.

"Can't make out a blessed thing that's written in it," he told them eventually. "It's all in some kind of foreign language."

"Like French?" Paddy asked, to whom foreign meant Calais, which was the furthest he'd ever travelled.

"Or Latin?" Bob asked, who'd done four years of it at Grammar School a long time ago and could just about remember Amo, Amas, Amat.

"Take a look," Sam told him, but when Bob sidled over to peer at the book he shook his head. "I don't think it is Latin," he said finally. "Or if it is, it's in some kind of code."

The men shook their heads in consternation.

"D'you think this has anything to do with what's happened tonight?" Tom asked.

Sam stared at him. "That blackness?" he asked.

"I know it sounds mad," Tom went on. "But before what

happened to Jim and Harold that would have sounded mad too."

"But why?" Bob asked. "And how?"

Tom shrugged. "You'd have to ask Sam's absent lodger that, if we ever get chance to meet him again."

"I'd like just one chance to meet that bastard again," Sam muttered as he gazed at the mutilated remains of the rat nailed to the floorboards. "He'd not forget it if we did."

While they were upstairs, they checked the rest of the bedrooms and Sam's living room, but the sheer solid blackness outside never changed. By the early hours of the morning they had all gone to sleep in the two other bedrooms besides Durer's, though none of them felt secure enough to undress. Whatever was happening to them, they were sure there were more surprises in store. And none of them, probably, good.

Sam was the first up. By half eight he had prepared breakfast for them all of fried eggs and bacon.

"There's plenty of food in the freezer, but I can't promise many more days of bacon and egg," he told them as they sat about the table in the kitchen.

"Do you think we'll be stuck here that long?" Tom asked, his sallow complexion now grey, with dark shadows under his eyes.

"Who knows?" Sam said. "We're still stuck now, aren't we? Which makes it nearly twelve hours already. Who knows how much longer this'll go on?"

"Much longer and I think I'll go stir crazy," Tom muttered. "We might've joked sometimes about how grand it'd be to get locked inside a pub, but the reality's not quite the same."

"The lock-in from Hell," Bob said. Like Tom, his plump face showed signs of strain.

"I never thought the Potter's Wheel Paradise, but I never reckoned to compare it to Hell," Sam said with an attempt at levity, trying to put out of his mind what they saw in Albert Durer's bedroom.

Levity, though, had come into short supply by mid-afternoon

and the view through the windows was still pitch black. There was a creeping atmosphere of fear in the pub. And claustrophobia.

There were strange anomalies. Though they could neither send nor receive telephone calls, and the TV and radio were dead, there were still supplies of electricity and water. Arthur Renshaw said it was a pity the water pipes weren't big enough to crawl along, otherwise they might have been able to get out that way, till Bob pointed out that, however big the pipes might be, they would drown in them anyway because of the water - and still get nowhere. Sam organised for the two bodies in the lounge to be wrapped and taped inside bin bags, then he and Tom dragged them into the cellar, where it was cold enough to keep them preserved - and where, more importantly, they weren't in constant view.

By evening there was real fear.

"We should have heard something from someone by now," Tom insisted. "Surely somebody knows we're stuck here, that something's wrong."

Sam shrugged. "Who knows what it's like on the outside? Perhaps it's as dangerous to get into the Potter's Wheel as it is to get out."

They drank slowly and steadily that night. Talk petered out long before ten; after that they sat around the bar in desultory groups, each consumed by their own gloomy thoughts for the future. Before they knew it, it was midnight, they all felt slightly drunk, and went to bed grumbling about the bloody absurdity of it all.

Five days passed and the situation hardly changed, though the bacon and eggs for breakfast had long since run out and Sam was beginning to look increasingly more worried whenever he went to the freezer. His initial optimism about what it held hadn't taken into account that it would have to cater for five grown men, with no additional food coming in from any other source. Now it was beginning to empty with ominous speed. Two days later the freezer was down to an already opened bag of peas, three fish fingers, some ice cream in a battered tub and a very old packet of boil-in-the-bag spinach.

Within the next few days they were all beginning to feel hungry and beginning to realise that they were facing the grim prospect of starvation. If being imprisoned within the pub had been enough to make them feel afraid to start with, their food running out increased this till there was hardly a moment when they weren't aware of it. It dominated their thoughts. But there was nothing they could do about it. They had long since searched the pub for every possible scrap of food, from half eaten packets of biscuits to the snacks hung on cards behind the bar. Even dusty jars of out of date cherries for cocktails that had never been popular in the Potter's Wheel had all been consumed. Their ill assorted diet led them to feeling queasy as well as hungry, depressing their spirits even more and making all of them irritable.

By the end of the second week tempers, as well as hunger, were at breaking point...

"This is bloody ridiculous," Bob said eventually as the five of them sat around a table in the lounge. With empty stomachs, they had stopped drinking alcohol till later at night; and each of them now held a bottle of fruit juice from behind the bar. "We've got to do something. If we don't, we're going to starve to death within the next couple of weeks, unless we turn to cannibalism."

"And with only five of us that wouldn't last long," Sam put in with a rueful smile, though his attempt at humour met with little response from the drawn faces of the four old men, who stared at him in silence

"We've got to try something," Tom said. "Even if it means risking what happened to the others. If we don't..."

"If we don't, we're doomed," Bob said flatly.

Sam went behind the bar and poured them five beers. "If we're to plan getting out of here we need something stronger than orange juice," he told them.

Their first plans, though, were vague impracticalities that were soon dissected and tossed to one side. It was Tom who came up with the first and only practical suggestion.

"Have you ever wondered why we've still got water and electricity?" he asked.

"Good job we have them," Arthur said. "We'd have been well buggered if we hadn't."

"I agree with you there. But *why* have we still got them," Tom went on insistently. "That's the important thing. That's what I've been wondering. After all, we've no TV or radio signals."

They sat there watching him, waiting.

"And?" Bob asked. "What answer have you come up with? Or is this going to be twenty friggin' questions?"

"Two things," Tom said, and, despite the hunger that was aching in his stomach, he managed a smile of monumental smugness. "Electrical cable and lead pipes - or whatever they make water pipes from these days."

"It ain't lead, I know that," Sam said. "But I get your point. Electricity and water get through because they're protected in some kind of casing."

"And?" Bob asked. "Am I being a bit thick, but how does that help us. We can't get out of here through either of them, can we?"

"But we might be able to make some kind of casing through the darkness," Tom said. "Something that'll protect us inside. It's just a matter of finding something that'll stretch out into the darkness that we would be safe inside."

"It's more than just worth a try," Sam said. "Better than sitting here, starving to death."

Putting aside their beers, they set out foraging about the pub for materials they could use to construct a tunnel.

"I hope that darkness doesn't stretch too far," Tom confided in Sam, but the landlord shrugged. "We've got to try, Tom. It's the best idea so far, and if we don't make a stab at it we're doomed anyway."

It was in the beer cellar they came up with the solution. At one time, during the late eighties, a previous landlord had made an attempt at building up the catering side of the pub, and with that purpose in mind had started work on a proper professional kitchen. Things had gone well, till he was told he would have to construct a ventilation system. Spiralling costs, at each new demand from the local council, had resulted in him eventually abandoning the project. In the cellar, though, were the aluminium panels for an unconstructed ventilation system, ready to be connected together to form a two foot square metal shaft.

"If we could connect these together we could lead them from the front door out into the darkness. Hopefully they'll make a shaft long enough to let us crawl out of here," Sam said, as they relayed the open-ended boxes up the cellar steps to the bar.

Opening the front door was a ticklish operation as no one wanted to risk suffering any of the mutilations that struck those who had already tried to get out that way. The deep, almost cosmic darkness that confronted them, with its cold, black depths, had become no less awesome - or frightening. Gingerly, they pushed the ventilation shaft, a twelve foot length of aluminium squares, inch by inch out across the doorstep into what should have been the street. Their first attempt, though, was a dismal failure. As they shone a torch into it, they could see that the inexplicable darkness had entered it from the far end, filling it till it was in line with the darkness at the doorstep.

"We'll need to seal the far end off," Sam said as they pulled the shaft back into the pub. "Perhaps that'll keep it out."

They found some sheets of aluminium in the cellar which fitted on the end of the shaft. With a soldering iron, it did not take long before they had it in place.

"Make sure you seal in every gap, otherwise the darkness might seep through," Tom suggested while Sam worked on it. "But not too strongly. It has to break off."

This time, as they slowly, carefully pushed the delicate shaft into the darkness, the inside remained clear. Even when most of it stretched out from the pub, its outside swallowed by the darkness around it, as if it no longer existed, its interior remained bright, unsullied by even the slightest hint of darkness.

The five men exchanged cheers of jubilation. They sat back and admired their work for a moment.

"Do you think the far end's reached the other side of the darkness?" Arthur asked, dampening their spirits. None of them knew how far the darkness reached. For all they knew it might have stretched only inches from the pub - or gone on for eternity. There was no way they could tell from staring into it. It was black and impenetrable to their gaze.

"There's only one way to tell," Sam said. "One of us is going to have to creep along that shaft and batter the end off with a hammer. Then, either the darkness will flood in, or there'll be the real world again."

"You make it sound so simple," Bob said. "But you do realise, don't you, that if the shaft doesn't reach safety and the darkness does coming flooding in, whoever's in there will be swallowed by it?"

"And be dissolved like poor old Jim Bartlet's face or Harold Sillitoe's arms," Tom said, unable to hide the horror in his voice as he said it.

"Thanks, Tom," Sam told him. "I was trying to forget that alternative."

"Well, one of us will have to try it, whatever the risks. Otherwise we've just wasted our time." Bob wiped his hands on his knees. He looked down at his stomach, which still loomed large despite their enforced diet. "Though I don't suppose I'll be able to volunteer. I might manage to squeeze down that shaft, but I don't think I'd be able to move my arms enough to use a hammer to force the end off."

"I think we'll need someone somewhat slimmer, I agree." Sam looked at the others, conscious that, even though he was youngest here, he was not much slimmer than Bob, and would have a problem in the tunnel too. "Well?" he asked. "Who is it going to be?"

There was a long moment of silence. The others knew the dangers involved, that whoever crawled along the shaft and knocked off the end would be risking his life.

"One of us'll have to do it," Arthur said. "Perhaps we should toss for it or pick a short straw or something like that."

The only ones slim enough to make it, Paddy, Arthur and Tom, exchanged glances.

Sam nipped behind the bar. He returned a minute later with a pack of playing cards.

"Lowest card wins - or loses, depending on your point of view," he said, shuffling the cards. "Aces low."

One by one, the three Grudgers reached for the cards and selected one.

"Looks like I'm the one," Arthur said, flatly as he gazed at the three of spades in his hands. Tom had the five of hearts and Paddy the king of clubs.

"Would you like to do best out of three?" Tom asked.
Arthur shook his head. "Only putting off the inevitable. It's got to be one of us. Anyway, if it doesn't work, perhaps I'm the lucky one, eh? At least I wouldn't have to starve to death. Or end up eating one of you lardy arsed buggers."

"When do you want to try it?" Sam asked.

"I doubt if I could sleep tonight knowing I was going to have to crawl along that friggin' tunnel in the morning, so I might as well do it now," Arthur said, his face deadpan. "What have I got to lose - apart from my nerve?"

"Here," Sam said to him. He went to the bar and handed him a large whisky. "Just to steady you a bit, eh?"

"Many thanks." Arthur smiled, thinly, and took a long swallow of the whisky. "Good stuff too, for once."

He looked at the galvanised tunnel, squared his shoulders, then stepped towards it. Sam handed him a heavy hammer. "A couple of hard bangs should be enough to snap the solder. If someone will help me, two of us will take a firm grip of this end of the shaft to make sure it doesn't slide forward."

"Take a bloody firm grip," Arthur said as he stooped and stretched his hands into the tunnel, then began gingerly to crawl on all fours along it. He could feel the cold metal beneath the palms of his hands. There was an intensity to the coldness which he supposed was because the blackness surrounding it was drawing out any heat into whatever voids of nothingness there were outside.

"Are you okay?" Sam called as the old man shifted his knees into the shaft.

"Feels cold but firm," Arthur told him; he looked back with difficulty over his shoulders. "Feels as if it's resting on something solid."

"Take care," Bob told him, as he crouched down to watch him crawl foot by foot down the shaft.

Sam gritted his teeth as he and Bob held onto the shaft to make sure it didn't move. Arthur moved only slowly, not daring to jar the shaft from their fingers, conscious at every move he made of the terrifying blackness surrounding him beyond the thin metal sheets. The shaft felt so fragile he half expected it to come apart every time he moved. Even though the shaft was only twelve feet long, it took him at least five minutes to inch his way to the end. Eventually, though, he was close enough to reach out and touch it.

He pulled the hammer from under his belt.

"Two sharp blows should snap off most of the solder," Sam called to remind him.

Arthur nodded, though he knew that if the shaft wasn't long enough, if the blackness extended even further than its end, it would rush in and kill him. The thought of it made the hair prickle along his arms and neck, while his stomach tightened with apprehension into a small, icy nugget of fear.

"Two sharp blows," Arthur muttered to himself beneath his breath as he manoeuvred the hammer so that he could grip it properly and swing it far enough back in the cramped space inside the shaft to hit the plate at the end.

"Hold onto the shaft for me," Arthur shouted to Sam and Bob. "I'm going to hit it now."

He closed his eyes, tightened his grip on the hammer, made a swift, uncharacteristically sincere prayer, then swung with as much force as he could muster.

There was a dull metallic thud.

Nothing.

He gritted his teeth and swung again. Even harder this time.

One corner of the aluminium sheet pinged free and a thin shaft of light shone through the gap.

For a second Arthur stared into it, a sick feeling in the pit of his stomach, till he realised he was looking at light, however dim, not darkness.

Light!

He could barely take his eyes away from it.

"What's wrong? What's the matter?" Sam called out to him, alarmed at his stillness.

Arthur took a deep breath as relief flooded through him.

"There's light," he shouted down the shaft. "Light!"

Buoyed up by the cheers of encouragement that broke out madly behind him, Arthur swung at the metal again with determination. A couple of good, strong blows and he'd have it off. Just a couple, that was all, he thought to himself. The first blow parted the sheet from one side, and the light grew brighter. He aimed a blow at the opposite edge. Just one, he thought. Just one more blow. Make it good and hard and he'd be out of here. Out of here for good.

Back inside the pub, Sam looked at Bob as he tightened his grip on the edge of the shaft before Arthur could strike his next blow. "Nearly there," he whispered. Bob grinned, then looked down the shaft as Arthur wriggled into position, before bringing the hammer down with a resounding, echoing thud against the metal.

A dim grey light shone down the shaft as the metal fell free. It was a cold light, almost shadowy in substance. Carefully,

Arthur crawled further along the shaft, till his head and shoulders were free of it. If he had expected to see any sign of the streets or houses that lay beyond the front of the pub, there was no sign of them now as he craned his neck to see as much as he could, though everything seemed to be little more than dimly seen differing shades of grey. There was an impression of vast stone walls somewhere in the distance and high above him, as if he was in an enormous cavern. He screwed up his eyes, wishing that he had brought his glasses with him when he came to the pub, but none of his friends had ever seen him wearing them - none of them even knew that his eyesight had worsened over recent years. Out there, though, he felt sure that something moved. Something large and dark.

"Are you okay, Arthur," he heard Sam call to him as he wriggled free of the shaft and crawled onto the hard, cold surface of the stone outside. He turned round and looked back down the shaft. "It seems okay here," he called back. "But I've no idea where I am. It's not Edgebottom."

"Not Edgebottom? But how do you know?" Sam asked.

Arthur saw his face disappear for a moment as Sam discussed things with the others. He reappeared again shortly. "Hold on to your end of the shaft," Sam told him. "We're coming through."

Arthur glanced around the darkness uncertainly. "I don't know whether it's all that safe," he told him. "I keep seeing something move in the distance. Something large. I've no idea what it is, though."

"But we can't just stay here," Sam insisted.

Arthur sighed. "Okay. I'll take a hold of the shaft."

The shaft stood out a few feet from a dark, glistening mass of blackness like that surrounding the pub. He would have called it a pool, but it rose in front of him up against the side of a wall of rock. He flinched as the shaft tugged his fingers; Sam had squeezed himself into the far end of it, his pale face almost filling it as he stared at Arthur.

"Take it slow," Arthur told him. "Don't risk damaging the

233

joins. They're not all that strong."

One by one the rest of them slowly made their way along the shaft, till all five of them eventually stood on the rough stone at the end of it. Bob shivered theatrically. "It's a damn sight colder here than in the pub," he grumbled.

"You can always go back if you like," Sam said.

"I'm not sure yet whether that wouldn't be a good idea," Bob retorted. "I thought this might lead outside the pub, but God knows where it is. It doesn't ring a bell with me. It's like nowhere round Edgebottom that I've ever seen."

"Nor me," Tom said, his voice quiet, as if he felt intimidated by the vastness of the gloomy depths around them. "Oh, my gawd," he mumbled.

The rest of them followed his gaze as he stared with a look of horror into the distance.

"What is it?" Arthur asked, though he felt sure that he knew. It was that thing - that large, dark shape he had seen move when he first climbed out of the shaft. He screwed his eyes in an effort to make out what it was. It was large in the distance. Immense. Too large to be real.

The rest of them saw the creature at once, though none could have even started to describe what they saw. It was impossible for them to fix it in their gaze, as if it did not even fully exist within reality, but partially slid between dimensions even as they stared up at it. It was a leviathan of Biblical size, perhaps octopoid, perhaps insectile, perhaps neither, or both, or many other forms of life simultaneously - or beyond all forms of life, something the like of which none of them had ever heard of or seen or imagined.

They felt fear deprive them of thought as they gazed up at it.

An impossibly long, thin tendril or limb reached towards them from the creature, dark, bristly, covered in rows upon rows of millions of tiny, moving suckers. Arthur shrank back against the rest of the men as it moved towards him. Sam pushed him to one side, then mindlessly scrabbled to get back as far as he could away from it. Panic infected them all as they ran about against the rock face in an effort to elude the nearing limb. Paddy was the first to scream. It was a pitifully pathetic, terror-filled scream of gut-wrenching horror. The rest of them were halted for an instant as the tiny suckers transfixed themselves to Paddy's face. His arms and legs flailed in helpless agony as he tried to tear himself free, as his face seemed to be drawn into all the suckers simultaneously, followed by the rest of his head, then shoulders. Sam felt sickened as blood erupted from all the tears that were ripped about the old man's body as it was wrenched apart into the hundreds of suckers consuming him. Sam grabbed at one of Paddy's arms, though he knew he was too late to save him. He tugged at the arm, but there was no give. The immense tendril that was drawing him violently into it was far too strong for his efforts to have any effect upon it.

More of the tendrils or octopoid limbs were emerging from the distant creature. Sam saw Tom trip as one of them soared down at him, attaching itself to his back. His screams rose in a terrible falsetto.

Bob made a bolt for the ventilation shaft to get back to the pub. But the old man was too fat and too slow to make it in time, and another tendril grasped him with its carnivorous suckers.

Was this why they had been trapped in the pub? Sam wondered. Had all this been part of some terrible plan, created by that bastard Durer?

Sam pushed Bob's writhing body to one side, then dived down the shaft. The brighter light of the pub was ahead of him, and he moved with reckless speed down the shaft towards it, conscious of the possibility that one of the tendrils and its deadly suckers might only be inches away behind him.

He slithered out of the end into the pub, scrabbling at the ground to tug himself as fast as he could from the shaft. The metallic structure was moving behind him, and he knew that something else was inside it. A scream was stuck in the back of his throat as he stared at the exit, his fists clenched in a useless

235

gesture of defence, when Arthur thrust himself out of the shaft.

"Help me!" the old man shouted. And Sam saw the thick tip of the tendril that had attached itself to one of his feet emerge from the shaft as Arthur crawled across the floor into the pub. Blood burst from his leg as the suckers commenced their terrible, relentless, irresistible work on him, consuming him even as he struggled to get as far as he could from the shaft. "HELP ME!"

Sam pushed himself to his feet and ran behind the bar into the kitchen. He tugged out the cutlery drawer by the sink. Then ran back into the pub, a carving knife clenched in one fist.

Without hesitation he hacked at the tendril, but the thing was so tough it was like trying to cut through seasoned mahogany. Sharp though the blade was, it barely scratched the surface of the tendril.

"Sam!" Arthur screamed at him, the foot and ankle of his left leg a ruin. "Do something, for Christ's sake!"

Sam threw the knife to one side.

"What can I do?" he asked him, agitated and frightened. He kicked at the end of the shaft, then on an impulse he reached down and tugged it. He felt it come free as he pulled the far end that was still in the cavern back into the darkness. The tendril, still trapped inside it, disappeared in an instant as darkness filled it. The rest of the tendril flopped onto the floor, falling away from Arthur's ruptured foot, its severed end oozing thick black fluids that hissed and bubbled on the floor of the pub.

Sam dragged Arthur away from the tendril and up onto a chair near the bar. He wrapped a towel round his injured foot. The old man moaned, but he was still conscious.

"What's happening to us, Sam?" the old man asked.

"I don't know for sure," Sam said. "But I intend to find out." He looked towards the stairs.

"What're you going to do?"

"Something I should have thought of days ago," Sam muttered.

Clenching his fists, Sam strode up the stairs till he stood in the doorway to Albert Durer's bedroom. He stared in at the painted pentacle and circle and the dead rat nailed in the centre of them. He stepped into the pentacle and kicked the stiffened carcass from the nails pinning it to the floorboards. He then kicked at the painted lines and curves and obscure symbols, scuffing them with the hard leather soles of his boots. He went out into the upstairs kitchen and found a knife. Back in Durer's bedroom he set to work scraping and slicing as much as he could of the pentacle away. Then he went to the sash window, pulled back its curtains and pushed up the bottom of the window frame. Outside, the ominous, threatening blackness loomed before him. He reached for the book on the dresser. For a second he looked down at its stained, old pages, with their obscure, thickly printed lines of writing and strange drawings. Then he raised the book and threw it with as much force as he could muster out into the darkness.

He sank to his knees. There was nothing else he could think of to do. After this, all there was left was to return to the bar and give what help he could to Arthur. A feeling of helplessness seeped through him as he raised his head and looked at the window - through which the first rays of dawn were starting to emerge from above the dark grey roofs to the east.

No one amongst all the scores of police and local and regional government officials who had gathered about the outside of the pub over the last few days was able to give Sam any reason for the 'Strange Anomaly' (as they termed it) that had isolated the Potter's Wheel from the rest of the normal world. Nevertheless, it was only a matter of minutes before Arthur was whisked away in an ambulance to the nearest hospital to have his injuries treated, while Sam showed a small group of the most senior investigators about the pub.

In the months that followed the reality of what happened became blurred through layers of 'official' explanations, denials, claims that the whole thing was some kind of hoax, and an inability of the two survivors from inside the pub to grasp just what had happened to them, as it began to seem, as they looked back on it, as a strange kind of dream or nightmare or, as some experts suggested to them, mass hallucination.

Of his late lodger, Albert Durer, Sam never heard anything more. The odd man appeared to have disappeared completely as if he had never existed. That he had almost certainly used a false name was soon pointed out, when someone mentioned that he must have taken it from the German painter Albrecht Durer, dead for over four hundred years.

"He'd wish he'd been dead that long too if I ever get my hands on him," Sam would mutter to himself when well in his cups. But he knew there was little chance of that. If he was still alive, 'Durer' would be well away from here by now, his mischief done. Though whether he would do what he'd tried to do in the Potter's Wheel elsewhere... Sam shuddered at the thought. Especially when Arthur hobbled into the pub at night for enough drinks to help him sleep. Then the two of them would talk into the early hours of the morning of those terrible events and marvel that even two of them had survived.

LAST CHRISTMAS
(I GAVE YOU MY LIFE)

Franklin Marsh

Kate drove into the empty car park, brought the Astra to a halt and slumped over the steering wheel. Fear, elation, disgust, horror and a wonderful sense of freedom chased each other around her nervous system. She leaned back, exhaled slowly and began to think about what she had done. There was no turning back. All bridges had been burned. Sighing, she leaned over to the back seat and grasped the handles of the cheap holdall, containing the cheap clothes.

Kate stepped out of the car, and surveyed the building in front of her. The Bide-A-Wee Guest House. They'd got to be kidding. She smiled to herself and started walking towards the front door. A noise distracted her. A soothing, calming sound. She quickly crossed the road and looked at the broad, slow-moving river. A sense of peace flowed into her. It would be easy.... No. She retraced her steps and entered the Guest House.

A dimly lit foyer containing an unmanned reception desk. Kate walked in, and prepared to ring the old-fashioned bell. Her hand was still a few inches above it when a sour-faced woman entered the foyer through a door behind the desk. She was tall, thin and her eyes looked Kate up and down with something approaching contempt. An uneasy silence fell. Kate felt compelled to break it, and got as far as opening her mouth when a figure pirouetted around the woman.

"Hell-O, Hell-O, Hell-O-Oh!" trilled a rotund little man with a bad comb-over, ruddy cheeks and tiny glasses perched on his fat nose.

"Welcome to Bide-A-Wee! I'm Mr Pottinger. Please call me Henry. This," he gestured at the tall, silent woman, "Is Mrs Pottinger. What brings you all the way out here on Christmas Eve?"

Kate was a little taken aback by the contrast between the Pottingers. She managed a smile.

"I'm... er... on my way to family for Christmas. I'm not expected until tomorrow. I'd like to stay here tonight, and continue my journey tomorrow. Do you have a vacant room, please."

"Of course, of course," beamed the little man. He fished a register out from under the desk, flipped it open at a new page and pushed it toward Kate. "Twelve pounds a night. In advance." He sounded almost apologetic.

Here goes, thought Kate. This is the beginning of the rest of your life. Goodbye, Kate Dyas. She signed the register Mrs H Robinson, and added a false address. She'd toyed with the idea of using a pun or a famous address but decided a non-existent one would suffice. She then opened her handbag and dug out a ten-pound note and two pound coins.

"Thank you." The money disappeared into Mr Pottinger's pocket. He unhooked a key from the rack behind him. "And now I'll show you to your room."

"Oh, that's OK, Mr Pott... er... Henry." She glanced at Mrs Pottinger, who appeared to be made of stone. "Please don't trouble yourself. Just give me directions, and I'm sure I'll find it." She bent and retrieved her holdall.

"Oh... very well." The disappointment sounded in Pottinger's voice, and showed in his face. "It's first on your left. Second floor."

"Thanks," said Kate. She marched toward the stairs.

"Mrs Robinson?"

She turned to see Henry Pottinger, hands clasped together, smiling.

"I'm afraid we can't offer you a meal tonight, but we're having a little get-together with our other guests. There will be food and drink there."

He gestured vaguely at a door further down the lobby. "In the dining room. At nine o'clock. Please say you'll come." A note of pleading in his voice. Was Mrs Pottinger attempting to

240

smile? Although her expression hadn't changed noticeably, it seemed less forbidding. One of her eyebrows was higher than the other.

Kate paused, one foot on the bottom stair.

"I'll see, Henry." She offered. "I'm very tired with all this travelling, but I'm sure I could pop down for a short while."

"Oh, marvellous!" squealed Mr Pottinger, clapping his chubby little hands together. "'Till nine then! See you!"

Mrs Pottinger turned without a word and disappeared through the door behind the desk, followed swiftly by a waving Henry.

Kate hurried up the stairs. Great! A Christmas party with those two crazy old coots. What a way to start a new life. They'd certainly made an effort in the foyer of the Guest House. There wasn't even a piece of tinsel.

She unlocked the door of room 7 and walked in. As she sat on the bed and looked around the dingy little room, realisation caught up with her and the sobs started. She fished out her mobile phone and turned it on. 13 missed calls. 13 messages. She selected Gerald's home number. Her... their old number. It was picked up before the first ring finished.

"Kate! Kate! Is that you?"

"Gerald? I…"

"Where the Hell are you? Where are the boys? What do you think you're doing?"

"Gerald, listen…"

"What are you playing at, Kate? Mother's here. We've been going frantic. There's so much to do…"

The concern had turned to anger. She pressed the button with the little red telephone and laid back on the bed. Mother was there. Well, he was alright then… the boys? His little darlings. Do anything for them, he would. And nothing for her.

She hurled the mobile against the wall. It bounced across the room, slid along the dressing table and dropped into the waste-paper basket. Kate had to laugh - you couldn't do that again if you tried.

She closed her eyes.

Her eyes opened and she looked at the fly-specked ceiling. The urgent rapping at the door came again.

"Mrs Robinson!"

Who…?

Kate sat up and everything became clear. Had she really….?

"Mrs Robinson? Are you alright?"

"I'm fine."

"Henry Pottinger here. It's gone nine, you know."

The party. Oh well, let's get it over with.

She swung her feet off the bed and stood up.

"I'll be down in a minute, Mr.Po... Henry."

"Look forward to seeing you!"

She glanced at her reflection in the dressing table mirror. She hadn't even changed her hair! Some secret agent you'd make. After all, she was now a fugitive….

Kate walked downstairs and headed for the dining room. Strange, all she could hear was a buzz of static. No polite murmuring. Don't say she was the first... no, there were quite a few people scattered around the room. All seated and quiet. She barely glanced at them as she made for the serving hatch that apparently was the bar. Pottinger was there fiddling with a radio. Music suddenly blared out. Wizzard. What a surprise! It was Christmas.

"Ah! There we are! This'll make the party go with a swing!" crowed Pottinger.

Fat chance thought Kate.

"Mrs. Robinson! Good of you to come. What can I get you?"

"A vodka and lime please."

"Of course!"

The old rogue poured a hefty slug of vodka into a chunky glass and added a dash of lime.

"There we go."

"Thank you."

"Compliments of the season." Pottinger raised a glass of

beer.

"Cheers."

Mrs Pottinger swept through the doorway from the kitchen, seemingly wreathed in smoke. She put down large plates of sausage rolls and vol-au-vents, then returned to the kitchen.

Kate swigged the vodka. Crikey! She'd get plastered at this rate. A surreptitious glance around the room at her silent, miserable fellow guests. An old man. An old woman. A young, studenty type of boy. The rest huddled at the end of the room in an amorphous mass. Drink up and get out, Kate, she thought. Phew! It's hot in here. And old ma Pottinger must have burnt something. It stinks. Another drink. God, it's hot. She ran a finger around the collar of her T-shirt. It's getting uncomfortable. Smell of smoke. What's the old witch doing in there?

An old classic came on the radio, much to Pottinger's delight.

'Dashing through the snow,

In a one-horse open sleigh...'

Kate drank again. And saw Pottinger humming away, studying her.

'A day or two ago,

I thought I'd take a ride...'

No, it was too much. She had to get out. She turned as Mrs Pottinger re-entered the room. Smoke was streaming from her. In fact, it was all around the room. Her eyes stung. Was nobody else affected? She looked at the silent guests. And saw the ropes around their wrists. The plasters over their mouths. Their eyes on her, beseeching. Mrs Pottinger's hair and clothes were blazing merrily. She smiled (yes, smiled!) at Kate. Pottinger's glasses shattered and his eyes melted. He advanced towards the terrified woman, face blackening, strips of flesh peeling away, crooning, "'Jingle Bells... Jingle Bells... Jingle All The Way... Oh What FUN...'"

Kate turned for the door. The paint was blistering, the wood cracking.

Heat. Smoke. Pottinger's blackened, smouldering hand on her shoulder....

The police motor-bike turned into the cracked, weed-strewn former car park and halted beside the Astra. The helmeted figure walked around it then plucked the radio from the bike, pushing the helmet back. "Sarge? Dawes. The Doob was right - it's here. Over"

"He knows, you know. Can you hang on 'till he gets there, Stace? Then you're free to go. Over."

"Will do. Over. And Out"

WPC Stacey Dawes looked at the car again. How did The Doob know these things? That's why he was a Detective Inspector, she supposed.

Ten minutes later, a Jag pulled into the car park, and pulled up beside the motor-bike. A middle-aged, bewildered looking man in a dark overcoat climbed out. He clamped a trilby on his head and produced a pipe from an overcoat pocket. Stacey grinned. So this was The Doob. DI Malcolm 'Jock' Doobie.

The man held out a hand, and they shook.

"WPC Dawes? Good work."

"You knew it would be here, Sir."

"Yeeessss." Doobie scratched the back of his neck with the pipe stem then fumbled for his tobacco. "They're always here, Dawes. Always at this time of year..."

He looked as though some thought had suddenly struck him.

"Good heavens! It's Christmas day, isn't it?"

"Yes Sir."

Doobie looked at Dawes. "It always happens this time of year." He waved his pipe at the river. "It'll go down as a suicide. But they'll never find her." He thought about it. "We'll never find her."

A pause whilst he filled his pipe and got it going, then he strolled towards the flat, black expanse of land adjacent to the car park.

"You familiar with this area, Dawes?"

"No sir. It's a bit off my beat. I'm covering as it's a holiday."

"Yes. Of course." The DI seemed deep in thought. He strolled back towards Stacey.

"You know, there used to be a Guest House there. The Bide-A-Wee." A snort that could have been a laugh. "Burned down twenty... two... or three... How old are you?"

"Nineteen, Sir."

"Good Lord, before your time then." Another pause as Doobie turned back to look at where the Guest House had been. "Seventeen people died in that fire. The two proprietors and fifteen guests. You know, it was a funny thing..."

A pause to allow for some pipe sucking. The odour of his tobacco reached her.

"...we received no calls about missing relatives. Couldn't find any ID - for anyone. Took a while, and a lot of work, to find out anything about anybody in that fire..."

Another long pause. Stacey watched a crow alight on the fence surrounding the car park. She noticed how quiet it was out here. Apart from the gentle trickling noise from the river.

"First one we learned about was... Hjalmar Dvornik. A Czech, or a Yugo, or something. Turned out he was a war criminal. Worked in a concentration camp. The Jews, old Simon Wiesenthal, had a file on him. One of their youngsters had gone to confront him. He lived out in the back of beyond. We traced Dvornik's address and found the poor lad lying on his doorstep. Shot through the head."

Doobie was gazing at the land next to the car park with a mild expression, but his voice was gaining in intensity.

"Then there was Andrew Scott. Poor old Andrew. We didn't look forward to contacting his parents. No one had seen them for a couple of days. Eventually we broke in. There they were. Dead at the dinner table. Andy had cooked them Christmas dinner. With Paraquat. He had the decency to leave a note though. Seems his parents thought his University results weren't good enough. Seems they thought everything about Andy wasn't good enough. He took it until Christmas." Doobie

245

puffed on his pipe. "Always Christmas. Annie Coombes. Eighty if she was a day. What was she doing out here on her own at Christmas? At her age? We tracked down her husband, Bertie. He was eighty-two. They'd been married for sixty years. He wouldn't answer the door. We broke in. He was in bed. Smothered with a pillow. He'd had Alzheimer's for years. The neighbours told us. Annie was a saint, they said. What she'd had to put up with from old Bertie. And she never complained. Their kids were on a Caribbean cruise."

Stacey wondered if there was a point to this. Doobie was on a roll.

"The people who ran the guest house. Called themselves Pottinger - at the time. Seems they'd had a variety of names over the years. Acted as carers for the elderly. Who didn't last long in the Pottingers' care. It was only a matter of time..." He broke off, seemingly in disgust.

Stacey was aware of him looking intently at her. "It hasn't ended yet, WPC Dawes. You see, people come here. They leave their cars in this car park and disappear. We mark the cases as possible suicides because of the proximity of the river. Two years after the fire, on Boxing Day, we found an old Ford Zephyr here. Belonged to David Hirst. He was an armed robber. Killed a number of people in furtherance of theft. Sub-Postmasters mainly. Two year after that it was a little Mini Cooper. Owned by an Army Corporal. Suspected of bullying one of his troopers to death."

Stacey glanced at the Astra. "What about this one?"

Doobie sighed. "We're looking for Mrs Kate Dyas. She left home with her two sons yesterday. We found the boys not far from here. In Farley Woods. Both strangled."

WPC Dawes yawned.

"What time are you off duty Dawes?"

Stacey glanced at her watch. "About ten minutes ago, Sir."

Doobie stared at her stone-faced. "Cut along Dawes. No reason why we should both waste Christmas Day."

"Thanks Sir."

Last Christmas (I Gave You My Life)

Dawes straddled the motor-bike and glided towards the road. She glanced back. Doobie was once again gazing at where the guest house had been. Silly old sod. Living in the past. If he was the best, no wonder their clean up rate was so poor. A few drifting white flakes showed up against his dark coat.

She looked to the future as she gunned the bike, and roared out onto the road. Her mum-in-law's Christmas dinner - and the present from her darling Neil. She couldn't wait to plug it in to her computer and start loading up her music.

"SHALT THOU KNOW MY NAME?"

Daniel McGachey

As a collector of folklore and accounts of legend and superstition, my old friend, Dr. Lawrence, has always made it his duty to seek out the unusual and arcane, and for him such a find is generally cause for celebration. What is by and large less pleasing, indeed, often uncomfortably alarming, he once told me, is when the unusual and arcane seems actively to seek him. Lately, even his own rooms at the college have apparently provided no safe haven.

He had barely begun to make an in-depth study of a most interesting text, accompanied only by the reassuring crackle of the fire in the hearth and the soft whisper of the pages as they turned, when his musings were rudely disturbed by an insistent clamour.

Over the loud and frantic knocking on the study door, Lawrence heard a familiar shrill voice raised to an unfamiliar level. "Lawrence! Are you in? Open up if you're there, man!"

He laid aside his reading matter with a rueful sigh of, "So much for Night 37. How I'm ever to get through all 1,001 at this rate..." But he got no further with the thought when the pounding at his chamber door grew louder and the voice on the other side grew yet shriller, causing him to hasten his steps across the room in order to silence this commotion before it roused every fellow who lodged along the same corridor.

"Lawrence? Dr. Lawrence!"

Lawrence turned the key with a mutter of, "Hold on there, would you? I'm coming as fast as I can," though he had no very real desire to face the owner of that strident voice.

"Lawrence, thank providence!" cried his visitor when my friend finally did open the door and the look of relief that flooded his face may have softened Lawrence's response just a little from the retort he had been formulating.

"Dower! Are you trying to knock a hole through my study

door? I have quite enough ventilation as it is."

Mr. Dower, for that was indeed the name this caller rejoiced in, looked at Lawrence and past him and all around himself in quick succession, while demanding, "Are you free to talk? You are alone, aren't you?"

"Well," Lawrence began, rather taken aback, since in all the years he had known Dower he could never once recollect hearing of him making a social call. In fact, from the description he gave me, social is not a word anyone could ever equate with this man, Dower. "Well, I suppose…"

"You suppose?" Dower practically spat the words; his eyes narrowing with a look Lawrence could only ascribe to suspicion. "You are either alone or not!"

"I was," Lawrence replied icily, before realising that bickering in the corridor would only prolong this encounter, not hasten it to a conclusion. With an inward sigh, he pushed the door wider and stepped back, saying, "Do come in, Dower. It is, as always, a pleasure."

"What?" exclaimed Dower, the barely disguised sarcasm obviously registering even in his agitated state. His tone softened as he entered the study, though he paced so furiously, Lawrence feared he would wear a threadbare patch in a rather attractively decorative rug of Eastern origin that he had won in a wager with a particularly eccentric baronet. "Oh, I am sorry, Lawrence. You must think me mad to make such a fuss in your own study."

"Mad? Not at all," Lawrence replied, closing the door and allowing himself the whispered addition of, "insufferably rude, most definitely!"

In that instant the softened tone was gone and Dower cried, "Are you talking to someone? Is there some other here?"

Lawrence had already made for the brandy and he offered Dower a glass, while surreptitiously doubling the size of his own measure, should the remainder of this visit prove as trying as its opening moments. "I was simply asking if you would care for a drink…" Dower accepted eagerly, draining the glass

249

in a single gulp. "...which you obviously would. A top up?"

This too was accepted with alacrity, though Dower had never been known to be a drinking man. Indeed his attitudes toward partakers and his strict temperance were the subjects of several cruel, though not entirely inaccurate jibes in those bars frequented by the college men. "Thank you," the visitor croaked, his face blooming with the warmth of the drink. "I needed that, I truly did. And, again, my apologies for bursting in and for burdening you."

"Really," Lawrence said, taking a sip from his own glass, "you haven't burdened me."

Dower fastened him with a serious gaze, saying, "No, but I am about to."

"Oh," said Lawrence, suddenly thirsty, "perhaps I'll have a top up myself."

Dower stopped pacing for just a moment, declaring, "I would recommend it. I cannot imagine what I have to tell you will not affect your nerves."

Dr. Lawrence shuddered, despite the fire's warmth. "Has it grown colder in here? Oh, no, I see, Dower! This is some joke. A prank to raise the hairs on the back of my neck with some spookery. Well, I warn you, I'm rather hard to impress in that respect, given the superstitions in which I'm daily immersed." He waved airily at the shelves that took up most of the wall space; each one crammed with tomes and tales from times and cultures both near and distant.

Dower nodded, with barely a glance toward the books. "Indeed, this is why I come to you."

"Very well," said Lawrence, seating himself and indicating that his guest also should take a chair before the fire, if only to spare his rug from further wear. "The fire is lit and the brandy is pleasant. Let's have your ghost story, then. It'll serve as an amusement."

Dower sat, and the expression on his face, the shadows cast by the flickering of the flames and the low tone of his voice combined to eerie effect, well suited to the telling of ghostly tales. "There is a ghost involved, yes, or a daemon or whatever you may call it. But, answer me this, Lawrence, when have you ever known me to joke about anything?"

The eye that regarded my friend as this question was posed, was one in which he had never yet seen a trace of humour. "You have a point. Make yourself comfortable and begin, then." Lawrence stood, eager to break from his visitor's gaze. "I'll fetch the brandy closer... and maybe I'll just turn up the lighting a little."

As he sat once more, glass refilled, Lawrence found that the hiss of the gas and the crackling fire made for a warm and convivial atmosphere, though it was not a feeling that would last as Dower's tale progressed. Yet, for the moment he sat back and made himself as comfortable as possible as his guest began his preliminaries.

"Now, I know full well my reputation. 'Dour Mr. Dower' is the usual remark, and I admit that I have never been one for levity. Personally, I do not regard a soberness of spirit as any flaw, but I am evidently in a minority on that count. I never have been popular company and have never sought to be. This goes back as far as my boarding school days and continued throughout university life."

Perhaps Lawrence's expression betrayed the fact that none of this was news to him, for Dower nodded and said, "What I have just admitted does have bearing. But, I shall begin by telling how I found myself on a working visit to Seachester."

*

Seachester is a picturesque coastal town, if somewhat untroubled by modern conveniences such as flat roads, adequate transport or comfortable hotels. I had taken myself there for the purpose of seeing what might be found amongst trunk loads of antique volumes deposited with the local museum following the death, at 102 years of age, of the last member of a very old and long established family of

251

landowners.

Even as I describe the place, I still seem to smell the salt in the air and to hear the waves and the cries of the gulls. But, as I do not propose to reminisce about the town itself, I must let these sensations fade, to be replaced by the musty smell of too many old things gathered in one space. The waves are drowned out by the scratch of my pen's nib on paper and the dull, echoing tick of the museum clock. To me, such sounds are the sweetest music as they are the sounds of my diligent toil. Typically, though, it was not long before a voice broke in upon my quiet work.

"How are you getting along, Mr. Dower?" The speaker of these words, the curator of the museum, stood grinning expectantly, rubbing his hands together and bending altogether too close to my ear.

"Slowly, Mr. Burnstow," I replied, adding pointedly, "and I am not aided by your solicitous interruptions."

The intention of this remark was seemingly lost on the fellow, as was the faint but distinctive jangling of the entrance bell to the small building which housed Seachester's only museum. Instead his grin widened even more as he looked at the piles and packets of papers I was attempting to sort through. "Old Squire Hesketh was never the tidiest of men, which can't make the work much easier." Thankfully, before he could continue stating this blindingly obvious piece of observation, there was an impatient ringing on the desk bell and with a cheery, "Oh, excuse me, sir. I'm wanted at the desk," he shuffled off in search of a fresh victim on whom to inflict his presence. My work was frequently hindered by the ever-present Burnstow, so I was not in the least sorry to lose his company. But, mere moments later, I encountered a yet bigger disturbance.

The museum was a quiet building, quieter than most as, apart from Burnstow; I had not yet encountered another soul within its precincts in those few days in which I had been based there. This, I imagine, was why Burnstow was forever interrupting my work, though I imagine Mr. Burnstow's interjections may also have been the reason behind the lack of customers in the first place. But the point I make is that the building was quiet, thus the voice that issued from beyond the bookcases that obscured my view of the main desk seemed unnaturally loud and garrulous and my every attempt to ignore it was in vain.

"You see, my dear fellow," this newcomer was declaring, "my job is much akin to the life of the crow. One pecks and pecks at the dirt around oneself until, voila, one finds the worm. And I feel there are worms aplenty to be found here, worms grown fat and ripe after being buried away in the dark for so long!"

This nonsense continued until I could only declare the situation as intolerable.

"As I said, sir," Burnstow wheedled, "I'm afraid someone is already examining the Hesketh archive at the moment."

"Well, I'm sure if I just have a word with him," began the overconfident reply, raising my hackles yet further. I could already picture the owner of this voice; brash, arrogant, smug. I knew the type only too well.

Burnstow sounded anxious. "Mr. Dower isn't keen on being disturbed." I could not help but marvel that the curator was incapable of heeding his own advice.

There was a brief pause. Then, "Dower? Well, well, speaking of worms... Perhaps I'll just take a stroll round your fine museum."

It was more than I could bear. What was this din? I sought out the curator to have words with him.

"I do beg your pardon, sir. It was a gentleman... not that I'm suggesting you aren't a gentleman, of course, sir. Enquiring after the Hesketh papers. I'm afraid his manner rather overwhelmed me. A very cheery sort."

"Good cheer seems to breed noise," I observed.

Burnstow's brow furrowed as a thought surfaced. "He knew you, sir. When I mentioned your name, it struck me he recognised it."

"He knew me? And did you get his name?"

The curator shuffled toward his desk, muttering, "He left his card. Was most insistent that I take it. Here we are. Well, well, it's not often we get two learned gentlemen visiting our little museum."

He brandished the card triumphantly and my heart sank as I read the name printed on it in a florid font, *Edgar Bright Esquire.*

*

It was here Lawrence interrupted Dower's account, "Bright? Wasn't he the fellow they found...?" A grim memory took shape. "Of course. Seachester! I knew I'd encountered that name recently. That was a gruesome business. My dear chap, I should have realised you'd know Bright, really. You were both schooled at Rhodes House, weren't you?"

Lawrence remembered well the exuberant fellow and his flamboyant ways. He scarcely struck him as the type of associate Dower would relish. "I only crossed swords with him once. Literally. It was a heated debate at mediaevalist society function, over an infamous duel. The only way to settle the matter was to re-enact it with a rolled up newspaper and a five iron. In fun, of course. But I proved my point and he accepted my interpretation of the historic event."

Dower laughed. It was a noise Lawrence had not heard him make before and it was not a pleasant one. "Accepted it? Yes, I imagine he would. He was always very good at accepting the theories and notions of others. And not always when they were offered."

It took only seconds for the implication of Dower's words to settle in. "Are you suggesting plagiarism?"

"I am not suggesting any such thing," his guest replied angrily. "I am stating it as a fact! I loathed the man and finding that he was on the same mission as I filled me with fury."

"Mr. Dower, are you quite well, sir? You've grown very pale." There was concern in Burnstow's voice, even if that foolish grin of his seemed never to be far from his lips.

My own voice, if it even came, was lost to me, as I was aware only of footsteps approaching from one of the small side chambers and an all too familiar and hateful voice that crowed, "No need to worry, old fellow. You run along now. Probably just the shock of running into an old friend. Am I right, Dower? Surely you haven't forgotten your chum, Eddie Bright?"

I did not turn to acknowledge this most unwelcome arrival, and instead concentrated on watching the reluctant curator slowly wander away with the vague pretence of putting some books on a few shelves.

"Dower?"

"I haven't forgotten," I replied coldly, turning now to face him. "How are you, Bright?" It was a ridiculous question, as I could judge from his expensive clothing and his easy grin that he was doing undeservedly well for himself.

"Splendid," he confirmed. "I have a new book shortly to be published."

My reply was instant. "Really? Who's it by?"

For a few brief seconds the smile faltered around his lips in a most satisfying manner and his eyes darted to Burnstow at his shelves. Then, with a laugh he clapped my shoulder. "Touché, Dower! And you? We haven't heard much of you in the academic journals. Still grubbing away, I see. I should have known you'd get here first. You always were an eager little chap."

"I am rather busy, Bright," was my lame response and I turned to walk away.

Bright, never one to take a hint, continued in his well remembered arrogant tone, "Eager but dry as a stick. Don't you ever relax? What say we have a chat about old times? I saw a most inviting looking public house across the square."

I spun round sharply, fighting to stop my voice from rising to a shout. "No! Thank you, no. I really do not think we have anything to 'chat' about, do you? You and I do not have any old times that bear discussion."

Bright attempted an appeasing smile, "Oh, now, surely—"

But I cut him off with a quiet threat of, "Unless you would have me talk loudly enough that anyone might overhear, of how you once sought my company and declared friendship..."

"I was merely being companionable to a fellow student," said he, defensively.

"You lured me from my studies and urged me to..."

"To live a little," he insisted. "You were young. You shouldn't have been closeted away with nothing but dusty books for companionship."

I glared at him, unhappy memories washing over me. "Live a little? Yes. That was the phrase you used. 'Try this.' 'Try that.' 'Live a little.' 'Just one more glass.' 'Just another tankard.' Oh, yes. Under your guidance I lived a little." I was no longer concerned with keeping my voice hushed. "You plied me with drink till I was insensible, then watched over me as I thought I would surely die."

"I watched as a caring friend would," he said, affecting a wounded nobility. "I fetched you water and broth and mopped your brow."

"And kept me bed-bound while you had the run of my rooms and access to my work. My work! My thesis paper, with the deadline mere days away. And, while I sweated and shivered, you were hard at work, copying it all down. While I was still weak and poisoned by excess, you submitted your own version of my paper."

Bright sounded dismissive as he said, "Dower, we had enough of your fantasies at the time," but there was a glimmer of worry in his eyes as he glanced toward Burnstow.

I would not be silenced, though. "Was it a fantasy that I submitted the results of months of research and was accused of cheating? Oh, you may have couched your facsimile in more elaborate and fanciful terms yet the work was mine and I was the one accused of stealing it!"

"I spoke up for you, didn't I?" he replied hotly.

"And had the board of the college convinced I was an inveterate drunkard who was scarcely able to control his own actions as he cheated and stole."

By this point, Mr. Burnstow had looked across, with a plea of, "Gentlemen, please! Think of the other visitors... if we had any other visitors..."

Bright, aware now of our approaching audience replied breezily, "You're entirely mistaken, my dear Dower," before adding; under his breath before the curator could draw closer, "And, even if you weren't, there is nothing you can do to prove the claim. So, were I you, I'd just keep quiet about it."

"I cannot prove it, true," I responded, equally quietly, "but can you disprove it? If that curator you are working so hard to charm was to suspect what I know, how would that affect your dabblings here?"

For the first time, I saw Edgar Bright admit to defeat, as he sighed, "I would ask you not to joke about it, but I see there has been absolutely no change in your humour over the years. What would you wish?"

"That you find whatever flimsy and facile treasures you need and give me and my studies a wide berth."

He nodded, placing his hat on his head and moving toward the door. "So be it. I'll bid you good day, Dower."

I waited until he was at the door before responding, "Goodbye, Bright."

As I have already said, and as most who have met me already know, I'm a far from jocular person. Yet to finally see Bright's unbearable confidence falter and the smugness slip from his face made me almost dance with joy. Indeed, it put me in such good humour that, when I returned to my work, I leafed merrily through the mouldering papers and laughed with uncontrollable mirth when I found one that I would ordinarily

257

have discarded as some piece of local superstition.

Yet, on this day, this paper put me in mind of a joke I might play, should Bright make his presence too closely felt.

Yes, you may very well be surprised. Can this really be dour Mr. Dower playing a joke? I admit that my mood must have been unusually heightened. Yet, as you must surely see, the joke has worn off.

It was hardly an amusing jest to begin with and the outcome was far from comical. For it was this joke that led to Edgar Bright's violent and unnatural death!

Please. I know the questions that must be forming already but I beg of you, let me tell the tale in my own way in my own time. I can only apologise if I occasionally slip ahead of myself or if the chronology of the events becomes distorted. Or, indeed, if my account seems to stray into realms normally reserved for lurid fiction. But, as you will discover as the tale progresses, the stress I am now under makes it sometimes hard to keep a clear mind.

As you are surely only too aware, if anything is more of a hindrance to a historian than a lack of recorded evidence, it may just be an overabundance of documents, papers, dockets, inventories and receipts, all of which require sifting and sorting and assessing. And, clearly the last of the Hesketh line had hoarded papers like a miser hoards gold.

I found this particular document by chance, as I was attempting to make order out of the chaos of papers that had been thrown carelessly into one of the old trunks. The entire mass had been heaped and crammed in, not with thought of preservation, it now seems, but more with the intention of concealment or confinement.

I had scarcely noticed the page as it was hidden between the folds of an old newspaper, and was in such poor shape that it was practically in the waste-paper basket before I realised there was writing on it.

It was a leaf torn from a book of prayers from the middle years of the century before last. I had seen many like it before, naturally. But it was what was written on the other side of the page that caught my eye. In a spidery, untidy hand... yes, spidery, that is entirely the apt term... Well, in this disorderly hand, the marks near faded and invisible in places, I shall tell you what I read.

'Some shall call me wicked for writing these words in a book of prayers,' it began, *'but, I, Meriel Pearson Hesketh, in the hours approaching my death, have no use for books and no recourse to prayers. I have been given the book, they say, that I might repent my sins as the judgement approaches, but I shall not be hung in their noose nor locked in their madhouse, and these are surely the only fates that may await me. In my grandmother's day, it would have been fire or ducking in the pond that must follow. Perhaps it is best that I leave only a son and no daughter and that I am last of my female line.*

'For the crime I am charged with and the crime of which I am guilty is one that goes against all laws of man and church. I, Meriel Pearson Hesketh, like my mother before me and her mother and all the mother's mothers in my line, am guilty of witchcraft.'

Meriel Pearson? The name seemed faintly familiar to me, but the details were vague. Had I fleetingly encountered that name as I trailed through these endless papers? I rifled through them frantically, the urge to know more growing strong inside me. Then I had it!

'The trial against Mrs Meriel Hesketh, formerly Pearson, continues on this day, with much that is unusual and uncanny being spoken of.'

The local news sheet, little more than a few loosely bundled pages, dated Seventeen Hundred and Fifty Four. And surely I had spied some bound transcripts.

A confession of witchcraft and a trial. More a tale for our celebrated Dr. Lawrence, with his myths and mysteries, which is why I bring the tale to you now. I wasn't remotely interested in this type of matter. Normally, at any rate. Normally I'd have dismissed it. Give me facts, not fables. But something in the tone struck me as ominous and strange. The gaps in the tale filled me with curiosity and, if there was more to be learned, I wished to know it. I was like a man in the grip of an obsession... though, I now wonder if possession might not be a more accurate description.

But I must return in my tale to that dingy museum, where I was so utterly engrossed in trying to decipher a most peculiar word... was it, 'Arch'? Perhaps, 'Arachnid'... that I had no idea of anyone approaching until Burnstow loomed down at me, asking, "Mr. Dower? Still busy, sir?"

That word, could it be, '...necron...?' Curse the man, could he not see I was deeply involved in deciphering this name? Did I even know it was a name at that point? Why would he not go? "What? Burnstow? What is it?"

"I'm about to lock up for the night," said the curator and I was suddenly aware that he was dressed in his outer clothing and that the sky beyond the windows was darkening. But surely it was too early to lock up? Yet there it was the on the clock, a few minutes to six. "Good grief, where has the day gone?" I cried.

Burnstow shrugged, "You looked so absorbed, sir, I scarce wished to bother you. And after your friend's arrival seemed to disturb you so..."

My friend? I had completely forgotten about Bright's arrival. "Has he been back?" I demanded. "Well? Tell me, man!"

Burnstow looked uncomfortable. "I believe I may have caught sight of him passing outside on more than one occasion. Should I be on my guard against him, sir?"

"What? Oh, no." Already a thought was forming itself in my mind. "No. Indeed not," I assured him.

The curator looked at me uncertainly. "Are you quite all right? You have a strange expression on your face."

"Oh, I'm quite in the pink, Burnstow," I smiled. "But, no. I don't think you need worry about Mr. Bright."

This did not seem to convince him. "But if he is in some way disreputable..."

Then justice will be served, said a thin, hard voice in my darkest thoughts. But I said nothing of this, instead turning back to the contents of the late Mr. Hesketh's trunk, with the words, "A few moments, if you please, Mr. Burnstow, and I shall bid you goodnight."

"Do you require assistance in tidying these away?" he asked, but I shrugged the offer away.

"No need. I shall be here at first opening tomorrow and I have my doubts that anyone should attempt to make off during the night with some old pages and dockets. There is nothing of interest in them, anyway." Then, as he drew away from me, I called out to him, waiting for him to turn back before adding, "And, should Mr. Bright enquire again, you may tell him that. Nothing of interest at all!"

Again those questions form. Nothing? What was I trying to hide? You are eager to know more of what I had discovered. And so, you see how easily the trap was baited.

Pausing only to scribble a few notes and place them with my day's work, I wrapped my coat tightly round myself and shivered in the gusting wind outside before setting out into the gathering gloom. But it was more than cold that made me shiver. It was the excitement of my discovery and the use to which I intended to put it.

You have realised that I had found something of importance, of course. What I had were fragments, no more, but with enough connective strands to allow a narrative to form. I had found a meagre type of journal and had read, in the hand of Meriel Pearson, married into the Hesketh family, how there had been two families of wealth that vied over which was to own more of that area. The words are still clear to my recall.

'Sannox has his mind set on the grove, my Nathaniel says. It's an age-old dispute. Bartholomew Sannox argues that the grove and the trees in it are rightfully his, while Nathaniel swears the land is Hesketh property. In truth, I know Nathaniel to be right, for I know the land was once my family's land. Not the Pearsons, but the land of my mother's

261

female kinfolk, way back when. It was bequeathed to a Hesketh in dark times and if I could but prove it I would. But those times aren't to be spoken of.'

And I read of how the dispute grew more bitter.

'Our labourers have fled, in the midst of the harvest. They say they won't be put upon by the thugs that has been set upon them. Though he denies it and calls them scum, I know they work for Sannox. I seen him talking to their leader and I seen the coins in the leader's hand. Sannox aims to ruin us by force but there are forces more than he knows. Nathaniel tried to have it out with him but Sannox calls him an ill-bred peasant. He writes down Nathaniel's words, lording his educated ways. He says he's keeping an account and that it'll be evidence should Nathaniel take action.'

There were appeals to magistrates to settle the matter, without success, court appearances, brawls, quarrels and assaults, until the matter was taken out of Hesketh's hands.

'The grove is gone. It burned and Sannox's hand is the one that lit the flames. Them few trees what didn't burn have been felled and piled. The heart has been burned out of the place and the heart has also gone out of my poor Nathaniel, who is beaten and broken. He is a decent man who has tried to stand up against a foe with no human decency. But, being as he is so inhuman, we shall see how something even less so than he shall despatch with him.

'I have mixed the draught, as my grandmother's grandmother described it and as the knowledge has been passed down. I shall drink of it and dream and on awaking, I shall know the name that I need to aid me.'

I read how imbibing some distillation of herbs and roots lead her to dream of the hidden identity of some monstrous being. And I read of the frightful spectre that, it was said, had been summoned up against that landowner.

'In the courtroom they told of a great wind that gathered up in the courtyard and which stirred the leaves and branches that littered the ground. And these appeared to gather up in

the air and take on a form, like that of a scarecrow but growing thicker and more solid and more like a living thing. And it fastened itself upon old man Sannox and rained blows upon him.

And his wife spoke of how, as the blows fell, the outer clothing of leaf and wood fell away... and what horror it was that was revealed within. And, as she told it, there were screams in the court and cries of terror.

And I know why they cried out for I saw it, that dark avenging thing, in my mind. I saw it as the leaves fell away. Something dead and decayed but full of dark movements...'

*

Dower shuddered and Lawrence silently refilled his glass, his own thoughts racing through accounts and legends, "Many is the ancient belief which held that to have knowledge of an entity's true name gave the possessor of such hidden knowledge control over that entity and called it to follow in his wake and do his bidding."

Dower nodded, gravely, "So the story went. As I read it, *'It was I who left the name for Sannox to find, chalked on the stone that broke the ankle of his prized steed. I know he took note of it in his evidence book. Now he has accepted it in. He has prepared the invitation and it always answers the summons to its name.'* So it went."

Lawrence asked, already knowing the answer, "The words of Meriel Hesketh's confession?"

"As I read it," admitted Dower, "and as Bright read it also."

With a degree of dawning horror, Lawrence asked, "You let him find the name?"

Dower jumped to his feet, pacing in agitation, his voice rising in desperation. "There was no name there! I constructed it myself, from fragments of words Meriel Hesketh had scrawled in the margins around her final confession. In one or other of the ancient languages. Something about spiders.

About death. Something about time. I merged these words into a suitably imposing name and left it to be found. I took the notes that seemed of value and left the dregs for Bright to find. If he were to take this nonsense, the ravings of a delusional peasant, and attempt to publish them with this invented word, he would be exposed for the sham he was. He would be the joke, you see?"

But neither man was laughing.

*

I had not gone to the museum until late that next day, leaving the bait in plain sight to be found. When I did set foot in the place, there was the curator, Burnstow, positively bursting with some piece of tittle-tattle.

"Sir, while it's far from my custom to pry," he wheedled.

I could not resist a barbed, "Yet, pain you as it does, I know you force yourself."

"But it was your acquaintance, Mr. Bright, sir," he continued, oblivious to my remark. "He was here. Or rather, in there, sir, where you were working."

"I trust you sent him on his way."

"I'd no need, sir. I'd been through in the back, you see, and when I came through... Well, as soon as I saw the door was open I went to speak, thinking it was you, sir, as you're so diligent in your studies. But I'd scarce cleared my throat to make my greeting when he came scurrying out, as if in fright. When he saw it was me he laughed and said how it was a gloomy business surrounded by old bones and such like and how he needed some air. Then he was gone and didn't even wait for his companion."

This news unsettled me somewhat. "I did not know he had company with him."

"Well, I didn't meet this person but, as Mr. Bright came through I thought I saw something shift behind him and, when he went, I reckoned I heard someone laugh in the darkness.

But, then, I was so distracted by Mr. Bright's peculiar nerviness and his sudden departure I forgot to look. And when I remembered, there was no-one to be seen. Though how they got past me..." The curator shivered and shook his head slightly. "Maybe I was mistaken and what I heard was the rustling of your papers as Mr. Bright ran off. I do hope everything's in order, sir."

"Oh, yes, Mr. Burnstow," I replied. "Everything's quite in order."

My happiness that all had gone to plan must have been evident, as Burnstow remarked, "May I say, sir, it's a change to see you smiling so?"

I was indeed smiling. The trap had been sprung. Burnstow's interruption had almost spoiled matters, though I was sure Bright would have recovered his wits sufficiently to offer a bribe to ensure his silence. For, then at least, I believed his panic was due to him being almost caught in the act of theft. I was rather pleased to imagine his discomfort.

But, though I wished Bright to suffer, I had no idea of how much suffering my actions were to bring about until I saw Edgar Bright again. Or, at least, what he had become. But it was not until the next morning, as I left my lodgings, that I was to witness for myself the effects of my joke.

"Dower. Thank God! I thought I had missed you," yelped the shambling figure who nearly bowled me over on the doorstep.

"Bright?" I was startled more by the change in his appearance than his sudden presence. "What are you doing here? I told you to leave me be! I am in no mood for your pretence at friendship, not after the night I've had."

His response was practically hysterical, though whether it was a laugh or a sob I could not judge. "The night you had? Did you sleep?"

In truth, I had slept all too deeply. And my dreams had not been pleasant ones. Full of half glimpsed night-things and... dark movements. The dream, only dimly remembered yet refusing to be wholly forgotten, seemed to cling to me, like

265

strands of some dark web.

Bright let out a cry which was unmistakably a sob. "I don't think I shall sleep again."

As I said, his appearance was dramatically altered. Instead of the puffed up, dapper and arrogant Bright of old, he looked appalling! His eyes were rimmed with red, his face was furred with stubble and his clothing was disarrayed. There were also cuts and grazes on his face and hands, as if he had come off the loser in some scuffle. Had he been drinking? I took a step back, warning him, "If you intend to cause a scene or threaten me..."

He stumbled toward me, his hands outstretched. "I must know what it is."

"What what is?" I demanded, though a dark suspicion was already lurking. I dismissed this thought, however, insisting, "Speak sense or step aside."

"Dower, I must know! What is it that's after me?"

I shrugged him off, insisting that I had no idea of what he might possibly mean.

His next words chilled me. "Something dead..."

'*... dead and decayed but full of dark movements,*' were the words of Meriel Hesketh that seemed to be whispered in my mind from across the centuries.

Even though I knew that the revelations he might make would terrify me, I flung the door wide and ushered him into the hall, saying, "Come inside, Bright. Tell me what you mean."

Once inside my rented room, Bright looked fearfully round the evidence of my studies lining the walls and taking up much of the available space. "Books? So many of them."

"Never mind the books. They cannot hurt you," I told him.

He laughed shrilly. "And I bet Bart Sannox thought leaves were gentle." But he did not laugh when he flopped exhaustedly into a seat and looked up imploringly at me. "What was it? What did Meriel Hesketh conjure up? What did her witchcraft summon?"

I was surprised, and I confess a little frightened, at the coldness in my own voice as I looked down at him and prompted, "If you know of this, then I must assume..."

"Yes," he sighed. "I admit it! I copied the papers you had been looking at. I couldn't resist it. You were clearly hiding something. What if it had been something of value? I'd have used it properly, sold it to an eager audience. With you, it'd have been collated and filed and forgotten, preserved for a posterity of no interest."

I shook my head slowly. "And this is you asking for assistance?"

His voice cracked as he finally said words I had waited many long years to hear. "I'm sorry. For copying your notes, now... and then."

I leaned closely to him, demanding, "You will finally admit to it?"

"Yes! I'll admit it! Whatever you ask," he sobbed. "But, please! This isn't the time! Something is following me!"

He stopped suddenly, looking round himself, as though something might have concealed itself in the room, waiting for its moment to bear down upon him. When he had satisfied himself that we were alone, he continued, struggling to keep his voice from trembling, "I first became aware of it in the museum. I thought someone was watching me, spying on me as I worked. Several times, I turned to face this watcher, half expecting to find you at my shoulder, quivering with rage, but there was never a soul there. Yet still I heard whisperings and movement and glimpsed something. Only glimpsed it, yet I felt sure it was always close by me. After an hour or two of this worsening feeling of something closing in on me, I left the museum.

"I hurried back home. All the way along the narrow lanes and unlit avenues I sensed a storm about to break at my back, a gathering darkness and a fearful and violent force set to be unleashed upon me.

"I slammed the door, locking it, just as the storm's first

267

howls reached my ears. Just in time. But, whatever tempest I may have escaped, there was worse awaiting me that evening. Some…" He took a ragged gulp of air before he could continue. "Some presence had been in my rooms! There was a great mound of books and papers piled high atop and around my desk. Something in the arrangement made them seem placed and precise, as if stacked by hands other than human.

"As I searched for other traces of this intruder, I became aware of some other presence in the room. There was no harsh breath to betray it. Instead, the sound was of a whispery scuttling, softer than the scratching of rats in the walls, yet amplified in the unnatural silence following the storm outside. The room shifted and distorted in the glow of the swinging lamp. Shadows lengthened and shrank back. And, within these shifting shadows, I was suddenly keenly aware, other things moved."

Yet again Bright's words seemed to echo those committed to paper by that young woman in her prison cell those many years past, *'Darkness within the dark. Shapes blacker than the shadows. Shapes that move.'*

Even as I recalled these phrases, Bright's next words made me start; they were so in tune with my thoughts of the instant. "Shapes that move! Shapes that run! There! And there!" He was whirling and pointing, his eyes wide, his words jumbled in his terror. "More there! From every corner, larger than mice but with more legs. Moving toward that mound of books. An infestation of crawling, creeping things!"

I had no brandy to offer and could scarcely leave him alone in this condition while I fetched a bottle of the landlady's sherry, so water was all I could offer and I thrust it upon him, insisting, "Bright, calm down and drink this! You are safe here!"

His shaking hands spilt more than he managed to get to his lips, and all the while he babbled on, "In a daze of horror, I leapt forward... just as the pile of books leapt at me!" He cowered back from the bookshelves, tears springing from his eyes. "I saw it between the pages as they fell away..."

I tried to reason with him but I could see that all reason was gone and only horror remained as he cried and gestured and sought the words to convey the darkness that had engulfed his mind.

"...creating motion... Motion toward me! Unstoppable, unrelenting... I ran screaming into the night and kept running till I could no longer breathe. I collapsed and fell into a daze, but it was a stupor with dreams. Such dreams! No matter how hard I run, it will never rest until it has me!"

I had to try to get through to whatever semblance of rationality might still be present. Grasping his shaking hands, I urged, "I can help you. I know! I know what you must do!"

"Nothing can help me against that! Listen! You hear it? It's speaking to me. *'Shalt thou know my name?'* You hear it?"

The wind was rustling the leaves outside the window and even I had to admit they stirred like something furtive. And, when I turned my head back, Bright was gone, the door flapping in the wind behind him. I ran to the door and tried to call out to him, "Bright! Come back, man! It can't hurt you!" Whether I believed that, I cannot say.

The wind was fierce and stung my eyes and throat and, as it intensified, it truly did seem to be filled with whispering voices. As I shielded my face I was sure I saw Bright disappear into an alley, leading to the seafront, while rubbish and papers were whipped up in a frenzy at his back. I thought only the mad or foolish, like poor deluded Bright would be out on such a night. But in the gloom I seemed to see another figure, though it may have been a jumble of rags or a grey mass of discarded and sodden newspapers thrown up by the wind.

But, really, did I fear it was something summoned to follow in his wake? Following, but not to do his bidding! You see, I did know something! Something that might help him!

I had also read that there are further laws, if control is to be maintained. Sacrifices must be made and tributes laid. Yet I had not left the pages with that information upon them for

Bright to find. Imagine, then, that you have presented control over such an entity to someone with no knowledge of these other, vital laws.

It... the entity would turn on them. It would be like a wild beast in captivity, ever prowling, testing the limits of its confinement. The captor would become the prey. It would claim its tribute one way or another.

I tried to tell him. I can still taste the salty wind and hear its rush as I called to him, "Bright, It can't hurt you! I can stop it, Bright!" If he even heard me, I cannot say. Nor can I honestly say why I did not follow after him, though I shudder to think that the sound I heard as I closed my door on the storm outside was not the wind rising but a distant scream.

Of course, the death was reported and naturally Mr. Burnstow had much to say on the subject when I returned to the museum to pack up my belongings. "They said that when his body was finally found and dragged from the sea that something had gotten to him, crabs or some such creeping scavenger."

Could this be true? When they dragged him from the foam, he had only been in the water for a matter of hours. But Burnstow had his answer to this. "Well, there are mysteries in death as well as in life. But, it is a truly a sad day for us, sir. And you're to be leaving us too?"

"Yes," I told him, feeling that some sort of explanation was necessary and that a lie would suffice. "I have... business to attend to, elsewhere."

Burnstow nodded, the grin returning to his lips if not to his eyes, "Life does go on. For some, at any rate, I suppose. Let's be thankful some departures are less drastic than others."

*

Dower stopped his pacing and stood before the fire, his back to Lawrence. "The implication was that it was a suicide. But, if he truly died by his own hand, mine was the hand that guided his."

Lawrence prompted him, "By dagger? By bullet? By poison? That would have been murder, but by pen and ink and paper?"

Dower turned to him, stating, "By writing its name, he called it forth. Yet by not offering it the sustenance it needed, the prescribed sacrifice, it was not bound to his control so it took payment in due. I held back that knowledge. That is my guilt!"

"Well," said Lawrence, after a moment's silence had passed uneasily, "you promised me a tale."

"More than a tale," insisted Dower, reaching into his jacket pocket. "I have the proof here! You see?" With a rustling sound, he drew out a folded sheet of paper.

"What's this? A confession to murder?"

Dower shook his head wearily. "No, but a death warrant, nonetheless, signed in my own hand." His voice remained dangerously low as he continued, "The first time I wrote it, I was spared a visitation. At least, spared a visit outside my dreams, as I had made an... an offering... of Bright. This time..."

"You've written it down, haven't you?" Lawrence cried, appalled. "You've written the name of the being down." He could make out Dower's neat and precise writing quite clearly. "Arachrononec..."

"No!" Dower crushed the paper into a pellet and threw it into the flames. "Don't read it! Into the fire with it! Let it burn like Meriel Hesketh's words burned. As she herself would have burned if she hadn't sealed her own demise."

"She escaped the witch-finder?" Lawrence asked, surprised. "How?"

Dower reached once more into his pocket, explaining, "She eluded him by summoning her own executioner. Her journal is burnt to ashes in my study grate but I've brought you this."

It was a news sheet, just a few yellowed and mouldering pages, from which Lawrence read, *'Let it be known now that Meriel Pearson Hesketh, complicit in the unlawful death of Bartholomew Sannox by means of witchery, was this evening*

271

found dead within the confines of her locked cell. Her body was badly torn about and the wounds were such that she was scarce recognisable as a person, even one bethought possessed of evil. No sign of human entry has been found into the cell but the jailer has sworn oath that a 'dark shape or shade' did seem to him to be present around the jailhouse in the hours leading to the death of the witch.'

Lawrence held the page out to Dower, though the visitor showed no interest in taking it back.

"She admitted in her journal that Sannox was the sacrifice and the entity did depart after claiming him. But she had called it back yet one more time. This time, it would not have far to look for its prey. *'Already I have dreamt it.'* Those were her words."

Dower stared into the flames, his voice more even than it had been since his arrival. "It is my reckoning that some things are not found but find us; that some instruments we think to use to our own ends are using us to achieve aims of their own. I went back to Meriel's final confession, looking for the words I had found scrawled there and which I had used to create that dreadful name. There was no writing there! I feel I was used to call this thing forth once more to our world. And Bright was the cost. I know what must come for me. You see, Bright described it, shortly before it caught him up."

*

As he prowled and paced in my room he never stopped speaking, even when it seemed that his voice would desert him. "In a daze of horror, I leapt forward... just as the pile of books leapt at me! I saw it between the pages as they fell away, the books dropping like a shedding skin. What stood there was a corpse. Little more than a skeleton, though it was given the illusion of solidity by the masses of web that sheathed and festooned it, webs of unnatural thickness and strength, many of them ancient, hanging with the dust of decades long gone.

"How did the witch girl put it? *'It is grey and gaunt and whatever life it once lived it was not as human life.'* Yes! That was it!

"Through the curtains of webs I could dimly spy something that moved, something that might once have been mistaken for a spider, yet one grown huge over the years. Whatever it was, it was dark and many-legged and it moved within the hollows of that desiccated form with purpose and intent.

"And the wind seemed to change, the whispering voices shifting. *'Shalt thou know my name?'* they had demanded, even though they already knew. For now they answered, *'Then thou shalt see my face!'*"

Meriel's words were in my own mind as Bright shrieked those words at me. *'Something dead and decayed but full of dark movements... I have seen its face! It has no face! Just the skull beneath and the things that crawl within!'*

Bright continued his description, barely giving himself time for breath. "Things that moved, acting like a puppeteer, controlling through the merest twitches of countless strands of web, radiating through the cadaver, coiling in their thousands through and around the bones like silken muscles, guiding them, creating motion... Motion toward me! Unstoppable, unrelenting..."

*

Dower paused, and in this silence, Lawrence was aware of the wind outside.

"Sannox's crime was the destruction of the grove! Bright's was the theft of my notes! For me it won't come clad in the form of some rustling thing of leaves or paper. It will be an entity of darkness, inky-black and full of spiders."

Although the paper had long since curled up and burned in the grate, Dower's gaze remained fixed on the flames. The reflected firelight seemed to be the only spark of life in his eyes. When he left, it wasn't racing out into the night like poor

273

Bright, hurtling blindly toward his brutal fate. He went calmly, his terror seemingly spent in the effort of telling the tale. His parting words, much gentler than his opening words, were, "My apologies once more, Lawrence. I hope... I pray I have not burdened you."

When Lawrence told me of this visit, a week had passed and he hadn't seen Dower since that night. Nor had anyone he had spoken to and he can be found neither in his rooms nor at his studies. My friend had no doubt that he will be found but, whether what is found will be recognisable, he would not speculate.

As to the night of Dower's visit, he did tell me this. As he sat to write what Dower had told him, endeavouring to jot it all down while still fresh in his memory, Lawrence began to attempt a phonetic spelling of that daemonic name he had heard described. Even as his pen traced the letters, he became aware of some movement around the edges of his vision and turned to see the most enormous spider creep slowly across the bookshelf and into the darkness.

Fair enough, you may say, all studies in old buildings have their spiders. But, my friend assures me, he was not entirely convinced it had only eight legs.

As Lawrence says, "I wonder now if Dower's need to confess was truly at his own volition, as I also wonder if he hasn't, indeed, burdened me with a terrible knowledge!"

Suffice to say, the remainder of the tale remains unwritten.

TO SUMMON A FLESH EATING DEMON

Charles Black

"*The Book of Setopholes*, pah!" Professor Ernest Mellman snorted in derision. The archaeologist leaned back in his armchair. "Next you will be telling me, you believe in Lovecraft's *Necronomicon*," he said, shaking his head.

Professor Julius Greydin glared at his seated guest. "Don't be ridiculous Mellman. Lovecraft's book is a mere fiction."

Mellman laughed. "Oh, and *The Book of Setopholes* isn't?"

"Of course not," snapped Greydin.

Although the academics were aged similarly - in their fifties - they were quite different in appearance.

Professor Greydin stood by the fireplace smoking his pipe. He was a tall, slim, and rather handsome man, with sleek dark hair. His colleague was shorter and broader. He wore a large pair of glasses, and what little remained of his hair was white.

One other man was present - although he was many years their junior - one of their students named Tony Danziger. He was quietly studying some of the curious tribal masks that adorned one wall of Professor Greydin's study.

"Really Julius, you know as well as I do that that book does not exist."

"That's where you're wrong Mellman, The Book of Setopholes does exist," insisted Greydin.

Professor Mellman glanced at Tony Danziger, and winked. "Have you tried Arkham's Miskatonic University, Julius?" he asked his host.

Greydin did not bother to respond to his flippant comment.

"No I'm sorry Julius, but the only place it exists is in the minds of a few poor deluded souls." Professor Mellman chuckled. "You're not one of those are you Julius?"

"You'll eat those words before the week is out Mellman."

"Well I know I have a healthy appetite," Mellman slapped his ample belly, "and I'll try almost anything when it comes to food, but I doubt I'll find a few words very filling."

Greydin muttered, "Oh you'll taste humble pie."

Tony Danziger - a fine example of youthful vitality - had been listening with interest. His curiosity in need of satisfying, and fearing that the professors would come to blows, the tall and broad shouldered student decided that now was a good time to interrupt. "Excuse my ignorance, but just what is this *Book of Setopholes?*" he asked, seating himself in one of the leather armchairs.

Professor Mellman answered, "It's a fantasy, haven't you been listening Tony?"

"Pay no attention to him, Danziger. You are aware of course, that Plato tells us Solon learnt of Atlantis from an Egyptian priest," said Greydin. "More brandy?" he offered.

"Of course." Mellman held out his glass.

Danziger nodded in response to both statement and question.

Greydin refilled their glasses, then began to pace the room. "*The Book of Setopholes* is a legendary book of knowledge written by an Egyptian priest. Among the wisdom it contains, is an account of Atlantis and its fate."

"You mean of its drowning?" Danziger asked.

"Yes, but Setopholes tells us that the Atlanteans worshipped dark and evil gods, with unholy rites and human sacrifices. But then - for some unknown reason - they gave up their bloody worship of these foul beings. It was then that Atlantis was drowned by the waves of the sea, as a punishment for turning away from their evil gods," explained Professor Greydin.

"A slight difference from Plato's account then," mused Danziger.

Professor Mellman, poured himself another glass of brandy, and said, "Ah, but that's not all is it Julius?"

"You've probably assumed that Setopholes was the name of the Egyptian priest, but you would be wrong. His name is lost to us," continued the anthropology professor.

The student asked, "Then who, or what, was Setopholes?"

Professor Greydin went on, "He was the man who told the

nameless priest all of the arcane knowledge contained in the book."

"Come on man; get to the best bit," urged Mellman.

"All right, all right, Mellman, I'm getting to it." Greydin glared at his colleague.

"Setopholes was a wizard who passed on his wisdom to the priest, by the use of a spell, and the knowledge was revealed to the priest in his dreams."

Unable to restrain himself, Mellman interrupted, "But the best part of this fantastic tale is that the things the priest learnt from these spell sent dreams, happened on another world."

Greydin again glared at the archaeologist.

"Isn't that the most outrageous thing you've ever heard, Tony?" Mellman was laughing again. "No, wait a minute, what's more outrageous is that anyone would believe such a thing could possibly be true."

Unwilling to offend either professor, the student remained quiet.

As did a scowling Greydin.

"But of course it's all a hoax," said Mellman.

"So what is the origin of this book, then?" Danziger asked.

"There are references to it in a Victorian book called *Mysteries of Dark Wisdom*; you have a copy haven't you Julius?"

"Of course I have," Greydin replied. "Would you like to see it?" he asked Danziger.

"Yes Professor, I would."

As Professor Greydin went to retrieve it from one of the many bookcases contained in the room, Mellman went on, "It claims that there were translations and copies of *The Book of Setopholes* made through the ages, among them Greek and Latin, and even some medieval copies. Unfortunately for Julius, this Victorian book is universally considered - not to put too fine a point on it - a load of old tosh." Mellman laughed again.

Greydin snorted, "Huh! That's what you think." The

anthropologist had taken the book to his desk.

"Not just me old boy." Mellman remained seated but Danziger went to take a look.

Greydin said proudly, "This is Charles Roland's, *Mysteries of Dark Wisdom,* published in 1890. Not many copies survive."

"Charles Roland? I've never heard of him," admitted Danziger.

"Few have," Greydin conceded. "And to be honest little is known about the man himself. He was born in 1843 and died, or at least, was last seen in 1907. But what is certain, is that he was an expert on the occult."

Professor Mellman snorted again, "Hah! He was a charlatan and a crank."

"Few men have dared delve as deeply into such matters as Roland," contended Professor Greydin.

"This book is a compendium of sorcery and the occult, but its primary interest is the information it provides upon *The Book of Setopholes*," Greydin explained.

"So apart from Atlantis being on another world, what else is in *The Book of Setopholes*?" Danziger asked, carefully turning the pages of the Victorian book.

"It's a collection of magical spells and rituals, information on gods and demons, and records of the history and events of Setopholes' world."

Professor Greydin ignored Mellman's snort. "Roland intended to publish a translation of *The Book of Setopholes*, and a more detailed book about it and its contents. Alas neither were to appear."

"Bloody good job if you ask me." Professor Mellman's opinion was scathing, "Roland was no more than a mere writer of fiction, and not very good fiction at that."

"Well I for one would like to read it," said Danziger. "May I borrow this please, Professor?"

Greydin was pleased that the student was showing such an interest. "Yes, but please be careful with it."

"I will; don't worry."

Mellman groaned, "Oh for goodness sake Tony, you don't want to be wasting your time reading that."

The clock struck the hour - ten o'clock.

The student smiled. "Speaking of time, it's time I was off."

"Yes me too, Julius. Thanks for the brandy, excellent as always. I will see you tomorrow."

"It's been an interesting evening Professor Greydin, thank you. And don't worry about your book, I'll return it in a couple of days, if that's okay?"

"Yes, that's fine. And I may have something very important to tell you then."

"Oh? And what might that be?" Mellman asked.

But despite Mellman's enquiry, Greydin would say no more on the matter and wished his guests goodnight.

Student and professor shared the same route for part of their journey to their respective homes.

"Well what do you suppose that was all about, professor?" Danziger asked.

Mellman smiled. "Can't you guess?"

"I've really no idea."

"You know; Julius has never been married?"

"No, I didn't know that," admitted Danziger. "Do you mean; he intends to announce his engagement?"

Mellman shook his head. "It's rare for Julius to let someone borrow one of his precious books."

Professor Mellman's apparent change of subject had Danziger puzzled.

"He likes you, young Tony."

"You mean..." Danziger was dumfounded, momentarily lost for words. "Just what are you suggesting Professor?"

"Suggesting? Was I suggesting something? Ah, I have to go this way now, and much as I'd like to continue our conversation, it's much too chilly for me to hang around here. I'm off home, young Tony. No, I'm none the wiser than you.

We'll just have to wait and see what revelation Julius has to make."

A couple of days later an uncomfortable Tony Danziger was back in Julius Greydin's study. He had only intended returning the professor's book, but Greydin had insisted he come in. Professor Mellman was again sitting by the fire.

"Well Julius what's this all about?" Mellman asked.

"I told you last time you were here, that I might have an important announcement to make."

Danziger looked worried. He had assumed that with Professor Mellman present there would be no embarrassing declaration by Professor Greydin. Surely, the professor was not going to reveal that he was in love with him, in front of his colleague.

Greydin spoke, "As Mellman knows, I have been searching for many years, for what I suppose you could call my hearts desire. It has proved to be a most elusive search; one that I feared would never find fulfilment. But now, and I can scarcely believe it, my quest has come to an end."

Danziger glanced at Professor Mellman, Mellman smiled back.

"After all this time I have finally found it." Professor Greydin paused dramatically, before announcing, "Gentlemen I have *The Book of Setopholes*."

The student breathed a sigh of relief; he thought he saw Mellman wink at him. The old devil had been kidding him all along.

Mellman was saying, "Really Julius, you don't expect us to believe you've managed to locate a copy of that damned book, do you?"

"Not just found Mellman. I have it. Well don't just sit there come and see; you too Danziger," urged Greydin unlocking one of his desk's drawers.

From the drawer he carefully removed a large book, and gently laid it upon the desk. The other men gathered round.

The iron bound book was easily identifiable of being of great antiquity.

"My God!" Mellman gasped.

Greydin opened the book turning to the title page. "This is what you have refused to believe in for more years than I care to remember, Mellman. This is probably the only surviving copy of the only printed edition of the legendary *Book of Setopholes,*" he announced, pride evident in his voice.

For once Mellman was speechless. It was left to Danziger to ask, "Where on earth did you get it Professor?"

Greydin was reluctant to reveal how he had come by the book, "A dealer in antiquities and antiquarian books that I know located it for me. But that's not important, what is important is that the book exists," was all he would say.

Danziger had read all about the different editions of *The Book of Setopholes*, but he had never expected to see one. Especially not the printed version of 1510.

The book was nearly five hundred years old, and had been included on the Index of Forbidden Books by Pope Paul IV in 1559. Quite naturally, it was not in good condition, but it was a miracle it had survived at all.

Neither Mellman nor Danziger pressed Greydin for further information on his acquisition of the book; they were too eager to see what was written on its fabled pages.

At first Mellman was convinced the book was a fake, but reluctantly he had to admit, "Well Julius it appears to be genuine. Though of course it will have to be analysed to prove whether it is or not."

Although Danziger did not know much Latin, especially that of renaissance Italy, the three men studied the ancient tome late into the night. The student having to content himself with the translations made by the other men, and the grotesque woodcuts that illustrated the book.

"The book may date to the sixteenth century but that doesn't mean that there's any truth to what's written in it," Mellman pointed out.

"Ever the sceptic Mellman."

"Of course my dear fellow. But just because the book exists, it doesn't mean that this story of Atlantis being on another world has any validity."

Mellman paused a moment in thought, and his grin grew broader. "What if we were to put some of this arcane knowledge to the test?"

"What do you mean?" Greydin asked.

"Why, a spell of course Julius. It won't prove anything about Atlantis ever having existed on another planet, but there's no reason why we couldn't attempt one of these so called magical rituals from this book of yours."

"Well, I'm not sure we should..." Professor Greydin began.

Mellman interrupted, "Come now Julius, think of it as an experiment."

"But these things should not just be gone into lightly," protested Greydin.

"Quit stalling, Julius. Anyone would think you were afraid your book is about to be exposed as the usual hotchpotch of unworkable nonsense that all these grimoires invariably are. What say you Tony?"

"Well..."

Not giving the student time to finish speaking Professor Mellman continued, "Have you so little faith after all in your book of marvellous magics, Julius?"

"I really don't think..."

Mellman interrupted, "Yes, you're right of course, we'd only be wasting our time."

Greydin sighed. "Very well," he reluctantly agreed.

"Splendid, then if we reconvene here tomorrow evening about nine, that will give you plenty of time to select one of the rituals, and make whatever preparations are necessary."

"Very well that suits me. How about you Tony?" Mellman asked.

"Me?" The student had not expected to be included.

"Yes of course you'll join us," invited Professor Greydin. "I insist."

"Then in that case, yes, I'll be here," he accepted

It was approaching nine o'clock when Tony Danziger arrived at Professor Greydin's house. He had thought about backing out and instead asking Michelle Chalmers - one of his fellow students - out on a date. But he was hoping to go on one of Professor Mellman's archaeological expeditions, and so he thought he had better appear keen - even though Mellman was not Danziger's favourite person right now.

He had to admit, that he was curious about what would happen when they tried one of the so-called spells from that mouldy old book - probably nothing, but wouldn't it be something if it did.

The student smiled - perhaps there would be a spell he could cast on Professor Mellman - a day or two as a frog might do the professor some good.

Just as Danziger reached the top of the steps to Greydin's front door, it started to rain. Danziger reached out and rapped on the door with the gargoyle shaped knocker. He did not have to wait long for the door to open.

As usual, Professor Mellman had arrived first. "Tony, at last, what kept you? I was beginning to think you had changed your mind about joining us." He handed the student a glass of brandy. "Julius refused to reveal what tonight's act of necromancy is, until you arrived."

"I'm sorry I kept you waiting," apologised the student, although he was not late, and he felt that if anyone should be offering apologies it was Professor Mellman.

However, Mellman was oblivious of the student's mood.

"Really Mellman, I have no intention of indulging in necromancy." Greydin paused dramatically, then said, "At least not yet."

Mellman was taken aback. "You're not serious?"

Professor Greydin smiled.

Danziger laughed. "You should have seen your face

283

professor."

"Well yes, I knew you were joking really," blustered the archaeologist.

Greydin's smile had quickly vanished. "Enough levity, we must be about our business."

"And just what is our business Julius? What dark rite have you in mind to perform tonight?" inquired Professor Mellman.

"A summoning," was the reply.

"A summoning? Are you sure?"

"Of course I'm sure."

"That's only about one stepped removed from necromancy isn't it?"

"Demonology, my dear Mellman."

"Well I'm surprised you've chosen such an ambitious venture, old man. I would have thought you would have chosen something more simple, like a love spell. What do you think Tony?"

Danziger frowned, "I'm sure Professor Greydin knows what he's doing."

"Will you stop prattling, Mellman."

"Very well old boy, let's get on with it then, shall we?"

Mellman and Danziger finished their drinks and followed Greydin out of the room. He led them along the oak panelled hallway towards the rear of the house. "I thought we would make use of the basement," Greydin explained as he opened a door. "More room, and it seemed more appropriate," he explained as the three men descended into a large cellar.

The centre of the room had been cleared, boxes and crates lined the walls; another door led out of the room.

Mellman laughed. "Behold the lair of the sorcerer."

On the floor a pentagram had been drawn in red and purple chalk, a lectern stood outside the pentagram between two points of the star.

"Is that where you keep your wine?' Mellman asked, pointing to the other door.

"Never mind that Mellman, you've had enough to drink

already," snapped Greydin.

Outside thunder rumbled ominously. "Ho, a portentous omen," laughed Mellman.

Danziger asked, "What exactly are you planning to do in this experiment, Professor Greydin?"

"Apart from make a fool of yourself," Mellman whispered to Danziger. The student could not help smiling at Mellman's comment.

"I have chosen a ritual that will prove the Book of Setopholes is a genuine work of magical knowledge."

"And what ritual is that?" Danziger asked.

"Really Tony, I sometimes think you go around with cotton wool stuffed in your ears. Julius already told us he plans to summon a demon, no less."

"It's entitled *How to Summon a Flesh Eating Demon*," Professor Greydin announced, opening the book that lay upon the lectern.

"Is there any other kind old man? Have you ever heard of a vegetarian demon, Tony?"

"Er, no." Danziger was beginning to feel foolish.

"If we do summon anything, I insist on checking it out to make sure you haven't got one of your students to dress up to play the part. I'm sure you could get that fool Brown to do that." Mellman laughed.

Danziger felt that of the two professors, only Mellman would resort to such an act.

Professor Greydin was becoming irritated by Mellman's comments, "Will you take this seriously Mellman?"

Danziger shook his head. He did not know why the Professors spent so much of their time together, Mellman was continually trying to provoke Professor Greydin, and he usually succeeded.

"Right you are. Well then Aleister Crowley, lets get on with it," urged Mellman, eager to complete the ritual and thus have Greydin fail.

"What do we have to do Professor?" Danziger asked, also

eager to get things over with.

"Stand at the points of the star." The Professor pointed to the points to the left and right of him, "Stay outside the pentagram, don't walk through it," he commanded.

From the lectern, Greydin took two pieces of paper and handed one each to the two men.

"What's this, professor?" Danziger asked.

"It's your part in the ceremony. When I give the signal the pair of you chant the incantation written there."

"Chant it?" Mellman looked doubtful. "I can't even understand it. It's just gibberish."

"Probably the Atlantean equivalent of abracadabra," grinned Danziger.

"Hocus-pocus," muttered Mellman. "What's the betting Julius fails to even conjure up a white rabbit?"

Ignoring Mellman, Greydin turned to the other door, opened it and went through.

"Where are you going now?" Mellman questioned.

Greydin did not answer.

"Of course, the wine cellar! A bottle of your finest vintage, Julius."

Greydin returned, carrying a small crate. He opened it, and pulled out a black chicken.

Mellman asked, "What on earth are you doing with that thing?"

"It's the sacrifice of course," answered Greydin.

"You're not serious are you Professor?" Danziger was shocked.

"Of course I am. Now let's begin shall we?"

"Let the ceremony begin," declared Mellman.

Professor Greydin picked up a knife that lay beside the book. He held the struggling chicken above the centre of the pentagram.

"My God man!" Mellman cried, as Greydin deftly wielded the knife, and allowed the chicken's blood to spill onto the floor. Mellman and Danziger watched in distaste.

"There we are, simple," he said, leaving the chicken lying in the widening pool of its blood. "That should do it."

Danziger asked, "What now?"

"Quiet both of you," Greydin ordered.

Professor Greydin began to read aloud an incantation he had translated from the *Book of Setopholes*. He spoke in a commanding voice, "Oh hear me, creature of the pit. I, your master Julius Greydin speak. Accept the red offering. I summon; you must obey. Come to me, obey my command." Greydin continued speaking, chanting strange words that neither Mellman nor Danziger recognised.

Greydin pointed the bloody knife at his acolytes, his signal for them to join in.

Mellman and Danziger looked at each other, and then feeling somewhat foolish took up their part in the incantation - chanting more of the strange words.

Greydin continued to speak for about five minutes repeating the incantation.

Mellman began to speak, "Well Julius, you've tried your best, but you've got to admit..."

An incredibly loud boom of thunder drowned out his words, the house shook as if it had been struck and the light went out.

"My God!" Mellman staggered.

Danziger yelled, "What was that?"

Greydin was performing the incantation again, but shouting the words now. The light flickered back into life, but the pentagram remained empty.

Professor Greydin fell silent.

"Look upon it as a successful experiment. You've conclusively proved that magic does not work. You tried your best, but it was never going to work," said Mellman, trying to console his colleague.

The three men were back in the study. Greydin was slumped in his chair; head held in his hands. Danziger refilling their glasses.

Mellman added some coal to the fire. "Although I'll admit for a moment, even I thought it was going to work."

"No Mellman, it was my fault the ritual did not work. I allowed myself to be pressured by you. I should have been more patient: these things work better at their appointed times. In my eagerness to prove you wrong I adapted the ritual as I thought fit. Next time I will perform it correctly."

"Next time?" Mellman questioned. "You're not serious are you Julius?"

"But of course. I intend to try again."

"Julius, you proved that sorcery does not work, that demons do not exist."

"My first attempt was flawed; it cannot be considered a legitimate attempt. I must try again."

"Julius, give it up," Mellman urged.

"I must make one more attempt. I have to perform the ritual again, but next time I must do it precisely as it is written in *The Book of Setopholes*. Though I do not expect either of you to attend."

Tony Danziger had had no intention of attending Professor Greydin's next attempt at demonology. Instead, he asked Michelle Chalmers for that date, and she had accepted his invitation to go to the cinema. But when the night in question arrived, she never showed up. After waiting for her for an hour, Danziger finally had to admit he had been stood up.

At a loose end, the student found himself somewhat reluctantly again at the Professor's house.

For a change, he had arrived before Professor Mellman.

"Can you follow this, Danziger?" Professor Greydin handed the student a piece of paper.

Danziger examined what was written on the paper.

"No! Don't even mouth the words," Greydin warned. "You understand it?"

"Yes, I think so."

"Good. Would you care for a drink?"

"Please."

"This spell certainly seems to me to be medieval in origin. So tonight we perform the ceremony in the original Latin." Professor Greydin poured Danziger a drink.

"Learn the incantation, but remember do not utter it until I say so. Now, I have some things to prepare, if you will excuse me."

When Professor Greydin returned, he made an unexpected demand that shocked the student. "Get undressed, there's a good fellow."

"What?" Danziger spluttered.

"Put this on." Greydin threw him a long, red, hooded robe. "We're doing this rite right this time," the professor smiled briefly. "Don't worry we'll all be wearing them. I'm going up stairs to change into mine now."

Both men had changed into their scarlet cowls when Professor Mellman arrived.

"Hello, what's this?" Mellman grinned. *"The Masque of the Red Death?"*

"Here you are Mellman." Greydin handed him one of the garments. "I want you to wear this."

"What's all this nonsense then?" Mellman asked.

"As I said, this time we do the ritual exactly as it says in the book."

"Have you got a bushy white beard for me then?"

Greydin sighed. "What are you on about now?"

"So I can be Father Christmas," laughed Mellman

"Have you been drinking?"

"Just a tipple, old boy. Why? Are you offering?"

"Just get changed."

"Oh very well, if you insist."

"I do."

Mellman went upstairs to change. And Danziger wondered, somewhat concerned, how Professor Greydin would react, when the ritual failed again.

"Well how do I look?" Mellman asked, coming down the stairs.

"Good. I was worried it wouldn't fit." Greydin glanced at the clock. "It'll soon be midnight, high time we got on with things."

"Isn't there time for a drink?" Mellman asked.

"No. I have calculated that midnight is the optimum time to attempt this ceremony." Greydin opened the door to the cellar. "Now, down to the basement, both of you. And put up your hoods."

Mellman led the way, Danziger went next, Professor Greydin followed, locking the cellar door before descending.

"So, what else are we doing differently this time Julius?" Mellman asked. "Oh! I see." Mellman had reached the bottom of the stairs.

Danziger expressed his surprise more forcefully, "Bloody hell!" he swore.

Instead of the electric light this time the cellar was lit by smoky candles that stood on skulls - most were animal but some looked decidedly human. Black drapes covered the walls, hiding the assorted clutter that was stored in the cellar.

Mellman gestured at the skulls. "Where on earth did you get those, Julius?"

"For heaven's sake, from the biology department of course. You don't think I've been grave robbing, do you?"

"Isn't this all a bit *Hammer House of Horror*, Professor?" asked Danziger.

"I'm following the instructions to the letter this time. Even if it means using all this paraphernalia."

"Well I must say it's very atmospheric." Mellman was examining a skull. "Monkey?" he queried.

Greydin nodded. "The others are, cat, dog, sheep, goat, horse, and bull, and those three are of course human: male, female, and child," he indicated each in turn.

"Take up your positions as before." Greydin instructed

290

crossing the room, pulling back a drape to reveal the cellars other door.

Mellman groaned. "Not another unfortunate chicken."

Danziger whispered to Mellman, "Judging by the lengths Professor Greydin is going to, I expect he's got the other ten members of his coven waiting in there."

"You may be right Tony." Mellman replied, as Greydin returned accompanied by another red robed acolyte. Face hidden by the hood of their robe, this fourth person moved slowly and unsteadily. As Mellman had predicted Professor Greydin was again carrying the small crate containing a chicken.

"Aren't you going to introduce us, Julius?" Mellman asked.

"Is he all right?" Tony asked, concerned.

Greydin put the crate down, then leaned close to his companion, and whispered instructions.

Obeying, the newcomer moved to the middle of the pentagram, and allowed their red robe to fall to the ground - to reveal their identity, and their nakedness.

"My God!" exclaimed Mellman, averting his eyes.

Danziger gasped, amazed, "Michelle! What are you doing here?"

Michelle did not reply, just smiled vaguely.

Mellman pulled Greydin to one side. "Julius, what is the meaning of this?"

Greydin shrugged. "She is a vital component of tonight's ceremony."

"She's been drugged!" Danziger had picked up Michelle's robe, and was trying to get her to put it back on.

"So, she's not doing this willingly?" Mellman asked.

"Hardly. I couldn't very well advertise for a young virgin to take part in a black magic ritual could I?"

"But that's monstrous!" Mellman was appalled. "Now look here Julius I cannot allow this to proceed."

"Why ever not?" Greydin was surprised by his friend's attitude.

"You don't seriously expect us to allow you to sacrifice this girl do you?"

"Sacrifice? Really Mellman, don't be so absurd. Do you really think I'm going to plunge my knife into this young girl's heaving bosom?" Greydin snorted. "Now who's being all *Hammer House of Horror*?"

Mellman asked, "Then just what is Miss Chalmers role in all of this?"

"Yeah, just what are you intending Professor?" Danziger snarled.

"She is part of the lure to bring the demon into our dimension. The scent of the chicken's blood and virgin flesh, don't you see?"

Danziger was angry. "And what's to stop the demon from devouring her when it obeys the summons?"

"The creature will be disorientated on appearing, I have only to speak the word of power, and the creature will be utterly under my command." Greydin smiled. "She will come to no harm, and will remember nothing."

Mellman shook his head. "Have you taken leave of your senses?"

"I won't allow it. It's too risky."

"I don't need your permission Danziger."

Danziger's hands were clenched fists. "What about Michelle's permission? You haven't got that either. You could be charged with kidnapping."

Mellman pulled the student away. "Calm down Tony. It's all right. No harm will come to Miss Chalmers. After all it's not as if the incantation is going to work now, is it?" he smiled reassuringly. "She'll be perfectly safe."

"God, how stupid of me, you're right of course. All of this black magic paraphernalia had me thinking it might actually work. Talk about getting carried away, it's just that I really like Michelle, the thought of anything happening to her..." The student shrugged, embarrassed.

"I understand, but she'll be fine."

"Nevertheless, he shouldn't be doing this without Michelle's say so."

"Please Tony; I think it will be better if we let Julius carry on. No harm can come to Michelle; I assure you. As for Julius, he is obviously unwell; I'm worried what he will do if we try to prevent this going ahead."

The student considered, and decided that Mellman was right. There was no real danger to Michelle if they carried on with what he now realised was a madman's farce, but there was no knowing how Greydin would react if they attempted to prevent him enacting this ritual. "Okay then Professor, but he's crazy, and you better make sure he sees a shrink."

"Don't worry I'll make sure he gets the help he needs."

"Well are you taking part?" demanded Greydin, impatient to begin.

"Tony?" Mellman asked.

The student nodded in response.

"Good," said Greydin. "Then let us proceed."

Naked, Michelle lay in the pentagram, head and limbs corresponding with the five points of the star. Mellman and Danziger each stood by her hands, whilst Greydin stood at her head.

As before Greydin sacrificed the chicken, allowing the blood to flow freely, splashing himself, and spilling onto Michelle's body.

Michelle writhed and groaned softly.

Tony realised how aroused he was, and hoped neither of the other men would notice. He was thankful that candles and not the more powerful electric light lit the room.

But in the light of the candles, the blood splattered Julius Greydin looked decidedly sinister. The student had doubts about the man's sanity, and had second thoughts about allowing him to continue. Would it be worse to try to stop this now, or let it proceed, only for Greydin to fail in his sorcery?

Professor Greydin began to read the incantation, speaking

first the words in Latin, and then the strange words of an unknown language.

Mellman started chanting at Greydin's signal, but Danziger missed it, joining in slightly after Mellman. The student was unable to keep his gaze from the beautiful Michelle's blood stained body.

Mellman realised he was sweating. It seemed unnaturally hot, and the air smelt unpleasant - a smell of sulphur.

Suddenly darkness descended as the candles went out, inexplicably extinguished. Professor Greydin stopped speaking in mid-sentence.

Something growled.

"Julius? What was..." Mellman's scream was shrill.

Danziger shouted, 'What the hell?" as something wet splashed him. "The lights Professor, where's the light switch?" He started to move towards the foot of the stairs; taking a chance on a light switch being there. He collided with someone - "'Professor Greydin is that you?" Or something!

Danziger staggered away from whatever he had bumped into. Groping in front of him, he found the wall, running his hands over its surface he found the lights switch. He flicked it on, and turned around.

Professor Greydin was crouched over the fallen Mellman; there was more blood on the floor than just the chicken's. There was no sign of a demon.

"What the hell happened, Professor?"

Professor Greydin turned and looked up, he was drenched in blood, his mouth smeared crimson. Greydin stared at the student, chewing on something, drool dribbling from between his lips.

"Jesus!" Danziger caught a glimpse of Mellman; blood spilled freely from the gaping wound in the archaeologist's neck. "Oh my God!" he gasped.

In horror, Danziger began to back up the stairs; Greydin had been so obsessed with summoning a demon that he had finally flipped. Then he remembered Michelle - he could not leave her at the mercy of a madman.

Greydin ripped Mellman's robe open, stroking a hand over the archaeologist's plump belly, watching the student as he did so.

Danziger slowly came back down the stairs. Michelle lay oblivious. Greydin swallowed, then bent his head and began lapping at Mellman's blood.

Danziger edged his way around Greydin. "It's okay professor, me and Michelle are leaving now."

The student crouched down next to Michelle, warily watching the professor, afraid that at any moment the lunatic would leap at him.

Michelle opened her eyes, "Oh hi Tony," she said, slurring her words. "Where am I?" she mumbled, a confused expression on her face.

Danziger smiled at her, "It's all right Michelle. I'll soon have you out of here."

Michelle's eyes closed again.

Greydin raised Mellman's limp arm, and sank his teeth into the flesh, chomping noisily.

Danziger lifted Michelle, and began to rise. Greydin snarled. The student paused a moment, then continued to rise. Greydin snarled again, releasing Mellman's arm.

Danziger crouched back down, lowering Michelle gently to the floor. The student considered. Greydin was not about to let him take Michelle. Would the professor let him go alone? Could he risk it? Would Michelle be safe? There was plenty more meat left on Professor Mellman, enough for the maniac to dine on, surely he would not need to start on Michelle. There had to be enough time to get help. He had to try. Then he saw Greydin's knife, it lay discarded on the floor. Of course, he could always overpower the professor. Greydin was in shape for an old guy, but he would be no match for the student. But just in case, he began to reach for the sacrificial weapon.

Greydin watched him, smiling again, still gobbling human

flesh - pieces of Professor Ernest Mellman.

"You crazy bastard," Danziger muttered. The student felt sick.

The knife was almost in his grasp, when Greydin leapt at him. Danziger was fit and healthy, and physically Greydin's superior, or at least he should have been. He struggled against the elder man who was possessed of a strength far greater than a man his age should have.

Danziger was grappled to the ground. There was no trace of the Professor in the man who lowered his face towards him. Madness shone in his eyes; the mouth came closer to Danziger's throat. His teeth were fangs, and he could smell the foulness of the possessed man's breath.

The student screamed as he felt searing pain in his body - nails grown sharp and long, ripping and tearing through his bloody red robe and lacerating his chest.

Danziger locked a hand in a stranglehold around Greydin's throat, and squeezed. And squeezed. His other hand scrabbled for the knife.

And then it was in his hand, and again and again he stabbed, plunging the blade into the professor's back.

The Professor howled, and the student managed to throw his tutor off. Greydin landed with a crash in a pile of splintering crates.

Gasping for breath, Danziger realised that incredibly Greydin was rising. The student got to his feet, and ran up the stairs. He told himself he was not running away, but luring Greydin away from Michelle.

Behind him he could hear the Professor in pursuit, could almost feel the maniac's breath on the back of his neck. He reached the top of the steps and the door, he turned the handle, but the door was stuck and refused to open.

He clawed frantically at the door, then remembered Professor Greydin had locked it. The student threw himself at the door in a desperate attempt to force it open. Then Greydin was upon him; the Professor had launched himself up the last

296

few steps.

For a brief moment, the two men struggled at the top of the flight, then they fell, hurtling down the steps.

Falling together, Danziger screamed in agony, as five sharp points tore through his robe and skin, piercing and ripping the flesh of his stomach. He hit the stone floor first; Greydin fell atop him and was cushioned from the impact.

The possessed man reared above the stunned student. For the first time since performing the spell, Professor Greydin spoke, or rather growled, "Not Greydin. Not professor. Am Karkasoz." And then he made a sound that might have been laughter. "Am hungry!"

Groggily Danziger unsuccessfully tried to evade Greydin's next attack; he shrieked in agony as Greydin lashed at his face, sharp claws tearing at his eyes.

Yelling, Danziger flailed blindly with the dagger, stabbing frenziedly.

It was the screaming that made him stop. Danziger realised that there was someone else screaming. Someone other than himself - Michelle.

He pushed Greydin's unmoving body off and slowly rose.

"Michelle? It's all right. It's all over."

"Keep away." He was unaware that Michelle cowered on the floor, trembling, frightened. She did not know where she was, or what had happened to her. "Just stay away from me."

Guided by the sound of her voice, Danziger staggered blindly towards her.

His robe so tattered he was virtually naked, blood stained and bruised, face ruined, flaps of skin hanging loose, Danziger was a hideous and terrifying apparition.

Michelle was backing away from him. "You're insane; keep away from me." She was sobbing. "You've killed Professor Mellman, and Professor Greydin. And God only knows what you've done to me."

"No that was Greydin, I saved you."

"You're a liar and a murderer!" she shouted. "I saw you kill Greydin."

"The ritual worked," Danziger explained to an uncomprehending Michelle. "Greydin wasn't mad. He summoned the demon; only it possessed him. He must have meant it to possess you, but it didn't, it took his body instead. I wonder why."

He had a sudden realisation, remembered something Professor Greydin had said about why Michelle was a vital requirement for the ritual. Danziger laughed wildly - Michelle was not a virgin. But apparently, Professor Greydin had been.